RUSSIAN WINTER

Also by Daphne Kalotay

Calamity and Other Stories

A NOVEL

RUSSIAN WINTER

Daphne Kalotay

HarperCollins Publishers Ltd

Published by HarperCollins Publishers Ltd.

First Canadian edition

Grateful acknowledgment is made for permission to reproduce the following:
Excerpt on page 212 from *Shostakovich and Stalin* by Solomon Volkov, published
by Knopf © Solomon Volkov 2004.

Excerpt on page 311 from *Galina: A Russian Story* by Galina Vishnevskaya,
English translation copyright © 1984 by Galina Vishnevskaya and Houghton
Mifflin Harcourt Publishing Company, reprinted by permission of the publisher.

HarperCollins books may be purchased for educational, business, or sales
promotional use through our Special Markets Department.

HarperCollins Publishers Ltd
2 Bloor Street East, 20th Floor
Toronto, Ontario, Canada
M4W 1A8

www.harpercollins.ca

Designed by Renato Stanisic

Library and Archives Canada Cataloguing in Publication

Kalotay, Daphne Eva
Russian winter / Daphne Kalotay.

ISBN 978-1-55468-672-8

I. Title.
PS3611.A455R87 2010   813'.6   C2010-903137-7

Printed in the United States of America
RRD 9 8 7 6 5 4 3 2 1

For Mamuka
And in memory of Imre and Bambi Farkass

It was then that I first came to know that love is not merely a source of joy or a game, but part of the ceaseless tragedy of life, both its eternal curse and the overwhelming force that gives it meaning.

—Nadezhda Mandelstam

Her husband had archaic ideas about jewels; a man bought them for his wife in acknowledgment of things he could not gracefully utter.

—Willa Cather

RUSSIAN WINTER

BOOK I

BOOK I

LOT 7

Diamond Earstuds. Each 4-prong-set with a round brilliant-cut diamond weighing approx. 1.64 and 1.61 cts., color and clarity H/VS2, 18kt white gold mounts, Russian hallmarks. $20,000–22,000

CHAPTER ONE

The afternoon was so cold, so relentlessly gray, few pedestrians passed the long island of trees dividing Commonwealth Avenue, and even little dogs, shunted along impatiently, wore thermal coats and offended expressions. From a third-floor window on the north side of the street, above decorative copper balconies that had long ago turned the color of pale mint, Nina Revskaya surveyed the scene. Soon the sun—what little there was of it—would abandon its dismal effort, and all along this strip of well-kept brownstones, streetlamps would glow demurely.

Nina tried to lean closer, to better glimpse the sidewalk below, but the tightness in her neck seized again. Since her chair could not move any nearer, she bore the pain and leaned closer still. Her breath left patches of fog on the glass. She hoped to spot her visitor ahead of time, so as to better prepare herself.

Cold rose to her cheeks. Here came someone, but no, it was a woman, and too young. Her boot heels made a lonely clop-clop sound. Now the woman paused, seemed to be searching for an address. Nina lost sight of her as she approached the door of the building. Surely this couldn't be right—though now the doorbell buzzed. Stiff-backed in her wheelchair, Nina rolled slowly away from the window. In the foyer, frowning, she pressed the intercom. "Yes?"

"Drew Brooks, from Beller."

These American girls, going around with men's names.

"Do come up." Though aware of her accent, and of the cracking in her voice, Nina was always shocked to hear it. In her mind, in her thoughts, her words were always bright and clear. She rolled forward to unlatch and open the door, and listened for the elevator. But it was mounting footsteps that grew louder, closer, until they became "Drew," in a slim wool coat, her cheeks rosy from cold, a leather satchel hanging from a strap diagonally across her shoulder. She was of good height, with a posture of self-respect, and thrust out her hand, still gloved.

It has begun, Nina thought, with a slight drop of her heart; I have begun it. Knuckles wincing, she briefly grasped the outstretched hand. "Please come in."

"It's a pleasure to meet you, Ms. Revskaya."

Miz, as if she were a secretary. "You may call me Nina."

"Nina, hello." The girl gave a surprisingly confident smile, and creases fanned out from beside her eyes; Nina saw she was older than she had first thought. Her eyelashes were dark, her auburn hair tucked loosely behind her ears. "Lenore, our director of fine jewelry, is very sorry that she can't be here," she was saying, removing her gloves. "Both her children came down with something."

"You may put here your coat."

The girl extracted herself from her coat to reveal a short skirt and a fitted high-necked sweater. Nina assessed the short skirt, the long legs, the low boots and pale tights. Impractical, showing off her legs in weather like this. And yet Nina approved. Though most people knew the phrase "Suffer for beauty," few truly embraced it.

"We will sit in the salon." Nina turned her wheelchair, and a current of pain shot through her kneecaps. It was always like this, the pain, sudden and indiscriminate. "Please have a seat."

The girl sat down and crossed her legs in their thin tights.

Suffer for beauty. It was one of the truer maxims, which Nina had lived to the fullest, dancing on sprained toes and rheumatic hips, through pneumonia and fever. And as a young woman in Paris and then London, she had of course served time in finicky gowns and treacherous heels, and in the 1960s those hopelessly scratchy skirt suits that seemed to be made of furniture upholstery. In 1978 she had undergone what was known as a "mini facelift." Really it was just a few stitches behind the ears—so minor, in fact, that on the day that she was to have the stitches removed, it had occurred to her that she might as well do it herself. And she had, with a magnifying mirror and a tiny pair of pointy nail scissors.

Smoothing her skirt, the girl removed invisible lint with a light, flitting hand. Petersburg airs, Nina's grandmother used to call them, these little feminine adjustments. Now the girl reached inside her satchel to pull out a clipboard with a leather cover. Wide cheekbones, fair skin, brown eyes flecked with green. Something about her was familiar, though not in any good way. "I'm here to compose a basic list. Our appraisers will take it from there."

Nina gave a small nod, and the knot at the base of her neck tightened: at times this knot seemed to be the very heart of her illness. "Yes, of course," she said, and the effort made the pain briefly stronger.

Opening the clipboard, the girl said, "I have all sorts of things I'd love to ask you—though I'll try to keep it to the business at hand. I love the ballet. I wish I could have seen you dance."

"There is no need to flatter me."

The girl raised an eyebrow. "I was reading about you, how they called you 'the Butterfly.' "

"One of the Moscow papers was calling me that," Nina heard herself snap. "I dislike it." For one thing, the image wasn't quite accurate, the way it made her seem, weak and fluttery, a rose petal blown about in the air. "It is too . . . sweet."

The girl gave a winking look that seemed to agree, and Nina felt the surprise of her coldness having been acknowledged. "I've noticed the butterfly motif in some of your jewelry," the girl said. "I looked back at the list from the St. Botolph's exhibit. I thought that might make our work today simpler. We'll go through the St. Botolph's list"—she indicated the pages in the grip of the clipboard—"and you can let me know which ones you'd like to auction and which ones you might be keeping, if any."

"That is fine." The knot in her neck twinged. In truth she possessed something close to affection for this horrible knot, which at first had been just another unrelenting pain. But then one day, only a few months ago, Nina happened to recall the way her grandmother used to tie her winter scarf for her, back in Moscow, when she was still too young to do it herself: knotted at the back, to easily grab at if she tried to run off. The memory, which Nina had not alighted on for a good fifty years, was a balm, a salve, a gift long ago lost and returned at last. Now whenever Nina suffered the pain there, she told herself that it was the knot in her old wool scarf, and that her grandmother's hands had tied it, and then the pain, though no less severe, was at least not a bad one.

The girl was already handing her the clipboard. Nina took it with shaking hands, as the girl said, conversationally, "I'm actually one-quarter Russian, myself." When Nina did not respond, she added, "My grandfather came from there."

Nina chose to ignore this. Her Russian life was so very distant, the person she had been then so separate from the one she had become. She set the clipboard on her lap and frowned at it.

In a more confidential tone, the girl asked, "What inspired you to put them up for auction?"

Nina hoped her voice would not shake. "I want to direct the income where I like, during my lifetime. I am almost eighty, you know. As I have said to you, all proceeds shall go to the Boston Ballet

Foundation." She kept her eyes down, focused on the clipboard, wondering if her stiffness hid her emotions. Because it all felt wrong now, a rash decision. The wrongness had to do with this girl, somehow, that *she* should be the one to sift through Nina's treasures. Those primly confident hands.

"Well, these pieces are sure to bring in a good sum," the girl said. "Especially if you allow us to publish that they're from your collection." Her face was hopeful. "Our auctions are always anonymous, of course, but in high-profile cases like this, it often pays to make it public. I imagine Lenore mentioned that to you. Even the less valuable items can fetch a good price that way. Not that we need to include keepsakes, too, but—"

"Take them."

The girl angled her head at Nina, as if in reassessment. She seemed to have noticed something, and Nina felt her pulse begin to race. But the girl simply sat up a bit straighter and said, "The very fact that they're yours would bring in so many more potential bidders. And there's of course the added allure that some of these pieces were smuggled out of Soviet Russia. In life-or-death circumstances."

Here it came, as it always did, the part of the conversation where Nina would be molded into that brave old woman, the one who had escaped oppression and defied her government in the pursuit of artistic freedom. It always happened this way; she started out an artist and ended up a symbol.

"When you escaped, I mean."

Those soulful brown eyes. Again Nina breathed a whiff of the past, the recollection of . . . what? Something unpleasant. A faint anger rose inside her. "People think I fled Russia to escape communism. Really I was escaping my mother-in-law."

The girl seemed to think Nina was joking. The creases showed again beside her eyes as her mouth pressed into a conspiratorial smile. Dark lashes, broad cheekbones, the wise arch of her eyebrows . . . It came to Nina in a swift, clear vision: that luminous face, and the shivering wave of her arms, a delicate ripple of muscle as she drifted across the stage.

"Is there a . . . problem?"

Nina flinched. The girl from Beller was watching her intently, so that Nina wondered if she had been staring. Taking a breath to collect herself, she said, "You remind me of a friend I had. Someone from a long time ago."

The girl looked pleased, as if any comparison with the past must be a flattering one. She dealt in antiques, after all. Soon she was discussing the St. Botolph's list with a brisk professionalism that whisked Nina past any tug of emotion, any last-minute regrets. Still, it felt like a long time until the girl finally donned her coat and went tromping confidently down the stairs, her inventory pressed tightly between the covers of the clipboard.

WARM MOSCOW MORNING, early June, school will soon be ending. "Can't you sit still?" A yank at the top of Nina's head, prickling tips of a comb on her part. The question is purely rhetorical. Nina learned to run as soon as she could walk and never tires of hopping from step to step in the dark stairwell of their building. She can cross the courtyard corner to corner in a series of leaps. "Stop fidgeting." But Nina swings her legs and taps her heels against each other, as Mother's fingers, precise as a surgeon's, briskly weave her own hope, her own dreams, into two tight plaits. Nina can feel her mother's hope folded into them, the tremor of quick fingers, and rapid heartbeats through the thin fabric of her blouse. Today is of too much importance to allow Nina's grandmother, with her poor eyesight and sloppily knotted headkerchief, to fiddle with her hair. At last the braids are done, looped up onto the top of her head and fastened with a big new bow to secure all the hopes and dreams inside. Nina's scalp aches.

Vera too, when they meet in the courtyard, has new ribbons in her hair. Strong gusts of wind flop them back and forth and worry the morning glories on the sagging balconies. In mere days the weather has gone from a cold drizzle to so hot and dry that Nina can't help being concerned about the dust, that it will ruin the cotton dress Mother has sewn for her. Vera's grandmother, dark eyes glowering from below a white headkerchief, keeps frowning and pulling Vera close to her. Like all grandmothers, she is permanently displeased, calls Gorky Street "Tverskaya," and gripes loudly about things no one else dares lament even in a whisper. The skin of her face is all tiny broken lines, like the top layer of ice when you step on it for the first time.

"We were up very late last night," Vera confides to Nina. The way she says it suggests Nina ought not ask why.

"How late?" Like Vera, Nina is nine years old and always being put to bed too soon. But Vera just shakes her head, a movement so small and terse her auburn braids barely move. On one of the balconies a woman who lives in the same apartment as Vera leans over the railing, shaking out bedding. With an upward glance, Vera's grandmother conveys something to Nina's mother so quietly, it could be another language. Murmurs, back and forth, nothing Nina can make out.

She worries the day will be ruined—and after such a long wait, ever since Mother first explained about the ballet school. The vague, dreamlike description might have come straight from a fairy tale, a land where little girls wear their hair in high, tightly pinned buns and study not just the usual reading and geography and history but how to move, how to *dance*. In the old days, girls like Nina would not even have been allowed to audition. Now, though, with thanks to Uncle Stalin, any child old enough can apply for an entrance exam.

But not everyone will be accepted to the school, Mother has explained. She has taken this morning off specially, asked for permission from the doctors' clinic where she is a secretary. When at last she looks back to Nina and Vera—"All right, girls, it's time to go"— Nina is relieved. Vera's mother was supposed to ask to be excused for today too, but off they go without her, following Mother through the courtyard gate into the alley, a scrawny cat sneaking away as Vera's grandmother calls after them, "I know you'll be the best!" Her voice seems to catch behind the iron bars as the gate clangs shut.

Hot, windblown street. Wide boulevards coated with dust. Each gust brings the gray fluff of poplars, and Nina and Vera have to keep plucking it off their hair and their dresses, as Nina's mother walks briskly ahead.

"I'm cold," Vera says glumly, despite the sunshine and warm breeze. "I don't feel well." Mother slows down and puts her hand out to feel Vera's forehead. Though she seems worried, she tells Vera, with a sigh, "It's just nerves, my sweet little chick." She gives Vera a squeeze.

Nina wishes Mother would put her arm around *her*, where it belongs. But soon enough they are at the corner of Pushechnaya and Neglinaya streets, looking up at a four-story house with a sign posted over the entrance:

MOSCOW CHOREOGRAPHIC SCHOOL OF THE BOLSHOI THEATRE

The Bolshoi is where Nina's father worked before he died, when Nina was still a toddler. He was a painter of stage scenery. Mother's voice whenever she recalls this sounds proud, as if she wishes she too worked at the theater, instead of at a desk in the polyclinic. But neither Nina nor Vera has ever been to the Bolshoi. The first time Nina saw ballet was just this year, at a pavilion in Gorky Park. That too was Mother's idea. After all, Nina is always jumping and twirling, trying out cartwheels and handstands—and then one day last year, playing in the courtyard, Vera went up onto the top of her toes. Not the balls of her feet; the very tips of her shoes. Of course Nina had to try it too. The glorious sensation of balance, of taking little steps and not falling. All afternoon she and Vera went up onto their toes like that—until Vera's grandmother yelled at them for ruining their shoes. By then Mother was home from work and, instead of scolding, told them her idea.

When Nina told the other girls at school she might be going to a school for ballerinas, they didn't seem envious. None of them has seen ballet, and Nina didn't quite know how to describe what she saw in the dance pavilion. Sometimes, on nights when she lies in bed trying to fend off the frightened feeling—a dark chill that blows through the building and dims the grown-ups' faces, colder and darker the later the hour becomes—she pictures the ballerinas on the stage in the park, their gauzy skirts rippling out like waterfalls, and imagines her own hair in a tight little crown on her head, and the ribbons of pointe shoes wrapped around her ankles.

Now, with a whole troop of girls, she and Vera are taken to a large room where a row of men and women sit behind a very long table. A slip of paper with a number written on it has been pinned to each girl's dress; when their numbers are called—in small groups, by the thin, strict-looking man seated at the very end of the table—the girls must step into the center of the room. The wooden floor slopes down toward a wall lined with tall, framed mirrors.

Already, without having danced at all, some of the girls are being dismissed. But Nina and Vera are in the group that is ushered to one corner of the room, where the strict-looking man explains that they are to walk, one after the other, across the floor so that their footsteps match the music. That is the only instruction they are given, and now, seated at a shiny piano, a woman with her hair piled high on her head begins to play—something pretty but also somehow sad, the tinkling of the piano keys like drops of rain splattering. One by one the girls make their way across the room. But at her turn Vera remains still, eyes wide, and Nina, waiting behind her, begins to worry. "Come on." Nina grabs Vera's hand, and the two of them move forward together, until Nina feels the tension in Vera's fingers relax. When Nina lets go, Vera continues ahead, airy and at ease, while Nina returns to her slot behind her.

Now that everyone has reached the other corner of the room, they are asked to go across once more—this time with one large step and two small ones, over and over. The music has changed to something faster and very grand. Hearing it, moving along with it, Nina feels herself shifting into a new being.

Back outside afterward, the air carries the scent of lilacs. Warm sun through the cotton of their dresses. Ice cream scoops from a street vendor. For a short while Vera, too, seemed happy about the dance exam, aware that, like Nina, she performed well in the end. But now she is oddly quiet, and Mother's thoughts are clearly elsewhere, so that Nina feels it creeping back, the dark nighttime feeling—so unlike the visible lightness around them, the sunny June freedom, everyone outdoors without a coat or hat. She tries to will the feeling away, thinks about the ballet school, about the man who came to her at the end to yank her leg up, this way and that, and examine the soles of her feet, asking her to point and flex her toes, and was pleased with what he saw. Vera too, unlike most of the other girls, was inspected from head to toe with approval.

When they pass the grand hotel at the corner, the sidewalk café is open, the first time since the long winter. "Look!" Vera says, pausing. A woman is exiting the hotel, ushered through a wide glass revolving door—the only revolving door in the city, pushed round by two dour-faced men in long jackets.

The woman is unlike any Nina has ever seen, wearing a dress suit of a fine pale gray-blue color, with a small hat at a slant on her head, and on her hands short clean white gloves. Gloves in springtime!

And the delicacy of that grayish blue shade . . . Nina knows only a few fabrics, the same dark plum colors in winter and cheerily ugly patterns in summer, nothing in between.

And then Nina sees the most remarkable thing: the woman has jewels in her ears. Diamonds, small yet twinkling mightily. For a moment Nina is almost breathless. The only earrings she has seen are big dull beads that hang down from clips: pearls, heavy-looking, or glassy lumps of brown or marbled green stone. And so these tiny glittering diamonds are startling. And they are in her ears!

Nina's mother looks away as the woman passes, but Vera asks, "Who is she?"

"American, I suppose." Mother reaches her hand out to Nina to show that it is time to continue on. But Mother's perfect oval face and slender waist must have impressed the guards—or perhaps they are bored and want to show off. They gesture to Nina and Vera, to allow them a turn through the doors.

Utter silence as the men solemnly escort them round. Nina glimpses, for mere seconds, the hotel's immense lobby, its gleaming floor and thick runner of carpet, and an enormous mirror with a heavy gilt frame. The ceiling is impossibly high, with glittering lights shining down. It is the first time Nina has seen such things, a whole other world—but the slow rotation continues, and now the marble floor, the plush carpet, the gold mirror and chandelier, are already behind her. That twinkling shower of lights—and the American woman's diamonds right there in her earlobes, tiny and bright, like stars.

Outside again, the tour over, Nina asks, "Did you see the lady's ears?"

Mother just gives a look that reminds her to thank the doormen.

"Thank you very much." Nina and Vera curtsy as they were taught at the audition, one foot behind the other, hands lifting the edges of their skirts, and turn away from the fascinating door, that

entrance to a whole other world, and only then does the understanding come to Nina, strongly, acutely—much more than at the Bolshoi
school—that something momentous has occurred.

WHEN THEY RETURN to the courtyard, the old woman who cleans
the building looks quickly away. Frown of her mouth chewing sun-
flower seeds. Eyes shifting as she sweeps. She moves toward the only
other people in the courtyard, a young couple who live in the same
apartment as Nina and her mother and grandmother.

Mother has said to stay and play, she will send Nina's and Vera's
grandmothers down to fetch them. But Nina keeps one ear listening
to what the old woman is saying. She hears Vera's parents' names,
and then, "There was always something odd about them."

Nina has heard this before—not about Vera's parents but other
people in the building, who now are gone. Whispers in the courtyard, *something odd . . .*

Vera turns and runs to the other side of the courtyard, where her
grandmother has appeared.

Nina's grandmother, too, has arrived, her kerchief loosely knotted beneath her chin. "Come here, Nina!" But Nina continues to
listen. "What did they do?" the young couple is asking, as the janitoress splashes a bucket of dirty water around the entryway. At the
other side of the courtyard, Vera's grandmother is taking Vera back
inside, without even letting her say good-bye.

"Ninochka! Come!" Her grandmother's voice is shrill instead of
warm and slightly annoyed, as it usually is. The old janitoress repeats herself: "I always knew something wasn't right about them."
Nina looks up, past the crooked little balconies, to the window of the
room where Vera's family lives. Pale morning glories tremble in the
breeze. Nina turns and runs, straight into her grandmother's arms,
to lean against her chest and feel the warmth of her body.

. . . .

BY THE TIME the girl from Beller had left, the sky was black, the salon gloomy. In her wheelchair, Nina went about tugging the cords of various lamps, shedding weak saffron rays down upon themselves and little else. Instead of relief at having taken care of things, she felt the same wariness, the same anxiety she had for a fortnight now.

She rolled the wheelchair up to her desk. With the little key she kept in her pocket, she opened the top drawer. She hadn't looked back at the letter since first receiving it two weeks ago. Even then she had read it just once, hastily. She had always been one to make rash decisions; it was her nature. Now, though, she unfolded the typed page slowly, trying not to look at the photograph it enclosed.

I am sending you this letter and the accompanying photograph after much contemplation. Perhaps you have already
recognized my name on the return address, recalled even
the very first letter I sent you, after our brief meeting three
decades ago, back when I—

There was the click of the lock on the front door, the sound of the heavy door swinging open. "Hello, you!" came the voice of Cynthia, the wiry West Indian woman who came each evening to cook Nina's dinner and ask embarrassing questions about her bodily functions; days she worked as a registered nurse at Mass General. Nina slid the letter and photograph back inside the envelope as Cynthia called out, in a voice still tinged with the genially arrogant accent of her native country, "Where you at, sugar?" She often called Nina "sugar." Nina supposed it was some sort of private joke.

"I am here, Cynthia, I am fine." Nina returned the envelope to the drawer. To think that there had been a time when she was left to do things for herself, unattended, without the worried ministration of others . . . For over a year now Cynthia had been necessary, the last person Nina saw each night after being helped from her wheelchair to her bath and back out again. Of some indeterminate early-middle age, Cynthia had a boyfriend named Billy whose schedule and availability directly dictated which meals she prepared. On nights when she was to see him, Cynthia would not cook with onions, garlic, broccoli, or Brussels sprouts, lest the smell cling to her hair. Other days she had no ban on any particular vegetables.

Nina could hear Cynthia hanging her coat, taking her little sack of groceries to the kitchen. The situation was appalling, really. Especially for someone like Nina, who had once been so strong, and was not yet even truly old. All the time now, it seemed, octogenarians went traipsing around the globe on cruises and walking tours. But Nina's once-supple body, now eerily stiff, allowed no such diversions. Even this afternoon, the auction house girl had been unable to refrain from saying, at one point, "You must miss dancing," as she eyed Nina's swollen knuckles. She had looked horrified, actually, the way young people do when faced with the misfortunes of the elderly.

"I do miss it," Nina had said. "Every day I miss it. I miss the way it felt to dance."

Now Cynthia was calling out again, threatening to tell all about her day, brisk steps in her white nurse's shoes as she approached the study. Nina slid the envelope more deeply into the drawer. Her knuckles ached as she twisted the lock with the tiny key. She felt no better than before, knowing the photograph was still there.

GRIGORI SOLODIN SAW the announcement on the third day of the new semester. He liked to be at his desk before eight, while the Department of Foreign Languages was still quiet and the secretaries hadn't yet arrived to unlock the main office. For a half hour or so the wooden hallways—cold from the heat having been off all night—remained peaceful, no trampling up and down the narrow stairway whose marble steps were worn like slings in the center. Much better than being home, that still somehow unfamiliar silence. Here Grigori could read the newspaper in peace and smoke his cigarettes without his colleague Evelyn berating him about his lungs or Carla, the secretary, wrinkling her nose exaggeratedly and reminding him that the campus was now officially "Smoke-Free." Then at eight thirty Carla and her assistant Dave would arrive to flick on all the photocopiers and printers and anything else that hummed.

Grigori reached for his lighter, the cartridge small in his hand. First it had simply been for support, something to soothe him while Christine was ill. Now it was one of his few daily pleasures. And yet he hadn't allowed himself to bring the habit into his home, too aware of what Christine would have said, how she would have felt about it. Anyway, he didn't plan to keep it up much longer (though it had been, now, two years). Installed behind his desk, he breathed the comforting aroma of that first light. He wore a tailored suit, clean if lightly rumpled, with a handkerchief poking up optimistically from his breast pocket. This costume he had adopted twenty-five years earlier, during his very first semester teaching here, when he had also tried growing a beard and smoking a pipe—anything to appear even a year or so older than his actual age. Even now, at fifty, his face had few lines, and his hair, thick in a way that seemed to ask to be mussed, remained dark and full. Tall, trim, he still possessed something of his youthful lankiness. Yet just yesterday he had been interviewed for the university newspaper by a spotty-faced sophomore who asked, in all seriousness, "How does it feel to be inaugurated into the Quarter Century Club?" For his twenty-five years of service Grigori had received a heavy maroon ballpoint pen and a handwritten note of gratitude from the provost; to the sophomore with the stenography pad and the serious question, Grigori answered, with the merest glint in his eye, "Horrifying."

He often adopted this tone (dry, poker-faced, with a slight and enigmatic accent) in his communications with the student population—yet they liked his deadpan delivery, his faux-curmudgeonly jokes, indeed seemed even to like Grigori himself. And he liked his students, or at least did not dislike them, tried not to show dismay at their sometimes shocking lack of knowledge, of curiosity, as they sat there in their Red Sox caps and zippered fleece jackets like members of some prosperous gang. In the warmer months they wore flip-flops, which they kicked off during class as if lounging on a gigantic beach towel. It was just one of the many signs that the world was plunging toward ruin. Grigori, meanwhile, continued to dress for class in handsome suits, because he had not yet abandoned the notion that what he did for a living was honorable—and because he retained the same worry he had first developed as a young teaching fellow studying for long hours in the privacy of his rented room: that he might one day mistakenly show up for class still wearing his slippers.

Now he took a puff on his cigarette and unfolded his copy of the *Globe.* The usual depressing stuff—the president intent on starting his second war in two years. But in the Arts section a headline took Grigori by surprise: "Ballerina Revskaya to Auction Jewels."

A noise issued from him, a low "Huh." And then came the sinking feeling, the awful deflation.

Though a month had passed, he had not given up hope—not really, not until now. He had believed, or tried to believe, that there might be some sort of movement toward one another.

Instead, this.

Well, why should he have expected otherwise? It was what he had been purposely avoiding, really. For two years the idea had gnawed at him. But grief had paralyzed him, and then only as it lifted did he find he could imagine trying again. And yet it hadn't worked. There would always be this distance. He would never get any closer.

He tried to read the article but found he wasn't taking in the sentences. His heart rushed as it had the last time he had seen Nina Revskaya, a good ten years ago, at a benefit for the Boston Ballet. From the grand lobby of the Wang Theatre, he had watched her stand on the great marble stairway and make a brief, perfectly worded speech about the importance of benefactors to the arts. She held her head high, if somewhat stiffly, her hair still dark—nearly black—despite her age and in a bun so tight it pulled her wrinkles smooth. Next to him, at their spot at the back of the crowd, Christine held lightly on to his arm, her other hand holding a champagne flute. Nina Revskaya seemed to wince as she spoke; it was clear that every movement pained her. When the ballet director led her slowly down the magnificent staircase and through the lobby, Grigori had thought, What if? What if I approached her? But of course he didn't dare. And then Christine was leading him in the other direction, toward the company's newest star, a young Cuban dancer known for his jumps.

Grigori tossed the newspaper down on his desk. That she could want to be rid of him so badly—so badly as to rid herself of her beloved jewels.

He pushed his chair back, stood up. A slap in the face, that's what this was. And really she doesn't even know me. . . .

The cocoon of his office was no comfort to him now. Grigori realized that he was pacing, and forced himself to stop. Then he grabbed his coat and gloves and ducked out the door to make his way down the narrow stairs and out of the building.

IN THE CAMPUS café, the morning shift was already in place. Behind the counter a skinny girl with dyed-black hair served coffee and enormous bagels, while the stoned assistant manager, singing happily along with the stereo, took too long to steam the milk. A few conscientious undergraduates huddled around one of the round tables, and at the back of the room a knot of visiting professors argued amicably. Placing his order, Grigori viewed the scene with a sense of defeat.

The girl at the counter batted her eyelashes artfully as she handed him a thick wedge of coffee cake. Grigori took it up from its little flap of waxed paper and felt immediately guilty; as with his smoking, Christine would not have approved. He thought of her, of what he would give to have her with him at this moment.

"Grigori!"

Zoltan Romhanyi sat at a table by the window, plastic bags full of books and papers all around him. "Come, come!" he called, gesturing, and then hunched down to scribble something in his notebook with great speed despite his shaky, aged hand. For the past year he had been composing a memoir about his escape from Hungary following the '56 uprising and his subsequent years as a key figure—if somewhat on the sidelines—in the London arts scene.

"Zoltan, happy New Year."

"Are you sure, Grigori?"

"Does it show on my face, then?"

"You look dashing as always—but tired."

Grigori had to laugh, being told he looked tired by a man twenty years his senior—a man of delicate health, who had spent much of Christmas break in the hospital, recovering from undiagnosed pneumonia, and who the previous winter had slipped on the ice and broken his shoulder for a second time. "You put me in my place, Zoltan. I have no right to be tired. I'm frustrated this morning, that's all. But I'm glad to see you. You're looking much better."

Perhaps it was odd, that Grigori's favorite colleague and friend was nearly a generation older than himself—but he preferred that to the opposite phenomenon, professors who mingled with their students in the pub. Zoltan's deeply lined face, the sags of skin beneath his eyes, the tremor in his hands, the small cloud of grizzled hair resting lightly atop his scalp . . . none of this spoke of the man

Zoltan had once, briefly, been: the pride and dismay of literary East-ern Europe, symbolic hero to the enlightened West, a young, skinny émigré poet in borrowed clothes. "I'm feeling much better," he said now. "I love this time of morning, don't you?" His anomalous accent (hard Magyar rhythms tamed by a British lilt) made him sound almost fey. "You can practically feel the sun rising. Here, sit down." He pushed ineffectually at some of the papers atop the table.

Grigori took a seat. "I can't stay long. I have a tutorial at eight thirty."

"And I have mine at one."

"Do you?" Grigori tried not to show disbelief. He had heard whispered in the department that Zoltan's only class for the semester had been canceled; just two students had registered, insufficient for a course to go ahead.

"Poetry and the Surrealists," Zoltan said. "Two young students of truly interesting minds. There was some talk of the course not running, you know, but when I proposed to the youngsters last week that we continue to meet either way, they agreed. Who needs official credit? I admire their enthusiasm."

"They know what's good for them." They knew that this was a once-in-a-lifetime chance, to study with a man who had known in person some of the very poets whose work he taught, and whose most off-the-cuff remarks contained not just nuggets of wisdom but often a morsel or two of world-class gossip. Zoltan's first book of poetry had been translated by a popular British poet shortly after his arrival in London, briefly turning Zoltan into Europe's—well, cer-tain circles of it—new enfant terrible. Zoltan had been something of a dandy then, with his sleepy eyelids and a confident smile; Grigori had seen photographs in subsequent translated editions (all of them now out of print). And though Zoltan wasn't one to name-drop, his own name turned up in more than a few memoirs of painters and playwrights, art collectors and choreographers, muses and stars of the stage. Just a line here or a paragraph there, but Zoltan had clearly made his mark. Subtle probing of his memories teased out reminiscences of Mary Quant and Salvador Dalí, and sighing, surprising asides ("Ah, Ringo . . . He had those long eyelashes, you know").

The problem was, with the new Web sites that students used to publicly evaluate professors, word had spread that Zoltan's classes were demanding and odd, more like prolonged conversations, for which students had to be impeccably prepared. He expected them to have not simply read but pondered, analyzed, even dreamed about the assigned works. And so students warned each other to stay away from Zoltan's courses.

Grigori had resisted the temptation to look up what his own students said about him. At any rate, he tried to stay away from the Internet. His most daring online escapade had taken place four years ago, when he made his first and only eBay purchase: a 1959 *Hello* magazine containing an article all about Nina Revskaya's jewels. A four-page photo spread of earrings and watches, necklaces and bracelets, the majority of them gifts: from admirers and international diplomats and self-promoting jewelers. A photograph on page three of an amber bracelet and matching earrings had confirmed—in its way—what Grigori had long suspected. He kept the magazine in his office, in the top drawer of the filing cabinets reserved for his Russian Literature notes, behind a folder labeled "Short Fiction, 19th C."

Now, though, the jewels were to be auctioned. So much for proof. So much for confirmation. Grigori must have sighed, because Zoltan's voice shifted to concern and asked, "How are you, really, Grigori?"

"Oh, fine, please don't worry." The sad widower role was fine for a year or so, but after that it became tiresome. As for the news item about Nina Revskaya, he was not about to add today's disappointment to his list of grievances. For some time now the adamant chatter of Carla and Dave and his friend Evelyn (who always made a point of inviting him out and taking him with her to movies and other cultural diversions) had made it clear that Grigori was expected to behave as so many men did after six or twelve or eighteen months alone—find a new woman and settle down and stop looking so glum all the time. Accordingly, Grigori had over a year ago stopped wearing the little pink ribbon pin from the hospital. Now that the second anniversary of Christine's death had passed, he had even removed his wedding ring. The gold band lay in a small covered tray with a few tie clips he never wore. It was time to buck up and stop being tedious. To Zoltan he added, "No new complaints."

"Who needs new complaints if you have a good old one?" Zoltan's eyes were smiling, but his mouth frowned. "Odd, sometimes, what the whims of the universe cast at us."

"And you?" Grigori asked.

"Go on and eat that cake," Zoltan said. "You nibble, as if it's on someone else's plate."

Grigori smiled. It was true. Just give in, give up.

Give up. Give it up.

Grigori realized that he was nodding to himself, as much as he disliked the thought that came to him next.

But it was the only way. If nothing else, it might prove . . . what? That he was done with it. That he respected Nina Revskaya, and that she need not be afraid of him. That he had surrendered.

Yes, he knew what to do. Feeling much lighter, he finished the cake, while Zoltan immersed himself in another fit of scribbling. Then Zoltan looked up, and his voice became suddenly serious. "We must talk—at your earliest convenience."

Grigori paused. "I'm sorry, I thought that was what we were doing."

Zoltan shook his head angrily, whispered, "Not *here*."

"Oh." Grigori looked around, but there was no one listening. He wiped the crumbs of cake up with the waxed paper. "Then shall I call you at home?"

"No, no, in person."

Grigori shrugged, perplexed. "Well then, you let me know when. I'd best get going." He stood and pulled on his gloves, as Zoltan nodded furtively. Two more café patrons took a seat at the next table, but now they murmured something and moved to another one, farther away. Grigori realized that this was due to Zoltan, that they thought him a vagrant, with his dirty plastic bags and stained, if perfectly tailored, gabardine pants, and his silk cravat with its many escaping threads. Well, that was America, the great equalizer—where revered poets were mistaken for homeless men. Grigori said, "All right, Zoltan. Until then."

"I look forward to it." Grigori heard a genuine hopefulness in Zoltan's voice. He tried to recall, as he turned away, when he himself had last looked forward—really, truly—to anything.

He had been young and hopeful, once. He could still see in his mind the stiff canvas backpack he had carried with him from Princeton, the one with the long thin straps that never fit him properly and the stains at the bottom from so many floors and sidewalks and lawns. He remembered how his T-shirt had smelled after all the hours on the Greyhound, and how hungry he was as he made his way along the avenue. He was nineteen years old, tall and long-limbed, his hair shaggy and less than clean. He had gotten off at the wrong T stop and so went a longer distance by foot than planned. The only cities he knew were Paris and New York, and in comparison the old Back Bay buildings looked both quaint and stately. All that mattered to him, though, was the address he had written down, the building with the tall stoop and the wrought iron railings. The big front door, of thickly carved wood, was propped slightly open. Grigori took a deep breath and wiped his hands on his pants. But he was still sweating, so he pulled his handkerchief from his pocket and wiped his brow.

In the front vestibule, he took the large manila envelope from his backpack, holding it anxiously, ready to put it back into the pack if no one was home. Inside were the various items he had come to think of as "proof." Grigori found the intercom and the correct button beside it. All of his hope he aimed at that one button.

He could still hear, in the remote bays of his memory, her voice on the intercom, suspicious, doubtful: "Yes?"

In Russian he announced himself.

"Your name again?" she asked in Russian. She sounded perplexed but not annoyed.

"Grigori Solodin. My parents knew neighbors of yours. In Moscow." It wasn't exactly true, but it sounded true enough. "I was hoping to speak to you about something important." He had a brilliant thought and added, "Briefly."

"Wait, please," she said firmly.

The wait for her to arrive . . . watching through the glass partition, his heart pounding as he eyed the elevator, waiting for its narrow doors to open, to reveal her. But then she emerged from around a corner on the stairs, that elongated neck, the long thin arms, and there she was, stepping down as if floating. She looked at him through the glass, politely inquisitive, her face a perfect oval, her dark, dark hair pulled back sharply. Those incongruous hands, already old though she herself wasn't yet, pushing the door open just a crack, their knuckles already enlarged.

"Now, who exactly are you?" she asked in Russian. She seemed to have a tiny smile in the corners of her mouth, perhaps at how young and bumbling he looked.

There Grigori always forced himself to stop, to prevent the memory from rolling forward. He had to. The rest was no good.

LOT 12

Platinum, Onyx, and Diamond Butterfly Brooch.
Solid platinum, wings comprised of six fancy cuts of black onyx 27.21 ctw, body comprised of approx. 7 ctw of old European cut diamonds. Center stone is bezel-set, pin detailed with milgrain edges, lg. 2 in., w. 1 ¹⁄₂ in., 11.5 grams, marked Shreve, Crump & Low. $8,000–10,000

CHAPTER TWO

It is decided—in that silent, abrupt way that adults make decisions—that Vera and her grandmother will go live with an aunt and uncle, in a town far north of Moscow.

That is what happens, Nina acknowledges, when your parents must go away. When two other people, ones you've never seen before, come to live in their room. It is what would happen if Nina's own mother were to suddenly depart. But maybe Nina could stay here with Grandmother instead. . . . She comforts herself with this thought as she and Mother accompany Vera and Vera's grandmother to the train station. It is a bright, mild morning, the second of September—the day before the first day of school. The streets are suddenly full again, everyone back from summer holiday, boys looking goofy and big-eared with their freshly trimmed hair, and all the girls purchasing the prescribed bows for their ponytails. The station, too, is crowded; at the track where Vera's train is to arrive, there is barely space for them among all the waiting people and tattered wicker hampers. All Nina can think is that now Vera won't be starting at the Bolshoi School with her, won't be here to play in the gritty courtyard, concocting elaborate games with convoluted, indispensable rules.

Vera, though, looks untroubled, proud of her cumbersome suitcase and little wrapped package of food for the train. Mother and
Vera's grandmother make polite, strained talk a few feet away.

"I got a telegram," Vera whispers.

Nina looks at her with wide eyes; she hasn't ever seen one.
"When?"

From the pocket of her overcoat, Vera takes a crisp square of
paper and unfolds it, her back toward the others, as if shielding an
important secret. "See?" Words typed in the center of the slip of
paper, very brief, so that the message seems rushed and all the more
important: *We love you Verochka Mother and Father.*

Vera looks at Nina proudly. "They're doing important work.
That's why they had to go away."

It is more of an explanation than Nina's mother has been able to
give her. Nina accepts it. Vera looks back at the telegram, reads it to
herself once more, then folds it and returns it to her pocket.

A loud clanking sound, and that hot coal smell—the train easing
heftily into the station, spitting puffs of white steam, and Vera's
grandmother saying, "Stand back, people are going to have to get off
first. Oh, well, now look at your hair." Old gray hands smooth Vera's
auburn braids, sweeping a stray lock back behind her ear.

"Well, girls," Mother says gravely, turning to gather up Vera's
grandmother's bags. "Time to say good-bye."

Vera does so tearlessly, while her grandmother laboriously pulls
herself up onto the train, not helped by anyone. Nor does Nina cry,
distracted by the rush of passengers, as Vera is sucked into the depths
of the train. Mother has said Nina and Vera can write letters and
stay friends through the post, but all Nina can picture, all the way
back home, is the train carrying Vera away.

Now they stop at the post office, where Mother asks Nina to run
around the corner, to get in the line for bread.

Nina hurries off and at the bakery joins the crowded, silent queue. She likes to watch the cashier counting on the abacus, the quick snap of the wooden beads back and forth on the wires. But after a few minutes, as the line moves slowly forward, she realizes Mother has forgotten to give her money. She scurries back to the post office.

Inside she finds Mother and runs to her side. But her mother hasn't noticed her; with great focus she is carefully printing something onto a special form. *Be good sweet Verochka. All our love Mother and Father.*

Nina turns and runs out of the post office, into the blinding September sunlight. Her chest feels cold, and the backs of her eyes ache. For a moment she wants to yell, to shout, to tell someone, anyone. The sad trick of it, this lie, this double secret. And that other, awful chafing feeling: that Mother must really love Vera, very much, to do such a thing. That she would do that, for Vera.

Waiting by the entrance, Nina tries to calm the pounding of her heart. It is a good thing Vera is gone, she tells herself, so that Nina cannot tell her what she knows.

THE TELEPHONE INTERRUPTED her thoughts. It had been ringing every few hours, but Nina refused to answer. More of those Charles Street estate jewelers, probably, nobody she need attend to. She was too exhausted to speak to anyone. These past few days had been bad ones, and nights of pain instead of sleep. Cynthia kept trying to make her take her tablets.

At her post by the window she took in the view, snow in heaps after this weekend's blizzard. Along the mall knobby trees, still strung with holiday lights crusted in ice, seemed to shiver; Nina could see past their branches to the other side of the avenue, where parked cars crowded up against thick banks of snow. Nina often sat here, in the salon. It was her favorite room, with its tall windows and good light—and the stereo sounded best from here. The only bother was the cold air that leaked in from the crack above the middle window. This had been going on for two years now, ever since the top pane had somehow slipped down an inch, but Nina hadn't bothered to mention it to anyone. In the warmer months it didn't trouble her, except on breezy days, when it caused the Venetian blind to make an ominous flapping noise.

Today the blind was up all the way. From the open space at the top of the window, a long-dead leaf, remnant of autumn, slipped in and fell quietly to the sill. It lay there like a secret missive, brown with age, and for a few minutes Nina simply looked at it. Then she reached out and with cold fingers felt the crisp delicacy of its tiny, cracked veins.

Would anyone other than herself ever notice the gap at the top of the window? The thought seemed to Nina profound. She rarely had visitors anymore. Cynthia was the only other person who ever spent time in this room, when her casseroles were baking and she came to sit and ask Nina lots of nosy questions. The cleaning women— Marya and a nameless crew of helpers who loudly, hastily blew in and out of the apartment once every three weeks—did a less than thorough job, taking no notice of details. Not to mention that they had yet to clean a single window.

No one else had any reason to enter this room. Nearly a decade had passed since Nina had entertained. When it came to Boston friends— real friends, close friends—in this last and longest chapter of her life, she had never really made any. There were plenty of acquaintances, of course, and colleagues from the ballet, but no friends as she had loved in Paris and London. No one she cared about as she cared for her Russian friend Tama, or dear Inge, "the Berlin girl," as she still thought of her. Well, there was Shepley, whom she had known, as astonishing as it sometimes seemed, for forty years now. But ever since his move to California, Nina had felt less connected to him.

Like Veronica back in England, Shepley was a fan who had gradually become a friend. As a young lawyer and balletomane, he had insinuated himself into Nina's life in a gentle, measured way, through small gifts and intelligent, respectful notes. His attention was never overbearing, nor disturbingly selfless, but wise and reserved. Even Nina—who, despite shedding fully and completely the first third of her life, never could meet a new person without feeling wary—had liked him immediately. She still thought of him as a skinny young man with a calm, youthful voice; on his annual visits it always shocked her, at first, to confront a gray-haired fellow in his sixties.

Back when her illness began to take hold, over a decade ago, Shepley (who had not yet met the love of his life in L.A.) had become doting and indulging, a pleasing combination of nephew and servant, driving Nina to her doctor's appointments and tests by specialists, visiting her regularly, and always including her in holiday celebrations. But it had been eight years since he moved west to be with Robert, and Nina had grown used to his absence. Only rarely did she miss him, mostly after one of his visits, when he took her to tea at the Four Seasons and shopping at Saks in Prudential Center (though she didn't need to buy anything and always felt exposed in public). At her apartment he would cook roasts and bake cakes and freeze things for her to eat for months to come, and afterward his joyous babbling and lurid anecdotes hung in the air—clung to the apartment itself, like cheery wallpaper—for a few days, and then fell away.

Other than Shepley, Tama, a Russian-born journalist a decade younger than Nina, and whom she had known since 1970, was the only friend she still spoke to regularly. Tama telephoned often, long distance from Toronto, mostly to complain. But her complaints were the benign sort that always cheered Nina up, and the ease of gossip in her native tongue was a pleasure.

Shepley too telephoned regularly, but anxiously—to make sure she was still alive, Nina guessed. She suspected she was a bane to him. Not that he didn't truly care for her, but his care, his concern, was itself the bane, a weight on his shoulders, since of course Nina wasn't well and wasn't ever going to become well, and there was no avoiding that basic fact. That she continued to live was itself problematic, in a daily, logistical way that had ultimately led Shepley to step in and make arrangements with Cynthia. And yet Nina had no desire to die. She passed her time with interest, listened to the radio and read the papers—she took the *Globe* and the London *Times*—and each day chose a different album from her collection. Shepley had set up the sound system for her, and regularly sent new recordings of Nina's favorite works. Today's was a recent issue of Brahms's string sextets. If only the telephone wouldn't keep interrupting. Nina continued to ignore it.

No, solitude did not trouble her. She could spend long minutes gazing out the window, hours listening to the BBC on the public radio station. She relished the very texture of her privacy, its depth of space and freedom, much of an entire day hers alone. Her early life of always sharing, never a private moment or corner or closet shelf of her own, had left her hungry for this, ever appreciative of solitude's most basic sensations: rolling her wheelchair from one room to the other with not a soul in her way, and lying in her bed at night hearing only the occasional sidewalk voices or sporadic tire-swish of an automobile in the street.

This current infiltration (as she considered the newspapers and the auction house and the telephone calls of these recent days) threatened to destroy that peace. And ever since that girl Drew had been over, memories—so vivid, they left Nina feeling weak. Even now she could feel them lurking, and something horrible ready to sidle up to her. She tried to focus on the Brahms, and looked out the window. When the ringing started yet again, she felt the last of her patience crumble.

She rolled her wheelchair to the marble table to pick up the telephone. "Yes?"

"Hello, Miz Revskaya, this is Drew Brooks at Beller."

Though she would have preferred to simply ignore her, Nina said, "How do you do."

"I'm very well, thanks—excited, I should say. There's been an unexpected development."

Nina felt her heart lurch.

"An individual who wishes to remain anonymous has brought us a piece that appears to match your amber bracelet and earrings. A pendant, Baltic amber with inclusions. The mounting and hallmarks are identical to those of your demi-parure. The owner maintains that the necklace is not only from the same source but that it belongs with your earrings and bracelet. That they're a full suite."

Nina realized she was holding her breath.

"Miz Revskaya?"

"Nina."

"Nina, yes. We have all three pieces together here, and while we'll of course have to confirm that the pendant is genuine, our appraisers believe, based on the mountings and maker's mark, that these may indeed be a set."

Slowly Nina said, "Does it not occur to you that the appraisers maybe are wrong?"

"Well, of course, appraisal is always a matter of judgment, on a sliding scale, we like to say. Not to mention that clasps and chains can be removed—and sometimes even authentic mountings have had their gems replaced. So we'll be sending this to the lab to make sure it is indeed Baltic amber. But we wanted to call you in case you know anything about it. You see, the pendant's owner would like to include it in the auction. As a donation. It's quite incredible, actually."

"I do not know about it. I have one amber bracelet, with matching earrings. That is all. They are very rare."

"Yes, well, it occurred to us that perhaps you had owned the necklace, too, at some point. Or that you might have known that it was missing."

"I did not think anything missing. I have owned this bracelet and earrings since 1952. They came with me when I left Russia."

"The appraisers thought they might have been a gift, or something handed down in the family. And that perhaps they were divided up at some time."

Her voice tight, Nina said, "Then the appraisers I suppose will know."

"Well, that's the trouble with amber. Since the beads are formed naturally, rather than by a jeweler, it's nearly impossible to confirm which items began as part of the same collection. Some pieces—particularly the more exquisite ones—might be listed in the maker's archives, but without that data or a serial number, we can't be one hundred percent certain."

Nina's breathing relaxed slightly. "I have nothing to say of this."

"That's fine." Drew's voice was unexpectedly firm. "I simply needed to ask you, in case you might have . . . forgotten."

Nina felt the blood in her cheeks. "I am old, but I am not senile."

"No, no, of course, I didn't mean—"

"You must understand, Miss Brooks, that dancers remember. We must remember everything." Physical memory was what she meant, muscle memory, quite different from what Drew Brooks was intimating—but Nina wanted to put her in her place. "I have in me, still, entire ballets. I recall clearly where my jewels come from."

"Yes, of course." A sharp breath. "All right, then. I just wanted to see if you might happen to recall anything. If you do, please let us know."

"Of course."

"In the meantime, our appraisers are going to do their best to confirm the provenance of this additional piece and make sure to corroborate what the owner has suggested. It seems likely, with such atypical mountings. And if the appraisal is sound, we'd like to include the pendant in the catalog. With a note, of course, that this is a last-minute addition that appears to belong to, but was not part of, your personal collection."

Nina remained silent.

"Our appraisers are really very good."

"I do not doubt they are well trained. But I know also that people make"—she paused to formulate—"innocent mistakes."

For a moment Drew said nothing. But then her voice was suddenly bright. "It's a remarkable piece, you know. As uncommon as your bracelet and earrings, to be set that way. And with a particularly stunning inclusion. It's sure to draw not only jewel enthusiasts but specimen collectors as well. Which broadens our bidding pool significantly. Not to mention that something this rare could bring in quite a bit more money. For the foundation, I mean." She waited for Nina's reaction. "And I don't need to tell you that the fact that the donor wishes to remain anonymous . . . well, it's just the sort of thing the public finds intriguing. It's certain to bring more attention to the auction. And more bidders, of course. Which, again, means more money for the foundation."

Nina understood what this girl was doing. "Yes, of course," she said weakly, and then, as quickly as she could, "Good-bye."

HEARING THE DIAL tone rude in her ear, Drew replaced the receiver, took a long slow breath, and wiped a drop of coffee from the lip of her mug in a small, instinctual motion. She knew better than to take any of this personally.

Yet it was difficult not to. The Revskaya project meant more to her than most, not only because of how she loved the ballet. There was also that one haphazard branch of her lineage that to this day remained something of a question mark. And so it did not bother her so much that as usual all of the work (yes, all of it) would fall into her lap, while Lenore floated along unburdened. Drew rarely complained of it; such things weren't worth risking her job for. And as long as she continued to love her work, she found she was able to step back and, from that slight distance, view the job's more irritating aspects as simply amusing. In fact, she found this technique worked well in many of life's circumstances.

Now she looked down at her checklist for the day, the hastily penciled objectives, deceptively brief. Really some of those items might take weeks. As for confirming the provenance of the amber suite, Drew knew that such things moved incrementally, step by step. And of course the directory of Russian goldmarks was temporarily "lost" somewhere in the auction house; Drew had had to order another copy from a special library. Though Lenore had said that an approximate date of manufacture was perfectly fine, Drew hoped the marks might be traced back to a specific production batch. Perhaps then she might be able to say with certainty that the pendant was part of that same set. There was nothing quite like the satisfaction of uncovering a difficult answer, proving something concrete. So much else in the world was vague and impossible to pin down.

As if aware of Drew's thoughts, Lenore poked her head in. Hair in a loose, wispy chignon, a few faded strands framing her face. "How's my lieutenant?" She still called her that, though nearly a year had passed since Drew's promotion to associate director.

"I just notified Nina Revskaya about the amber pendant."

"Good, good." Already Lenore was turning away, a dreamy, distracted expression as she caught her reflection in the glass. Who knew if she had even heard Drew's reply? And yet Drew had to admire—had in fact, in her time here, absorbed—Lenore's poise, her effortless aplomb. She liked watching her at the auction block, her gentle command and easy, swift delivery, her slight accent as if from an overseas boarding school, and the way she nearly flirted with bidders, teasing out their interest, their paddles nervously raised past their avowed limits. "Whenever you're able to start getting some text together for the supplemental, I'd love to see what you come up with."

"I'm on it." Drew had in fact already begun drafting an introduction to the brochure that they would be producing in addition to the biographical notes in the catalog. She gave a small ironic salute, as Lenore drifted out the door like a breeze.

When she first took the job, four years ago, and Lenore called her "my lieutenant," Drew had still been in her twenties. But she was now thirty-two, had little lines at the outer edges of her eyes when she smiled. In the past month something had even happened to her voice: a distinct, if subtle, breaking sound at the back of her throat, that biological shift to some horrible new maturity. The other day the girl behind the counter at the Dunkin' Donuts had called her ma'am. Drew had gone straight to Neiman Marcus and purchased a minuscule tube of the face lotion her best friend, Jen, swore by, some clear, sticky substance that had ended up costing twenty-five dollars. Jen was knowledgeable about that kind of thing. A few months ago she had rubbed some cream that smelled like bubble gum through Drew's hair "to soften your look," taken a photograph, and, without asking Drew's permission, opened a subscription in her name on a dating Web site.

Drew mostly found the ruse humorous—after all, Jen meant well, and had found her own fiancé that way—and had even gone on a few dates, though really she wasn't looking for a husband. The one love she had known had been ephemeral and naïve, perhaps even a trick of self-delusion. And though four years had passed since her divorce, only in recent months had Drew's guilt finally begun to lift. Not that she felt any better about having hurt Eric. But she was growing impatient—with her family, who even from a distance continued to treat her with faintly spiteful pity, and with herself, for continuing even now to feel shame at having made a mistake and hurt someone, when really lots of people made such mistakes, and found themselves exiting relationships they had sworn to remain in forever.

It helped, too, that Eric had finally moved on. After two years of angry silence, and a brief spate of resentful letters, he had written an e-mail to say that he had fallen in love. In yet another reference to the notion he had clung to, that only some sort of insanity could have caused Drew to forgo their marriage, he described his new woman as "a solid person" who had "her head on straight" and "all of her ducks in a row." Then last month Drew's mother—who through sentimentality as much as love remained in touch with her former son-in-law and every so often accidentally released some tidbit of information—let slip that Eric had changed jobs and was moving to Seattle, and that the woman with the ducks was going with him.

And so Drew was all the more aware of time having passed, of having completed, without quite noticing, the passage from "girl" to "woman"—if without any great improvements or new wisdom to show for it. Since her move to Boston she had lived in a diminutive Beacon Hill apartment whose rent continued to rise in small increments, like a slow bleed, despite there being each year a few more splintered floorboards, and smudges on the walls, and cracks in the ceiling. When she first moved in, the ancient building had felt like a fresh start, so different from the sparkling Hoboken unit filled with wedding gifts: 1,200-thread-count sheets, thick towels of Egyptian cotton, Laguiole knives, a cappuccino machine she and Eric never used. Drew's "new" furnishings were secondhand and giddily substandard: stocky chairs of nicked wood, a table with one of its edges faintly splattered with gray paint, an assortment of mismatched cutlery she had found bundled together in a rubber band at a garage sale. She no longer possessed a television, an automobile. This pared-down life suited her, was proof to Eric and the others that there really was no one else, Drew had not left her marriage for some other, better draw. Proof to herself, too, that she had been right to leave; she did not need anyone else, did not need much at all. She was proud of her self-sufficiency, of being able to replace the fuses herself, just as she was proud of her spartan crockery, her found-on-the-sidewalk bookshelf, her yard-sale tea towels and wineglasses.

Jen called it self-punishment. But Drew liked the simplicity of her downsized life, this quieter existence. One needed, she saw now, only a few belongings, just as one needed only a few close friends, and a single passion—it need not be a person, necessarily. Though when she moved in she had purchased a thick cotton bedspread in a deep shade of violet, really she had little hope in that realm. It wasn't that she didn't believe in love; but she no longer believed in it for herself. And while she had, in her first years here, shared her bed with some perfectly nice men, she had gradually come to view her room as a place of solitude and silence. The bedspread had faded to a dusty purple. Every time Drew changed the linens, she told herself she should buy a new one.

The truth was, she always felt a bit separate from most people. Even in her marriage she had never felt, as she had yearned to, that she was part of a team, that she and Eric were partners. Though they had shared many friends from college, after the breakup Drew had given most of them up. Even now, at certain moments—nudging herself onto a seat on the T, or eating lunch at the narrow counter in the sandwich shop, or taking her leisurely twice-weekly (except in winter) run along the Charles—she looked at the people around her and felt not just that she was surrounded by strangers, but that she herself was strange, somehow, that something kept her from ever fully bridging the gap between who she was and who all these other people, making their way through the very same day, were.

According to Jen, this was due to Drew's being an only child,

independent and accustomed to doing things on her own. She had
not grown up with the closeness of siblings, of secrets and shared
genetics. And though she and her mother had once been close, her
father was a quiet man who had never been terribly communicative;
only when Drew graduated from college and became a member of
the workforce did he seem comfortable conducting in-depth conversations with her, asking lots of detailed professional questions, as he
might of a lunch companion or someone sitting next to him on an
airplane. For all these reasons—Jen put forth in her matter-of-fact
way—Drew possessed, or revealed, little need for companionship.
Well, Drew thought to herself, perhaps that was so. She turned back
to her computer screen.

Backdrop: History and Circumstance
behind the Jewels
By Drew Brooks, Associate Director of Fine Jewelry

During the years that Nina Revskaya danced with the Bolshoi
Ballet, her government kept files on a full two-thirds of the
population. By the time she left the USSR, that same government had killed nearly five million citizens. To anyone, these
numbers can be shocking. And yet along with Revskaya,
upon her escape, came objects of startling beauty whose

Drew waited for the next words to come to her. The problem
was that she did not know where to start. She suspected there was
much to say—despite the fact that Nina Revskaya insisted she had
no more information to offer. It was laughable, really. Especially
when she herself said that dancers had such good memories, that
she could remember entire ballets . . . In her mind, Drew could
hear the rising intonation of her voice, the hard rolled *r*'s and nasal
vowels—though her accent was really not so strong, and her English

nearly perfect. For that reason too her unwillingness to talk, paired with the sudden appearance of Grigori Solodin's matching amber pendant, made Drew suppose that there was something more to Nina Revskaya's story.

Not to mention that Grigori Solodin, too, was a bit of a mystery. A big man, tall and slim yet weighty somehow, with a wide thoughtful brow and pensive eyes. Thick hair slightly messy like a boy's. Even now Drew could picture his firm, even tense, jaw, the definition in his face and around his mouth. He had an odd, light accent, not Russian so much as something else Drew didn't recognize. When she asked if he had any documentation to support his assertion that the pendant had belonged to Nina Revskaya, Grigori Solodin had pursed his lips almost as if he were biting them, so that his jaw tightened toward the back of his cheeks, where he had something like dimples. "I am sorry to say that I have no documentation."

But Drew was accustomed to this sort of tricky situation. It was part of what she loved about the auction house, the mysteries and dramas, who originally made that piano, who really painted that portrait, the conflicting versions of family histories from sisters selling their dead aunt's collection of perfume bottles, or a father's humidor full of sought-after cigars. What was it, though, that prevented Grigori Solodin from explaining anything more about how the necklace had come into his possession? When Drew tried to ask him, gently and without insinuation, as they sat in one of the little one-on-one meeting rooms, he said only that the pendant had been handed down to him. "I've owned this necklace my entire life. But for various reasons, and particularly after seeing Nina Revskaya's amber earrings and bracelet, I'm convinced that it too once belonged to her. Or, rather, to that same amber set."

Drew wondered how old he was—late forties, early fifties? Not of Nina Revskaya's generation. She found it intriguing, perhaps even somehow suspect, that besides having a Russian name and living here in Boston, Grigori Solodin, like Nina Revskaya, was reticent, holding something back.

If Lenore sensed that there was anything to all this, it was nothing she would make time for. Her priority was not the hidden details but outward appearance: putting on a successful auction, running a solid business and a good show. Drew, though, loved the stories behind the objects, gossip she heard from clients auctioning off a relative's estate, or of a little-known muse to one of the Group of Eight painters, or the jazz musician who owned a trumpet Miles Davis once played.

The fact was, she hadn't at first had much interest in jewelry. As an art history major she loved paintings and drawings and once had dreams of becoming a museum curator; after graduation she had worked in a gallery in Chelsea and interned at Sotheby's before finding a better-paid position. The job at Beller was simply the first one she found when her marriage ended and she wanted to leave New York. She had revised her professional fantasies accordingly, into a new vision of herself as one of the experts on *Antiques Roadshow*, cheerily informing people that the watercolor they had found in their attic was a rare one worth thousands. Her first opportunity for advancement, five months later, had been as Lenore's associate. And so Drew had refashioned her dream once again, and begun studying for her gemologist certificate through a correspondence course.

In fact the only jewelry she wore she had purchased just three years ago, her very first auction win: a garnet ring that, due to a minor flaw in the stone, had found no bidders. Drew was able to purchase it afterward with a bit of money left her by her grandmother. It remained her only ring, the garnet small and round-cut, propped up by short prongs on a band of white gold. Drew wore it on her right ring finger, as a reminder of Grandma Riitta, whom she still spoke to in her mind sometimes. She was the only one who had not been accusatory when Drew decided to leave her marriage. "You kept growing, didn't you? You grew up," was all she had said, one of the last things she said to Drew, so that Drew knew she understood.

In her mind she still heard her grandmother's voice sometimes. Though she recalled her accent clearly, the few Finnish words Drew knew were already fading. Drew's mother, having come to America as a toddler, had always insisted on responding to her own mother in English. And so in these past years not only Grandma Riitta but an entire language had been lost to Drew.

Looking up from the garnet ring, Drew again read to herself. "Backdrop: History and Circumstance behind the Jewels." That at least had a nice ring to it.

The way Nina Revskaya had denied, so vehemently, that the amber pendant might be hers, not to mention the fact that she and Grigori Solodin apparently did not speak to each other. Or acted as if they did not. Drew wondered what the connection between them might be—or rather, between those three amber pieces. With enough research, and some luck, she supposed, she might be able to figure it out.

Buoyed by the thought, Drew placed her fingers on the keyboard and began to type. "Diamonds may be a girl's best friend, but in the case of Nina Revskaya"

Drew paused, waiting for inspiration . . . and pressed delete.

IT HAD SNOWED again, five more inches. That morning's radio played a clip of Mayor Menino saying that though it was not yet February, Boston's entire annual snow-removal budget had already been spent. As for today's weather—the newscaster announced oddly gleefully—the high would be just two degrees, with a wind-chill factor of ten below.

Americans, always needing to know the exact temperature before deciding how hot or cold to feel. Grigori would have said it aloud;

entering the kitchen he felt—ridiculously, embarrassingly—the familiar disappointment of not finding Christine there sipping her decaffeinated coffee, simultaneously grading a batch of ESL exams and eating a portion of yogurt. She had been one of those people who woke easily and immediately, never needed time to warm to morning, to rub sleep from her eyes.

He poured himself a glass of tomato juice, took a cold gulp, and went to fetch the paper from the front step. Atop a narrow sidebar on the front page was a headline: "Intrigue at Auction House," and in smaller print, "Mystery Donor Brings Rare Gem, Increased Interest."

In his mind he heard Christine, so clearly: *I can't help but dislike her.*

"Well, now," Grigori had always said, whenever the topic of Nina Revskaya came up, "let's not be too hard on her." His instinct was always one of defense. He knew it took restraint for Christine not to simply do something about it herself. That was the main reason he had hesitated, all those years ago, when he first chose to confide in her about Nina Revskaya. Not lack of trust, or shyness, or embarrassment, so much as the knowledge that a woman like Christine would never be able to sit back and let things continue unresolved. A can-do, glass-half-full optimist, she had majored in education—that most idealistic of professions—and was considering a master's in social work. At first Grigori told Christine only the substantiated facts, about his parents, about being an only child, adopted, growing up in Russia, then Norway, then France, and the final leap, in his late teens, to America. When he finally told her, back when he was twenty-five, after they had been together for a full six months, about the ballerina Revskaya, he first made Christine swear to him that she would not intervene, would not take any action, would let Grigori deal with things on his own, in his own way.

Not to mention the fact that you're the only person who ever took the time to translate Elsin's poems into English. And *got them published. I don't see how she could be so apathetic about her own husband's legacy.*

Ah, Chrissie—my advocate, I miss you.

Not so much as a thank-you . . .

That his curiosity about Nina Revskaya's life with her husband had transmutated into Grigori's topic of scholarly expertise—the poetry of Viktor Elsin—was one of those rare happy outcomes born of personal obsession. Whenever the topic of Nina Revskaya's reticence arose (not just with Christine, who knew the full story, but with anyone who inquired about Grigori's translations and scholarship), Grigori had been able to say, without emotion, "It was a harsh time for her. You can imagine how she might not want to be reminded of . . . certain things. It could be like opening Pandora's box, for her to look back at it all the way a scholar likes to. That kind of scrutiny."

Asked if he had requested Nina Revskaya's help in his studies of her husband's poetry, the phrase Grigori used was always, "Not in any detailed way." If pressed he would add, "She knows that I've translated his work, yes, but . . . she hasn't played any *active* role as the holder of Elsin's literary archive." In fact she claimed not to possess any of Viktor Elsin's papers or personal matter. Grigori had decided to believe this to be the truth. After all, plenty of scholars faced such challenges. Not just biographers; any researcher with someone standing between him and his subject. It was part of the job description. And anyway, the poems themselves, and the truths they held, meant more to Grigori than any book he might produce about them or their author, more than any of the finicky papers he had published or the lectures he had presented at various conferences. And so Nina's refusal to help when he approached her, years ago, as a scholar and professor—rather than as that young, innocent college student—he had not taken nearly so personally. Not like the first time. Standing there in the vestibule, waiting for her to come down . . .

As for the translations, they were enough, they would suffice. The poems themselves were enough to maintain his continued interest. At some point they might yield their own secrets, with or without the help of Nina Revskaya. In the meantime, Grigori was perfectly aware of how he came across: nothing atypical, just one of those petty, unbrilliant academics worrying away at some esoteric and ultimately meaningless subject.

The way it felt to press the bell on the intercom, like detonating a bomb . . .

Grigori closed his eyes. If only he knew the truth. Impossible ever to be fully himself until he knew his own history.

He sighed. The pendant was being sent to a lab. "To make sure it's not copal or, you know, a reconstitution," the young woman at Beller had said at their meeting. She had a pleasant, businesslike manner Grigori found calming. "This is really just pro forma," she had assured him. "With rare mountings like these, we have little doubt it's genuine amber. But Lenore always says that if two decades in the business have taught her anything, it's that even the best collections can have something wrong with them."

"Something wrong?" Grigori had felt a kind of panic.

"Something fake, or falsified. Anyone can be duped."

Duped. Just recalling her words, Grigori couldn't help wondering if he himself had somehow, for all these years, been fooled.

"Especially something of this era," the woman had explained. "The Victorians loved remembrance jewelry, and amber with specimens was the ultimate. Demand really spiked—which is of course when imitations start to crop up. Again, though, it's not that we're *doubtful* the pendant is genuine amber. We just want to be able to state in the catalog that it's been verified. With luck, the lab should even be able to confirm where the amber is from. The chemical makeup of Baltic amber is pretty specific."

It was during that conversation that Grigori had for the first time consciously viewed the pendant as a jewel with its very own private and organic past. A gemological creation of the natural world, nothing to do with human travails. Until that moment, he had simply considered it a clue.

In a way it had always tinged him with the shame of a fetishist—not necessarily because it was a woman's jewelry, but for the significance he had placed on it, and the nearly unbearable weight of what he suspected yet could not prove. Only Christine had known all about it. Sitting beside her on the floor of the room he rented, years and years ago, in the big rickety house just over the river in Cambridge, Grigori had told her all he had managed to piece together, and showed her the few bits of evidence. When she first touched the amber, it was with a small stroking motion, almost as if the thing were alive. "It's sort of eerie, isn't it?" She took the pendant in her palm, felt the weight of it. And then: "Can I try it on?"

Why had this surprised him? It hadn't occurred to him that anyone might ever actually wear it. Uneasily he said, "Sure," sounding calm enough that Christine hadn't noticed his hesitation. Leaning forward, she reached behind her head to lift her hair as Grigori draped the necklace and fiddled with the clasp, his hands grazing her neck. He could smell the soap she always used, rose-scented, from Chinatown. "Okay," he said, and she turned around so that he could see the necklace.

It didn't look right on her. Christine said so herself. "That's why I only wear silver," she had explained as she stood to examine herself in the long mirror attached to the bedroom door. "Gold doesn't work with my coloring. Neither does amber, I guess."

Grigori had gone to stand behind her, drawing his arms around her—already, somehow, not quite so jarred by the girl he loved wearing this old and mysterious object. Relief was what he felt, that Christine was so separate from that fraction of his world. In the long mirror he saw, with surprise, a young couple in love.

From that moment the questions that had once seemed to him so central became less urgent; life with Christine overtook those other mysteries, grew larger than the past, created a *new* past, a *new* history—with Christine, who knew him as no one else had, Christine, the place where his search had finally ended.

Ah, Chrissie.

Grigori gulped down the rest of the tomato juice. These past two years had been that much worse for the way that hole had reopened. Larger every day, it seemed, the wanting, the needing to find his way back, somehow.

He placed the empty glass in the sink. This was the moment when Christine would have looked at the clock, said Yikes, gotta go, and kissed him so that he tasted the coffee flavor of her tongue.

Fighting the thought, Grigori went to fetch his coat and gloves from the closet, and braced himself for the cold, cold day.

LOT 16

Antique 14kt Gold and Lava Brooch, depicting St. Basil's
Cathedral. Russian hallmark of 56 zolotniks, in original
fitted box with Cyrillic label. $1,500–3,000

CHAPTER THREE

Again the phone was ringing. First it had been the *Herald* and the *Globe*, but now came the piggybackers: the *TAB*, the *Phoenix*, not to mention the local television and radio stations. All because of that second press release from Beller. You would think there was nothing else happening in all of Massachusetts. But of course that was Boston, its essence, everyone excited about what was really not much at all. Local reporters sniffing around for news . . . At first Nina simply applied that universal yet somehow disingenuous phrase: "No comment." But it felt weak, wrong, and each time she said it, she felt less in control.

"Do you have any idea who the anonymous donor might be?"

"No comment."

"Were you surprised to learn that someone else owned amber jewelry that matched your own?"

"No comment."

After nearly a full day of this, Nina realized what a fool she had been not to turn the ringer off. When she found the little switch, she felt as she imagined a scientist might upon making a simple yet brilliant discovery. And so she had a day and a half of quiet—until Cynthia discovered the switch and made that sucking noise through her teeth that she always used to show disapproval, and turned it back on. Then she scolded Nina with a long spiel about safety and the rules of her job at Senior Services. When the ringing started up, she scolded Nina again, for not having an answering machine.

It was the next day that Cynthia said, "You know, sugar, if you just give them one interview, I bet they'll stop calling."

"I have given quite sufficient interviews in my life." The problem was, Nina knew, that she was "theirs." Other once-famous dancers resided in New York, Paris, Majorca, but Nina was Boston's very own grande dame of ballet. Yet she had no desire to speak to anyone, least of all some poor scribe from the *Worcester Telegram & Gazette*. These days she sometimes found herself talking too much, saying things she hadn't even wanted to say. It was those tablets. They made her not just groggy but loose-tongued, caused her to chat with Cynthia for much longer than she had meant to. One day last week she had found herself in the middle of a detailed story about her studio in London before realizing that it was Cynthia, and not a friend, she was talking with.

"I'm just saying," Cynthia went on, "as long as you don't talk, they'll keep calling. But you give them what they want, they'll quiet down." She must have seen that Nina was considering. "An exclusive," Cynthia added, as if she worked in the industry and used such terms all the time.

That was how Nina came to talk to Channel 4 News. It was arranged in no time, simply by returning their call. When Cynthia heard that June Hennessey and her crew would be taping at the apartment the next evening, she assessed Nina with new appreciation and said, "Wait till Billy hears!" Apparently June Hennessey had been the *News 4 New England* entertainment reporter for decades and was something of a celebrity herself; Cynthia said she was the last person to have interviewed Rose Kennedy before she died. Nina would have raised an eyebrow, had her face not been so painfully stiff. "I suppose she plans to kill me off too."

To her credit, Cynthia didn't bother laughing. "Something tells me it would take more than that to do you in."

The afternoon of the taping, Cynthia showed up wearing not her usual nurse-pajamas but sleek black pants, a form-fitting purple sweater, and lipstick of a cheery mauve color. Nina chose not to acknowledge her efforts, and to treat June Hennessey, the two cameramen, the slim, frowning producer, and the sound technician with similar indifference. Microphones and large freestanding lights were set up with some sort of reflective panel, and Nina's face powdered and rouged, while the producer stood with his arms crossed, bossing everyone around. But all that mattered to Nina—seated on the divan where Cynthia had insisted on arranging her among a cluster of firm little velvet pillows—was that she had her answers ready. When June Hennessey, sitting next to her, asked, "Isn't it surprising that the amber necklace that matches your set should also happen to be here in the U.S., and not back in Russia?" Nina barely paused.

"It is mysterious. But I am sure there are many instances of this. Matching sets of jewels—or anything, why not?—become separated, because of theft, or perhaps they ended up to be sold at commission shops, or . . . desperation, bribery . . . who knows?" The bright light from above the first cameraman hurt her eyes.

"Bribery," June Hennessey said in a dramatic voice, and Nina knew she wanted more of that.

"In the Soviet Union, it was how much was done."

June Hennessey gave a deliberate, knowing nod so that the second cameraman could be sure to catch her reaction. "You mentioned theft. Do you think the pendant was stolen?"

"It is very probable. The bracelet and earrings were handed down, you see, to me through my husband. They belonged to his family, but in the civil war many of their valuables were lost." That very last bit, at least, was true.

"Such a tragic history." June Hennessey arranged her face to look stricken, and the second cameraman did something with his lens to zoom in. "Your husband lost his life, didn't he—not in the revolution, but—"

"According to official records, yes."

"Terrible, just terrible." June Hennessey shook her head, the waves of her carefully set hair moving stiffly side to side. "And when you defected, these absolutely *gorgeous* jewels came with you."

"They came with me from Russia, in a situation of great danger and hardship." Nina could hear the light hum of the first cameraman's lens moving in for a close-up.

"In a way they're mementos, aren't they?" June Hennesey's brow rose into a hopeful expression. "Not only are they incredibly rare, and completely *gorgeous*, not to mention extremely valuable. But for you they have an emotional value, too. They were from your husband's family, and when you lost your husband, the amber that he had passed down to you was all you had left of him."

June Hennessey seemed thrilled with her own insight. In a small voice Nina said, "Yes. All I had left of my husband."

IN 1947 SHE is twenty-one, and has been in the company three years. Five counting wartime, when she was one of the group that stayed to dance at the Filial; the rest of the Bolshoi had been evacuated to a town by the Volga. Back then Nina was one of just two new graduates hired for the corps—a dream come true, if not, perhaps, a surprise.

After all, Nina excelled from the moment she entered the ballet school, never questioned the grueling repetition, ten years of pliés and *relevés* and holding her buttocks tight. ("Imagine you're gripping a tram ticket there," the teacher said in the very first class, "and don't ever let it drop!") Ten years of chassés across a raked wooden floor dark with wet spots from the watering can, ten years of studio windows steamed with sweat. Always some ache or pain. From that first year with the other little girls dressed all in white, having to curtsy each time an adult passed in the corridor, to the years of black leotards and pale tights (to reveal every shadow and line of the leg muscles), Nina has withstood the exacting comments of her ballet instructors, their constant minute corrections, the light, uncompromising touch of a fingertip here, there—shoulder back a bit more, chin tilted just so—and been buoyed by their approval, the glimpsed delight in their faces at her quick turns and jumps, asking her to demonstrate a *saut de basque*: "Nina, please show the class what I mean." The very fact that they always remembered her name revealed that she had impressed them. Even as a small girl, with no family connections to pull strings for her, she was always selected for dance scenes in the Opera, or for the ballets with children's roles—a mouse or a flower or a page. Meanwhile her muscles strengthened, tendons elongated, she grew lean, her spine supple, every movement imbued with poise and sense of space. But it was her devotion, her ambition, her strict self-discipline that set Nina apart. An intensity of concentration that could draw rivulets of sweat down her face, neck, arms, chest, no matter how seemingly simple an exercise. The tyranny of her own perfection, of wanting, always, *more*, of knowing the limits of her body even as she sought to push beyond them, her limbs trembling with fatigue. Always dancing full-out, her diagonals across the floor nearly sending her into the wall. Staying on after class until she learned to land her *tours jetés* without a sound, practicing triple pirouettes until her face turned a purplish red. Practicing her autograph, even—as if that too might ensure her future. By the war's end she was a soloist.

Yet when she thinks of all the hurdles she has cleared, the sometimes humiliating classes, the sternly judged exams, the frustration of injuries (tender right kneecap, and a recurring corn between her fourth and little toes), it seems nothing short of miraculous that, from the dusty courtyard of the building where she still lives with Mother, she has somehow, finally, arrived here: not just onstage but in this new life, a dancer, permitted—by her own doggedness and exacting training as much as by luck and the various whims of the universe—to do for a living the thing she loves most in the world.

Now it is December. Winter darkness, like a candle blown out. All month a flu has stalked its way through the company, as always, just in time for the endless *Shchelkunchik* performances, half the corps shivering with fever, mucus flung from noses with each pirouette. Tonight all three principals are ill, and Nina at the last minute finds herself dancing the role of the Sugar Plum Fairy, holding forth well enough in the big adagio but still worrying the audience might begrudge this eleventh-hour switch.

Her pulse continues to rush after the heavy curtains have swung shut, and then she is back in the chilly dressing room she shares with Polina now that they have both been promoted to first soloist. Polina is Nina's age, with freckled skin, spidery eyelashes, and a long, thin neck. Tonight she danced the part of the Snow Queen and has glitter all through her hair. Peeling off sweaty tights with trembling hands, trying to hurry, hoping the silk doesn't snag. An official from the Ministry of Foreign Affairs has requested two dancers for a reception tonight, and in the absence of any principals, Nina and Polina are to perform.

Only after company class this morning did the director explain: a foreign delegation; a Party official's private residence; a car and escort to be sent for them . . .

"You of course understand what an honor this is, to entertain our leaders."

Of course she is honored. While the top-tier dancers (and actors, writers, singers) often perform at government functions, not until this year has Nina been included in the lowest reaches of this category. Yet even now, as she quickly washes and powders herself, she hears the implication in the director's words: that it is her duty to perform, that both she and Polina are at the service of the state. If only she weren't so tired, if only the hour weren't so late. Already this week she has performed double her usual bill. Her pointe shoes, crusted with rosin, are starting to wear through.

"I'm so excited," Polina is saying, stuffing pink tights and leg warmers into her drawstring bag. "I just wish I had something better to wear."

"They'll only see our costumes, anyway." Changing into her one good dress, though, Nina too feels plain. Just last week her mother fixed her coat up for her—sewed a yard of braid to the cuffs and hem—yet the elbows are so worn, they shine. At the last minute, though, she has an idea.

"Well now, where did that come from?" Waiting in her own shiny-elbowed coat, Polina raises her overplucked eyebrows.

"Where do you think?" Across Nina's shoulders is a fur, white and lush, taken from the costume stash. "I'm just borrowing it." She rubs her chin against the animal's small head as she and Polina, carrying the hangers with their costumes, and the drawstring bags with their shoehorns and leg warmers and rubbing alcohol, and the clutch purses with their perfume and lipstick, make their way outside, where their escort—a shivering, glum-looking man in a thick-shouldered coat—waits.

The snow has been coming down since afternoon, wet flakes beginning to turn icy. Polina keeps exclaiming about the weather as she and Nina are driven along in a long black ZiS limousine. This is the first time either of them has ridden in one. Only once has Nina been inside a private automobile—back before the war, when a friend's cousin was visiting and took them for a drive in an old German Opel. Now Nina supposes the cousin must have gone off to the war, wonders, with that familiar, vaguely sick feeling in her chest, if he made it home or ended up in a steel box. Or maybe he is like the beggars she sees on the streets, with stumps for limbs. Nina always stops to give them a few kopecks. In her mind she still hears the line—it comes from a poem—everyone knows: *better to return with an empty sleeve / than with an empty soul.*

They arrive at a handsome gray stone building (none of the usual peeling paint or sagging roofs) and soon are in a changing room yet again, pulling on silk tights and stiff tutus, stuffing thick butcher paper down into the toes of their pointe shoes, where the fabric is worn out. They will be performing variations from *Swan Lake.* Just a year ago Nina's top roles were the dance of the six swans or of the four cygnets—but already this year she has danced one of the lead swans, and the act 1 pas de trois, and the Hungarian Bride in the third act. Still, she dreams of no longer being among the crush of girls in feathered headbands, the cramped queue starting at the front stage right corner and curling all the way backstage. . . .

Tonight's stage is a vast, twinkling ballroom, the rough wooden dance floor laid atop a marble one shiny as ice. Nina's heart pounds so intensely surely everyone, seated at tables all around, can hear it. Her mouth has gone dry, her hands cold and clammy. She glimpses plates heaped with food, and circles of men in dark suits: people with official posts, executive powers. Her heart seems to be right between her ears. There are even a few women here, wives in long gowns. But now the pianist has begun to play, and the guests become a blur as Nina, her body moving as of its own will, begins to dance.

Not until Polina's variation, while Nina catches her breath, does she note the ballroom's high vaulted ceilings, the vast buffet, the many candles, lanterns, and flowers. As if the barrenness of these past years, the fatigue, the hunger, no longer exists. And to think that this is someone's *home.* Clatter of cutlery, of dishes being re-filled, even as Polina dances. Watching, the guests smoke cigarettes, and fill their mouths, and chew and swallow, and clink their glasses.

Nina feels her legs already beginning to cool down; there is a bad

draft from somewhere. But now it is her turn again, adrenaline rushing as she tries not to stumble on the seams of the gritty makeshift
floor. *Chink-chink* of dishes, the chewing mouths. Already it is over,
Nina and Polina taking their carefully choreographed curtsies before
being shooed back to the changing room.

"Did you see the food?" Polina whispers, already untying her
shoe ribbons, her tights smudged with dirt from the dance floor.

Nina nods, and her stomach gives a twinge; she hasn't eaten for
hours. Now that she acknowledges it, she feels immediately famished.

"I recognized some of them," Polina adds, stepping out of her
costume. Her legs and arms are splotched pink with cold.

Nina too recognized some faces: the deputy foreign minister with
his winged white hair, and the chairman of the Arts Commission.
But they were eating, some of them barely looking, gulping and mas-
ticating while she danced. . . .

"They've seen both of us now, up close," Polina says excitedly,
and Nina wonders why she herself doesn't feel that way. She has
never been interested in politics, her enthusiasm for such matters
limited to the watching of parades and air shows. She attends as few
Komsomol meetings as possible; as a young girl her only interest in
the Pioneers was for the folk dancing and the neat red scarves. Even
now she has to force herself to sit through the mandatory Marxist
lectures, and rarely sings along to the Party songs with the rest of the
troupe on the touring bus. Because what does any of *that* have to do
with dance?

She has just finished dressing when a servant taps on their door:
Nina and Polina have been invited to the table of the deputy minister
of foreign affairs.

Polina's eyes open wide, while Nina quickly takes up her small
pocketbook and drapes the white fur around her neck. Her heart
gallops all over again as they are led back out to the great ballroom.
The twinkling lights of the chandelier make the room seem warmer

than it is, softening everyone's skin, so that no one looks quite so sallow. At a table with a small group of others, the deputy foreign minister, red-faced and jolly, introduces Nina and Polina to the guests of honor. They are from Holland, the wife in a dress of a style Nina has never seen before. Its fabric, when the woman stands to shake her hand, rustles like aspen leaves. "This is Nina Timofeyevna Revskaya. Our Butterfly."

He must have read the newspaper article—the review that called her that, just last week. "N. Revskaya's buoyancy, her seeming weightlessness, the boundlessness of her leaps, make her look, at times, caught in the air. Her every movement contains a wholeness that is not simply physical but also emotional, of the mind as well as the body."

The guests say something that the translator, a flustered-looking gray-haired woman, turns into a compliment about Nina's dancing. The very sounds of this strange language make Nina anxious; normally even the briefest chat with foreigners could mean a trip to the secret police. At the same time, Nina cannot stop staring. These are the first Westerners she has seen close up. The only foreign cities she has been to—with the ballet—are Budapest, Warsaw, and Prague.

"For you," the deputy foreign minister says boisterously, as he offers them goblets of red champagne. His wife, a stocky woman with a fox fur around her neck, emits a smell—something unpleasant yet familiar. Could it be perfume? Nina's own scent, Crimean Violet, always evaporates as soon as she puts it on.

Now everyone at the table is raising their glasses: "To peace." Nina clinks her glass with the others, but there is no food in her stomach to soak up the red champagne. It is with relief that she and Polina are ushered over to the buffet. Polina exclaims at the cold meats and salads, and smoked sturgeon, and black and white bread, and blinis with caviar and sour cream . . . Baked apples, too, and in the middle of it all, an enormous half-eaten salmon. Nina's stomach growls, though she is used to hunger. Only this month was the complicated rationing system terminated. Mother still stretches milk with water and brews carrot peels in place of tea, and returns from the markets having struggled over a few rotting potatoes and a wizened parsnip or two. Yet now, here, all this . . . Their escort has stepped away, no one is watching as they fill their plates. Breathing the distinct aroma of coffee, Nina arranges the delicate chain strap of her purse over her shoulder so that she can help herself to bread that she spreads with real butter. Even the cutlery—gleaming forks and knives and serving spoons—is stunning. Nina spreads the butter thickly, eagerly, so hungry, her hands shake. The knife slips from her grasp.

"Lucky you," Polina says when it lands on the floor. "A man is coming to call." She ascribes to numerous superstitions. "And I'm going to meet my Prince Charming tonight. I feel it in my bones."

Nina bends down for the knife. "How do you know it's not the flu?"

"Ha! I have a good sense for these things. I can smell it in the air." Polina is always falling in love; for it not to be in the air, she would have to not breathe. "You might meet yours, too," she adds, in a tone that makes it clear she doesn't really think so. She knows that the only kissing Nina has ever done has been in ballets, her brightly painted lips pressed dryly against her partner's. And although as a dancer Nina is used to being touched by men, guided, lifted, tossed high in the air, she has rarely felt physical attraction toward them, with their wrestlers' bodies—thick thighs from so many squats for the *prisiadka*, bulging pectorals from all the acrobatic lifts. Andrei, her adagio partner, has legs like mutton drumsticks. He sometimes flexes the muscles of his buttocks just to make her laugh.

"Do you see anyone?" Nina asks, though of course the question is moot. Any men close to their age would have been eaten up years ago by the war. The only healthy young men Nina ever sees are danseurs in the ballet, and even some of them have lost their teeth to scurvy.

The rest were killed in action, or exiled if they happened to have a German name. Nina's romantic fantasies are just that, fantasies, childish ones, of brave parachutists, aeronauts, deep-sea divers—no one she's ever met. She looks out at the clusters of military men and Party officials, members of the Secretariat, all of them twice her age. Dessert has officially begun, petits fours and scoops of ice cream. Nina spots the foreign diplomats, visibly alien in their fitted suits and neat haircuts, eating contentedly. No chance, of course, for any one of them to be a Prince Charming. A new law has made it illegal to marry non-Soviets.

Her own countrymen look comparably scruffy, their suits rumpled the way only men are allowed to be, their cuffed trousers pooling at their ankles. Nina watches the Dutch wife, who with her clean new shoes and prim dress looks so different from the Russian wives in their furs and long gowns of panne velvet. "Do you know anyone?" Polina asks, her chin high.

"No. Oh, well, there's Arkady Lowny." Aide to the culture minister. A face like the fat pink boiled hams at the Gastronom. He goes around with a broad, inexplicable smile, as if he has just been told good news—but his hands, Nina has noticed, are always trembling. Now he is approaching them, grinning.

"Good evening, ladies." Brushing his hair to the side with a shaky hand. Polina says a bright, "There you are!" clearly relieved to know someone. Soon she and Arkady are deep in a back-and-forth of meaningless chatter, Polina's freckles disappearing as she blushes. "Oh, but you do!" "No, I don't!" "I'd say you do!"

Just a step away from Nina are two other couples in conversation, one of the women slightly familiar. It is Ida Chernenko, the famous wild-animal trainer, older than in the posters. The other woman is younger, with a shapely bust and a long wave of golden hair, her hand resting just above her hip in a way that makes her waist look slender. Like many of the women she wears a big flashy oval ring on her index finger, and a string of amber beads. The man next to her is different from the others, younger, and tall rather than stocky, somehow elongated, not a Muscovite at all. He is telling a joke; Nina can tell because of the way Ida and the other man are listening, the corners of their mouths already upturned, their eyes crinkling, certain of a punch line. On her bosom Ida wears an enormous brooch, and when the man finishes his joke, she laughs so hard, the brooch flops back and forth like a small, severed head.

"Please, no more," the other man is saying, cheeks red from drink or from laughter. "Your jokes are a strain on my liver."

The younger woman just smiles in an elegant, amused way. The handsome man must be her husband. Square jaw, aquiline nose, thick gleaming brown hair. Long-limbed, so that his baggy suit drapes him in a way that seems refined rather than poorly constructed. He must not have served in the war. He looks too healthy and content.

He has noticed Nina staring and glances up, a pleased look spreading across his face. Opening his mouth to speak—

"Oh, good, you're still here!" Lida Markova, who runs the State Archive for Literature and Art, beams at Nina. A thick wall of a woman, with coarse hair and a booming voice, and glass beads hanging from her earlobes. Lida loves the ballet, always seeks out the company of the newer dancers, who are not as aloof as the more senior stars. "So wonderful to see you dance tonight."

"Thank you. How nice to see you." Nina tries to look past Lida, to see if she can catch the man's eye.

"And I absolutely adored you last month in *Coppélia*. You have such a lightness to you." Nina danced the "Prayer" variation (though she dreams of one day having the role of Swanilda). "It's my favorite ballet, I must say. Because it has such a happy ending. Simplistic, I suppose, but isn't a happy ending what we all really want?"

"Yes!" Nina laughs. But past Lida's shoulder she sees, with a droop in her heart, that the handsome man is no longer there.

"It's so wonderfully comic," Lida is saying. "Even stupid Frantz is happy at the end."

Lida smells just like the foreign minister's wife. A heavy scent, some kind of perfume, dying flowers mixed with overripe fruit. There is something familiar about it, something Nina has smelled before.

"Oh," Lida says, "there's my husband signaling to me." She nods at him, and the fur across her shoulder nods too. Nina cannot help but notice that it is slightly decayed.

That's what the smell reminds her of. A dead rodent.

Nina looks down, somehow dismayed, and strokes the borrowed fur on her shoulders.

Under her breath Lida says, "Time to go."

"Already?" Nina hasn't even tasted the desserts, and quickly pours herself a cup of coffee. But Lida says, "Have a good night," and hurries to her husband.

Sipping her coffee anxiously, Nina sees that the other Party folk also are leaving. A mass departure, as if choreographed, the men with their five o'clock shadows and their suits from the Moscow Tailoring Combine, and the wives who smell like their furs. Like in *Cinderella*, when the clock strikes midnight. The coffee tastes of chicory.

Not far from Nina, a woman is making stiff commands at a Siamese servant. Perhaps this is *her* house, not the foreign minister's at all. Or perhaps it too is a sort of theater, a temporary haven like the Bolshoi, grand and lush—and now everyone is being kicked out. Nina notices that the curtains on the window across from her are frayed, and that the glass itself is cracked. "*Nyet!*" the woman hisses to the servant, who hurries off, looking confused.

That is when Nina sees Polina leaving with Arkady Lowny. Probably the tall, handsome man, too, has left, along with his shapely wife. Nina hastily spreads more bread with butter, eats it hungrily—though there is something ruined about the food, now, too, the salmon and sturgeon picked to bits, and a trail of something pinkish where the desserts were. From a large wooden bowl holding a pyramid of tangerines, Nina plucks one off the top and holds it in her palm. It fits there exactly, its skin smooth, cool, perfectly orange; the only things Nina ever sees this bright in winter are the Pastorale costumes in *Shchelkunchik*. She thinks of her mother at home, her same old black bread and cabbage soup, her net shopping bag limp with a few bruised root vegetables. Looking quickly about, Nina opens her purse and drops the tangerine inside. She shuts it, then takes another and cuts the skin with her thumbnail, releasing its bright, sharp scent. Holding it up to her face, she breathes in.

"Good for congestion, is it?"

The man—the tall one—is next to her. Nina feels her heartbeats rush, wondering what exactly he saw. But she manages to calmly peel another swatch of tangerine skin, white veins pulling away from the orange flesh, and hands the piece of peel to the man. "Just pinch it a little."

He takes the peel from her as carefully as if it were gold leaf. Then he folds it back, bringing it up to his nose and closing his eyes. Watching his nostrils flare, his lips curling slightly, Nina supposes he must look like this when he is asleep and having pleasant dreams. Just thinking it makes her feel she is witnessing something private— too private for someone she has just met. But then, he might have witnessed her taking the tangerine. When he opens his eyes, she looks down, afraid that he has noticed her staring.

"For you," she says, pulling apart the tangerine, holding a half out to him. They eat the wedges in silence. The sweet juice prickles at Nina's tongue, and all at once she is overwhelmed, by the bright taste in her mouth, and by the distinct sensation that she has entered someplace she isn't quite meant to be.

When he has finished the last of the tangerine, the man grins at her, as if they have shared in a prank. This grin is stunning in its boyishness, the grin of someone utterly unworried. Nina has not seen such a grin in an adult *ever*. It is as if he has never seen hardship, never felt hunger. Even the way his teeth pile into each other pleases her, because it is the only thing she has seen of him that isn't smooth and aligned. She finds it attractive on him, this very slight crookedness.

Perhaps this is why she decides she can ask him. She makes her voice so quiet it isn't even a whisper. "Why is everyone leaving all at once?"

The man looks like he might laugh. "New to these events, I see." More quietly, he adds, "It's always this way. Show up as is your duty, get as drunk as possible, and leave as soon as you've filled up on dessert."

His frank talk emboldens her. "But the guests from Holland—"

"You yourself know, surely, not to be friendly with strangers." Again he looks as if he has told a joke.

"Ah, Viktor Alekseyevich, there you are."

Coming toward them is Vladimir Frolov, from the Society for the Dissemination of Political Knowledge. A frequent presence at the ballet, he is a short, beaming man with a friendly, somewhat doughy face. Hair parted in the middle and graying at the temples. "I've been meaning to give you my congratulations. Oh, good evening, Butterfly, you're still here, how wonderful." He lifts her hand—the one that mere minutes ago held the tangerine—to kiss it, while Viktor says, "I agree. Quite wonderful."

"Did you know," Frolov asks her, "that our dear friend here has received excellent notices for his latest book?"

Nina doesn't dare ask what kind of book. It appears she should already know.

"Excellent notices," Frolov continues. "I look forward to reading it myself. Nina, beware of this man. He is a poet of devastating talent."

Nina says the first thing that comes to her: "You don't look like a poet."

The man named Viktor raises his eyebrows. "And what should a poet look like?"

"Sleepy" is what comes to mind. Both Viktor and Frolov laugh.

"Rumpled, I mean. But in an otherworldly way."

"It's you who are otherworldly," Vladimir Frolov exclaims. "Isn't that right, Viktor?"

Viktor gives a slow nod. "Like you've drifted in on a raft of stars."

"See that?" Vladimir Frolov says, his eyes comically wide. "He really is a poet."

Nina says, "Or perhaps he just has a way with words."

"Words have their way with *me*," Viktor says. "Sometimes they won't even let me sleep."

"Well," Nina says, "I congratulate you on your new book."

"I'll give you a copy."

"Oh, I'm afraid I never read anymore." Though it is the truth (the ballet leaves her no free time), she worries it sounds rude, and adds, "I used to love to read when I was little, but now all I have time for are the notices on Gorky Street."

"We'll have to change that."

Frolov looks annoyed at having been briefly excised from their chatter. "More than a poet, you see?" he says. "He has a good eye, not just a good ear; see how quickly he managed to find the most beautiful woman in the room? I forbid you to monopolize her. Come, both of you. I'm taking you for a snow drive!"

He ushers them away from the buffet table, toward a small cluster of people he has already rounded up. Nina can't help feeling uncomfortable, surrounded by so many new faces. There is a woman who sings in the Opera, and another functionary like Frolov, from the Central Council of Trade Unions, with thick, wild hair and rosy cheeks. His wife, looking like something out of the past, wears dark lace and holds a gold lorgnette. To his other side is another man, larger and stockier, with a yellow mustache, looking very drunk—he is a character actor from the Moscow Art Theatre. "Good evening," they all greet each other, with practiced, if false, poise, while Nina realizes, with the thrill of surprise, that for the first time in her life she is in a group of the privileged few. The very spontaneity of this outing—not part of a club or association or organization of some kind—is a privilege.

"Yes, yes, bundle up, let's go," says Vladimir Frolov, taking from his pocket a key, dangling it in front of them.

Nina retrieves her bag and costume and coat and follows the group outside, where the street is white. It has continued to snow, and now the flakes are tiny, like sparkling dust. "Oh!" Nina slips on ice. To her disappointment it is the big stocky character actor, not Viktor, who catches her.

"You're light as a feather," the man says, and she can smell the alcohol on his breath.

"Here we are." Vladimir Frolov's face glows with pride. In front of them is a big black Pobeda crowned with fresh snow. The men brush the drifts off with their hands until the car is uncovered, round and shiny. Opening the back door, Frolov cries, "Please, hop in!"

Three of the others pile into the front, and for a moment Nina worries that Viktor is among them. But no, he is still here, and Nina slides in beside him, on this seat that smells like tobacco. She can practically hear the wardrobe mistress scolding her, for dropping her costume in a crumpled mass at her feet. On Viktor's other side are the thick-haired man and his wife. Very casually, Viktor drapes his arm around Nina's shoulders. She is shocked; the most any man ever dares in public is to take a woman by the arm. But Viktor's face shows nothing. His arm might as well be resting on the back of a chair and not her shoulders with the borrowed white fur. Nina decides to act as if she doesn't notice.

The car is cold, and her breath makes a mist. Frolov turns the key and gives a few tries at the motor. Though the streets and sidewalks have been cleared earlier, a new sheath of snow has accumulated. Now the motor roars. Frolov pulls wildly out into the road and begins driving toward the center of town, and Nina feels herself tossed lightly, first toward the door and then toward Viktor. The others are oohing and aahing at the glittering night, and at Frolov's swerving.

Looking out the window, Nina thinks, For once the city looks beautiful. Most of the year she finds it drab, everything covered with a gray-brown film of mud or dust. Now the snow has made it clean, sparkling. "Moscow never looks quite so beautiful, does it, as when it's all covered with snow." She says it quietly, so that only Viktor will hear.

"The opposite of a woman," Viktor answers. He too speaks almost in a whisper, his breath warm on her ear. "Our city looks best when everything's covered up. And a woman is most beautiful when there's nothing in the way."

Nina feels her shoulders tense, at his nerve, his insinuation. But she follows her instinct and removes the white fur from around her collar, placing it on her lap, where the folds of her coat open in a V. As she does so, she affects a bored expression, in case Viktor is watching her face.

He moves his hand just the slightest bit forward. Nina feels his fingertips touching the side of her neck, stroking her skin. Heat shoots through her, while Vladimir carries on a commentary from up front, calling out, "There is nothing like it, I tell you, nothing like driving in fresh snow!"

She wants to look at Viktor but doesn't want to turn her head. She can see at her periphery that he is still facing forward, as if she weren't even there.

Frolov and the others are laughing at something, and Nina sees

that they are now on the Arbat, sliding past movie theaters and book-
stores and commission shops. "Overtake and Surpass" banners ripple
tensely in the wind. It is so late, only the plainclothes police are out,
looking forlorn among the drifts of snow. In the windows are New
Year's trees covered in tinsel, and glittery images of Father Frost. With
the decorations sparkling, the street itself looks like something out of
a fairy tale. And although music filters as usual from the big outdoor
speakers, the snow mutes it, makes it sound far away.

The drunk man in the front seat is mumbling the words to a song
Nina doesn't know. She isn't drunk at all, cannot afford to be, with
her dancing. What about Viktor, she wonders: Is he drunk? Is that
what has emboldened him to put his fingers where they are now,
stroking her neck, so lightly, as if they just happened to land there?
And what about that woman, the blond shapely one . . .

In the front seat, the man's singing becomes louder. He has
switched to a song from the end of the war, "Glory to Comrade
Stalin." Nina feels herself tense; the man's drunkenness makes the
song sound, just slightly, mocking.

"Too bad it's not our operatic friend instead," the man next to
Viktor says, clearing his throat somewhat anxiously, as the drunk
man continues, off-key.

Frolov, clearly eager to set everyone at ease, calls out, "The green
snake gets the best of us." He has to raise his voice over the man's.
But the man must sense the problem; he switches his singing, to a
folk song that quickly fades into nothing.

Snow floating down again, flakes bigger than before. The Pobeda
skids through the white streets, but Nina feels safe despite the speed
and these strangers and this man's fingertips on her neck. Odd, how
protected she feels—by the snow, the sidewalks glinting with it, and
by the warmth and absurdity of all these bodies packed into the car,
tossed against each other with each swerve, this random congrega-
tion, like characters in a joke.

Now the Pobeda has slowed. Slinking along, past floodlit Red Square—empty and vast, the poor stiff soldiers freezing on each corner, guarding Lenin's tomb and the old round-walled execution block and the spruce trees lining the walls of the Kremlin. "It's coming down harder now," the woman in the front seat says. "Look how thick the flakes are."

But Nina is looking just ahead, toward the south end of the square, where St. Basil's Cathedral, marvelous and absurd, stands like bonbons on display. The rest of the city may still be in tatters, but St. Basil's is dazzling, freshly restored, its striped domes patterned with bright swirls of color. "Somebody made that," Nina says, with surprise. "People made that." Her realization is genuine; she has never, so clearly and precisely, thought of it that way. Seeing it in the midst of the incredible snow, she is aware, unmistakably, that that vision in the distance is the product of human effort.

It is at that moment, as the car creeps past the whipped peaks of St. Basil's, that Viktor lifts his hand away from Nina's neck.

She feels him swoop a lock of hair back over her ear. Then he pulls his arm back, no longer around her shoulders, and with one easy motion slides his hand under the white fur in her lap, to where the edges of her coat meet, and then between the folds, lightly pressing the fabric of her dress between her legs. It is the back of his hand, as if it just happened to land there, his knuckles against her, nudging her thighs apart. Nina takes a quick breath, but says nothing.

The car swerves to the right, and Frolov gives a yip of delight. The couple in the back laugh fearfully as he fishtails toward the bridge. Nina closes her eyes, alarmed by the new feeling inside her. She leans her head against Viktor's shoulder.

"Aha!" cries Frolov. "You see what this car can do!" The other women squeal, while Nina swallows hard. In the front seat, the drunk man has begun to protest, saying he does not feel well. "It's too much," Nina hears him say, and Frolov says, "All right, then, I'll stop." He drives more slowly.

Nina closes her eyes against the new feeling overtaking her. The couple next to Viktor is debating something about the desserts at the reception, while the drunk man in front continues to make complaints. Nina feels her hips shifting, her neck tightening. She is terrified of what is happening. The feeling is rising, her stomach fluttering, and without a thought she reaches out toward Viktor's other hand, to grab it. Holding it tightly as the car continues forward, she struggles to act as though nothing is happening.

When they drop the drunk man off, Nina lets go of Viktor's hand and moves hers away. His other hand moves only slightly, opening up so that his palm now rests on her thigh. It remains there as Nina's pulse gradually slows, as Frolov stops to drop the older couple at their building, and continues on to deposit the opera singer at hers. By then the pounding of Nina's heart has returned to normal. "And you, Miss Butterfly?" Frolov asks, as he again swerves out into the street. "Where shall I deliver you?"

Nina gives him an address, not of the building where she lives with her mother, but of the larger street that abuts it. Viktor's hand pulls away then, out from under the coat and back to his own lap. Nina straightens herself and reaches up to tidy her hair, as if it too has been flustered.

"Here we are!" Vladimir Frolov cries happily, slowing the car to a stop.

Nina picks up the fur from her lap and brings it back to her neck. She does not want to leave the side of this man whose very existence was unimaginable to her just hours ago. It is the first time in her life that she has felt this way, the first time she has wanted to feel someone else's skin against hers, the first time the heat inside her has become something all of its own.

"Good night," she tells them, as Frolov steps out of the front seat to open her door.

"Indeed," says Viktor, and takes her hand, not at the palm but further down, facing up, so that his fingertips are at her wrist bone. Nina is speechless, because of what he has done to her body. Surely he can feel her pulse.

He kisses her hand—but on the inside, toward the top of her palm, as Frolov opens her door. Nina eases herself away from Viktor, takes her bag and purse and costume up from where they have been crushed beneath her knees. She really will get a talking-to from the wardrobe mistress. She finds her voice again to thank her host. "Good night," as Frolov returns to the driver's seat. Then she steps toward the building that is not hers, where a guard stands passively on patrol. The car lurches away with Viktor inside, and Nina reaches for her neck, for the borrowed fur; it feels ruffled, as if having gone through a blizzard.

It must be five in the morning. Along the sidewalks the old women are shoveling snow, chipping the ice underneath with heavy spades. In their felt boots and coats of wadded cotton, they do not look up when Nina walks by. She turns back toward her alley, where the snow has collected in thick drifts, and sees the lights shining weakly through her building's windows; with so many people inside, the windows are always lit, always some kind of activity, no matter the hour.

Glancing back, Nina takes one last look at the glittering street. The streetlights and the snowflakes make everything clean and pure. Behind the whiteness, though, is the endless scraping sound, the determined *chip, chip* of the old women's spades. Nina thinks again, as she will from now on: My city looks best in winter, everything hidden under snow.

LOT 20

South Sea Pearl Necklace, composed of 29 white pearls
with rose overtones, graduating in size from approx. 10.28
to 14.10 mm, completed by an 18kt white gold and diamond boule, lg. 18⅝ in. $30,000–35,000

CHAPTER FOUR

Amber is one of the few organic gems, formed not by the human hand but by nature. Specifically, it is oxygenated, fossilized pine tree resin, often containing remnants of the biological world. In Lithuania it has been called *gintras,* from a form of the word "protection," because it was thought to ward off evil; indeed, in the mid-nineteenth century Europeans wore "specimen" pieces (those with fossilized insects or forest life preserved inside) as amulets, to protect them from the perils of life.

Ensconced on her sofa, in the corner closest to the old, hissing radiator, Drew added the word *amulet* to her notes and underlined it twice, not so much because she thought it might lead anywhere as because the idea—that a simple bead could protect from life's many dangers—appealed to her. Though she did not think herself superstitious, she knew that she treated her garnet ring that way. While she often removed it to cook or clean and before she went to sleep at night, she always made sure to wear it whenever she left the house, to the extent that when, more than once, rushing out the door, she realized she had forgotten it, she had always made a point of going back to slip it on, even when she was running late. In fact nothing truly terrible had ever happened to her, either before or since she had owned it. But there were so few things one could control in life; the garnet ring on her finger had itself become comforting.

Drew shifted on the cushion and took a sip from her drink, an inch of bourbon in a small, low glass. The bourbon's color was that of the amber pendant exactly—though without, of course, the surprise inside, that somehow shocking spectacle. Drew thought again of Nina Revskaya's bracelet and earrings, wondered if perhaps even more pieces had belonged to the original set. If so, and if they were still somewhere out there to be found, it was possible—if unlikely—Drew might somehow track them down and come to the answer from that other direction. The key was to keep her mind open to these other avenues, to gather as much information as she could without overlooking the details. To make sure not to miss some clue, even the smallest idea or suggestion that might be of help.

Sometimes called "Lithuanian gold," amber is found most prominently in the Baltic regions, south of Finland and Sweden and east or north of Gdansk, and washes up not only along the Baltic shores but also in the forests of Denmark, Norway, and England. Amber can also be mined: open pits of glauconite sand are dug out with steam shovels and dredges and then poured through grates at a washing plant, where streams of water are used to separate the amber boulders from the sand before shaping them with a slow-turning drill. In Ukraine, amber is found in marshy forests near the Volyhn-Polesie border and comes in a variety of colors, as seen in the restored "amber room" of Catherine the Great's summer palace in Tsarskoye Selo.

"Specific mines—traceable?" Drew liked the scratchy sound the tip of her pen made against the notepaper, the rasping sensation vibrating up into her hand. It was an old refillable cartridge pen she had miraculously managed never to lose, and she found the sound, the feeling, reassuring, confirming something, a concreteness of existence—the reality of Drew and of the pen in the world.

Of all the locales where amber may be found, none yields more than Russia's Kaliningrad region, where waves in the Baltic Sea dislodge amber from the depths of the ocean floor and carry it shoreward. At low tide, foragers use nets and rakes to dredge the shallow waters and find bits of amber caught in silt and seaweed.

In her mind Drew saw again those rich, smooth beads, and around them—unusual for amber jewelry—gold braiding meant to look like twisting vines. It was a startling combination: delicate human handiwork surrounding tiny globes formed by nature. She wondered who had first commissioned them, or if the jeweler had come up with the design unbidden. Her imagination found horse-drawn carriages on their way to country estates, toboggan rides in winter, men whose bushy hats flapped down over their ears, women with their hands poked into enormous fur muffs. Since beginning the Revskaya project, Drew had been reading Chekhov, short stories in a book she seemed to have always had, with a pen-and-ink nature scene on the cover. Its print, small and dense, was packed tightly onto pages darkened with age. And though she knew that the stories had been written in another time, Drew felt she understood the confused schoolteachers and reluctantly betrothed daughters, the aging widowers and poor farmhands, whose main misfortune was simply to be human—to fall in and out of love, to grow old or die young. She had been reading one or two stories each night before bed and, when she at last closed her eyes, felt she had been there with those people and suffered their small agonies. Sometimes, on the path to sleep, she found an image of her Russian grandfather, his face roughened by life, with thick eyebrows and a mischievous smile framed by a big fur hat. In reality Drew had never seen a photograph of him. Grandma Riitta used to have one, she had said, but it had been lost when she moved to the States.

> Containing a high concentration of succinic acid, Baltic amber is distinct from all other types. When newly minted, it is of a yellowish color, but over the centuries oxidation darkens it, giving it an increasingly reddish tint. The many insects that often appear in Baltic amber are proof of swamplands in past eras. The frequent presence of butterflies indicates pieces derived from pines situated near grassy fields.

Butterflies. That would have been perfect for Nina Revskaya, Drew considered. If the amber suite had been purchased for her specifically, it would have been appropriate for one of the beads to contain a butterfly, or some kind of moth, something with wings.

But there were no butterflies in the three auction pieces. Well, after all, what were the odds of finding such a thing, amber with the very specimen that matched the person in mind? What were the chances that it would be not only available but also something one could afford? Before the revolution those wealthy enough might have had access to such things through travel and commerce, but to find and purchase a matching suite like this, in Soviet Russia—or wherever it had been purchased . . . Where, after all, had Grigori Solodin first been handed that pendant? Why did he too insist on remaining so secretive? Feeling her frustration bubble up, Drew reminded herself to stay focused. But again she found herself wondering—about Nina Revskaya, and what her life must have been like in Russia, as an honored artist, a most prized ballerina. In which case, Drew considered, there would have been no pressing reason for her to leave, despite her nation's troubles. . . . And yet, the horrors around her must have been evident. They had reached Nina's own husband in the end. Drew was still unclear about the exact chronology of what had happened. Had Nina known what was about to occur? Clearly something awful must have already been in motion. Was that why she left? Or was it Nina's disappearance that caused things to unfold as they did?

A huge leap she had taken. Perhaps it hadn't even felt like a choice, so much; some of the bravest acts, Drew supposed, were not choices but reflex reactions. Yet Nina's story made Drew's own decisions seem piddling. After all, nothing really terrible had happened. She had simply married too young, been swept up in the idea of a romance that was in fact little more than friendship, and landed in a life that was not so much a conscious choice as one more wedding gift she did not necessarily want.

She took another sip from her glass, glanced at her watch. In an hour she was to meet her friend Stephen at the second-run cinema over in Somerville. He was one of the people she had kept in her life. There had been an awkward period during which he had tried repeatedly, unsuccessfully, to be more than a friend, but Drew had explained to him why it was impossible. For anything more than friendship—for real romance, passionate love—she would have to feel something very strong, strong enough for her to want to try again. And that wasn't anything she felt about Stephen.

The telephone rang, and Drew gave a start. She considered not answering, then supposed it might be Stephen.

It was her mother. Drew's heart sank slightly. "Any good news?" her mother always asked, her tone more dubious as time went on. And though Drew knew her mother worried about her—with her poorly paid job and stubbornly unmarried life—she knew too that some of that worry came simply from wanting her to succeed in some clearly measurable way. Drew's promotion to associate director had taken care of that for a bit. Now, feeling the relief of having something more to offer, she prepared to tell her mother about her progress on the Revskaya project.

Instead her mother said something completely unexpected. "Where did you put it?"

Drew took a long, tense breath, and reminded herself that someone else, someone not directly involved, might find all of this curious and perhaps even amusing. "It" was a photograph, a large, professional—if candid—one, from nine years ago, of Drew on her wedding day.

"It's just such a beautiful picture of you," her mother had said, when Drew first noticed it still there on the bookshelf in the family room a year or so after her divorce. The sky behind her a perfect Wedgwood blue, Drew looked even younger than twenty-three, her cheeks full, the bright sun on her face revealing not a wrinkle. Drew's mother's face, when she gazed at the portrait, seemed itself to change. Though Drew had asked her once, years ago, to please remove the picture, it remained downstairs, in the big heavy crystal frame that had been a year-end gift from her father's company.

Funny, really, how people seized on things, things that others might not think twice about. Clearly the photograph meant more to her mother than Drew could understand. Drew had tried to remove herself from the equation, to see simply what that gown and veil represented, something so different from her parents' brief appointment with a justice of the peace and two friends as witnesses, followed by slices of cake at a tea shop. Even Grandma Riitta had never had a proper wedding; as for her first husband—Drew's grandfather—Riitta had never legally married him.

But this past Christmas, spending four days with her parents, Drew had decided to put an end to the photograph once and for all.

Her decision was nothing premeditated. It had to do with that heavy cloud of guilt that seemed at last to be shifting away. Drew had removed the picture from the frame and, unable, in the end, to discard it, hid it upstairs at the bottom of one of the drawers in her old room. Then she decided that she never wanted to see the big crystal frame again, either, and moved it too upstairs into the drawer.

"You just noticed now?"

"I'm hurt, Drew. You know how much I love that picture."

"Because you love the person in that photo more than you like me." It was nothing she had ever thought quite so clearly, but as she said it, she realized it was true.

"That's a horrible thing to say! Would you say that about your baby photos? I keep those too." Two of them were on that same bookshelf, next to a photograph of her parents cycling through Lyon.

"My baby photos mean something. But the one of me in my dress—"

"I love it because you look happy!"

"Because *you* were happy, when you thought you could be proud of me." If she thought it would make a difference, Drew would have tried to explain that she too still felt that loss, not just of a husband, not just of love, and of a place, a way, to direct that love, but even of her in-laws, whom she had also loved and continued, if in fewer and briefer moments, to miss. Instead she said, "Please let it go."

Her mother was silent for a moment. "Drew," she said, her tone adamantly bewildered, "if I had known your thoughts about it were so . . . fraught!" This was typical of her mother, the switcheroo, as if Drew had created a problem that otherwise would not have existed.

"Look, I have to go," Drew said tiredly. There were other things she wanted to say, but she knew too well what it might mean to state her thoughts, to act on her feelings. The last time she acted on her feelings, she ended up with an ex-husband and two sets of parents mad at her. "I'm meeting a friend."

She hung up, and decided to put the conversation out of her head. After all, it was a small thing, and now it was over, and if she managed to think of it that way, as a chapter that had come to a close, then it might at last become nothing much at all.

HIS FIRST MEMORY was of winter.

A Sunday, with his parents after a heavy snowfall, walking past Red Square. Everything snowy; everything snow. The square is vast and quiet. There is just one area where people are allowed to cross, and in the distance they look like black dots—black dots slowly moving across an expanse of white. Grigori is just three years old. He stares at the people-dots, entranced, while his mother urges him to keep moving, to keep warm. He hears the crows cawing as they fly overhead, and looks up. The sky too is white, except for the birds. When one swoops down lower than the others, Grigori says, "Look at the bird," because it is something he knows.

"*Voron*," says his mother. The word for raven, the biggest and blackest of all.

"*Voron*," he repeats, but Feodor corrects them, as is his nature. "No, *vorona*. See, they have a little gray on them." Looking up, pointing.

"*Vorona*," Grigori repeats. Caws in the thick white sky. "*Vorona*," and people small as dots filing across the big white square. Not a male *voron* but a female *vorona*. Just a touch of gray. That very slim difference between two such similar things.

Making his way along the poorly shoveled sidewalk of St. Mary's Street, Grigori considered that his vocation—his attention to the smallest details of language and image, slight shifts in words and meaning, the difference that a single letter could make—must have begun there in the square, in that moment, on that other snowy day. Subtle changes in sound and sense, words contained in other, different words . . . Even now Grigori often found himself noting tiny surprises in written English, that "intimates" contained "inmates," just as "friend" contained "fiend." . . . This was an attention that he had carried first into Norwegian, then into French. And yet it had been a shock to discover, at the lycée, that these interests far outweighed his talents in mathematics and sciences, and that despite the long hours he spent on homework in order to be in the *supérieure* group, he never excelled in those other subjects. "But aren't your parents scientists?" a bewildered teacher had asked when Grigori performed poorly on a physics exam, as if the one thing naturally followed the other.

He hunched his shoulders against the thought, shoulders to ears in the frigid air—but still that other memory came slipping back. The way she opened the glass door between them, only slightly, her knuckles protruding as on a much older woman. The door propped in front of her like a shield, the cold finality of her voice.

I'm not the person you want.

With relief Grigori entered the fluorescent-lit Dunkin' Donuts to meet Zoltan.

There he was, the back of his head, the grizzled thinning hair, hunched over a booth by the window, the tabletop spread with many sheets of paper. Grigori took a seat across from him on the hard scoop of bench and removed his gloves, quietly clearing his throat.

"Ah!" Zoltan looked up as if shocked. "You!"

Grigori said, "You know I'm always punctual." To Grigori, Zoltan had said, on the telephone, "Meet me at the new café I've found, much better than that other one. Across from the St. Mary's T stop. With the pink and orange sign."

Zoltan would spend all morning here, with the businesspeople and shopkeepers and construction workers rushing in and out and the television buzzing from its perch up on the wall and the bag ladies rustling about and the employees gossiping in Portuguese. Grigori unbundled himself from his coat but remained in his hat and scarf; the place was not well heated.

"You know what a woman just said," Zoltan asked, "a minute ago? She said, 'Days like this, keeping warm's a chore.' Oh, it doesn't sound the same with my accent. But you hear the poetry, don't you? 'Warm's a chore . . .'" He wrote it into his notebook. Grigori had to smile; not only was Zoltan able to see cafés where others did not, he found poetry, too, in unexpected places.

As if aware of Grigori's thoughts, Zoltan said, slightly defensively, "There's good light here for reading. Not like that ghoulish campus place." He rippled his shoulders in a theatrical shiver. "The murmuring of so many overactive egos . . . I hadn't realized how it was weighing me down, Grigori, the deadening chatter of academics all around me."

The truth was, Zoltan had been kicked out of the campus coffeehouse. Just the other day; Grigori had heard it from one of the Spanish professors. In a prolonged burst of creativity, Zoltan had spent even longer hours than usual there (which explained why Grigori hadn't heard from him for over a week). The new café management apparently thought Zoltan some kind of squatter and requested that he no longer spend all day there, at his favorite seat in the front, showcased by the window.

Zoltan took a sip from his Styrofoam cup. "Excellent coffee here, Grigori. You really must try it."

"I'm afraid I don't have much time. You said you had something to discuss."

"Yes! Very important. I would like to ask you, respectfully and with friendship, to be my literary executor."

It was nothing he had expected.

"Thaddeus Weller had agreed to do it, you know. An excellent chap. But I've recently had the sad news that he's passed away."

"I'm so sorry." Grigori had never heard of him.

"Tragic, really. Barely sixty years old. He never did write the brilliant novel he had inside him. You could practically see it there, in his gut, bursting to get out. Others simply called it a beer belly. I asked myself, when I heard the news, Who else do I know who truly understands me—without, of course, there being any odd tension between us? That's the problem, you know, with my fellow poets. There's competition, rivalry. Envy, you know. With you that's not an issue. Even though you're not a poet, as a translator you understand poetry thoroughly and emotionally. Not to mention that your translations are superb. And then, you and I, we have a common sensibility."

"Well," Grigori said, "this is quite a flattering surprise." Normally such a job might have gone to the writer's offspring or spouse, but Zoltan had neither. (Nor had Grigori and Christine had children; Christine's pregnancies had never lasted past eight weeks.) "I'm very honored. Although I am curious to know just what you see as our 'common sensibility.' "

Zoltan leaned forward on his elbows. "You have that past buried inside you that most people can't see." He nodded. "I was older than you when I left my country, but I think the upheaval of starting over, with that other history still a part of you, that heavy weight, is something we have in common. Don't you?"

Grigori thought of how this country, one that offered a fresh start to all who washed up on its shores, had somehow diminished not just Zoltan but Grigori's parents, too—in a way that the other countries along their trajectories had not. Lessened their authority, muted their brilliance; fine qualities of the mind simply were not as appreciated in this home of the brave. Looking into Zoltan's eyes, for a frightening moment Grigori felt that rare but seizing impulse: a distinct, nearly physical, longing to tell his story. Yet all he said was, "A common sensibility. Yes."

"Which doesn't mean, of course," Zoltan said quickly, "that you have to agree to be my executor. There's no need to decide right away.

No rush. Although this is of course something I need to take care of. It's not an enormous oeuvre, by the way. The poetry collections, various essays, and the untranslated works—I realize you'll need help with those. My journals are in English, though I don't know that you'll want much to do with them." He gestured toward a thick faded hardcover notebook on the table. "Twenty-three volumes. But they've been extensively pillaged these past few years, by yours truly, in service of the memoir."

"Any good dirt?"

"Oh, a divine lot. State secrets, broken hearts . . ." He laughed. "I look forward to your decision, Grigori. You're just the man, you know. I hope you know how much I admire your work. You've brought a long-dead poet's words to life again. And in a whole new tongue."

A snatch of Grigori's own rephrasing flew through his thoughts: *Black velvet night, pinned wide and high by pinprick stars . . .* "I just did it for myself, really."

"The best reason, of course. The best writing happens that way."

Patchwork shade, pine needle carpet, ocher-resin drops of sun. The air hums . . .

"If I weren't writing for myself," Zoltan continued, "I wouldn't bother at all." Though his first and second books had been translated into various languages, none of his subsequent volumes of poetry had found life outside of the Hungarian. Grigori supposed it must pain Zoltan to think that his most mature work, the fullest blossoming of his talent, happened to have been composed in a tongue that, despite its beauty, many viewed as a linguistic joke.

"Yes, well, I suppose there's no sane way," Grigori said, "to account for the hours we devote to these obsessions."

Really Viktor Elsin's poems had been a pleasure to translate. His language was simple, his imagery rarely ambiguous. Grigori hadn't had to spend much time grappling with linguistic puzzles or ponderous questions of meaning and intention. Except for the final two poems: "Night Swimming" and "Riverside." Those, too, Grigori had once viewed as clues—like the *Hello* magazine, and the black-and-white photographs, and the hospital certificate with the Soviet emblem at the center. Like the letters and the stunning piece of amber . . .

That tawny resin, slow-motion tears, as if the tree itself knew the future.

All of those things Grigori could have offered to Nina Revskaya—had tried to, once, had made his best effort, years ago, at her doorstep and in the slightly pleading letter he then sent her. But what could they prove, really? Just as the photographs contained other people, too, no way of verifying that they belonged to her or that they were not someone else's duplicates (though surely, Grigori told himself, she would recall their origin), the letters were cryptic, with their nicknames and initials and at times vague phrasing, so clearly aware of the censors. The letters were the only items Grigori had ever shown to anyone other than Christine—proving what a mistake it was to show them to anyone at all.

. . . cool and delicious, the checkered shade of those branches. I sometimes think, that *is what I live for, days like that, perfect.*

Back then he was twenty-one years old, and never had he been quite so proud of any paper he had written. It was with real excitement that he handed over "The Pines Weep: A Reinterpretation of Viktor Elsin's 'Night Swimming' and 'Riverside' Sequence, Based on an Unpublished Letter."

He was in his first year of graduate school. His professor was a short, big-eared fellow with a Mongol last name, which Grigori later erased from memory. It was with trembling hands that Grigori handed him the paper he had typed, feverishly, on his Brother typewriter.

"Thank you," Big Ears had said, without even glancing at the cover page. "I'll let you know when I've read it."

Grigori had waited and waited, though really it was less than a week later that the phone rang in the hallway outside his rented room. Big Ears had just one question, he said, but it was a significant one: Where *is* this letter whose text you've included?

"I'll show it to you," Grigori said, eager, delighted, and just the slightest bit apprehensive.

When he handed him the handwritten pages (photocopied from the original), Big Ears read for a while before saying, "How *interesting* . . ." Grigori couldn't help looking over his shoulder at the first paragraph.

My dear, please forgive me. I don't suppose you believe me
when I say I love you. And yet you know I do. You understand what it means to be overtaken, that big net so wide
and inescapable—like the sun on the lake that day, when
all we wanted was to take refuge under a tree. And then the
ground was damp and you worried you wouldn't get the sap
out of your skirt. I can still smell the pine needles, winter
hidden in them, cool and delicious, the checkered shade of
those branches. I sometimes think, *that* is what I live for,
days like that, perfect. But of course there was the tree sap
staining your skirt. That tawny resin, slow-motion tears, as
if the tree itself knew the future.

As Big Ears continued to read the letter, Grigori paced the room, his heart thrumming.

"Fascinating, yes," Big Ears said when he had finished. And then, "But what makes you think Viktor Elsin wrote this?"

"He signed it."

"Yours and yours alone" was how the letter was signed, but Grigori had no trouble making the mental leap.

"There's no *name*, Grigori. This could be anyone. And we don't even know who it's addressed to."

"Well, that would be his wife," Grigori said. "They often corresponded by mail. She was frequently on tour, and he traveled, too. And often stayed in his cottage at Peredelkino." The writers' village outside of Moscow; Grigori had done the research to prove it.

Big Ears nodded, but he was frowning. "The problem is, how do we know that Viktor Elsin wrote this letter? Really, Grigori, anyone could have written it."

"But . . . the paper I just wrote. That's the whole point. I was showing how the same things he refers to in the letter are in the poems!"

"Because you were looking for them, Grigori. Don't you see? It's not difficult to draw parallels when one tells oneself they're there. You'll need more than a few related words or similar phrases to convince me that these images are the same exact ones. Or that someone hasn't simply cribbed from Elsin's work." He gave a deep, impatient sigh.

Grigori closed his eyes slowly. Perhaps when he opened them . . . "But—"

"How is it, again, that you have this letter? I see it's a photocopy. Did anyone actually tell you that it was Viktor Elsin who wrote it?"

"I figured it out myself." But Grigori's voice, instead of sounding proud, seemed hurt.

"How did you figure it out?"

"It belonged to his wife, and then—"

"Really? Well, now, that's good and concrete. If you can just provide some sort of testimonial from her, then—"

"No, I don't think I can."

Big Ears made a face. It was the face that Grigori would see again and again, for years to come, each time disappointment assailed him.

Big Ears letting his eyes droop into mock sadness, his mouth pinched into a small, demeaning pout, the way one might approach a small child who has made an adorable mistake.

"Grigori." He shook his head. "Without any evidence, this letter could be written by . . . anyone. My uncle Vassily could have written it! Or some old lady neither of us knows. How do we even know which came first, the poem or the letter? The writer of this letter might simply have read Elsin's poems and borrowed some images." Seeing Grigori hanging his head, he added, "Listen, Grigori, your paper is very well written, an excellent example of clearly explained textual analysis. I've given it an A."

Grigori's rage bubbled up. An A? Was that all this would ever come to? An A?

"Please," Big Ears continued. "Accept my congratulations on a job well done. But I do suggest that you leave it at that. Until you find some more concrete way to support your supposition about this most interesting document."

Grigori had thrown the essay away, in the smelly trash bag filled with empty cans of the beef stew his housemate always ate.

Yet the letter—along with the other one in his possession—meant as much to him as before, even the parts that had nothing to do with the poems.

I like to close my eyes and remember. Kissing in the park
where that scrawny policeman came and scolded us. The
hours, the days and weeks, were nothing but markers—
between each chance I would have to kiss you.
　　Our dear V. says you might take a friendly jaunt together.
Lucky we are, to have such friends! But please, dear, only if
the weather is clear. And don't forget to bring ID. A song
keeps running through my head, the one about the husband

missing his wife like a wave misses the shore—over and over again. That's how I miss you.

It had all made sense when he explained it to Christine. From the very first moment that he showed it to her, she had believed him.

As for the amber, I used to doubt I would ever meet the woman who could move me to pass these things on to her. Little glimpses of sunshine . . . The earrings especially. Each piece has its own little world inside. They remind me of the dacha (all those insects!) and the sun in the late evening, the way it would just drop right into the lake. The impossible perfection of that summer . . . I was waiting for the perfect moment to give them to you. I wish I hadn't waited so long.

Seated in the drafty booth, Grigori tried to dodge the thought, that same old recollection. Across from him, Zoltan was saying that poetry was one of those paradoxes: "Something seemingly useless that people nevertheless continue to create, unbidden, all the time."

"Well," Grigori said, "I'm honored by your proposal. I can't see why I wouldn't agree to it."

Zoltan smiled, clearly pleased. Even now, viewed from a certain angle, one could still find the dandy there, as much as he might blend in with the other dubious characters who whiled their time away at the Dunkin' Donuts. "Think about it first. Although I do hope you'll say yes."

As Grigori stood to button his coat, the bag lady who had been sitting at the table behind Zoltan rose and shuffled past. Beyond her, from its perch on the wall, the television showed a perky dark-haired newscaster going on about some local transportation debate. Then, as if noticing Grigori there, she said brightly, "A famous ballerina, a jewelry auction, and a mysterious necklace. Join News 4's own June Hennessey for an exclusive interview with dancer Nina Revskaya. Tonight at six, only on *News 4 New England*."

Good god, it was inescapable. Grigori found himself avoiding the newscaster's eyes, even as the image switched to some other announcer and a menacing stream of words moved relentlessly across the bottom of the screen: *Shoe bomber sentenced to life in prison. Weapons inspector says Iraq not cooperating.* Grigori pulled his gloves on. "All right, Zoltan, I'm off."

Hunched over his notebook, Zoltan paused to look up. "Good day to you, Grigori." Already his gaze had returned to his notes. "To you, too," Grigori said, and headed out the door.

STEPHEN HAD ONE of those flat-screen televisions Drew had heard about but never seen. Since she possessed no television of her own, she went to his apartment straight from work to watch the Revskaya interview. In exchange she brought with her a bottle of the merlot Stephen liked, which he poured into two enormous wineglasses.

"*Cin cin*," he said, clinking his glass against hers, his expression one of simple happiness, at having Drew next to him on the sleek gray sofa. Drew felt a pang of guilt, that she could not love this man who wanted to love her.

On the television screen a sixtyish woman in a bright red skirt suit, standing in the News 4 studio, gave a somewhat breathless introduction, speaking directly to the viewer:

Nina Revskaya, the renowned Russian ballerina known
as "the Butterfly," has long been a fixture of awe and
inspiration for balletomanes all over the world. A principal
dancer with the Bolshoi Ballet, and wife of the populist
poet Viktor Elsin, Revskaya became in 1952 the very first

of what, in the decades after her escape from the USSR, was to become a string of Soviet dancers who defected to the West.

A series of photographs briefly flashed: Nureyev, Makarova, Baryshnikov.

Though Revskaya's brief career with the Paris Opera Ballet was cut short by illness, after teaching in London she ultimately settled in Boston, becoming ballet mistress for the Boston Ballet at its inception in 1963, as well as artistic consultant, a role she held until 1995. She has been known as both a great patron of the arts and as the owner of a formidable jewelry collection.

Now the woman gave a sly little smile as if to say that thank God there was something truly interesting to talk about. On the screen there appeared a photograph from the 1960s or so, of Nina Revskaya wearing a diamond necklace.

New Englanders were awed to see her array of jewels— gifts from friends, fans, government envoys, and famous jewelers themselves—at the St. Botolph's Club fund-raiser five years ago. Now Beller Auction House is auctioning the collection of over one hundred items, valued at close to one million dollars, with all proceeds going to the Boston Ballet Foundation. Adding to the excitement, last week it was announced that an anonymous donor had reunited a necklace of Baltic amber with a matching bracelet and earrings in Revskaya's collection. I had the great pleasure of speaking to Nina Revskaya at her Back Bay home about her life and about the mysterious necklace.

The screen shifted now to a prerecorded interview, Nina Revskaya and the woman together on a settee. Drew recognized the Commonwealth Avenue apartment and the displeased look on Nina Revskaya's face. At the same time, she felt the keen curiosity that overtook her whenever she came upon celebrity interviews in magazines or the newspaper—the way she landed avidly upon this random fact and that odd aside, as if such minor confessions might somehow hand her the key to another person's life. It was as much a search for clues, she knew, as her research for Beller—to glimpse how someone else had forged a life, what someone else had managed to carve out of this world. Really, Drew supposed, all that she read and researched, even her work for the Revskaya auction, fed that more general quest: for how to live, how to be.

"This auction, to benefit the Boston Ballet, is extremely generous of you," the News 4 woman began. "The arts are so underfunded. It must make a substantial difference in the dance world to have your generous support."

"That is my hope." Nina Revskaya seemed to be looking away.

The News 4 woman continued unfazed, admirably relaxed, as if she chatted on this settee all the time. "Now, many of these absolutely gorgeous gems were gifts from jewelers and admirers after your arrival in Paris and then London. But I think our readers will be interested to hear that a few of them came with you all the way from Russia."

Jaw tight, Nina Revskaya said, "Yes, some of them are very particular of Russia."

"She's not going to make this any easier for her than for me," Drew told Stephen.

The News 4 woman nodded encouragingly. "It seems to me that in a way the value of these jewels is symbolic. They're beautiful artistic creations that survived an authoritarian regime in the same way that you, a beautiful and talented artist, ultimately escaped oppression."

"Please understand," Nina Revskaya said, looking peeved, "we all were in danger, everyone, all of the time, not only artists like myself. That was the world where we lived. Anyone could turn in anyone else, for any thing. Small things. Owning more than one's neighbor. Speaking the wrong thing, telling the wrong joke. You must understand how common these arrests were. It was impossible *not* to know someone who was arrested."

"Horrible, horrible!"

"Jesus Christ," Stephen said.

Nina Revskaya said, "It was a method for the government to warn us, you see, to make sure we behave."

"Thank goodness you got out of there!" The News 4 woman shook her head, her gold-tinted hair barely moving. "I think our viewers will agree that the jewelry that came with you represents, in a very moving way, that tragic past."

"Tragic, yes. For millions of citizens."

"The amber in particular is symbolic, in that amber literally captures and holds moments of the past. In its resin, I mean. Because the little insects and things that are caught in it are extremely old, aren't they? In that way these amber pieces are more than just gorgeous; they offer a glimpse into the past."

"I suppose."

"Do you have any idea who the mystery person is who owns the necklace that matches your own set?"

Drew felt herself leaning toward the television, as if about to be handed something new. All Nina Revskaya said was, "It could be from anywhere."

"Who's that?" Stephen asked, with a small laugh, pointing.

"Who?"

"There's someone in the back corner there, see? Just an arm, but—"

"Where? Oh, I see." In the shadow of the screen's periphery an arm, clad in purple, was becoming just barely noticeable, someone leaning slowly in.

"But isn't it surprising," the News 4 woman asked, "that the matching pendant would also be here in the United States, and not back in Russia?"

At the edge of the screen, the entire side of a woman's body, in slacks and a purple sweater, was now discernible, loitering at the rear of the room. As Nina Revskaya spoke, the person, a slim black woman, leaned more fully in, then looked straight at the camera and, for a split second, gave a smiling wave before quickly pulling herself out of the camera's view.

"You mentioned theft," the News 4 woman was saying. "Do you think the pendant was stolen?"

"It is very probable," Nina Revskaya said primly. "The bracelet and earrings were handed down, you see, to me through my husband. They belonged to his family, but in the civil war many of their valuables were lost."

"Oh, now you tell me," Drew said. If the jewels had been handed down through Revskaya's husband's family, their names might be recorded in the jeweler's ledger books. Why hadn't she said so before? Drew would have to call her tomorrow morning, or go there, have Nina Revskaya spell out her husband's relatives' names in Cyrillic, as far back in his ancestry as possible—in case Drew ever did manage to track down those records. To Stephen she said, "This woman is going to drive me crazy."

"Now, now." Stephen jokingly patted Drew on the shoulder—but quickly withdrew his hand, to show he understood the rules of their relationship. Again Drew felt her heart drop. If there were some sort of spark, she might at least try; but then there would just be more potential to hurt him. She simply could not imagine feeling about Stephen the way she would have liked to feel, that ideal that had been her undoing: true partners in love and life. Otherwise she might as well have remained in her marriage with Eric, just two people living in tandem.

She still recalled, palpably, the uncomfortable feeling of growing past him, and the moment when it had seemed there was no way back. It began with her first truly good job, one that paid, in the design department of a national insurance company; Drew was an assistant to the man who assessed and recommended art purchases for the company's many business properties. The man, Roger, was an older gentleman, soft-spoken and kind, probably gay although he made a point, in a somewhat strained way, never to mention his personal life. What mattered was that he liked Drew and took her with him on his many buying trips—not just to antiques dealers on Eleventh Street, or to auctions outside the city, but abroad, to sales in London, to Athens and Paris, to Bolivia and Turkey and Morocco. This was in 1996; the company was happy to pay. Drew had found herself emboldened, thought nothing of wandering alone through markets where voices chattered words that to her ears were little more than music. She bargained in pantomime, in high school French and guidebook Greek and *Sesame Street* Spanish, and felt the small, bright thrill of those minor accomplishments.

She took Eric with her on one of her trips, for a long weekend in London after her two days of work. On their first morning together, they went to take the Tube to Bloomsbury, and just as they descended the steps toward the platform, a train's doors slid open. Drew said, "This is the one we want!" and swiftly stepped onto the subway car, but Eric paused, asked, "Are you sure?"—and the doors slid shut. Amid the crush of passengers, Drew mouthed to Eric through the window the name of the subway stop where she would wait for him. But as the train pulled quietly away, she could not help but feel that something irreparable had happened.

Pushing the memory away, Drew found herself again on Stephen's sofa, in front of the enormous television screen. "I was looking through our archives," the News 4 woman was saying, "to find photographs of the amber bracelet and earrings, but I couldn't find any of you wearing them. I did find a number of amazing pictures, though—the one of you and Jackie Onassis made my day!"

When Nina Revskaya showed no reaction, the woman said, "I would have loved to see a picture of you wearing those gorgeous amber earrings."

"They did not suit me."

"The color, you mean? Amber?"

"Big beads need a broad face, and height, too. Otherwise they weigh you down. No, they were not for me."

WINTER'S GRIP, THE quivering gray mornings, perpetual dusk. Sometimes the Bolshoi tries to save money by not heating during the day; Nina rehearses in woolen tights and long knit sweaters and layers of leg warmers that make her thighs feel thick. Before performing, she soaks her feet in hot water. She still hasn't heard from the man named Viktor, though for a week now she has anticipated another meeting. Painted her nails a color called Pearl, and patched the soles of her good shoes. She even managed to find a nice rayon dress at a commission shop. Now she is in the little dressing room, scraping away some of the leather from the bottom of her toe shoes, to help keep them from slipping. Each time she pulls the rasp across the bottom, she tells herself not to think of Viktor. She must focus, prepare herself: tonight is *Sleeping Beauty*, and she is dancing the Lilac Fairy.

At the dressing table next to hers, Polina, who will be playing the Diamond Fairy, is gluing on false eyelashes, saying that she is in love.

"With Arkady Lowny?" Nina hears how incredulous she sounds. Really she sees this sort of thing often enough, dancers making as many Party "friends" as possible. It is a way to work one's way up the ranks regardless of actual talent. Not that Polina isn't talented. But she lacks that most elusive quality, the one that no amount of practice or training can guarantee: charisma, stage presence, the allure of a true star. Perhaps it is lack of confidence. There is something brittle about Polina, too studied, not quite natural, despite her long strong legs and perfect attitudes. She dances with her muscles but not her heart.

"No, not Arkady," Polina whispers. "His *friend*." Eyes open wide, only one of them lined with the feathery lashes, so that the other eye looks smaller and oddly beady. Like Nina she has already made up her face, so that her skin looks brightly false. "Oleg. He's a department chief at the Ministry of Trade." Polina always has a worshipful tone when she mentions people in government. She turns back to her mirror and dreamily applies the second strip of lashes, her smile small as if concealing mischief. "Arkady took me to dinner at the Riga, and this friend, Oleg, was there. He's so charming, Nina! He looked at me across the table in this way, I can't explain it except to say I just *knew*."

Nina has taken up her other toe shoe and is shaving the bottom in quick, almost careless, motions. "Knew *what*?"

"That something was going to happen with us!"

"So you're just going to drop Arkady, then?"

"Well, I'll have to tell him something." For a moment, with her long, skinny neck and bright makeup and feathery eyelashes, Polina looks just like an ostrich. In a whisper she adds, "He let me keep his cigarette case."

"Arkady?"

"No, Oleg!" From the drawer of her dressing table, she takes a slim silver box, a section of its lid ornately decorated in what looks to be ivory.

Nina examines the box, the swirl of flowered vines that decorate it. Looking closer she sees, with shock, that they are not flowers or vines but, rather, two human bodies: a man's and a woman's, naked, entwined. Surely that's why Polina has shown it to her, to prove some sort of maturity Nina doesn't possess. Pretending not to notice, Nina hands it back.

Polina slides the case proudly back into her drawer and locks it. Since their promotion to first soloists she and Nina have been allotted this more private dressing room, small and cold, without windows. Walls of cracking plaster, lightbulbs too bright. Tights hanging on pegs to dry overnight. Across the top of her mirror Nina has draped a strip of eyelet cloth, to pretty it up a bit. Polina's mirror has two small photographs tucked into the frame, and her dressing table is cluttered with twice the beauty supplies Nina has. Thick tubes of lipstick, square tubs of sparkling powder, eye paint in every color, cold cream called "Snowflake." A jar of "Persian mud" containing a secret ingredient from Georgia. Tacked to the wall is a newspaper article by Dr. Yakov Veniaminov, Cosmetician, whose prescriptions Polina follows religiously.

The wardrobe mistress is at the door. She hands them their costumes briskly and leaves.

"Well," Nina concedes, pulling on the lavender tutu, "I'm glad you met someone you like." As Polina helps her with the hooks on the bodice, Nina wants badly to tell her that she too has met someone, but already it seems she must have dreamed it. She takes up her toe shoes and at the sink runs cold water over the heels, so that they will bond with her tights. Then she sits down and, pointing her toes, fits one foot down into its shoe, toes crushing against each other as she nudges them all the way in to where she has layered a wad of cotton wool. Her debut in this role, hours of effort ahead of her, no time to think of Viktor . . . She works the back of the shoe up onto her heel, then takes up the second shoe. Even as she wraps and ties the ribbons securely around her ankles, she is convincing herself that she is prepared, she is ready. But when she tucks the ends of the ribbons in, quickly stitching them so that they won't slip out, she sees that her hands are trembling.

The bell. Tossing her cardigan sweater over her shoulders, Nina wishes Polina "No down, no feathers" and hurries to the makeup room, to have the little purple-flowered crown firmly secured to her hair and final touches of color painted around her eyes. Scent of talc, of nerves, as she warms up in the training studio. Even backstage, as the prologue begins, with the princes and pages in their capes, and the queen and king and their attendants all miming along to Tchaikovsky's stately march, Nina continues to warm up with plié after plié, holding on to a lighting boom for support, while the dressers flutter around making a last-minute check of hair ribbons and coronets, and the corps de ballet girls chatter like sparrows, and the stage manager shushes them and complains that they are tracking too much rosin onto the floor.

One of the prop men hands her a sparkly spray of lilacs—her magic wand—and now the harp strums the opening arpeggio that introduces Nina's first entrance. Giving herself over to the lullaby-like melody, Nina follows her retinue of tutu-clad girls as they move together on pointe onto the steeply sloping stage, into the bright lights of the Fairy Kingdom. Nina is in the center, the calm, soothing central force even as she introduces the other fairies, gesturing graciously, arms gently waving her lilac frond, lots of little bourrées here and there, none of the fast jumps and spins she prefers; this opening section is a very slow adagio, nothing terribly challenging, only one pirouette into arabesque. Since the Lilac Fairy represents wisdom and protection, Nina tries to infuse her every movement with the thought that good can overcome wickedness, that spells can be both cast and broken. For her first solo (to a grand, somewhat pompous-sounding waltz) she imagines each of her smooth opening *développés*—leg extending high up to the side until her foot is past her ear, as she rises on pointe—banishing the evil to come. As always when she performs, the minutes pass like mere seconds; already she is making her concluding diagonal across the stage, the repeated sequence of two little *sissones*, then rising up onto *relevé*, and then a double pirouette.

Only later, as she and the others stand patiently immobile waiting out a pas de deux, does she allow herself to look out at the many-tiered theater, past the footlights and above the heads of the orchestra, searching, as if amid the red velvet seats and darkness-obscured faces she might—if she wills it hard enough—find Viktor.

Instead, there is her tiredly beautiful mother, in the side loge where she always sits. Now that Grandmother has passed away, it is just the two of them in their bare-floored room. Mother still spends her days working at the polyclinic, afternoons filled with ongoing errands for friends and relatives too weak or old, always someone or other in hospital, not to mention Mother's brother in prison for three years now. (He is innocent, there has been some mistake; as soon as Comrade Stalin finds out, Mother always says, he'll put everything right.) Neither she nor Nina ever mentions a word of the brother's predicament, even as Mother makes her way from one end of town to the other in search of food and medicine for him—an endless quest, standing in queues in every weather, summers in her white cotton kerchief, winters in her dark woolen one. Yet she never misses Nina in a new role, attends at least one performance of every ballet she dances, happily flapping her program at her, watching each ballet intently, as if she has never seen it danced quite so well.

Tonight, though, Nina longs to see Viktor's face instead, his proud nose and almond-shaped eyes and the flare of his nostrils. Just thinking of him, she feels a small bird rustle beneath her rib cage.

Before her entrance in the second act, she puts herself right up against the front wing, just next to the stage, so that she can look out farther into the theater, although she of course knows the rule: If you can see the audience, they can see you. She looks out, searches the seats. And now the stage manager is telling her to step back, she is too near to the boom and might cast a shadow. . . .

The applause ends, the curtains have closed, the lights are up again. She has danced well—she knows it, the audience knows it, she hears it in their applause. Even her comrades onstage congratulate her.

Nina's mother is waiting in the rear hallway, beneath the "We Celebrate with Work!" poster. Her face is glowing, her shoulders pulled back straight in a way that she rarely holds herself at home, as if to show the dancers that she too, given a different turn of events, might have been one of them. "Everyone is saying how beautifully you danced, you should hear them!" Then, as always, come the complaints: "That blond girl was in the way. When you were all in a diagonal in the wedding section. I could barely see you."

Nina is used to this; none of it will ever be enough for her mother. "She's supposed to be in front of me. It's part of the choreography."

"She was showing off."

"I'll be sure to tell the director." Nina laughs, kisses Mother on each of her smooth cheeks. "It's late, I don't want you to have to wait for me." She embraces her again and wishes her good night, glad that she witnessed this important evening. Then she dodges the congratulations of the other dancers and heads back to the dressing room, exhausted. Cold stale air—perfume and old sweat. Nina unties her slippers, frees her tired feet, her poor blistered toes. She peels off her false eyelashes and places them back in their little case. On their little foam pillow, they look like centipedes.

A knock on the door. "Come in."

"You were magnificent."

Viktor, holding an armful of roses. Nina gives a start, nearly knocking the wooden stool over. "How did you find me?"

"An arduous process. I bribed the stage doorman. Here, these are for you."

Most bouquets are just something easily grown, marigolds or

lupins, in winter artificial ones—nasturtiums and violets of orange and purple fabric. But roses . . . "So many!" Nina says, and counts to make sure there is an odd number; an even number would mean bad luck. Viktor says, "I wanted to give you something as beautiful as you."

"They're perfect," she tells him, losing count. "Just like tonight. You've made it perfect."

"Well, that remains to be seen," he says. "Will you come dine with me?"

She manages to say, "Yes," but as much as she wants to sound calm, her voice is shaking. "Just let me wash up. All this awful makeup."

"I love it. You look like a Caspian call girl."

The wardrobe mistress opens the door to take Nina's costume, but seeing her still wearing it—and Viktor with her—turns away. "You go ahead and wash up, then," Viktor says. "I'll wait in the hall." He steps out the door as swiftly as he arrived.

Quickly Nina rubs oil into her face and massages off the makeup Viktor claims to love. Even as she showers—in the good hot shower that is so much stronger than the one at home—the bird rustles in her rib cage. Drying off, buttoning herself into the bright pink brassiere she barely fills, wishing she had thought to wear the rayon dress . . . Meanwhile Polina has returned and is perched on her wooden stool, examining her raw toes. Nina asks, "Do I look all right?"

"Lovely." Polina barely glances up, absorbed in bandaging her toes. Nina fits herself into her coat with its new trim and nestles a sheepskin turban tight on her head. But when she steps out to the corridor, there is only the long rack of costumes for tomorrow's show, covered with a sheet. Her heart sinks—until she sees Viktor behind the rack, leaning against the wall, smoking a cigarette in a re-laxed, slouching way, as if he comes here all the time. For the slight-est second, Nina feels a fleeting doubt, or perhaps it is fear—that this is some kind of a trick, that he is not who she thinks he is, that he doesn't feel about her the way she feels about him. And what about that fair-haired woman from the party? Then Viktor sees Nina and grins, and the doubt and fear flit away.

At the Aragvi they sit at the back of the room, where a band is playing Georgian songs. Nina has been to a fine restaurant only a few times, and so she lets Viktor order for them: a bottle of Teliani wine, and fish salad and caviar to start. Shashlik for the main course.

"Did you always want be a poet?" she asks him. "When you were a child, I mean."

"Not at all. Like every boy, I wanted to be a polar explorer." He laughs. The band, aware of having an audience, has become noisy, and he has to raise his voice to tell Nina about growing up in a town outside Moscow, an only child, with his mother and maternal grandmother. "More of a village, really. My mother was a teacher, and it was my grandmother who raised me, since my father died shortly before I was born. She loved the outdoors. My real home is the woods, I always say."

"My father died too," Nina says. "When I was three. He had some kind of blood condition." And then, "What subject did your mother teach?"

Viktor looks briefly surprised. "Languages," he says quickly, as if unsure of which ones.

"That must be where your linguistic talent comes from."

He smiles. "I suppose I have her to thank. Although I had no plans to become a poet. As soon as I was old enough, I enrolled in an FZU, to become a welder." He tells her about his years at the factory school, and that despite his efforts he never quite excelled. "I had no talent for industrial work—although I didn't want to admit it. The whole time I was apprenticed, I made up little songs and verses, just to keep me going. Or to keep me from admitting my own failure, I suppose. I wrote some of them down, and a teacher found them.

He sent them to a magazine that was printing an article about the Institute of Steel. I saw my poems there and felt a sense of accomplishment I never had as an apprentice welder. I'm still convinced my teachers purposely arranged things that way—so that I'd switch careers and get out of their school!" He takes a swig of wine. "Fortunately I was admitted to the Literary Institute after that."

When the kebabs are served, he tells Nina about the poet from Leningrad who mentored him. There is something warm and direct about the way he speaks, an ease, an openness, his eyes looking right into hers. He describes being evacuated to Tashkent during the war, and his three years there with other artists—musicians, actors, filmmakers. "I've never felt such heat," he says, gnawing contentedly on a piece of lamb. "It was the first time in my life I understood why people would want to sit in the shade instead of the sun." He tells her about riding camels with the local Uzbeks, about eating fresh apricots, and picking mulberries from a tree just outside his window at the House of Moscow Writers. "Seventeen Karl Marx Street," he says, dreamy with the memory. "And all around, almond trees."

Then his face becomes serious. "Of course it was nothing we could enjoy—knowing our brothers were losing their lives each day. I wish I could have fought alongside them. I would have, if they'd let me."

"Why wouldn't they let you?"

"I have a hole in my heart. That I was born with. The doctors can hear it with a stethoscope."

"A hole!"

"Well, that's the simplified expression. Really it's a valve that doesn't quite close. Nothing lethal, although it does make my heartbeat somewhat irregular. It made me exempt from service."

Nina recalls how she guessed, the first time she set eyes on him, that he hadn't served. Yet clearly it is his status, and not his heart, that kept him from battle. Because really, in the end almost anyone at all, no matter how ill or unqualified, ended up being sent to the front. Only his being a respected poet would have saved him from that fate—just as most of the Bolshoi folks were shipped off to Kuibyshev, far from harm's way. But Nina simply nods as Viktor continues his story, telling her about his return to Moscow, and living in an artists' building with his mother.

"That's why I wasn't able to see you until tonight," he adds. "She was unwell. For a week the doctor didn't know what to do. But she made it through, I'm happy to say."

For the slightest moment, Nina wonders if he is telling the truth. She pictures Viktor's mother like her own: a once-lovely woman running long errands, each day's frustrations caught in the knots of her shawl. At last she dares to ask that other question:

"That woman, with you at the party . . ."

"Lilya, you mean? A stunning woman, isn't she? An old friend. She lives in Leningrad now, but still visits her family here."

Nina tries not to show her feelings. *A stunning woman* . . . But Viktor seems to have decided the story is finished, and that his meal is too. He deposits his napkin on his now-empty plate, pushes the plate away, and smiles, that happy, untroubled look. The napkin, though, looks tormented—twisted tightly, as though Viktor has been wringing it all night.

"And you?" he asks. "What about your family?"

"There's just me and my mother now. She works at a polyclinic. My father was a scene painter for the Opera. In fact, I suspect that's why my mother married him. She's always loved the theater, but she wasn't brought up in that world. It's because of her that I'm a dancer. Only recently did it occur to me that the ballet must have been her own dream—for herself, I mean." As she says it, she pictures her mother's delicate ankles, her sinewy calves, narrow but strong, like a doe's. Immediately she feels guilty, wrong to have revealed Mother's private sentiments. She turns to watch the band.

Viktor doesn't seem to mind. "You have such an elegant neck," he says. "I suppose that's a prerequisite for ballerinas—part of the audition, even. Is it? Do they measure the length of your neck?"

Nina laughs. "It's an optical illusion. We're taught to go up on our toes and then, when we come down, leave our heads up there." Though it sounds like she is teasing, it is just what she means. "In a way it's a kind of magic."

"Indeed. Your neck is splendid. I would like to touch it again."

Blushing, the flare from her chest to her cheeks, Nina brings her hand to her neck, as if that might hide her hot skin.

"A neck like yours should have all kinds of jewels, to show it off."

His bold statement—the trust it implies—delights her. She has no patience for those types who oppose personal property on principle, who make a point of saying so, as if to prove some sort of superiority. Like the family across the hall at home, who always comment disdainfully about everyone else's belongings, anything not utterly necessary. Even Mother, with genuine humbleness, claims not to need more than she already owns. Never admits any longing for material goods, and ties a piece of rope around her skirt instead of a belt. Nina surely seems greedy in comparison.

But with Viktor she again feels the confidence of their first meeting, when they shared the tangerine. It seems like forever since she has felt such closeness with anyone. "What I've always dreamed of, actually," she says quietly, "are earrings."

"Earrings . . . yes." Viktor narrows his eyes, as if envisioning something.

"Ever since I was nine years old," Nina says, and tells him about the woman at the hotel, about the diamonds in her earlobes. Though it risks sounding materialistic, she guesses a man like Viktor can see beyond such judgment. "I'd never seen anything like her. She might as well have come from outer space."

Viktor says, "You too shall have jewels in your ears, Butterfly.

And strands of pearls so long they reach the floor. They'll lie there in swirls, like puddles." He grins then, the grin of a teacher's favorite, of the boy who always has his way. As if all of life were a lark. There is so much life in that grin, Nina feels her own smile trying to match it. At the same time something inside her is frightened—of the incredible confidence this man possesses, as though the entire world belongs to him.

And yet, that crumpled napkin, twisted tightly.

When they have finished their meal, Viktor offers to accompany her home. This time Nina allows him to see the alley that leads to her building, half hoping—and half terrified—that he might come with her and, in the darkness, touch her again the way he did in the Pobeda. Instead, Viktor says he will watch to see her safe inside the door; he has been nothing but gentlemanly all night, only once lightly taking her arm in his, a proper suitor. As Nina makes her way down the alley to her door, she feels slight disappointment at the same time that she is thrilled. Whatever this is between herself and Viktor seems to have become something respectable and real.

Only days later, when she is home, wondering when she will next see him, does Nina again recall the cloth of the napkin wrung tight. When a week has gone by and the roses have faded—and she still hasn't heard from Viktor—she clips a few inches off the stems. She brings a pot of water to a boil and dunks the fresh ends in, holding them there briefly as the steam reaches up at her hand. Quickly, her hand red from the heat, she transfers the bouquet back to the vase and refills it with cold water. Because if she can just keep these roses alive . . .

Within an hour the flowers have perked up.

LOT 23

Perfume Flask. Silver, marked sterling. 1 3/4 in. long from top of lid. Flacon 1 1/4 in. wide. Carnelian screw-off stopper. Handpainted butterfly design on off-white porcelain over glass. Weight 18 g. $1,000–1,500

CHAPTER FIVE

G ood god, Carla," Grigori said, entering the Department of Foreign Languages. "You smell positively edible."

"It's that new cleaner the janitors are using. Pineapple something."

Grigori's gloves as he removed them were stiff from the cold. "A whiff of the tropics—how subversive." Outside it was snowing again, tiny dry flakes that blew about in a faint shimmer. Grigori had taught his graduate seminar, "Poetry of the Acmeists," while still musing in frustration about the Revskaya broadcast last night. Yet his students, with their passionate readings of the assigned poems and their almost tender interest in the Russian language itself, had cheered him, distracted him, made his existence feel briefly necessary.

He entered his office and closed the door behind him, removed his coat and hat. This room too smelled like a piña colada. Lighting a cigarette, Grigori leaned back into the firm weight of the swivel chair. Across from him, framed degrees on the walls displayed their indecipherable calligraphy, the Latin that no one any longer knew how to translate. Since Christine's death he often found he needed to look back at them, to be reminded of his accomplishments. He was somebody, had made himself into somebody: Grigori Solodin, chair of the Department of Modern Foreign Languages and Literatures,

owner of a restored Victorian (the bottom floor rented out to another couple) and a sturdy Volvo that had made numerous trips to
Tanglewood, Jacob's Pillow, and various bed-and-breakfasts across
the Berkshires. The wooden plaque on the wall across from him declared him Professor of the Year, and though that year was long past,
it was a year that had indeed existed. At the same time, Grigori supposed he might just take down that plaque. There was something pathetic about it, like those faded newspaper reviews posted in dreary
restaurant windows.

No, he decided, tapping ashes into the little dish he kept in his
desk drawer, it was important to leave the plaque on the wall, for
those moments when his only comfort came through concrete objects: the thank-you letter, still tacked on his bulletin board, from the
Tolstoy specialist; the note of congratulations for his second book—a
comparative approach to three Soviet poets—from a revered editor
(now dead); the announcement about the award from the Academy
of Arts and Letters. He had been in this same office for so long, who
knew what he might find if he ever dared to clean it out. At least one
drawer of his desk contained mail dated from the previous decade.

He had expected too much, that was the trouble, he told himself
now. Even in giving in, he had expected too much. For he felt no
lighter, really, having surrendered the amber necklace. That chunky
oval wedge with the surprise inside . . . Of the small collection of
objects in his possession, the pendant was the only one Grigori
had ever shown to Nina Revskaya. After all, it was one of a kind,
the only one that felt truly powerful. Of course the letters too had
once seemed that way, utterly convincing, but that was when he was
young and stupid. . . . *cool and delicious, the checkered shade of
those branches. I sometimes think,* that *is what I live for, days like
that, perfect.*

Allowing the thought, Grigori walked over to the tall, broad
bookshelf—a wall of books, a pleasure to him. In one eyeful he

could take in the sum of his knowledge. Now he turned to what he mentally referred to as "the Elsin shelf." He slid out a slim volume in hardcover, *Selected Poems of Viktor Elsin: A Bilingual Edition*. In smaller print was "Translated and with a Foreword by Grigori Solodin." He was still genuinely proud of this work—unlike his dissertation, *Three Soviet Poets: A Comparative Study*, which he rarely looked back at, or *The Socialist Realism Reader*, an anthology that had required all kinds of annoying legal permissions in order to reprint the various selections. Thoughout his time spent on both of those projects, Grigori had been working simultaneously on the Elsin translations. They were a labor of love and had nothing to do with academic hurdles. The book had had a print run of just five hundred copies.

Perhaps that was why he kept all praise for his translations in a separate file in the big metal cabinet. These congratulations came not so much from scholars as from poets—artists whose talents Grigori could only hope to imitate. One had called his work "as close an approximation to Elsin's voice as I can imagine even myself ever producing." Another, in a review journal, praised Grigori's "fidelity to the formal constraints of Elsin's work while capturing the easy exuberance of his phrasing." Even Zoltan, who as a youth in postwar Hungary had been force-fed Russian in school, said Grigori had "a poet's ear" for the nuances of Elsin's verse.

The fact was, as popular as Elsin had been in his lifetime, he could never be called "major." Much of his work's beauty came from its simplicity, the very simplicity that had made him popular not only with the public but also with his publishers, who had of course worked according to government decree. His earliest poems celebrated the countryside of his youth with the direct simplicity of country folk, using humor and argot, playing with language while safely following official regulations of topic and tone; his lathe-turners were always handsome, his milkmaids always fair. As his writing matured, he had managed as well as anyone could while faithfully remaining within the stylistic and topical guidelines. Though, in selecting Elsin's poems for translation, Grigori had weeded out a good bunch of somewhat facile verse, other poems were quite moving—beautiful, even. *Patchwork shade, pine needle carpet / Ocher-resin drops of sun. The air / Hums . . .*

Sometimes it all seemed so futile—Grigori's efforts, his curiosity, each small discovery. His very profession, even, and the embarrassing fact that his dearest concern remained, in the end, closed to him. He had spent fifty years on this planet for what, exactly? To write endless letters of recommendation for students named Courtney and Heather and Brian, so that they could head off to their Semesters-at-Sea or wherever it was they went to continue the endless keg party that was an American college education.

A knock—probably Carla, to say something cross about the smoke. Grigori placed the book back into its slot on the shelf, then went to the door and opened it warily. "Oh, Zoltan, hello, come in."

Zoltan entered looking, as always, slightly hunchbacked, something about the way his broken shoulder had healed. Or perhaps it was from carrying the grubby plastic bags stuffed with notebooks and papers everywhere. "I found something interesting in my journal last night, that made me think of you. A reference to your ballerina. And a little thing she said about her husband."

Your ballerina. For years Zoltan had called her that, since Grigori was the "expert" regarding her husband's work.

"I was reading my journal and came upon a description of a party—quite a party, I must say, as proper as it supposedly was. Princess Margaret, well . . ." He laughed to himself about something he decided not to say, then reached into one of the plastic bags. "I marked it for you."

"It's very thoughtful of you," Grigori said, though Zoltan's past discoveries of Elsin-related diary references had never amounted to much. Although Zoltan had met Nina Revskaya briefly in London, he had known her only slightly. Now he opened a somewhat battered-looking journal and ran his finger down a page. "It's not much, really just . . . where did it go? Ah, here. Do you want to hear the whole thing, or just the mention of Viktor Elsin?"

"The whole thing, of course." Grigori retrieved his cigarette and took a long drag.

In a slightly louder voice, Zoltan read: *"The Butterfly" was there, looking more like a praying mantis—long and harshly folded into herself. It is always surprising to me how very slight these ballerinas are in person. She was positively draped in pearls, and herself possessed a pale luminosity. She speaks excellent English, always correct, if with syntactical quirks I cannot replicate here. At first our chatter was quite on the surface but then she softened. Isabel and Lady Edgar were at the other side of the room performing what I believe was a salacious song—despite my so-called "splendid" English, I did not catch many of the references—and Nina looked only slightly amused. I suspect she did not understand all the words, either. She confessed to me that she had been shocked the first time she attended one of Roger's soirées, said she had never seen people so casual, sitting on the floor and kicking their shoes off. One of those differences you notice then gradually forget, she said. I already know what she means. Little things I found fascinating just one year ago I've now nearly forgotten. But the Butterfly still didn't look comfortable, and when someone later brought up Margot—* Zoltan looked up at Grigori to add, "Fonteyn, of course"—*it was clear the rumors are true and the two no longer get along. Not that she said so, but it was evident from her manner, the sharpness in her eyes and her bones.*

Before that, it had come out that I was a poet, and I waited for her to mention her husband. But she did not. When I asked if she read poetry anymore, she said no, she had lost her taste for it. That was how she said it, lost her taste. I asked how that could happen, and she said she agreed with Plato, or at least Plato as summarized for her: that there was something dishonest about it and that he was right to want to banish the poets. I was of course horrified. Zoltan looked up at Grigori again to say, "I've never forgiven Plato for that."

He went back to reading: *What she meant, she told me, was that the only reality was life, real life, and that these beautified versions were lies and she no longer had patience for it. I dared to say that I supposed her husband would disagree. She said, No, it was he who had told her Plato's view, and that she thought he was well aware that his poems were not truth. The reality he wanted to believe wasn't anything that existed, she said, and so he had to create it on the page. She said, "He wanted to believe it, but I don't think he did." Then Roger came twirling at us with a Christmas ball hanging from one nostril—* Oh, that's it. That's where it ends."

Grigori nodded slowly, wondering if what Revskaya had said was true. "Thank you for letting me hear it. It definitely puts another spin on his poetry."

"I'll make a photocopy for you, shall I? Funny, isn't it, how one forgets these things. It's the auction that's made me think about her, all the buzz in the papers." Zoltan was already picking up his plastic bags, turning to leave Grigori's office. "Good day to you, Grigori, I'll leave the photocopy in your box. Funny how you can see things different ways, depending on what you're looking for."

Zoltan shuffled out, and Grigori reached over to close the door after him—but Carla was already leaning in to say, "You know this is a nonsmoking building."

A NEW YEAR begins, dirty icicles hanging from eaves, sun waiting until ten to rise. Windows shut tight for the season, wedged with wadded cotton that soon turns black with grime. Mother makes her rounds, to work, to the shops, to the hospital and the prison, to this friend and that relative, while Nina hurries back and forth, in the mornings to company class and the mandatory Marxist lectures, in the afternoons to rehearsal, and in evenings to perform. Not to mention compulsory "community service," long bumpy bus rides to distant villages to perform for peasant laborers, or for factory workers in big industrial plants. For extra money, there are private concerts at clubs, and performances at institutes and academies, scurrying from concert hall to concert hall. When she has worked her muscles too hard, her entire body feels as if it is trembling inside. Knots in her legs, hips, feet. Stockings bloody at the toes. Some days everything comes together beautifully, her body obeys and even surprises her with its achievements. Other days it disappoints her. She is forever cleaning her toe shoes and ironing her costumes, stitching elastics and ribbons onto her slippers. Listening to notes after rehearsal, shedding occasional tears. The frustration of unattainable perfection . . . She kisses her mother's cheeks and steps out into the twilight, past children playing hockey in the alley, their bright voices like chimes in the cut-glass air. In the street overstuffed trams roll slowly by, passengers clinging to the sides, as Nina heads to her world of tights and tutus, of makeup rubbed on and then off, of the Bolshoi curtains drawn apart and then together again, their gold tassels swinging. All the while, she is waiting to hear from Viktor.

Two weeks have passed since their dinner together. Wondering if she said something wrong, or he has met someone else—or has something horrible happened to him?

Then, one evening, she sees him.

Or thinks she sees him. She has just finished a matinee, not at the Bolshoi but at a much smaller concert hall, a private recital to supplement her salary. It is Sunday, a crisp, clear afternoon, cold but not painfully so, the sun barely starting to set. Nina joins the crowded sidewalk, everyone ambling along, enjoying their day off. And there, ahead of her, by a corner kiosk, is the blond woman—Lilya, *stunning*, in a gray fur coat, her hat dark and small as if to display her fair hair. And now Nina sees a tall, dapper man at the little wooden booth, buying cigarettes, obscured somewhat by his hat and scarf and the dense clump of people—but, yes, it is Viktor, tall and lean and healthy. Nina's heart sinks.

She will approach him, she will, she must, she is already working up the courage. But the busy sidewalk, the slow-moving crowd, blocks her, as the blond woman and the tall man merge with it and continue on their way.

Nina closes her eyes, tells herself she will forget this. She will forget him, she is young, she doesn't need that man. Instead of heading home she decides to walk on, as if she might walk far enough, past this fever, past her thoughts. Silently she confides in a friend she does not have, explains how it was with Viktor just two weeks ago, a closeness that was more than physical, that she thought was real. To trust someone that way, without doubts or misgivings . . . Impossible, perhaps. In a side street, children are squealing and shouting, trying to skate on the rough ice and packed snow. A wave of recollection curls over Nina: the dusty courtyard, with Vera, playing together for hours, laughing so hard they could not stop. And then the wave has passed and she is simply walking, alone.

She walks and walks, by the embankment along the Moscow River. Joyous voices of choral singers waft from loudspeakers. She watches the changing colors of the river, ice turning pale pink as the sun slides away. Then all at once she is cold, so cold, feet nearly frozen, face numb from the brisk air.

The next day, she finds a scrap of paper on the dressing room floor: a note, slipped under the door. *Very sorry for the long absence. My dear mother was ill again, I couldn't get away. Please accept my apology. And please let me take you out tonight. Yours, Viktor.*

Mother, indeed. But when, after the performance, Nina finds

Viktor slouching casually against the wall across from her dressing room, all she says—as frostily as possible—is, "I'd given up on you."

"Forgive me. I was housebound with my old mother—but please don't blame her!"

"Not at all. I blame you."

Viktor just grins. "And if I told you it won't happen again?"

"I won't believe you." Her voice is surprisingly calm. "I saw you with that woman. Lilya."

Viktor looks surprised rather than concerned. "You saw me yesterday? Where, in the restaurant? Why didn't you say hello?"

"I didn't want to interrupt a private moment."

"But we were with—you don't mean you think . . . I told you, she's an old friend." He laughs, as if none of it matters. "Butterfly, if it helps things, she's off to Ukraine, she's been offered good work there at a theater. But even if she lived right here, Nina, don't you understand . . ." He gives a small shake of his head, and then his face changes; for the first time in the short stretch that Nina has known him, he truly seems at a loss for words. "Something happened with you," he says, looking almost perplexed. "Something's happened."

"What happened?" She hears the alarm in her voice.

He shakes his head. "I just want to be with you."

To Nina's astonishment, this truly seems to be the case. From that night on, Viktor takes her out to dinner, to cafés thick with cigarette smoke, to a crowded nightclub buzzing with music, and his easy manner makes Nina feel at ease. The invisible barrier that ordinarily separates her from any new acquaintance does not exist. A new appetite has overtaken her, one more than physical: the hunger to know this person to the core, to discover his many layers, his incongruities. For the first time in her life Nina feels not just curiosity but the need to discover the heart of another person.

Viktor has become eager, a courteous and reliable suitor, and only the suddenness of his transformation makes Nina uncomfortable.

Yet it really does seem there is no one else. In snatched moments of rare privacy—the dressing room when Polina isn't present, or a briefly vacant hallway, or the cold blackness of cobblestone alleys late at night—Viktor kisses Nina lingeringly, surreptitiously, murmuring in her ear. Sometimes he touches her, the way he did in the car, and it amazes her that she has lived her life until now without the pleasure of such surprises. She arrives home very late, to her mother's lightly whistling snores, and slides happily under the covers of her narrow iron cot.

Some nights Mother wakes up, slight worry in her voice as she calls, "How late you are."

From her cot across from her, Nina says, "Sorry, I tried not to wake you."

"A mother hen never sleeps until her chicks have made it safely home."

"Ha! You should hear yourself snoring."

Mother laughs lightly, her voice high like a girl's. "You're happy, I can tell." Then her voice shifts. "I just want you to be safe. To be sure you're with people you can trust."

"Please don't worry."

Mother sighs. "You're still my little girl, you know." And then, though Nina hasn't yet mentioned a word about Viktor, "Is he handsome?"

"Very."

"*Very!*" A pause. "If he does anything, you know where to kick him."

"Mother!" But she can't help laughing.

The long dark waves of winter, the extreme cold and melancholy sky, snow blackening, hardening, melting, freezing again . . . It all seems beautiful to her now, because of Viktor. She meets his friends and acquaintances: a married couple that does literary translation; a cocky young novelist from Siberia; a pale, nervous playwright who always manages to spill something. The slightly older bunch includes bald Academician Rudnev and Architect Kaminsky and the woman who runs the State Archive of Serfdom and the Feudal Epoch. But Nina still hasn't been to Viktor's apartment, and still hasn't met his mother.

One friend in particular, the composer Aron Simonovich Gershtein (friends call him Gersh), is Viktor's closest friend. He teaches at the Moscow Conservatory and lives in the same building where Viktor and his mother have their quarters, a large one owned by the Bolshoi, right near Theatre Square. It is reserved for composers, performers, and artists, and is in much better shape than the moldy wooden structure where Nina and her mother live. Like all big apartment houses, this one has militiamen at every side, and inside smells of frying oil.

On each of the three stories is a long dark corridor with many doors all along. Whenever Nina and Viktor come to visit, all the doors open a crack, and from behind each one an uneasy pair of eyes peeks out. No matter the hour, there is someone smoking in the hall, someone on the telephone, someone yelling about something, and someone cooking potatoes on the stove. Gersh's room is halfway down the hallway, much of it taken up by a grand piano.

Gersh himself is a broad-shouldered man in his early thirties, with thick but receding brown hair. Gray-green eyes bright behind small round glasses, one eye angled just the slightest bit toward the bridge of his nose, as if a punch to his head has shifted it there. Yet he is not unattractive, perhaps because of the glint in his eye. "Come in, come in," he says the first time Viktor brings Nina to meet him. "How lovely to see you in person, Butterfly," lifting her hand to his lips. "You as well, Viktor, as always. You're just in time to try the new tea Zoya's concocted."

"Zoya?" Viktor mouths silently at him, and Gersh gives an apologetic little shrug. But Viktor's eyes give Nina a warning look. She glances uneasily over at the petite dark-haired woman busying herself at the other side of the room.

Zoya, looking up, says, "Viktor Alekseyevich!" Hair short and curly, dark ringlets framing her face. "It's been much too long, actually. And how nice"—turning to Nina—"to meet *you*. I've seen you dance. Amazing, I always say. Won't you take off your coat? I love the ballet. In a way I've always fancied myself a dancer." She speaks very quickly, with a slight lisp, and Nina feels the effort of trying to keep up. "Your timing is perfect, actually. I hope you'll have some of this tea. It's the first time I've made it." She learned it, she explains, from a Chinese doctor, who gave her the buds himself. "He said if you drink it every other day, it can add ten years to your life."

"Goodness," Viktor says, "what will we do with the extra time?" and Gersh says, "The question is, what happens if you drink it *every* day?"

"The buds only open once every twenty-four hours," Zoya continues. "Or something like that. I forget the name, actually, but it's very good for you and all that. He explained why."

"Why?" Nina attempts to take it all in—this woman's quick chatter, and the unfamiliar apartment, and Gersh with his one slightly wandering eye. She can smell how strong the tea is, an unfamiliar bitter scent.

"I can't remember, actually. But it has to do with rinsing out your intestines and all that." Zoya's ringlets bob earnestly. Her eyelashes too are curled, and she bats them in a way Nina has only ever seen onstage.

"You don't have to drink it, you know," Gersh tells them. "Zoya won't be offended. Right, noodle?"

Nina can't help watching Gersh's one just-slightly-crossed eye; behind his glasses, it makes him look either bookish or tough, she can't quite decide which. "Of course we'll try it," she says, not daring not to. "I need all the help I can get to stay healthy through the winter season."

"He's never been sick at all, the doctor told me." Zoya pours the dark tea into chipped ceramic cups, her hands small as a girl's. The samovar is the new cheap kind made of tin.

"Please, have a seat," Gersh tells them, and sits on one side of the divan (from which some stuffing is escaping), across from the bed with a down comforter covered in red silk. The rest of the furniture consists of three mahogany chairs, an armoire with a washbasin next to it, a big radio on a large, low cabinet, shelves stuffed with sheet music (lots of pages flapping out), and this small table, round, with beautifully carved legs. On the table are some eggs and a small dish of black pepper: treasured goods. Nina also notes that Gersh has his own telephone—atop the low, heavy cabinet—and a small portable stove. Such obvious privilege, Viktor and his ilk, favored, coddled as Fabergé eggs, so precious that they had to be shipped out to Tashkent.

"This cup's a bit chipped on the edge there," Zoya is saying, as Nina and Viktor seat themselves in the mahogany chairs, "so be careful of your lip. Oh, and this one, see, I told you it had a crack in it! Don't burn your mouth, now. Oh dear, I almost spilled. I hope it tastes all right." Zoya continues to fret about the china and about the tea as Gersh proposes the toast: "To long life and filled cups."

Not the most realistic proposal. Nina keeps the thought to herself as they raise their cups of tea. A sharp aftertaste hits when she swallows.

"You know, Zoya," Viktor says, "I may have to forgo those extra ten years."

Gersh hasn't any sugar, but Zoya suggests some milk might sweeten it. "Oh, dear, who knew, but it's Chinese and all that." She pours the milk from a dirty green bottle, and Nina watches the precious whiteness swim in her tea. "I bet this will help your dancing."

Her interest seems genuine; she works for the lecture bureau of the Moscow City Education Department, organizing cultural events for the public. "It's a wonderful program, actually, I'm so honored to be a part of it. We have such talent in this great nation." Nina recognizes Zoya's type—always showing her Party spirit and wearing something on her lapel. Now she is telling them about a variety show she recently arranged for a rest home of the Scholars' Aid Commission. "It was a huge success." A flat, matter-of-fact voice and little shake of her ringlets, as if success is only natural for her. "There was an accordionist, a magician, an absolutely fantastic singer, and such a funny juggler. And a talk by a senior lecturer from the teacher-training institute. Oh, and the cutest little trained dog—"

"I wonder how the poor lecturer felt," Gersh says from the divan, "squeezed between a juggler and a dog."

"You laugh," Zoya says, looking coyly hurt, "fine, I know you like to put on airs and pretend to be above all that—" But her face cannot hide that she finds Gersh charming.

"I'm not pretending at all. I truly believe that my work—despite anything the Central Committee might say"—his tone changes as he glances at Viktor—"is of a higher realm than that of a trained dog. Perhaps not the magician . . ."

Viktor's eyes twinkle; he clearly takes pleasure in Gersh's impudence. Zoya says, "Those magicians and jugglers are artists, too. Their art is entertainment, rather than . . . well, I don't exactly know what you think of as your art's goal, actually."

"Beauty, my sweet dumpling. Beauty and nothing less. Don't you agree?" Gersh turns to Viktor and Nina for support, but Viktor looks less at ease now that he's been drawn in, and Nina, surprised at Gersh's bold statement, doesn't know what to say. Officially, art has a much greater purpose: to educate the population and serve the Revolution. Without social context, mere beauty is insufficient—at least, according to the lectures Nina has to sit through at the House of Art Workers.

"You can put your work up on a pedestal," Zoya is saying, giving a little "humph" that could only be described, Nina supposes, as adorable, "but I can tell you, there are jugglers whose company I'd much prefer to certain poets. Not you, of course." Zoya gestures petitely at Viktor.

Gersh says, "Ah! I know what might sweeten this stuff," and leans over to the cabinet, to take out a bottle of liqueur.

Zoya turns to Nina. "If you would ever consider dancing for us . . ."

"Oh, certainly." She is still taking everything in, figuring out just who Zoya is, and Gersh too, trying to make sense of them, of why Gersh would air these opinions so freely in front of someone like her. Well, clearly she is smitten with him. Maybe opposites really do attract.

"Viktor has performed for us, you know. Quite a showman, actually, the way he recites. I love the one about the poppy fields."

Then her face changes. Quietly, turning back to Gersh, she says, "I hear that—" She pauses, as if to find the correct words. "Your old friend Zhenia has become a widow."

Gersh stops unscrewing the bottle top. Viktor mutters, "Yes, I just heard," looking down into his tea. Nina searches her memory, as if it might reveal who Zhenia is. But of course Zhenia isn't the person Zoya means to mention. It is the husband—the fact that he has died, in some sort of bad circumstance. That's what Zoya means.

"I didn't know," Gersh says in a low voice, turning his attention back to the bottle of liqueur. Nina feels a shiver, though in the ballet world it's no different, these quiet, coded revelations.

"Yes, well, I just heard myself," Zoya says.

Gersh is adding the liqueur to their cups, still looking down. His voice tight, he asks, "I don't suppose he was run over by a truck?"

This Nina knows, this she understands. Last month the wonderful actor who was director of the Jewish Theatre was killed in a car accident. At least, that's how the newspapers put it—but word has gotten round about the truck that hit him, that the MVD had a hand in it. Nina still doesn't know quite what to think. Why would they—how could they—just go and kill someone, an innocent person? Her heart sinks all over again, thinking of it. The Jewish Theatre, meanwhile, has been shut down.

"Not that I was familiar with his poetry myself," Zoya says, ignoring Gersh's question, as Nina tries to avoid his eyes. The slightly crossed one, she has decided, makes him look a bit off-kilter.

"His poems were heartbreaking," Viktor says very softly.

Taking a seat on the divan, Gersh says, with a kind of finality, "Yes. *That's* what I mean when I talk about art."

"It's for the masses," Viktor says, to no one in particular, and Nina can tell by his tone that he wants to switch topics. "Poetry, juggling, magic shows. They're all ultimately for the same good. It's not about the performers or their work so much as the people. No matter what the art." He sips his tea doubtfully. "Mmm, I can swallow it now, thank you."

"Well, right, 'for the masses,'" Gersh says. "But you know what that comes to." He shifts farther back on the divan, seeming to have recovered from whatever shock or anger or fear he feels. Then he reaches over and casually presses a cushion over the telephone. "For three days last month I sat with my fellow composers listening to the Central Committee reiterate its 'guidelines' for Soviet music. Three days of everything we're doing wrong: 'anti-people' this and 'formalist' that and 'Muddle Instead of Music,' et cetera, et cetera. Nineteen thirty-six all over again. We had to nod along while Zhdanov listed all the culprits in the audience: Shostakovich, Prokofiev, Khachaturian. Who knows why my name wasn't on that list."

Nina has heard about that meeting—quiet grumblings from the rehearsal pianists and conductors at the Bolshoi, whispers and frowns on the musicians' faces. She wonders if Gersh ought to complain in front of someone like Zoya, but decides that he must understand her well enough to know.

"The most middling, second-rate composers were of course delighted," he continues. "Good for mediocrity, you know. The speakers kept saying, 'The Central Committee wants beautiful, graceful music.' That was the phrase they kept using. 'Beautiful and graceful.' " He raises his eyebrows. "Well, who can argue with that?" Something almost like a smile crosses his face. "I was talking with poor Shostakovich later. He told me about when he and Prokofiev were invited to meet with Zhdanov. And Zhdanov told them that the most important element in music—" Though his tone is slightly scornful, Gersh's eyes seem to be laughing, crinkling at the sides. He stops, lights another cigarette, exhales. Now he affects an expression of exaggerated gravitas. "This is advice for our two greatest living composers. Zhdanov told them that what matters most in a piece of music is that it has a melody that can be *hummed*."

Nina and Viktor laugh lightly, while Gersh shakes his head in a sad way. Zoya's face seems not to know what to do, as if she wants to but cannot quite disapprove. Lips pressed together, her eyes, on Gersh, shine—the bright flash of fascination. Glimpsing it, Nina wonders if her own eyes, when she looks at Viktor, reveal her so nakedly.

Viktor, in his usual way, has begun telling jokes.

Nina has seen him do this before, deflect sadness or disagreement with some humorous story. He has an endless supply. Soon Nina too, she can't help it, is laughing.

"I know one," she says, happy to have remembered one—a cartoon from Polina's *Krokodil*. "A woman in a dress shop is trying on a dress. The shopkeeper asks have you made up your mind, and the woman says, 'I don't know. I like the way the fabric feels, but I don't like the pattern.' 'Oh, don't worry,' the shopkeeper says, 'the pattern will completely disappear as soon as you wash it.' "

The others laugh, but then Viktor says, "Patience now. You'll have your pretty dress soon enough."

Nina feels momentarily chided—but Zoya quickly says, "I've got one. A farmer is standing between two tractors, looking confused. He asks, 'Which one's been fixed, and which one still needs repairs?' 'Run them,' the other man says. 'I already did that,' the farmer says. 'Neither of them runs.' " Her lisp makes her seem innocent and very young. Viktor doesn't seem to mind her joke. A brief surge of annoyance courses through Nina, at the way Viktor always acts around women—how he courts their attention in small ways, even now, with Nina by his side.

Zoya offers to refill their cups. But only she takes more of the tea, with a small, contented sigh. "I'll have the other stuff," Gersh says, and Zoya pours him more liquor. That flash again, across her face, of adoration.

"Thanks, noodle."

"Please, Gersh," Viktor says, "the dear girl is not a comestible."

"It's because I told him I didn't like to be compared to an animal," Zoya says. "Even 'kitten' bothers me. So he started calling me other things."

"You see? She asked for it." Gersh reclines on the divan.

"He's quite a ladies' man," Viktor remarks to Nina afterward, as he accompanies her back to her apartment. "Collects women the way a tree stump collects mushrooms. Likes to have them around." Viktor says it in a prideful manner that suggests he once viewed himself, too, that way. "Lately he's calmed down, though," he adds, as if to appease Nina.

Yet Nina feels somehow sorry for Gersh; he has a musty smell—the stale, lonely odor of clothes left too long in a drawer. Quietly she asks, "Did he really need to put the cushion over the telephone?"

"Oh, you know," Viktor says, "people have been doing that for years."

"But why?" As much as she knows to be careful of what she says, she is ignorant, from so many hours of ballet, just ballet and home to bed, and little else.

"Rumors," Viktor tells her. "Of recording devices left over from the war. Confiscated from the Germans." He makes the face she loves, the insouciant, slightly obnoxious one. "People flatter themselves with the notion that their own quarters have been fitted with these things." He tosses the butt of his cigarette to the ground.

FROM THE FRONT hall came a shuffling sound and small thud, the usual shower of bills and catalogs that her across-the-hall neighbor always dumped through the slot in the door. Nina paid it little attention; she rarely wrote to anyone, expected no significant mail. Well, there were holiday cards from former students, and the odd package from Shepley or Tama, and once a year or so a long letter from Inge. Today's pile of mailings lay on the floor like litter—until Nina happened to glimpse, on top, a cream-colored envelope.

She rolled her wheelchair forward, closer, to see if she was correct. Yes, just like the other one, the address in confident, dark black ink.

At first she sat in her wheelchair just looking at it. Then she tried to bend down to reach it, but her hand went nowhere near the floor. This in itself was an embarrassment, an affront. Yet Nina tried again, first breathing slowly and deeply, as she had learned to so many years ago. She breathed and stretched, then breathed and stretched again, and indeed her hand was able to move closer. Nina took another breath, exhaled. Her hand moved closer still. But not close enough.

After a brief rest, she tried again. She knew that any physical challenge took time. Inhale, exhale, reach. She moved slowly, gradually stretching one inch, then another, by sheer force of will. Now her hand was nearly at the floor. Just one more inhalation, and then exhale. Her arm stretched impossibly, fingers trembling as they approached the corner of the envelope. But then her right side gave in, all at once, collapsing without warning. Nina crumpled over the armrest, pain shooting across her ribs.

She had to wait until five o'clock, when Cynthia finally showed up. "Here you go, sugar." Jade bangles on her wrist knocked against each other as she handed the pile over.

"Thank you." Nina tried to act as though she had little curiosity about any of it. But as soon as Cynthia had gone into the kitchen to start dinner, Nina took up the cream-colored envelope, carefully tore it open, and slid the letter out.

Madam,

I was, as you might imagine, surprised by the news that Beller is to auction your jewelry. And when I heard that you were including the amber that matches my own, I could not help but feel culpable.

Please believe me when I insist that I did not intend, in my original query, to create a situation of alarm. It was my intention simply to prove to you, through the incontestability of these beautiful objects we both own, that the ties between us are real and un-contradictable.

The fact that rather than recognizing this connection you have chosen to unload yourself of all concrete proof leaves me no doubt as to your feelings about me, or about that particular slice of your past. As painful as this is, I respect your wishes. It is for that reason that I too have decided to auction off my own small evidence of that past.

After all, while this object has for decades been invaluable to me, it has not brought me the answers I have longed for. At the very least I wish, therefore, to reunite it with its mates, so that the collection (unlike myself, my own history) may at last, if briefly, be complete.

I have come to this decision respectfully, without guile. At the same time, I continue to hope that you and I may at some point meet in person, and that you might clarify the questions that continue to haunt me. It is out of respect for your privacy that I have entered this auction anonymously. And it is my hope that, out of respect for me, you will grant me, at last, a meeting.

Respectfully yours,

Grigori Solodin

Something awful flared inside her. Across her hips, the pain was returning, despite the tablets she had swallowed three hours ago. She had taken them last night, too, had given in, though she often went without them for days at a time. But then the pain would become so extreme it would wake her, or simply prevent her from sleeping, or cause her to cry out—before she could stop herself—in the presence of some unwanted witness like Cynthia. The dark bedroom at night always made it somehow worse, when the walls were so black, she might have been anywhere. But the tablets brought with them their own muddied sleep, left her foggy-headed in the waking hours, given to long, rambling chats with Cynthia. Or she would catch herself dozing; once she had woken with drool on her blouse. And so she would again swear off the tablets, and again the cycle would begin.

With the new letter in her lap, Nina rolled her wheelchair into the study, to her desk, and unlocked the top drawer, where the first letter still lay shoved toward the back. Again Nina's urge was to crumple it in her cramped hands—but of course that would accomplish nothing. She slid the letter forward and removed it from its envelope, feeling once more that perverse urge: to see what she had long ago told herself she would forget. Unfolding the page, she took the photograph between her trembling fingers and thumb. The picture was in color, remarkably clear, the detail surprisingly crisp. Nina supposed it was one of those digital ones she kept hearing about. The girl from Beller, too, had said they would be taking digital photographs, to post "online" for potential bidders.

This one had been taken close up, showing the bead its actual size, a big thick spoonful of honey. Nina felt the same surprise as before, that even in this reproduction the color was exactly right, exactly as she remembered it, a clear dark reddish orange hue. She brought the photograph closer to her eyes, to better inspect the bead. Despite the trembling of her hand, she was able to find what she knew was inside. But it felt improper, somehow, to look. The brisk and horrible feeling flared again. She must put an end to it.

She turned the photograph face down. Then she slipped a sheet of creamy paper from the blotter before her and uncapped a nibbed pen. "Dear Mr. Solodin," she began, in thin blue ink. "I have received your correspondence." She saw how the letters cramped together, tightly, like her knuckles themselves. She brought the pen nib down again, trying to think what to write—something firm and final—but a spot of ink began to bleed where the tip met the paper. She lifted the pen and stared at the page, aware that she was doing the same thing as always: reacting too quickly, not stopping to think, not pausing to take a calming breath. She put the cap back on the pen and placed the paper inside the drawer, along with both of Grigori Solodin's letters. No more rash decisions, she told herself. This was going to take some time, to decide what, exactly, to do now.

NOT LONG AFTER that night at Gersh's, Viktor brings her back to the same big, square building, the same bored, chilly militiamen out front—but this time they enter on the other side, around the corner, and walk up to the apartment where Viktor and his mother reside. Like Gersh's it is off a gloomy corridor, this time at the very end, across from the telephone. A woman in a dressing gown is talking loudly into the receiver and only briefly glances at Viktor as he ushers Nina into his room. Dim, fusty, with windows facing Shchepkinsky Passage, it has been divided in half by a wall Viktor constructed himself, so that his mother has her own room. "But don't tell anyone!" Viktor warns Nina teasingly—because then he could be said to have two rooms, one of which would certainly be given to some other family.

"Shh, won't we wake her?"

"No, she barely hears anything. She's what I call 'willfully deaf.' "

"I suppose one has to be, with the phone right there." Nina can hear the woman's voice in the hallway: "You told me eighty rubles. I did not 'mishear.' " Though the hour is late, plenty of other sounds reverberate along the hall: a man coughing, a cat whining, the clatter of pots and pans.

The plywood door to Viktor's mother's side is shut, no light under the crack. "Anyway, she's fast asleep," Viktor adds—but Nina is self-conscious at being alone with Viktor, who now brings his mouth to the back of her neck, his hands on her buttocks, moving slowly. She glances toward the door to his mother's room, ready for it to swing open, while Viktor for the first time peels her clothes off and leads her to his narrow bed. The mattress is thin and the pillow heavy as a sack of sand, and then Nina feels just Viktor's hands on her skin, until his fingers find their way inside her, Viktor whispering, "It's all right," when she can't help but cry out. It is very late when he accompanies her home and she slips back into her own narrow cot.

After that, whenever they go to Viktor's apartment, it is always late enough that his mother's light is out and the other residents along the corridor have settled into their various nighttime routines. When one night Viktor for the first time presses himself against her, Nina makes a surprised sound. Viktor laughs and sits up, brushes back her hair—long ago loosed from its coiled bun—and looks at her with fascination. "It's true, then?" he asks, his mouth in a pleased smile. "You really haven't done these things before?"

"No," she says. "Not at all."

Viktor shakes his head, as if disbelieving. "But surely you must have had a love story!"

"Never." As for Viktor's love stories, she has no desire to know them. He is nearly ten years older, and it takes effort not to imagine the women he must have been with. Nina conjures them quite vividly sometimes—not only Lilya . . . A dark-eyed poetess in Tashkent, or an actress from the Vakhtangov Theatre. Artists and writers less naïve than herself.

"And yet," Viktor says, laughing, "the men you dance with put their hands all over you, all the time."

"I don't think about it that way."

He laughs. "But maybe they do."

She tries to explain to him that her partner's hands on her waist, lifting her onto his shoulders or tossing her high above his head, feel no more intimate to her than the dresser's fingertips on her back, pausing quickly at each hook and eye. At rehearsal the next day, though, she pays attention to the men in the company, to see if Viktor might be right. She has been so focused on herself for so long—her own image in the long mirrors, and her thirty-two fouettées in a row—that she hasn't wondered much about the others. Her most frequent partner, Andrei, whose hands she trusts more than anyone's (though the more difficult lifts leave bruises on her rib cage), clearly finds no particular thrill, other than a professional one, in placing his hands on her body. In fact, he doesn't seem interested in any of the ballerinas. Afterward, as always, he leaves with Sergei, a dancer in the corps.

Now Nina feels stupid, or small-minded, to have been so slow to understand. But this sort of thing is never spoken of outright. Nina feels suddenly afraid. They could be declared "socially dangerous" and handed five years of forced labor just like that.

As for Nina, it is becoming more and more difficult for her to hold herself, her body, back. This body she has spent over a decade perfecting, honing into the instrument of her art—and that Viktor's touch has now permitted new efforts and sensations. She thinks all the time about what Viktor does with her, about what they do to each other. The thoughts are soft powder running through her fingers; she picks up a handful over and over.

On a night in early spring she allows herself to give in. They are on his narrow mattress, her arms stretched above, grasping the metal bed frame. The air smells lightly of their sweat and of Peut-Etre—a gift from Viktor, authentic French perfume, along with a flask of silver and porcelain. Painted on the porcelain is a small butterfly.

"Can't you take this off?" Viktor whispers, tugging at her underpants. Nina tugs his off, too, and then there are just their bodies, the surprise of him inside her and her legs strong around his hips, holding him into her, rocking him closer, pulling his weight onto her, the ripples starting inside her. His mouth searches her face, her neck, her shoulders, as if only this will save him. Afterward, she can't help crying—not from sadness but from the release of her body, and a feeling of something like loss.

"Are you hurt?"

She shakes her head. "It's just . . . I wanted to save this for when I got married." She feels ridiculous for only now admitting this.

Viktor just says, "Then let's get married!"

His face becomes very serious, and he bends down onto one knee to take her hands in his. In a soft, grave voice, he asks her to be his wife.

Nina bursts out laughing.

"I had no idea it was such a comical proposition."

She apologizes, horrified to still be laughing. But after so many years of classical ballets, she cannot help seeing, in Viktor's artful pose, the usual overacted pantomime. "You know those scenes," she tries to explain. With exaggerated seriousness, she says, "I'll love you forever," lightly touching her chest with her fingertips, then reaching one hand forward, palm up, before pressing both hands to her heart. Her voice higher, she says, "But what if you leave me?" hands reaching out pleadingly. Shaking her head exaggeratedly: "I'll never leave you." Arms outstretched: "Promise me!"

Viktor catches her hands in his, pulls her to his chest with a flourish. Grandly he says, "I promise you." Then he bites her earlobe for good measure.

But hearing him say the words, Nina is struck, suddenly and powerfully, by their weight—the deep need for that promise, the solemnity of it, the many natural fears and anxieties it contains. She pulls away, in order to look Viktor in the eye. Her jaw is trembling when she says, "I promise you."

Quickly Viktor adds, "But I can't leave my mother."

Nina squeezes his hand. "It makes sense for me to live here with you. With the Bolshoi just two steps away."

When he walks her home that night, it is later than usual. Nina tiptoes back into her apartment and sits on a corner of the bed where her mother is asleep, chest rising and falling with each breath. "Wake up," she whispers, softly rubbing her mother's shoulders. "I have good news."

Opening her eyes, squinting at the faint beam of light slicing the darkness, Mother's voice is hoarse: "What good news?"

Nina opens her mouth to speak, but instead of words there comes a sob. Her mother sits up, alarmed, and brushes Nina's tears with rough fingertips. Then she holds her the way only she can, all warmth, the thin cotton of her nightshirt a flimsy barrier between them. That is why Nina is crying—the thought of leaving this: the scent of her mother's bed-mussed hair, and the indentations of the pillow in the flesh of her cheek, and the gentle scuffing of her leather slippers across the wooden floor. Her mother, who has given her this life, and woven her own hopes and dreams into her braids. Who every single night when Nina arrives home is here, always here, asleep in this bed. And so it is a few minutes before Nina is able to speak, to tell her, "I'm getting married."

. . . .

THEY ARE WED on a bright spring day when the city itself seems to be starting anew. Replanting has begun, new maples propped along the streets. The militiamen at each intersection have swapped their dark winter coats for white cotton jackets.

Viktor's mother does not join them, which is fine with Nina; the two have met just once, and it did not go very well. But she forgets that now, as her own mother and Gersh accompany Nina and Viktor to the registry office. Since first meeting Viktor two months ago, Mother has grown fond of him. Nina wears a new belted dress and holds a bouquet of white arum lilies from Latvia. Viktor wears his good suit, and in the buttonhole a lily from Nina's bouquet.

They have no wedding rings. The ones at the Mostorg are poorly set, even the good-quality stones, so Nina has told Viktor not to give her any of those. He instead presents her with an oval brooch bordered in gold. The lava cameo inside is not of a bust but rather, Nina sees when she looks closer, the tops of St. Basil's Cathedral. The tiny picture is exact, the cathedral's onion tops bizarre, minute, and perfect. And so Nina knows that Viktor has the same memory of the snow drive: the warm car, the glittering snow, and the absurd beauty of the cathedral there in the distance, another world just slightly beyond them.

Lot 28

Unmounted Colored Diamond, the yellow mine-cut diamond weighing 1.85 cts. $10,000–15,000

CHAPTER SIX

In the dream the letter arrived by special delivery, a thick white envelope like something you might see in a cartoon. Around it was a ribbon, as for a wrapped gift. Just Grigori's name there, no return address. The penmanship was somewhat shaky, that of an elderly person. This seemed perfectly natural, and Grigori felt as if he had expected it, had known all along that it would arrive. Yet he untied the ribbon slowly, so as not to betray his excitement. Even in a dream, he wanted to prolong that moment of hope, the heightened expectation. He slit the envelope open with the silver letter opener Christine's sister had bought for them at the Shaker Museum. The letter slipped out, and Grigori unfolded it eagerly—but more calmly than he might have in real life.

There were no words. Nothing written on it at all. Instead, like a blotch of black ink, in the center of the page, at the crease where the letter had been folded, was a large, dead, squashed spider.

In winter, when the air was too cold for jogging, Drew took long walks along the Charles River. She liked to watch its changing surfaces, crinkly, smooth, muscled, rough. In fair weather it would be dotted with the white peaks of sailboats, or in early morning the smooth shifting and gliding of sculls. Other days it turned a shiny dark metallic color, something cruel about it. At night, the gleam of city lights hopped about on the surface.

Today, a frigid windless afternoon, the water was very pale, an opaque grayish white that mirrored the snow on the ground. Just a touch of blue in the white. Drew walked briskly and every once in a while brought her hands close to her mouth, dosing the tips of her gloves in a brief puff of white, as if that might prevent her fingers from going numb. She liked the cold air on her face, liked its cold clarity, its sharp reminder of what life was, that glorious intensity that was also sometimes painful. Now that she had reached the footbridge, she turned away from the water and mounted the stairs to cross Storrow Drive, so that she could make her way along the north side of the Public Garden over to the farthest corner of the Common. Her lunch break was almost over, but she had a work-related errand.

Back in college the very thought of library research had at first made her stomach knot up. She had even managed to pass an entire semester without setting foot in the imposing, cathedral-like library that crowned her school's leafy green campus; inside, Drew had been told, were mazelike hallways and steep spiral staircases that led to closets and gables and far-off hidden rooms to which, for some reason, only the skinny albino guy in her dormitory possessed the keys. But a history course during her second semester, requiring the examination of various "primary sources," had meant that she could no longer avoid the library, and then, during her second year, for a class on developmental psychology, she regularly found herself in deep, low-ceilinged basements where mobile stacks rolled toward each other and apart when she cranked a handle. At some point in her third year, when she had switched her major yet again, back to art history, something changed. Her hands no longer felt dirty after reading the battered publications on reserve; she no longer cringed to touch the dusty covers of a portraiture book in the oversize stacks. She began to enjoy the hunt through dark, narrow labyrinths, climbing precipitous staircases to the upper galleries or tunneling her way to some obscure elbow of the building where the reproductions of fifteenth-century Japanese woodblock prints were confined. The sleuthing was as satisfying as ultimately finding what she was looking for, and as being told by the woman at the circulation desk that Drew was the first person in thirty-five years to have borrowed this or that book.

It occurred to her now, as she crossed past the old gold-domed State House and mounted the low gray stone steps of the Athenaeum, that maybe her conversion in that first library had been the first sign of her work to come, her appreciation of old, overlooked, and sometimes hard-to-find things.

Luckily the auction house had arranged for a group membership; the reference librarian was expecting Drew and had set the requested book aside. *Russian Gold and Silver Marks.* Lenore hadn't even worried when Drew pointed out that their house copy had been misplaced. She said that the information they already had was good enough. But Drew hated the thought of what they might possibly be overlooking. She had even thought to call in an entomologist, to identify the exact specimens in the amber.

Feeling hopeful, Drew took the book—heavy and square, with a thick shiny cover like a slab of tile—into the reading room, where two different old men in tweed jackets and bow ties did not bother to look up from their periodicals. She made herself comfortable in a firm leather armchair. If indeed the amber had been handed down through Nina Revskaya's husband's family, and if Drew were able to narrow down the possible date of origin, or the date of purchase, then perhaps . . . And yet Drew could not help wondering if what Nina Revskaya claimed was true. First she had said she knew nothing about the amber's origins, and then she seemed to just toss off that comment about her husband's family. Well, it wasn't the first time Drew had been given contradictory information by a client.

Scanning the table of contents, Drew first turned to the section on maker's marks, to see if by some (very) small chance there might be more than one mark for Anton Samoilov—if the mark might have changed over time. She had once seen this in the case of a goldsmith whose mark, in later years, had been slightly altered to indicate the addition of his sons to his business. Something like that might narrow down the time frame of when these pieces were made. But no, here was a photograph of the little AS imprint, same as the one on the suspension loops of the earrings, and on the clasps of the necklace and bracelet. (Well, the one on the bracelet was a bit rubbed.) Drew had to admit that it was as she had expected.

Now she flipped to the section on city marks. Here was what she wanted, toward the back of the book: "Town Marks before 1899." Two pages of little drawings of each town's crest or coat of arms, from Astrakhan (a cartoonish pointed crown floating above a horizontal sword) to Zhitomir (a palace of sorts, with three towers, looking in the reproduction more like a birthday cake with three candles). Since these were stamped images, they were difficult to make out, the ink as blurred as an imprint in silver or gold would be. Irkutsk's looked like a cat holding something dead in its mouth, while Kazan's appeared to be a duck wearing a crown. For Moscow there were ten different marks, beginning in 1677, first the Imperial Eagle—the one with two heads—and later on, the profile of a sword-carrying chevalier on horseback: St. George slaying the dragon.

Drew found herself pausing, wondering what Moscow would have looked like in those years. Not that she possessed an image of how it was now. But she had told herself that one day she would visit Russia, the country of her mother's father—whom her mother had never known; he had died shortly after her birth, after two years that Grandma Riitta called the happiest of her life. This was a story

Drew had heard so many times, she pictured it as clearly as if it were a movie she had watched over and over.

Grandma Riitta, at thirty the old maid of her village, had returned home for the weekend, as she often did, a dutiful eldest daughter. For years she had lived in Helsinki, where she worked as a lab technician, but she continued to visit her parents when she could and tried not to be bothered by the way that, each time she returned, she immediately became the person they believed her to be: a peculiar, impatient girl, attractive enough yet too old and odd for the village boys who had once been her friends.

Now it was springtime. She had just fetched the mail from the post office and was driving her family's three-wheeler back to the house. It had rained, and the route was muddy. At the side of the road she saw an old man walking slowly, and leaned out the window to call to him.

"Can I give you a lift, Uncle?"

The man looked up, and Riitta saw that he was not so old as she had thought. But his back was hunched, his clothes faded. He did not seem to understand her.

More loudly she said, "Your boots are right muddy, Uncle. Hop on up." She patted the seat beside her.

The man's face looked surprised and then softened into a smile, revealing gaps where some of his bottom teeth were missing. Yet the softening of his face made him look younger again, a young-old man. He pulled himself up onto the seat, and she smelled him. It was the smell of hard work and unwashed clothes, overlaid with a stronger smell, the one Riitta loved and missed in the city, of wet leaves and mud and hay. He must have done his sleeping out of doors.

He gave a grateful nod, said, "Thank you," with a heavy accent. So he wasn't deaf after all, he was a foreigner. Riitta saw, to her surprise, that despite the many lines in his face he was handsome. She said, "Someone roughed you up."

He gave her a helpless look, said, "My Finnish no good." An apologetic shrug of his shoulders. "Russki."

Russki. The enemy. Briefly, but not long ago at all; Riitta's own uncle had been killed in the Winter War.

But this man didn't look like an enemy—just a weary soul. Riitta tried English. It was the language she had studied in school, and she knew it well enough. But the man did not. Perhaps he was an escapee. A convict. Though he would have had to walk very far . . .

In Finnish, with hand gestures, she asked, How is it that you ended up here, of all places, old Russki who walked out from the woods?

He understood her question, drew train tracks in the air, made steam engine sounds. When Riitta said the word *train*, he recognized it, said, Yes, train. But then why was he here, in this village? He just shook his head, said, "I very dirty—sorry."

She took him home and fed him lunch. Nourishment turned him younger yet again; now he was perhaps in his forties. His thin gray hair still had some dark black in it. Riitta invited him to come along with her when she went to neuter the pigs.

It was the sort of farming activity she had lost touch with during her years away, and she was proud not to have forgotten. The pigs were still young and cute, and for a moment she worried the Russian might be upset at all the squealing. But he had done this before, too, had once been a country boy—and surprised her by stepping in to help her. Only later, thinking back on it, did she see the cruelty in what she had forced on him, this man who had himself been neutered, in a way, over those past years, and had for a time lost his own virility.

She collected the testicles, to cook for dinner. By then she and the man had exchanged names. His was Trofim. He did not offer up any information as to where he had been, but Riitta could imagine. It was becoming clear that he knew more of her language than he could speak. She invited him to stay, despite her parents' concern. He bathed and shaved and borrowed some clothes her brother had left behind when he moved to Turku. It was the first stage of what Riitta thought of as his rebirth—emerging from the washroom in trousers too big for him and a buttoned shirt whose sleeves puffed out like billows, his face glowing from the fresh shave, his visible relief at being clean. "A working-class face," she always called it. (Drew's mother always balked at that part.) "Good looks, but a roughness to them. You could see he'd never had it easy."

The second stage of his rebirth she thought of as that evening, at dinner, when, like bones carefully exposed by the gentle brush tips of a patient archaeologist, his personality began to emerge.

He was a joker. The fact of it, after what he must have been through, surprised Riitta as much as the realization that such things made themselves known with or without language. Within minutes of sitting down to dinner with Riitta and her parents, Trofim made them laugh. His first joke was about the testicles, with facial expressions rather than with words, but it was how Riitta first witnessed what would turn out to be his very core.

She took him back with her, to the city. He had no other place to go. Within a week he had found a job in a bottling factory. It was a longer time till he first kissed her, suddenly and boldly, one evening when she had just returned from work.

One of the old men cleared his throat very loudly over his bow tie and tweed jacket. Startled, Drew looked up, recalled where she was, reminded herself why she had come here. Looking back down at the big square book in her lap, to the list of town marks, she found Moscow again, and St. George on his horse. In some stamps he faced right, in others, to the left. Drew scanned the years, 1783 . . . 1846 . . . Here was the precise one from the amber suite: the little *zolotnik* number and, to its right, St. George's left-facing profile. This was it exactly.

According to the list, this was the mark used from 1880 through 1899. The same span of time Lenore had approximated, weeks ago, without even having had to refer to a book . . .

She had so wanted to narrow down her search. Yet even this was no help in finding a more precise date. Drew told herself to look on the bright side: if indeed she was lucky enough to locate the jeweler's records, nineteen years would not be *too* many to sift through. She tried not to be disappointed, as she returned the book to the circulation desk and made the brisk walk back to work.

NINA SITS AT the wooden table in Viktor's home, a week or so before they are married. It is the first time she has been in his apartment during daylight hours; she is here to meet his mother, as soon as she awakes from her nap. Viktor has stepped out into the corridor, to discuss something with someone from the House Management Committee. Nina can tell from their voices that the problem will not be easily resolved. She sits alone, sipping lukewarm tea, looking around the plainly furnished room where Viktor has lived for three years. Just as at her own home, the floorboards have been painted a deep orange color in place of a carpet. But along the hallway side of the room are a cupboard and a small portable stove and a broad shelf stacked with dishes and cookware. Then comes a settee and, tucked against the next wall, the bed Nina will share with Viktor. Past the large steamer trunk there is the window wall, with a low armchair and side table and a drying rack full of Viktor's socks, dripping onto the newspaper spread underneath. Finally there is the plywood wall—the one Viktor made to create a separate space for his mother—against which stand a tall wooden wardrobe and a narrow set of cabinets.

Now a loud coughing comes from the other side of the plywood door. It is the first time Nina has heard any sound from there, and she realizes that in all the times she has visited this apartment, late at night, she has managed to forget, in a way, that Viktor's mother really does live here.

The coughing is violent, a choking sound. Nina puts down her tea. The sound continues, and becomes worse, and then, all of a sudden, stops.

Nina looks slowly, fearfully, toward the plywood door. "Are you all right in there?"

No response.

Nina waits, then stands and walks over to the door, leans her ear against it. She listens, but all she hears is her own heart, pounding. She turns to go find Viktor in the hall—but what if there's no time for that? She pictures Viktor returning, opening his mother's door and finding—what? Something awful could have happened.

She knocks on the door.

Nothing.

She remembers, then, with hope, that his mother is hard of hearing. *Willfully deaf.* She knocks as loudly as possible.

"Yes?"

Nina's heart relaxes slightly, as the coughing sound begins and stops again. When she pushes the door slowly open, an odor escapes. She looks in.

Sitting in an armchair in front of the window, so that the sun lights her from behind, is a woman in a long dark dress. Billow of satin, all the way to her ankles. The sun makes her no more than a dark shadow, but as Nina's eyes adjust, she sees that the woman's hair is piled into a thick bun atop her head, and that her dress is a deep blue color, and her shoes of scuffed suede.

And then Nina screams.

Crawling up over the woman's shoe is a small rat. But no, it isn't a rat, Nina sees now, as her eyes become accustomed to the sunshine and the dark. It is a bird, squawking back at her scream, with bright green and white feathers, and short wings flecked with blue.

"I wanted to make sure you were all right," Nina says, loudly. The bird, in what seems very unbirdlike behavior, has begun climbing up onto the billowy skirt. It uses its beak to pull itself up, and the nails of its claws seem to catch, slightly, in the fabric. As Nina's eyes acclimate, she sees that the dress is covered with pulls.

Now a voice comes, slow, wary. "You're not Lilya."

"I'm . . . Viktor must have told you—"

"Your Excellency!"

"He must have told your . . . excellency—"

"I am Madame Ekaterina Petrovna Elsin, wife of His Excellency Aleksey Nicolaiovich Elsin." Her tone is proud, offended. "*S'il vous plaît.*" Nina can hear the phlegm caught in the old woman's chest. The bird has pulled itself up over her knee, continues toward her chest. And now another fit of coughing begins.

As the old woman struggles, Nina hurries to her, to knock on her back a few times—not too hard, in case her bones are frail. Soon the coughs come more loosely. The sound of phlegm caught there. But as the coughing subsides, the woman takes a deep, rheumy breath and then, more loudly than Nina would have thought her able, says, "You are NOT to touch my hair!"

"I didn't—"

"*S'il vous plaît!*" squawks the bird, wings flapping, still attached to the woman's plump satin bosom.

"No one touches my hair!"

Nina steps back. "I only wanted—" But she suspects no explanation will do. "I'm very sorry . . . Madame. I'll leave you, then."

She steps away from this woman sitting mountainlike in her chair, framed by dust-faded curtains. The bird clamors on as the woman coughs again, less violently, and Nina can't help but take one more look before she closes the door. The bird sits quietly now, on the woman's shoulder, leaning its head toward her, as if to better hear what she has to say.

Minutes later Viktor is back. When Nina tells him about the incident, he simply says not to worry. "It's just the way she is. The coughing will go away. I'm sorry your first meeting had to happen like this."

Nina frowns, raises her eyebrows. "She was disappointed to find that I wasn't . . . Lilya."

"Oh, now, don't worry about *that*." Laughing in a fatigued way, he tries to joke: "My mother always falls for those Leningrad girls."

Nina turns her head away—but she can no longer avoid the more looming question. Her voice is almost a whisper as she tells Viktor, "She said to call her Your Excellency."

Viktor closes his eyes briefly. When he opens them, he looks at Nina with a seriousness she hasn't seen before, not even when he asked her to marry him. "Since you're to be my wife, it's time you knew the full truth. My father was in the Imperial Guard."

Nina feels herself giving a small nod, as if she might have known already.

"He was an admiral," Viktor continues, his voice low, "in the Imperial Fleet. And my mother's father was a prominent banker. As was her brother. Both of them were shot in the first days of the Revolution. Then my father was killed, not long after my mother learned she was expecting."

Nina watches Viktor's face, wondering who else knows all this. Firmly, but just as quietly, she says, "It's not your fault who your parents were."

Viktor bows his head before looking up again. "My mother was nearly forty when she found herself pregnant with me. There she was, in a delicate condition, her loved ones either killed or fleeing. Nearly everyone she knew left."

"Why didn't she?"

"She's a stubborn woman, as you'll no doubt see for yourself. I'm not sure she fully believed what was happening. In a way she still doesn't. It's only because of one of the family servants, in fact, that she survived. This housekeeper had been with her family for decades, and had known my mother since she was born. Such loyalty. She took pity on my mother and hid her—along with my grandmother and my aunt—in an *isba* in the woods. It's where I was born. That's why I call the woods my real home. We only spent a year or so there, but that world is in my veins. In part it's because of my grandmother. She's the one who raised me. She had to, because my mother didn't know how. She had always been waited on, you see. The shock of losing her husband, right when she learned she was pregnant—it was too much for her. In a way she never recovered."

"But your grandmother did?"

"She was very different in constitution. She tried to make the best of things—by caring for me, I suppose."

"And your aunt?"

"Sonia. She managed the transition as best she could. She found work as a translator, from French and English. Both she and my mother were fluent in both. It was Sonia's salary we lived off— meagerly, of course, compared to how they had been raised." Viktor takes a long breath. He looks relieved to be telling the truth, and Nina understands what a burden it must be to have to hide the most basic facts about his family. The same way that Nina knows not to mention her uncle in prison. Only with Viktor it's everything, all that precedes him. Why, he could be arrested for "concealing social origins." People are sent to prison for that. It occurs to Nina that perhaps Viktor is hiding his mother, as much as caring for her, by keeping her behind that plywood door.

"What happened after you left the *isba*?"

"At first we were able to go back to the family home. There were other families living there, of course. We were pushed back into what had been the maid's quarters, and—" He stops, and Nina can see that the memory pains him. "We lived there until I was twelve. I've tried to explain to her—" But he doesn't continue.

"And when you were twelve, you moved again?"

"We were evicted, to make room for some government workers. But my aunt found us a room in the city."

"What happened to her? Your aunt."

A long sigh. "I miss her terribly. She's the one that put food in our mouths all those years. She died ten years ago, of pneumonia."

Nina recalls something. "You told me your mother was a teacher. Of languages."

"She ought to have been. Or she could have worked as a translator, like my aunt. She was raised by a French governess, and was tutored in English from the time she could talk. But she . . ." Viktor moves his hand slightly as if to indicate that it no longer matters. "You have to understand, she has always seen herself as a member of a superior class; it's how she was raised. That's why she asked you to address her that way. It's still her identity. Even now."

Nina tries to accept this. "Her dress, it's . . ." Nina is about to say ruined, but instead she says, "old."

"Until the age of forty she was surrounded by wealth," Viktor says. "It's hard for us to understand what it must have been like—to go from that to living communally. She'd had such an easy life. When everything was equalized, well . . . She doesn't understand why her world had to change." He takes Nina's hand, clasps it. "Please have pity on her. She never has adjusted to life as we know it."

"You're very protective of her." Hearing how this sounds, she adds, "It's good of you." After all, she too will soon be living with this woman.

But first, she and Her Excellency—or Madame, as Nina decides to call her—have a proper introduction. This time she has changed into a fresh dress, of slightly torn lace, the hem reaching the floor. She stands regally, if somewhat weakly, as Viktor pulls out a chair for her at the wooden table. "Thank you, dear." Mouth a frown, eyes sunken, scrutinizing Nina, who bows her head slightly. With Viktor, she and Madame sip tea and eat sticky pastries from a bakery.

"I always hide the silver," Madame tells her. "Thieves all around—the Armenians especially. Next door. Took every one of our forks. I found them, luckily. Otherwise we would be eating with our hands."

Viktor gives Nina a covert shake of his head, and Nina looks down at her fork, doubtful that it is of real silver. She focuses on her little tartlet, the pastry crumbling in her mouth.

"I saw their room," Madame continues. "Full of *our* furniture. The big standing mirror my father gave my mother. Oh, they might tell you it's all gone, that there's nothing left. Even the piano."

Nina doesn't know how to respond to this. "Do you—did you—play?"

Madame cocks her ear, and Viktor repeats the question for her.

"It was said I could be a concert pianist if I chose," Madame says. "But the real talent was Sonia. My sister. She sang like a nightingale. That is probably why people thought I played so well. They were fooled by Sonia's beautiful voice." A loud squawking comes from her room. "Lola too has a lovely voice—when she wants to."

"What kind of bird is it?"

"The annoying kind!" Viktor says, laughing.

"A macaw," Madame tells her. "All the way from South America. A gift from my husband."

This confuses Nina. "But—then it must be very old."

"Thirty-two years old," Viktor says, to Nina's astonishment. "Older than me. Still goes by the Julian calendar, just like my dear mother." He makes a joking face. "Don't ask me how the thing survives."

"Such birds have a life span of seventy years," Madame says proudly, and Nina finds herself glancing at Viktor, waiting for another dismissive shake of the head. But he does nothing; apparently it's the truth. Seventy years. So few people ever live that long.

"Like me," Madame continues. "*We* are from good lineage, you see." Her tone implies that Nina isn't. Well, Viktor did say to try to imagine what it was like for his mother, having to shift from one world to another, practically overnight.

Madame says, "Lola will always be by my side. That is what my dear husband told me when he gave her to me."

"In that case you'll have to live to be a hundred and ten," Viktor says.

"I won't die until I meet my grandchildren. That is what my dear father used to say to me: I won't leave this world until I've met my grandson."

Viktor helps himself to a tart, seemingly unhurt by the insinuation—that it was his own fault somehow, that he arrived too late.

"GRIGORI SOLODIN IS here for you."

Ellen, the receptionist, made her announcement the moment Drew stepped in the door. "He's up having a look around the gallery, but he wanted to talk to you."

"Just give me a sec to thaw out, and you can send him in." In her office she warmed her fingertips in her palms and curled her toes until the tingly feeling went away.

A soft rap on the wall beside her open door. "Miss Brooks, I hope I'm not interrupting you."

"I was just on my break, actually. Please have a seat."

He entered somehow humbly, though he was a striking man, tall and broad-shouldered, with an appealing face. As he fit himself into the chair, he brought with him a faint cigarette scent, not ashy-dirty but the mellow, almost sweet, aroma of tobacco. "I was in the neigh-borhood," he said, slightly awkwardly, "and thought I'd check in. I'm wondering if there's been any progress in finding out more about the amber."

"There's apparently some sort of backlog at the lab," Drew told him, hoping to hide her frustration at the unnecessary delay. She too wanted to finalize things, for the catalog as well as publicity purposes. And though the entomologist had been able to name nearly all of the inclusions in the amber set, for the pendant he had only a JPEG and couldn't confirm anything before seeing it in person. All Drew said now, though, was, "Nothing to worry about. We should have the test results by the end of the week. Again, it's simply pro forma."

Grigori Solodin did not look convinced.

"But I've been meaning to contact you, actually. I've started work on the supplemental, and I wonder if you might have any informa-tion for it."

"Supplemental?"

"The supplemental brochure, for the pre-auction dinner. A col-lector's edition type of thing, in addition to the photos and biographi-cal notes we'll include in the catalog. You see, for auctions of note we sometimes hold private events, and I'm creating an additional bro-chure, with some less official, more personal, information. I'd love to have something about the amber. Well, about all the jewels, but in your case, if you have any supplemental information . . ." Grigori Solodin looked down at the floor, and Drew felt she had somehow said something wrong. "I've already asked Nina Revskaya to provide any background she might have, about the people who gave them to her, or what outfits she wore them with. Even just memories of how they were purchased or passed down."

"Good luck with that," Grigori Solodin said drily.

"Yes, well, any level of cooperation is appreciated." Drew felt slightly piqued but tried not to show it. "Which is why I'm mentioning it to you, in case you have anything else you might share. Even information that might seem peripheral could be interesting. I'm trying to personalize things a bit. Since there's so much interest."

Grigori Solodin's face was oddly blank—as if forcing blankness on itself.

"None of this risks losing your anonymity," Drew assured him. "I'll be sure to write it in a way so that it's about the necklace, not about you. I'm hoping to even have photos—of things like the original box from the jewelers, or the gift card. That kind of thing."

With a tight nod, Grigori Solodin pressed his lips together so that the dimples toward the backs of his cheeks showed. "I see." But he didn't offer up anything of his own. "Is it common, to have a . . . supplemental?"

"For the more popular auctions, yes. Have you ever been to one of our auctions?"

"No. In fact, I believe I've only ever been to one auction, out in the Berkshires. My wife liked Oriental carpets, and there was—still is, I suppose—a rug place that would auction them. Nice stuff, not expensive, really. I went with her once."

His face was only slightly sad, so that Drew could not be sure if he was a widower or divorced. Whichever it was, he seemed to be accustomed to speaking of his wife in the past tense. Drew wondered again how old he was. He seemed to possess a certain wisdom she associated with age.

"And you?" he asked. "Are you allowed to bid in your employer's auctions?"

"Yes, but only as absentees—otherwise it could look like we're trying to raise the price. And if there are things left over afterward, sometimes we can buy them after the fact." She showed him the ring on her right hand, told him how her grandmother had left her a bit of money in her will. "Not terribly much, but for two years I kept wondering what I should do with it. She had specified that she wanted me to 'buy myself something nice.' "

"It's very nice." He smiled, and the dimples in the side of his cheek stretched into three lines.

"Thanks." She had never seen three dimply things in a row like that. "I bought one other thing. Just last year. A watercolor from the Japanese Paintings auction." Now it was on the wall in her bedroom, a simple picture, a small black bird alone, not flying but standing, though there was no ground, no earth in the painting, just an empty background, so that the bird stood out even more singularly. For some reason no one had bid on it; afterward Drew had been able to purchase it for less than two hundred dollars. She often found herself looking at the bird as if it were real and could return her gaze. It was just a plain black bird, but it was beautiful in its simplicity, its aloneness, its adamant there-ness, both proud and humble against the white space. But it would be too hard to describe to Grigori Solodin. Drew said, "You're welcome to come to the jewelry auction, of course. No one need know of your personal involvement."

"Thank you." He seemed suddenly uncomfortable. Taking up his hat and gloves, he said, "And, again, if you could tell me when you hear from the lab."

He looked about to step away, and Drew found herself speaking in a rush. "If you think of anything I might use for the supplemental, please do give me a call."

"Unfortunately," he said, looking away, "I don't believe I have any ancillary materials."

"Well, I just wanted to be sure to ask." Drew felt oddly disappointed, although really she hadn't expected much from him. But even after he had wished her a good afternoon and ducked his way out the door—as if he were too tall, too big-shouldered, for it—Drew felt somehow hurt that he had not wanted to help her.

. . . .

A MONTH LATER Nina is installed in the communal apartment, which she and Viktor share with thirty-three other people. A big kitchen with three stoves and six tables, and hanging laundry everywhere. The clunky black telephone, always either in use or ringing, at the end of the hall just outside their door. One toilet and washroom, always a wait. Now that she is right at Theatre Square, though, Nina simply runs to the Bolshoi when she needs a bathroom. It is one of the privileges she is daily thankful for—like the portable stove, which she and Viktor use to heat their room, and Viktor's stipend from the Moscow Literary Fund, and the bread they receive from the Writers Union, and the retired woman, Darya, who cooks and cleans for them daily.

On the same floor with them, each with their own family, are two other dancers, four opera soloists, a playwright, a painter, a cellist, and three actors. One of the ballerinas goes around in a silk dressing gown that is always flapping open, and the cellist's husband spends much of each day in the bathtub. The playwright is always screaming at his wife. Two of the opera singers, both tenors, with rooms at opposite ends of the corridor, practice at the same time, as if trying to drown each other out. The children of the family across the hall own a small, frightened cat that wanders the building mewing and whining.

"The Armenians," Nina discovers, are the family to their right, with three children. The father is an artist known for his paintings of Stalin.

As for Viktor's mother, she stays in her room much of the time, drinking tea brewed in an ancient charcoal samovar. (Viktor and Nina have their own samovar, a good brass one from one of the Tula factories.) When she does emerge from behind the plywood door, it is to boss tired, heavy-footed Darya, questioning whichever cut of meat the poor woman has managed to find at the market, or picking with dissatisfaction at whatever dreary meal she has set out on the wooden table. Quiet, uncomplaining, looking perpetually exhausted, Darya seems to think this treatment her due. She arrives each noontime having fought her way through the markets, and always seems genuinely surprised when she turns out not to have procured exactly what Madame wanted. Wordlessly, she changes Madame's chamber pot, rinses her laundry, carries in sloshing tubs of water when she wants to wash; Madame refuses to go to the public bathhouse like everyone else. And though now Darya cooks and cleans for Nina, too, she clearly understands Madame to be her mistress. When Nina increases her pay, now that she is serving three instead of two, Darya looks utterly surprised. But Nina has no talent for cooking and is grateful for her help.

Madame, meanwhile, always seems affronted to discover Nina there in the apartment, as though she were a guest who has overstayed her welcome. It is as if Madame spent most of her patience—her politeness—at their introductory tea, and there is little left for daily use. Although Nina is at work much of the time, and does little at home other than sleep, only the fact that Madame is hard of hearing gives her any sense of privacy. Madame is often unhealthy, frequently out of sorts. "Not so loud, please, I'm feeling a bit flu-ish," she says, her face flushed, her head heavy. Other times she declares that she is unable to find her heartbeat. "I've been trying all day, but I suppose this is the end for me." When Nina responds dubiously, Madame narrows her eyes, thrusts out her wrist, and says, "Just try to find my pulse!" At times she even manages to convince Viktor that she is gravely ill—but Nina is certain this is an act, to steal his attention from other things, such as Nina herself.

Sometimes Madame's hair is neat, the big, high bun thick and tight. But with the bird constantly climbing around on her head, picking at her tortoiseshell comb, Madame always becomes gradually disheveled, her dress peppered with bird droppings. So different from Viktor, who is always dapper and cleanly shaven, makes regular visits to the barber, polishes his boots each morning, and has his shirts cleaned and pressed at the Chinese laundry.

Sometimes Madame sits at the table and counts the silverware. Lola accompanies her, perched on her shoulder, pecking at the little buttons on the front of Madame's dress. Shiny things attract her: the pearls that dangle from Madame's earlobes, and the thin glass of her lorgnette. Little tap-tap-tapping sound—soon Nina has grown used to it. That and Lola's squawking. The bird is vocal and boisterous, saying, "Good day!" and "*S'il vous plaît!*" and chirping loudly. Madame, too, can at times become loud, both of them carping away like unhappy women.

On days when she is feeling loose-tongued, Madame reminisces about her childhood, growing up with a cook and a maid and a tutor and a nanny. For slow, tired Darya she describes in great detail the house where she lived, from the cut-glass door handles to the oil paintings that hung in heavy frames on the walls. It is as if she is taking a stroll through her old home, a private tour in her mind, pausing before every treasured object: the Dyatkovo crystal paperweight, the silver candelabra by Sazikov, the parasol with an enamel handle by Fabergé. Sometimes Nina too can picture it, the separate rooms for every activity: library, music room, dining room. Her mind follows Madame's through French doors into a salon hung with silk wallpaper patterned in vines, and an airy kitchen where cooks use only the best cuts of meat, and a high balcony overlooking a broad stretch of private grounds. "And then, when we returned, not a painting was left. Those beautiful paintings. I used to walk right into them with my eyes, the way one walks down a path into the woods." She looks momentarily bereft. "Our house—filled with boors. Muddy boots lined up all along the hall. You have never seen such rudeness. One could smell them through the walls. They never washed. Like the Armenians next door. Thieves." Saying so reminds her; she begins, again, to count the cutlery.

Well, the fact is, Nina's mother too stores cutlery and cookware in her room, won't leave even a bar of soap, hard and full of dark cracks, where other tenants might get to it. Madame's behavior is really only a step away from the usual hoarding of soap and salt and kerosene, the faint distrust of everyone else that even Nina, she has to admit, feels. The one difference is that Madame's complaints are loud, unconcealed, like those of Nina's long-gone grandmother, and of so many old grandmothers. The last of her kind.

"Does she ever go out?" Nina asks Viktor, when she has been living there for nearly three months. She is still trying to figure out just how much of a "secret" Viktor's parentage is, and just how quiet she ought to be about Madame. Because as much as Viktor doesn't speak of it in public, he has never specifically warned Nina about saying anything, and is clearly unworried about Darya spreading gossip. Perhaps his literary success has exempted him from such a thing being held against him. After all, he cannot help which family he was born into. "Does she ever leave the building?"

"I used to take her out to walk a bit, but it always upset her. She simply doesn't like the outside world." He seems to be thinking to himself. "There's a word she uses. *Base*. She isn't accustomed to seeing . . . oh, you know, drunks on the street. Unpleasant behavior. A lack of manners. It's because of her background, of course. No one treats her as she feels she ought to be treated."

After all, she is a woman raised on a private estate, a woman who has traveled abroad, a woman adept at musical instruments and foreign languages. No wonder she clings to her old title, her haughtiness, her ancient dresses of silk and lace. In a way, Nina realizes, she is like the demobilized men who, though the war has been over for three years now, go out in their military uniforms on Sundays to display their medals and their wounds. As if to remind everyone—or perhaps just themselves—who they used to be.

Lot 34

Chrome Diopside Earstuds. Round cut, 1.00 cts, 5 × 5 mm, 14kt yellow gold mount/posts, clarity VVS. $800–1,000

CHAPTER SEVEN

Evelyn leaned her head in around six o'clock, her blond hair feathering lightly away from her face. "Let me just go wash up, and then we can go."

"I'm ready when you are."

The other inhabitants of the Department of Foreign Languages had left earlier, but Grigori had used the time to grade three papers from his graduate seminar. He didn't want to risk spending time home alone today. Even this morning he had felt the need to hurry out of the house, hadn't dared listen to the radio, even, avoiding the songs they would be dedicating, this and that message read over the air. It would only make him miss . . . everything. Yes, everything. He missed the sound of the door closing behind her when she arrived home from work in the evening. He missed the telephone messages, loads of them, she had so many friends, Barb announcing that Bowie, her ancient pug, had died, or Amelie saying she was going to be in Boston next week, how about a drink at the Fairmount? He missed Christine's book club sitting in a chatty circle in the living room, laughing in a way he had always envied, sharing personal information he at times found almost shocking; it seemed no subject was too private to be mentioned around a cheese tray and bottle of chilled white wine. He missed what it had felt like to follow her upstairs, to peel off her clothes and make love to her lusciously in one of those spontaneous bouts of romance that Grigori considered a secret privilege of married life.

Of course he knew what kinds of thoughts these were: the not-always-true ones, conveniently forgetting the other times, when he and Christine had bickered at the smallest thing, aggravated by the other's mere constant presence, and sometimes even said awful things—irreversible and stinging—that lingered like a foul odor for a long time afterward. Then there were long stretches of calm. And yet the bickering, the irritation, that too was part of the delicate glue that kept them together, still feeling *something*, even when they grew, sometimes for long periods, bored with each other, tired of each other, before settling back into their more usual, tamed and tamped down but still real and extant love.

"Okeydoke, I'm good to go."

He looked up to see Evelyn in the long, sleek leather coat that matched her high-heeled boots, and around her neck a tasseled wool scarf, knotted affirmatively. "Don't you look elegant," he told her and, buttoned into his own coat, went with her out to the T.

She had suggested they eat at the Thai place near the Wang, and though Grigori had little appetite, he supposed it would return. He always had a good time with Evelyn, or at least a perfectly enjoyable time. She was smart and good-natured and not afraid to make fun of herself. Plus she had known Christine well and wasn't afraid to talk about her. At the same time, a new awareness had crept into Grigori's thoughts—just faintly, but consciously, on the last few occasions the two of them had gone out. There had been moments, saying good night, when Evelyn seemed to expect something more. It was not the first time Grigori had seen this look on her face, but until recently he had thought he was imagining it. Then things had become a bit awkward, a split second of visible disappointment from Evelyn last time, that he had not picked up on her cue.

But Grigori had never considered her as more than . . . Evelyn, petite and pretty and inexplicably single, with an honest laugh and expensive-looking blond hair and about thirty different pairs of high heels.

This morning, though, Grigori had told himself, as he rushed to dress and escape the house, to be open to the possibility of Evelyn. He had even put on his best shirt, one that Christine had given him, of soft thick patterned cotton, a visibly luxurious shirt, the kind that required cuff links. In the past he had worn it only for special occasions. Well, perhaps tonight would turn out to be one.

The thought made him nervous. At the restaurant, he realized he was tugging at his cuffs. But Evelyn looked relaxed and happy, and Grigori was relieved when the waiter took their order for drinks.

"Cuff links," Evelyn said. "Nice."

"They belonged to my father." A geologist who often worked in the field, he had rarely had opportunity to wear them. Feodor, quiet and contemplative, always patting down his little flap of hair as if it contained all the world's unruliness . . . And yet he could yell when he wanted to—grasping the sides of his head with exasperation when Grigori asked mathematics questions considered elementary. It was only after leaving Russia, when Grigori made friends with other little boys in Norway, that he came to understand that not all families yelled out their thoughts this way. A young friend, playing at the apartment in Larvik, had looked frightened to hear Feodor screaming at Katya in Russian. They were simply debating something they had heard in the news—but Grigori understood for the first time that this was not the way other people, other cultures, debated things.

"You look very dapper," Evelyn said, smiling in her easy, radiant way.

Perhaps this was his big chance, to move on—though he worried it might be too much of a risk, to try to convert friendship to romance. Also, Evelyn was younger than Grigori, at most forty—though the age difference apparently did not bother her. Perhaps Grigori was some sort of "catch." Well, he had been the object of student crushes often enough, though surely that was something different. The little notes he at times received on the last pages of essays or exams, "Can we continue this discussion in person?" or "Would you like to meet for a drink?" only slightly surprised him. He had assumed they would taper off as he aged, and for a few years, in his forties, they had. Then something happened, he still did not quite understand it, but the crushes suddenly returned, one or two students each term. Some were overt, some unintentionally obvious. E-mails suggesting coffee "somewhere off-campus?" or an exhibit of Russian painters they might go see together—in Connecticut. One girl last year had written a long message detailing the ups and downs of her heart, explaining that she was now "over" him—but would he like to meet up tomorrow evening?

It was his grief, he had decided, that attracted them. For as sad as he was, his anguish had its own terrifying energy, an electricity that must have shone from him visibly, infused his very being.

And now Evelyn, with the blond flyaway hair . . .

The waiter was back with their wine. "Cheers," Grigori said, clinking his glass to hers, and Evelyn said, "Happy Valentine's Day."

THE FIRST REHEARSAL of the new season, a cold wet day, Nina's second year as a wife. In the dressing room, she is stitching ribbons into a pair of toe shoes. At the small vanity across from her, Polina diligently applies moisturizing cream to her face, lightly tapping her skin with her fingertips to help the cream penetrate. This is just one step in a long complicated regimen that ends with her washing in cold water with a few drops of ammonia in it, to help diminish her freckles.

As Polina pats at her face, she tells Nina about her new love, a man named Igor. The way she talks about him, he might be a movie star, but really he's another Party functionary, the deputy director of a division of a branch of an office of some department or other—Nina can no longer keep track. "He treats me so sweetly, Nina. Like a kitten."

"Well, good, he ought to." What Nina wants to say is, You don't need him. You're a dancer; work on your technique, not your relationships with these . . . lackeys. That's the word, though she doesn't say it. Assistant bureaucrats trying to make their way up the ladder. Nina sees them often enough, in the theater's personnel department, where government agents in civilian clothes comb through everyone's paperwork for anything worth reporting to their superiors; and at her performances at the various ministries, where officials in dark wool suits say demeaning things to their subordinates; and even in the Bolshoi concert hall, agitprop men from the Central Committee every now and then silently watching from dark seats all the way at the back of the theater, while the poor director trembles his way through a dress rehearsal. Career types who will do anything to make their way up the ranks.

"I think he's the *one*, Nina. I really do."

"That's good, Polina, I'm happy for you." But she doesn't look her in the eye. Sometimes she gets the sense that for Polina, a career at the ballet is not so much about the dancing as it is about the concept—the idea—of being a ballerina.

The door opens. "They told me I'd find you here."

Nina stares, wonderingly, at a strikingly beautiful woman, and then drops the ballet slipper. It is Vera, standing there.

Yes, it really is Vera, smiling, pleased with her surprise. Very slender and long-limbed, no longer a girl. Nina gives a small yelp and embraces her, Vera's figure slight—though she is taller than

Nina—in her arms. The truth is, for a long time Nina hasn't even thought of her.

Now Nina says, "You!" because it is all she can manage. She cannot even find her breath to introduce her to Polina; Vera has to introduce herself, while Nina regains her composure and takes in the ways that the years and the war and who knows what else have altered Vera, who now tells Polina, "I'm Vera Borodina."

Nina has heard this name—the new young beauty of the Kirov. It's a different last name, a stage name, she supposes, and then recalls what happened so long ago, the day of the Bolshoi school audition. Vera's parents gone, and "There was always something strange about them. . . ." The first time in years Nina has thought back to them, that seemingly ordinary couple whose daily life divulged no inkling of where they would end up. Because only now, in adulthood, does Nina understand, in the way her childhood self could not, what must have happened. Not that Nina dares ask Vera—not in front of Polina. Whatever happened, it is in Vera's best interest to have erased any ties to her parents. And so she has become Vera Borodina. . . .

Nina regards her with surprise, notes that her face, though thinner than years ago, has blossomed, her cheekbones more prominent and delicately rosy. Front teeth surprisingly straight, with little spaces between them, giving her an air of youth as she stands there smiling. Hair a deep reddish brown. Big dark eyes set wide apart, something melancholy, almost strange, about them. Perhaps it is the way her eyelashes have been crafted with mascara into little clumps, making her look young and innocent, almost as if she has been crying.

She has in her hand the same small drawstring sack all the dancers are given, in which they all carry their tights and tunics and precious bars of soap. It must mean that Vera is joining the company. But at that moment Nina is still focused on other thoughts: Vera is *alive*; she has *survived*; she has *returned*. Polina says, "Well!" as if she too once knew Vera years ago and nothing could have surprised her more.

When Vera confidently drops the sack onto the chair of the vacant dressing table that for two years has been shoved into the corner of the small room, Nina feels a small proprietary flinch; now three of them will have to fit here. But it is *Vera*, she tells herself— Vera Borodina . . . Still, Nina's guard is up, as it always is in the presence of someone new. Vera, meanwhile, in brisk, distracted motions, flicks dust off the table. To be in this dressing room means she will be dancing solos and the occasional lead. Nina supposes the director must have recruited her, or that Vera knows someone in the administration—in the Kremlin, even. The Bolshoi pays attention to connections—friends, family, relationship to the Party. Just look at Lepeshinskaya, once the embodiment of youthful vitality, now almost forty yet still dancing lead roles; she is married to the head of the General Staff of the USSR, and everyone at the Bolshoi is terrified of her.

Vera too must know someone important. Nina can see that Polina is wondering the same thing, the way she keeps stealing glances at Vera, perhaps envious of her beauty, or simply curious, or fearful of who she might turn out to be. Because Vera is now one more person to have to compete with. She too, like any ballerina, must want what they want: to rise to the very top.

It becomes clear the moment they see Vera in class that she is indeed here on her own merit. Agile and precise, with feet quicker than theirs. Her beats are clean and sure, her pas de bourrée exact. More important, she has that quality—the elusive, magical one— that Nina too has been said to possess: the spark that makes people want to watch you.

And yet Nina witnesses how Leningrad-style dancing can be somewhat cold. There is a strictness to Vera's movement, all expression confined to her upper body (clad in a thin wool sweater, her delicate collarbone visible, her skin very pale). This contained perfection is a reminder to Nina: that not only have their experiences of youth, and of growing up, been different, but their bodies too have been variously trained.

At first Nina experiences something close to envy, not just of Vera's technique but also of her form—those long, delicate limbs and highly arched feet. Nina suffers a pang she has felt before, knowing she would do almost anything to have such a body (though it has been years since she and her classmates sat on one another's outstretched feet attempting to shape higher insteps, or massaged one another's bulging calf muscles to try to make them slimmer). From the tips of her fingers to the strong points of her toes, Vera is the embodiment of the quiet dignity the Kirov is known for. Her thin frame and her big soulful eyes make her look almost ethereal. Nina cannot help envy that otherworldly quality—not to mention Vera's wide cheekbones and thick russet hair. She reminds herself that she has her own strengths: energy and airiness; passion and musicality; fast turns and seemingly effortless jumps. Being petite and strong is a gift itself, and a more standardly pretty face, if lacking mystery, has its own allure. Really it is a blessing that she and Vera possess different styles and physiques; it means they will not, most of the time, be competing for the same roles.

She has to stop herself from asking too many questions that first day, as Vera arranges the contents of her sack in her locking drawer. But she asks where she will be living.

"With a family I don't even know. There's a bed in the pantry. Just until the ballet can find me someplace." Easier said than done, with the housing shortage. "The man and his wife play in the orchestra—and have *three* little boys." Vera makes a face, and Nina feels sorry for her, all of them surely crammed into one room. "It's almost funny, if you think about it: I'm actually lucky enough to have a permit"—a Moscow resident's permit—"but there aren't any rooms available. And meanwhile I keep hearing about people who are worried because they have an apartment but no permit!"

On her dressing table she has set a small framed picture—a young couple, so very young that it takes a moment for Nina to recognize them as Vera's parents. From the back of the frame Vera takes a yellowed square of paper, which she unfolds and tucks into the corner of the mirror. When Nina looks more closely, her heart gives a tug. It is a telegram.

Without having to read the words, Nina knows it is one of the messages her mother so carefully wrote, all those years ago, as if she were Vera's mother, too.

Her mother, alone in the room full of sighs . . . Now that she has been pensioned from her desk job, and without Nina at home to tend to, she seems less devoted to her own life. Even her many benevolent errands have lessened. Instead of being freed from prison, Nina's uncle last year was sent to exile in the Urals. And the old woman downstairs, whom Mother used to check in on daily, has died. Yet Mother continues to keep a spotless home, fills the windowsill with straggling plants repotted in tin cans. Her strength seems to come directly from caring for others, even though she herself has never been good at accepting help. Even when Nina buys new clothes for her, Mother continues to embroider the neck and cuffs of her baggy old sweaters, dons her same old fading flowered kerchief to make her way to and from the Gastronom—but these days she makes her rounds slowly, her shoulders stooped though she is barely fifty. She who with clipped, brisk steps led Nina and Vera like ducklings to the audition at the Bolshoi School . . .

Nina recalls how much her mother always loved Vera, too—and that they still have, against the wall, the iron cot with the cotton mattress where until last year Nina slept.

"If you could stay with my mother," Nina asks, "would you prefer that?"

"Oh, but surely she wouldn't want me taking up space?"

"She loves you, Vera. She'll be so happy." Nina glances at the telegram tucked into the mirror. How many of them did her mother send? And when did she stop? Nina wants to ask Vera, as much as she longs to tell her the truth, as evidence of her mother's love for her. But she knows that some secrets are meant to be kept.

A week later Vera installs her black karakul coat and five pairs of shoes and a large travel trunk in the apartment that Nina left nearly a year and a half ago. That the two of them have swapped places, in a way, seems right. After all, Vera had to leave here so abruptly, all those years ago; now she again has her hometown and her best friend and a mother, even if each of these things is now altered. Nina's mother is more than glad to have Vera there, and Nina and Vera often go back to the apartment together, sometimes with Viktor, to join her for tea. These first weeks are filled with confidences, the filling-in of so many years apart, a rush of stories exchanged, scraps of memories here and there, like knitting a big messy sweater together, watching it grow in bursts around them both. Soon they have found a new rhythm—much like the old, if only in that it continues day after day.

NINA WOULD NOT have even acknowledged that it was Valentine's Day except that Cynthia decided to celebrate it. Of course there had been a delivery of ridiculously expensive chocolates courtesy of Shepley, and a somewhat depressed phone call from Tama, but neither of those required comment. Now, though, along with that day's dinner ingredients, Cynthia brought a long-stemmed rose and a greeting card. The Senior Services people must give them to all their employees, Nina supposed—but then decided to allow that Cynthia might have arrived at the gesture on her own. The card stock was thick, with a photograph of a puppy holding a cutout paper heart in its mouth. Cynthia had signed it in red felt-tipped pen, drawing a heart and then printing her name out in big letters, as if Nina had trouble reading.

The rose she put in a tall thin crystal vase, which she placed on the table in the front hall, so that Nina could see it from the salon. The bud was already opening, from the heat of the radiator; Nina supposed it wouldn't last long. Well, wasn't that like romance itself—the sudden blooming, and then the petals falling, first slowly one by one, and then suddenly all at once.

Viktor, the surprise of him, there at the dressing room door, his arms full of roses.

"You okay out there, sugar?" Cynthia called from the kitchen. No onions today, of course. Billy had made reservations at a restaurant in the South End—a "brasserie," Cynthia called it.

Next to the rose, the puppy on the greeting card gazed out eagerly. "Yes, fine, thank you," Nina said, though already that other feeling was returning: a dark and overwhelming, if imprecise, shame. Cynthia went on to make lots of clanking noises with the pots and pans, as if to ensure that Nina didn't drift off again. And now the telephone started up, a loud clattering sound.

"I have it, Cynthia," Nina managed to say in a calm voice, though in her experience a ringing telephone most often meant something unpleasant.

It was Drew Brooks. "From Bell—"

"I recall who you are, Miss Brooks, no need to say to me."

"Yes, well, I'm just calling to let you know of a slight discrepancy in your collection."

A horrible staggering in her chest, dread of what more trouble there could be.

It was the stud earrings that the St. Botolph's list referred to as emeralds, Drew explained, her voice not the least bit anxious. "In going through the collection, our appraisers noted that they're actually chrome diopside."

The term was nothing Nina had ever heard of. Her pulse hastened at having been caught—if unwittingly—in a lie. "I did not know," she said. "I was misled."

"Oh, it's a common confusion," Drew told her. "In fact, the slang term is 'Siberian emerald,' it's so common in that region. I'm not surprised you have some of your own."

"Then they are emeralds after all," Nina said, with relief. "Siberian ones."

"Well, no, that's the thing. They're called 'emeralds' because of their color, but as stones they're only semi-precious. Much less valuable than emeralds."

"I see." Absurdly, her heart dropped—just as it had, if only for a moment, on the day she first opened the little square box and glimpsed the small green earrings there. The slight embarrassment of her own confusion.

"It happens often enough," Drew was saying. "With these and also tsavorite garnets. We see those a fair bit."

Nina's throat felt tight. Of course she couldn't help but wonder if Viktor had known. Siberian emeralds . . . Or had he, too, thought the earrings were real?

"Are you all right?" Drew's voice was loud in her ear. "Are you there?"

"There is no need to scream."

"Just making sure." Something in the way Drew said it made it sound like she might laugh. Even when she came by the other day, to fetch the written names of Viktor's family members, Nina had sensed in her only the briefest annoyance at having made the trip when really Nina had only one name to offer. Nina had printed it out for her in Cyrillic, explaining that other than her mother-in-law, she had never known any of the people on Viktor's maternal side, nor anything past his father. And yet Drew had remained unperturbed, as if her inquisitiveness could only work out for her in the end.

"I also wanted to remind you," she was saying now, "about the supplemental information for the pre-auction event we talked about. For the accompanying visuals, I'm hoping to include photos of any objects that might be related to the jewelry. Personal, memorabilia-type stuff, if possible. For instance, if a particular jewel was a gift, maybe you still have the card that came with it? Or a picture of the person who gave it to you? We can scan them for digital photos."

Again, digital photographs, they were everywhere. It was epidemic.

"Excuse me?" Drew asked.

"I do not have for you any of that."

Drew seemed to be waiting for something. "Yes, well, it doesn't have to be directly related. It could simply be something from the ballet. Or from when you moved to Boston. Or even just the names of specific people. In the meantime, I'm going to look for archived photos. It's of interest to the public, that's all."

"All right," Nina said, knowing that it was the only way to end the conversation.

Drew thanked her and said she was very excited about the project, and wished her a good evening. But as Nina put down the telephone, all she felt was frustration.

Siberian emeralds.

That was the very problem with the auction house, the catalog, these assessors . . . Too much unpleasantness to discover.

LAST BURST OF autumn warmth, of pale purple phlox, the whole city tinged yellow with fading leaves. Sweaty hands on the barre, endless morning drills and afternoon rehearsals, infinite anticipation of evening. In the dressing room before the second performance of the season, Nina sits with her feet resting on Polina's chair and watches as Vera beads her eyelashes. She learned it from one of the Kirov dancers. Over a candle, she heats a tiny skillet the size of a soupspoon, on which she melts a bit of blackish makeup. Then she takes a drop of it onto the tip of a little wooden stick, which she touches to the tip of one of her upper eyelashes. Now a tiny bead clings there.

"Painstaking," Vera tells Nina as she takes up the next tiny black drop, "but worth it. Especially for a night like tonight." The Bolshoi's prima ballerina *assoluta*, Galina Ulanova, has taken ill, and so her role—they are opening the season with *Swan Lake*—has been divided in two: Vera will play the Swan Queen, Odette, and Nina will play her evil double, Odile. "I can help you do yours," Vera adds, "if you want to try."

"Oh, I'm not sure." Hot waxy stuff, so close to her eyes. Though she hasn't said so, Nina is feeling slightly insulted, that the management doesn't think her—or Vera, either—capable of dancing the full, dual, starring role. Have they not the same faith in Nina's delicate bourrées and battements, in the way her body listens and responds to every shade of mood in Tchaikovsky's music, as in her double pirouettes and arabesques and fouettées? The ballet master has rehearsed them and given his pep talk, reminding them that the conductor can prompt them should they need help. The seamstress has refitted the black-feathered Odile costume to Nina, but for now she wears the loose pajamas that are her lounging clothes; she will not be onstage until after intermission. "It might affect my vision."

"Oh, you get used to it really quickly." One by one, the minuscule beads form at Vera's eyelash tips, and with each one Vera's face opens up, becomes more innocent, her eyes somehow larger and wider. Nina finds herself once again surprised, as she continually is, by Vera's beauty—by the very fact that Nina somehow missed, when they were children, just how beautiful she was. The surprise, and the small, slightly painful pang that accompanies it, is one of the new sensations Nina has begun to grow accustomed to, a natural consequence, she supposes, of having a true close friend her age, a girlfriend, a sister, this gift she hasn't known since childhood: the gift of female friendship. These weeks have been a readjustment not only to what it means to share her life this way, the give-and-take of it, but also to Vera herself, this new, adult Vera, who is, after all, a different person from the one who left Moscow so many years ago.

Tonight, though, she can't help but wonder: If Vera hadn't joined the company, would Nina perhaps be dancing Odette, too, and not just Odile? Don't be jealous, she tells herself, and goes back to darning her toe shoes, stitching around the edge of each point with thick pink thread to make them last longer. She will need her most sturdy pair tonight, for all the fast turns Odile performs. And she must focus, concentrate, think not about poor Odette but fierce, strong-willed Odile, about Von Rothbart using her to such evil ends. Her stomach gives a nervous turn, at the thought of performing the role in public for the first time.

Having perfected her eyelashes, Vera blows out the candle and wipes the mess of maquillage from the little frying pan before hiding it all in her drawer; the theater management doesn't allow candles in the dressing rooms. To finish things off, she adds a small red dot at the corners of her eyes.

How far they have come, Nina thinks to herself, from that June day so long ago, when neither of them even knew what a plié was. Nina recalls, quite suddenly, what she has long forgotten. "Your stage fright." As soon as she says it, she wishes she hadn't.

Vera looks up questioningly.

"I was just remembering. The audition. At the Bolshoi School."

A distant look comes over Vera, as if she just barely remembers. "It was a hard day for me. My parents had just been taken."

Her voice is meek, almost affectedly so, and Nina feels a surge of annoyance—that Vera has made this particular claim to grief. After all, everyone knows someone who has been taken away. Of the top three ballerinas here, Semyonova and Lepeshinskaya have both survived their husbands' arrests; Semyonova's was executed. Why, just last year one of the girls in the corps was called out of a dress rehearsal by a man from the secret police. Everyone could see from his jacket what he was. The girl never came back. After a few days her name was taken off the roster. No one has ever mentioned it.

And of course there is Nina's own uncle, off in a gulag somewhere. Yet Nina knows perfectly well that Vera's loss was much more extreme. She could have ended up at the NKVD children's placement center, living with delinquents. Just a year or two older, she might have been subject to the death penalty. Surely there is a file on her somewhere. Even for her to mention any of this, now, is brave. Of course, Polina isn't in the room to hear it. Still, it shows that Vera trusts Nina, that she knows she won't tell—since clearly the Bolshoi must not know. Or perhaps they do but are willing to overlook it. Like Semyonova, who for all her acclaim is still the "wife of an enemy of the people." Then again, maybe Vera's parents, whoever they were, whatever they did, were simply no one important. Not powerful enough, or famous enough, for anyone to pay any attention to their offspring. Just look at that couple in the photograph on Vera's dressing table, so humble and unassuming and young.

Whoever they were, whatever they did.

For the first time in years, Nina finds herself wondering. Very quietly she asks, "Did you ever find out what they . . ." She stops, unsure that she wants to continue. "What your parents . . . ?" She doesn't dare complete the sentence.

Vera's eyes close briefly, as if to avoid an unpleasant sight. "What they did, you mean?" She speaks slowly and very softly. "A few years ago an old neighbor who lived in our same apartment told me what happened. She saw the whole thing. It was the couple who lived in the room next to us that those men were supposed to arrest. They went there first, but the couple wasn't home. So they took the ones next door instead." She gives a little shrug of her shoulders.

"But then it's a mistake!" Nina is horrified. "How could— Somebody needs to—" She hears her own mother's refrain: *If Comrade Stalin knew—as soon as he finds out . . .*

Vera, though, doesn't look incensed, just sad, and Nina understands that it is too late, her parents cannot have survived so long. Perhaps Vera has already had word of their demise. Still, such a mistake. Not to mention that it is a permanent mark on Vera's record.

"Every time I take a train, or go over a bridge," Vera says, "I can't help but wonder, Did they build these tracks? Were they the ones who made these roads?"

Nina has never forgotten Vera's words, so many years ago. *They're doing important work. That's why they had to go away.* But now something else occurs to her: Perhaps the old neighbor made that story up, about the couple next door, so that Vera wouldn't have to know the truth. Perhaps it was the neighbor, not the NKVD men, who lied.

She feels suddenly, utterly confused.

The door opens, and the seamstress hands Vera her costume, onto which some errant feathers have been restitched. "Thank you," Vera says, calmly, almost regally, standing slowly to step into the stiff white tutu, adjusting it over her silk tights, pulling up the white bodice, slipping her arms through the feathery straps. The expression on her face is remote, unrevealing. Nina has noticed this about Vera in her interactions with others. She is one of those soloists who keeps to herself, does not chat with most other dancers—yet her aloofness, her reticence, somehow only makes her more alluring. As the seamstress does her up, Nina sees how well Vera fits not just this costume but this role, graceful yet fragile, something distant and haunted about her.

"Better go have your makeup checked," the seamstress tells her before bustling off.

In a rush, Nina wishes Vera, *"Ni puha, ni pera."*

"'K chortu!" and Vera follows the seamstress out the door.

THE LAST-MINUTE PATRONS, ushered into their seats just as the lights went down, kept ruffling programs and even talking during the overture. Seated next to Evelyn, Grigori found himself focusing not on Tchaikovsky's music but on the other sounds around him: the coughing of the aged, the wheezing of the overweight, the whispers of little girls in their heavy velvet dresses. A young mother behind him was explaining to her daughter that very soon the curtain would lift and there would be people onstage, while the daughter whined that she was scared of the dark. To Grigori's right, a line of young women passed a pack of gum back and forth, the sound of crumpling paper continuing up and back down the row. "You'd think we were at the circus," Grigori whispered to Evelyn. She laughed and patted his arm, in a stroking way that felt good. How long it had been since Grigori had felt that way. She left her hand there, and he looked down, surprised, so that the moment became suddenly awkward; Evelyn pulled her hand away. Flustered, Grigori turned to glare at the young women with the gum. They appeared not to notice.

At last the curtain lifted, and Grigori was able to lose himself in a world that was beautiful and also a bit comic, Prince Siegfried in his white tights, looking forlorn and pantomiming like there was no tomorrow. After the interlude things improved: the familiar dreamy melody, and the dark, misty forest, the dry ice slowly receding to reveal two dozen swan-girls folded over themselves. The dull trampling sound as they bourréed across the stage, Odette fluttery and fearful in her feathered earmuffs. Their seats were good, so close Grigori could see the trembling of the dancers' tutus—flat frilled things like white carnations. Evelyn sighed and leaned just the slightest bit into his shoulder. Perhaps it was unintentional; Grigori had broad shoulders, was a big man, perhaps he was simply in the way.

When the lights went up for intermission, Evelyn joined the rush for the bathroom. Grigori pushed his way down the aisle, out to the arcade, and bought a glass of red wine for each of them. Sipping his wine, he listened to the conversations that wafted by. Beside him a woman recited to a friend her busy cultural agenda. "Next week I have the ART," she said, pointing at the squares of her date book, "*and* the Huntington." She moved her fingertip along the following weeks: "Ballet, ballet, symphony, Huntington, symphony."

A man's voice was saying, "Odette seems a little off tonight."

"You think?" answered a woman.

"Less confident than last night's," said the man. "I wonder if she's injured." A loud put-upon sigh. "Not to mention that the swans sound more like a herd of elephants."

Oh, come on, Grigori wanted to say: You spoiled, spoiled people. The dancer was wonderful, just like the swan-girls, doing their best to deliver them magnificence. If she was "slightly off," it was nothing Grigori had been able to notice. These people—himself included—were all so thoroughly indulged, could they not simply accept the wonder of it, sitting in this lush, gilded theater while a live orchestra accompanied so much physical exquisiteness? And this man thought he had the right to be disappointed! That these people expected so much, that they *could* expect that much, and not be ashamed of their petty disappointments.

A little Chinese girl in a frilly dress was being plied with candy by her pale blond parents. "Anything to get her to like ballet," the mother said, laughing, to Grigori, when she caught him watching.

"Is it her first time?"

"Yes," the father said. "She's only four, so I'm not sure how much she's actually taking in."

"But I couldn't wait," the mother said, beaming. "I've been dreaming of this for ten years."

Grigori smiled back. Wonderful to see parents like this, basking in parenthood. This little girl would probably never fully know to what degree she had been wanted, loved, by these parents, before they even knew her. It was something Grigori understood, and still felt—reflexive memory, perhaps, that faint hope and longing. He and Christine had considered adoption, after so many failed pregnancies, but then Christine had said the years of waiting, the bureaucracy of it, the potential for it to all suddenly fall through, was something she no longer had the strength or will to contend with. As much as he had wanted to, Grigori hadn't had the heart to pursue the matter further. It wasn't anything he thought about anymore.

Last year, though, Christine's friend Amelie, whose twins were now three years old, had said something that remained with him even now: "Pretty much all my life I've wondered about my birth parents, wondered who they were, what they were like. But since I had my children, I don't wonder anymore. Because I look at my kids, and I can *see* the answer. It's right there in their features, in who they are. Everything that isn't Rick and his family must be from my side. It's my kids who are finally showing me where I come from."

Grigori's parents had not given him the full account of his adoption for many years. For one thing, his mother, despite her scientific nature, believed strongly in fate; she had not wanted, Grigori understood much later, to corrupt the miracle of his late arrival in her arms with the dour truth of the circumstances that had put him there. It was an unpleasant story, she had told him, of which they had only a few facts. As for his father, Feodor had always preferred to avoid unnecessary complications. Keep it simple, he always said—as if life might allow such a thing.

Grigori still saw in his mind, sometimes, his mother, the straight line down the middle of her scalp where she parted her long fading brown hair. As a child he had admired the neatness and simplicity of that line, the way it seemed to embody Katya's patience and concentration. Once, when he was very young, when they still lived in Russia, Grigori had witnessed his mother brushing out her hair at night; no longer twisted up into clips, her hair was suddenly longer, smoother, and Grigori had been shocked to see Katya become, all at once, a young girl. As much as wonder, he recalled, even now, his deep fear at the suddenness of the transformation, how quickly someone he thought he knew had become someone else.

Sudden transformations awaited all three of them. When Grigori was eleven, his father defected while attending a research conference in Vienna. As they had planned, Katya managed to transport Grigori and herself into Norway, where Feodor met them five months later.

It was in Norway, when he was still a boy, that Grigori overheard his parents' friend, the woman who lived in the apartment next door, tell his mother in a teasing yet matter-of-fact way, "Your problem is that you're Russian: you don't know how to be happy." That statement too remained with Grigori, though he did not necessarily believe the woman's words. If his mother—and his father, too—came across as somewhat grim, surely it was because they had lived in fear and left much behind: friends, some family (though there had been few relatives), rooms they felt at home in, language that rolled without effort from their tongues. Not until much later had Grigori understood that their departure from their homeland had something to do with their science, with what they knew and believed. So much about them Grigori had never really known. The three of them had lived in Norway for two years before moving to Paris, and then, when Grigori was sixteen years old, Katya had accepted a position at a university in New Jersey, where Feodor was offered good work at a lab. And so young Grigori, gangly and adolescent, became, to the degree that he could, American.

He had told Christine this, and all he recalled of the secretive trip to Norway, and about arriving in France not understanding a word. About his first time shopping, with his mother, in a non-Soviet store, the great shock of hearing the proprietor tell them "Thank you" when they made their purchase. About never having seen so many types of lettuce before he came to Paris. About the plane descending for landing in America, and viewing from above the rooftops all the shining blue circles and squares, and his disbelief when it was explained to him that these were swimming pools. He told Christine all of this on their third date, and from that night he loved her, because of how she listened, with complete attention, as if trying to picture it all. It was the first step, he recognized much later, in his own version of Amelie's experience—discovering one's hidden self through love for another.

He told Christine about his long-faced, intelligent parents, who after the move to America seemed to lose their former worldliness, as if having left it behind on some luggage rack. While they had managed to adjust to life in Norway, and then France, with few problems, they negotiated this last new country with timidity and incomprehension. Even the most benign American customs seemed all the more bewildering: the baffling "How are you?" to which no real answer was expected, the thank-you cards for dinners or birthday gifts for which they had already been thanked in person . . . Only much later did Grigori realize that much of their confusion came not so much from themselves as from how people viewed them and treated them: the older couple with the awkward teenage son—the one with the imprecise accent and odd sense of humor. Sometimes people thought they were his grandparents. Grigori supposed it had to do with their apprehensiveness more than their age. Or perhaps people sensed the progression of something Grigori had long felt: that despite his love for this tight little knot that was his family—the only family he possessed and was a part of, as stippled with complexities of emotion as any other family—the truth was that he had always felt a certain, if small, unbridgeable distance between him and his parents. Then, when he was in his late twenties, they had died.

"Oops, excuse me. Oh. Hello."

In front of Grigori, caught before a small cluster of people crowding the concessions stand, was—it took a moment for him to understand—the woman from Beller. "Drew. Hello."

Holding a plastic glass of wine, some of which had trickled onto her hand, she looked surprised. "Sorry to bump into you like that. At least I didn't spill on you. Oh—this is my friend Stephen."

"Pleased to meet you," Grigori said, firmly shaking the man's hand, as Drew said, "Excuse me," and blotted up the spilled wine by bringing her mouth to the back of her hand. "Stephen, this is . . . Grigori Solodin." The look on her face changed then, suddenly almost pained. Immediately Grigori understood that it was due to the auction house and Grigori's confidential status there. No one was supposed to know.

Grigori said, "So nice to see you here, Drew," to show that he had full faith in her and was confident she wouldn't goof up. As some other patrons squeezed by, the young man, handsome, somewhat slight of build but with a confident smile, put his hand lightly on Drew's back to nudge her forward.

"Are you enjoying the show?" Drew was asking, still looking uncomfortable.

"Very much. And you?" Past her shoulder, approaching them, Grigori saw Evelyn, and felt himself tense; hopefully Drew would understand that Evelyn, too, knew nothing of his involvement in the auction. She had stepped up to the three of them and was looking at Drew and Stephen expectantly, as Grigori handed her her wine. With luck she might think these two former students. Grigori said, "This is my good friend and colleague Evelyn Bennett."

Evelyn asked, "Are you students of Grigori?"

Drew looked to Grigori as if wondering how to answer, just as Stephen said, "Oh, you're a teacher?"

"We both are," Evelyn told him.

"Evelyn is a professor of Italian," said Grigori, "while I profess the Russian language and its literature."

"Oh, that's right, Drew told me how she once tried to learn Russian."

Drew's face had turned pink. "I'm afraid I'm no good at languages," she said awkwardly. "But I grew up with a romantic notion about Russia, so I finally signed up for an intro Russian course. But really I'm no good—"

The bell sounded, loudly, signaling the end of intermission. "Oh, there you go," Grigori said quickly, "I suppose we'd better get back to our seats," though he knew perfectly well that the lights would not go down for another ten minutes.

"Yes, us too!" Drew said, clearly as relieved as Grigori at having found an exit from the conversation. "Enjoy the rest of the show."

"Nice to meet you," added the young man.

"Oh, so they're not even your students," Evelyn said, laughing, as Grigori turned toward the auditorium doors. "Did you just strike up a conversation while I was in the restroom?"

"We were sort of thrust together by the throng," Grigori told her, happy not to have to lie, exactly. They made their way down the red-carpeted aisle and settled into their seats. Evelyn had reapplied her makeup and brushed her hair, so that she looked particularly bright and healthy. Yet Grigori found himself unable to chat as easily as he had before. The feelings that had warmed him during the first act were gone, or perhaps just submerged. Though Evelyn sat as close to him as before, there was a space, a discomfort, between them. It had to do, Grigori realized, with the young woman, Drew Brooks; how flustered Grigori had been, not knowing what to say, how to explain things. Even now he felt anxious, restless, aware that she was still here somewhere in the theater with him.

The conductor had returned. The orchestra again began its thankless task, and at last the curtain lifted, revealing the various princesses, and now wicked Odile made her entrance, masquerading as Odette. Though Grigori had seen *Swan Lake* numerous times (back when he and Christine were subscribers), something about tonight's performance—Odile's evil confidence, her consuming beauty, the wicked precision of her twirling fouettées—overcame the ridiculous setup and the interminable solos, the coy princesses showing off endlessly. The story really did feel tragic: How could anyone *not* fall for this gorgeous woman's trick? Quite suddenly Grigori felt real pity, not only for poor Odette, trembling hopelessly somewhere in the forest, but for Siegfried and his unknowing betrayal, a victim himself. After all, it was an honest mistake. Funny, Grigori had never really thought about it much before, hadn't cared enough to think more than, "Poor Siegfried screwed up." But now, having watched Siegfried jump and leap and spin himself to the hilt, Grigori understood the ballet in a new, felt way. The same thing sometimes happened when he read good poetry, or any great literature: the truth of it had reached his core, and would not let go.

"MY TWO BEAUTIES," Viktor says when Nina and Vera meet up with him and Gersh afterward, their cheeks rosy with success. The performance has gone splendidly—though Vera, always self-critical, insists she nearly tripped in a bourrée as she made her exit at the end of act 2. Yet Nina can see from her eyes that Vera feels the same pride and immense relief that she does. Their dressing room could

barely contain all the bouquets they received. Nina gave the largest and brightest, full of zinnias and calendula, to Mother when she
came backstage afterward—looking, in her maternal way, even more
proud than usual, not just of Nina but of Vera, too.

Vera, meanwhile, cut a blossom from one of her own bouquets
to pin to Mother's coat collar and, when Mother had gone home
for the night and Vera and Nina were washed and dressed, did the
same for Nina, pinning a gladiolus to her left lapel—the one over her
heart—so that the petals, white edged with pink, faced down. "To
show that your heart is already taken." For herself, Vera has chosen
a snapdragon, its many small petals pale white, and pinned it facing
upward.

Now they are at Kiev, a new restaurant operated by the Ukraine
Ministry of Trade, eating pork swimming in a sauce of carrots and
onions. A small band shoved into the corner of the room serenades
them boisterously.

"The way you moved your arms, Verusha," Viktor says, "honestly, I heard feathers rustling." He is always at his best in the presence of a beautiful woman. Though he has met Vera just a few times,
he already treats her like an old acquaintance; Nina has told him
about their childhood years, and about auditioning together for the
Bolshoi school—but she has not mentioned Vera's parents being
taken away. When Viktor commented, the first time he met Vera, on
the deep sadness in her eyes, Nina simply explained that although
Vera managed to escape Leningrad during the war, she lost her entire
family in the Siege. It wasn't exactly a lie.

Gersh, who has met Vera just once before, says, "I realized at
a certain point that I'd forgotten it was you. I mean, that you had
become Odette." Vera really did transform herself, became half
woman, half swan; at moments as she moved a feather would float
from her costume and drift to the ground, as if to expose her fragil-
ity. When she dance-mimed the story of how she and the other swan

maidens first became spellbound, her sad pleading seemed genuine, not corny at all. It took no leap of the imagination to understand Siegfried's obsession. Stroking invisible feathers with her cheek, plucking at her invisible wings, Vera seemed truly birdlike, enchanted, and even managed to make her spine quiver, that ripple across her back, from one arm to the other, as on tremulous feet she bourréed across the stage.

"And you," Viktor says to Nina, "I have to say it again, you took everyone's breath away."

It's true that the audience gasped when Nina did her thirty-two fouettées. They began applauding when she was just halfway through, so loudly that she couldn't hear the music and had to hope the conductor would simply follow her. With each whip of her leg she spun faster, beads of sweat flying, stinging her eyes—and yet she finished cleanly, precisely, and counted calmly to five before releasing the pose. Secretly, though, Nina finds it cheap, these technical feats. A cheap way to impress, nothing subtle or artful—just virtuosic display, demanding of applause and dropped jaws. Nina wants to do more than fancy tricks; she wants her body to sing, her eyes and her hands and the very angle of her head to convey every nuance of the music, and each facet of whichever character she is called upon to play.

Still, it was a good night. Even as she took her first step she sensed that it would be so, that her body would not let her down, that already she had the audience at her command.

"Well, then, we have multiple reasons to celebrate," she says, and explains to Vera, "Viktor's new book has got glowing notices." Gosizdat, the State Publishing House, has just published a new collection of his poems, which both *Izvestia* and *Pravda* have heralded with ecstatic reviews.

"Yes, a toast!" Gersh says, lifting his glass of Ukraine vodka. "To our two Pavlovas," looking to Vera and Nina with his healthy eye, "and of course," now toward Viktor, "our next Annabelle Bucar!"

They laugh; it's the name of the author of the big best-seller *The Truth about American Diplomats.*

Nina says, "I'm going to be serious now," and turns to Viktor. "I love your poems. I know I've told you before, but I don't know how else to say it." She finds his work beautiful and unpretentious, loves the unabashed joy in his language, the purity of his phrasing. Short lyrics, vivid imagery. "I'm proud of you."

Gersh says, "Ninulya, we're supposed to be celebrating you and Vera!"

"Please, Gersh, why stop them?" Viktor says. Vera is refilling their glasses with vodka. Lifting hers, she says, "To poetry!"

Viktor, putting on a mock expression of competition, says, "To dance!"

Nina, looking at Gersh with a laugh, says, "To music!"

Gersh, raising his eyebrows for suspense, waits a beat before saying, "To *love*!"

As they swallow their vodka, the music suddenly becomes confused; the band falls out of tempo, then loses the tune altogether. Within a few beats the melody has changed, become an American song everyone knows. Nina and the others glance toward the door. The song means that foreigners are present.

Indeed at the entrance are two foreign couples, the women in camel-hair coats, the men in long coats but no hats. The maître d' leads them in and seats them not far from Nina and Viktor's party, close enough that Nina can hear their voices. French, but not the familiar vocabulary of ballet, and nothing Nina can understand despite her mandatory language lessons at the Bolshoi School. Nina feels a tug of yearning, and an unaccountable shame—of not understanding, and of wanting to understand. "I wish I spoke another language," she says, very softly.

"You do," Viktor says. "The language of dance."

But all Nina feels is the rare, acute urge to know more than her own country, to see places she can only imagine, to hear the sounds of truly foreign tongues—not just the usual Georgian and Kalmyk, Latvian and Uzbek. She can't help being slightly jealous of Viktor, who has traveled more than she has, has even been to England; that was just last year, on a public relations assignment of sorts. He and two other writers (and their MVD escorts) were sent to visit a Russian poet who has been living there for thirty years. *Woo him back*, was the unstated goal—though Viktor and the others, despite their best efforts, were unable to change his mind. What they did accomplish was no less exciting: purchased suits of fine gabardine, turtleneck sweaters, gleaming ties of Liberty silk—and, more important, English penicillin, much better than the stuff at home. For Nina and the other wives, there were nylon stockings and Western cosmetics.

Nina's own travel, with the Bolshoi, has been limited to more familiar borders. The presence of these Westerners so close to her tonight reminds her that the world is large and full of mysteries. She recalls, as she often has since her girlhood, the woman stepping out from the grand hotel, with her jaunty hat and the tiny diamonds in her earlobes. That same feeling returns, a yearning, the understanding that Nina's own country, this majestic nation, despite its vastness, is but one piece in the great mosaic of the world.

The nightclub has become less lively now, the other patrons cautious—their conversation muted, their toasts brief. Only a young couple toward the back, inebriated, allows their voices to rise. As they begin to sing an old Gypsy song, loudly slurring the words, Nina feels, again, that odd shame; she wishes she were elsewhere.

Viktor and the others, too, are ready to leave, yet reluctant to say good night. They decide to stop at Gersh's. Nina much prefers to spend time in that room—smelling of cigarette smoke and reheated tea and Gersh's fusty shirts and old curtains—than in theirs in the opposite corner of the building, with Madame behind the plywood door feeling "flu-ish," or at the wooden table counting the cutlery, aloof

and disapproving, demanding grandchildren, thrusting out her wrist
for Viktor to palpate. Viktor nearly missed tonight's performance,
thanks to Madame's own little drama, a long coughing fit Nina is sure
she worked up on purpose. Sometimes the way Madame looks at her
makes everything painfully clear: that Nina is no different from the
other boors along the hallway, an average girl claiming what ought not
to be hers—Viktor, and even the physical space itself, the very proximity to "Her Excellency" and her noble blood. *You're not Lilya.*

But Viktor is devoted to his mother. There was a day, a few
months ago, when he filled a big basin with hot water for her to soak
her feet in. Nina peeked through the crack in the door, as if it might
help her understand something, to see Lola on Madame's shoulder,
avidly pecking at her earring, while Viktor lovingly (it is the only
way to describe it) placed the heavy sloshing bucket at his mother's
feet.

Since then, Nina hasn't dared spy on them together, hating how
it made her feel.

She wonders if Vera ever feels a similar reluctance to return
home, to enter the slightly sad (Nina always feels) room of Nina's
own mother.

At Gersh's, Vera drops wearily onto the hard, dark sofa facing the
piano. "You'll have to have more success like this," she tells Viktor.
"So that we can always have a reason to celebrate."

Though visibly delighted by her praise, Viktor manages to remain
nonchalant, asks, "Well, now, where did these come from?" seeing
an array of chocolates wrapped in fancy tinfoil.

"They're from Zoya, *actually*," Gersh says. "Help yourself."

Viktor peels the colorful foil from a chocolate, while Nina recalls that bright-eyed, curly-haired woman and the adoring way she
looked at Gersh. Such an improbable couple. Nina has asked Viktor
about her connection to Gersh, wonders where she is tonight. As
Gersh heats water for tea, Vera slips off her shoes and folds her legs

so that her feet are tucked underneath her. Nina and Viktor, after distributing the bonbons, take the love seat next to Vera, who asks, "Ninochka, do you remember our kicking contest?"

It was something they used to do, that last summer together, after they had been admitted to the Bolshoi School. "We would see who could kick her leg higher," Nina tells the men. "We didn't even know the term for *grand battement*."

"And then one day," Vera says, "I was sure I would win, and I kicked my leg so high, it lifted me right up into the air, and I landed flat on my behind!" She laughs, and rearranges herself just slightly on the sofa, her knees visible below the hem of her skirt. That she can be so comfortable here, so at ease, her feet tucked up under her like that, Nina takes as a compliment of sorts; that it is Nina's own presence, the fact that these men are of *her*, in a way, that allows Vera to be her full self, rather than the cool, composed version she usually presents. "Plunk, there I was, lying on the ground. Little did I know how many times that sort of thing would happen in my professional life!"

Nina remembers the episode another way. After she hit the ground, Vera had immediately begun laughing, and though Nina laughed too, even at that young age she knew that if she had been the one to fall, she would not have been able to laugh at herself. She wanted to win the contest, to be the best; she didn't want anyone to see her landing on her behind, ever. Already she felt—if in an inarticulate, unformulated way—the ferocity of her ambition, and the downside of pride.

"I wish I could have known you then," Gersh says, taking a seat, looking at Vera, his eyes dreamy behind the little round glasses, the lazy one veering off slightly.

Viktor has moved to the piano bench, and plays a few chords before attempting to bang out a tune. Gersh is asking Vera questions about her life in Leningrad. To Nina's surprise, Vera answers them openly. Closing her eyes, Nina listens to Viktor's enthusiastic, if amateur, playing, and to the growing conversation between Vera and Gersh. "Students and teachers were evacuated, too, not just the stars," she hears Vera say, of being sent to Perm during the war. "I suppose I got to dance more roles there than if we'd all stayed in the full company back at home. Still, we were so far away. And then when we came back, it was as if everything was just . . . finished. I remember seeing the theater. It was the feeling of my own home, my only home, having been ruined."

Nina's heart aches at the thought of Vera there, of what she might have suffered had she not escaped. She has heard the stories—of starvation, of children whose hair turned white, of bodies lying frozen in the streets.

Almost forcefully, Vera adds, "Well, it *was* my home. I'd lived there since the age of ten. Because the Kirov school takes boarders, and I'd already been accepted to the Bolshoi when I left Moscow—so it made sense for me to apply there. Since my aunt and uncle had no interest, really, in taking care of me."

"Your aunt and uncle . . ." Gersh says it in a wondering way.

"I'd been sent to live with them, after what happened to my parents."

Nina opens her eyes, surprised. She sees Gersh giving just the smallest nod of understanding, not asking what happened; Vera's eyes say the rest, glancing away to avoid more questions. "The other students were my family. I still remember which of us were the first ones chosen for the Opera—we danced in the ballet scenes, our first chance to perform onstage. My first was Queen of Spades." Vera has stretched her legs the length of the sofa and now lifts her knees slightly, bending them so that her skirt tents, revealing the long line of muscle where her shinbone meets her calf. With a faraway look, she says, "Fridays we went to the steam baths." Wrapping her arms around her knees, leaning forward, toward him, she looks straight at Gersh. Nina recalls how she felt with Viktor that first night she met him, the feeling that she could trust him. To Gersh, Vera nods in a final way and says, "The Kirov became my family."

"And yet you left."

"The Bolshoi is the best company in the world. How could I not accept?" But Nina wonders if it was that simple, if it felt less like an invitation than a command. Again her heart winces, at how difficult it must have been.

Viktor has finished his piano playing, so that the room is suddenly quiet. Gersh takes up a cigarette, and then his eyes move past everyone, brows rising. As if amused, he points toward the opposite corner of the room. There is a little pile of dust there, like an anthill, on the floor.

Not dust, he explains: "Cement." Looking up, he points to a small dark spot in the ceiling. Then he lights the cigarette, as if none of this is at all worrisome.

"Is it a hole?" Vera whispers. It might have been painted there, it is so small and black.

"Looks freshly drilled," Gersh says, exhaling cigarette smoke as if the whole thing is a game.

Nina is horrified. Viktor says, "You'd think they would at least clean up after themselves." He too lights a cigarette.

"No, that's the point," Gersh says quietly. "To let us know they can hear."

But what could they have heard? Nina thinks quickly to herself. No one here has said anything wrong, let alone done anything, and the piano playing would have covered everything up anyway. Vera looks up at the hole with a mix of concern and reverence.

Viktor turns his head just slightly, to blow a smooth stream of smoke across his shoulder. "Were you planning on sweeping up your little anthill?"

"Maybe more of them will turn up," Gersh says. "I'll start a collection."

Their light banter hides nothing. Clearly Gersh is on some list. There has been more harsh talk—in the papers, in official speeches— about people like him. Every week, it seems, a member of the Jewish intelligentsia is arrested, or some Jewish organization disbanded. Perhaps that is why Zoya is not with him here tonight; surely someone like her would not want to be too closely associated with Gersh now. And yet, those fancy chocolates . . .

At the piano, Gersh has taken Viktor's place and starts playing a Glinka mazurka. Nina calms herself, watching him. He is one of those musicians who, when engaged in his music, becomes a more vivid version of himself; his cynicism gives way to pure emotion, so that he seems suddenly stronger and more ardent. Nina has noticed this about him before, his passion suddenly visible, palpable. It is something the two of them have in common, she realizes—this physical, primal, connection to sound and rhythm.

Vera is watching Gersh with big dark eyes, head resting on her hand, and now Viktor leans back to listen. Nina can see in his very posture how badly he wants to believe that drill hole doesn't matter. After all, if Gersh isn't doing anything wrong, then what is there for anyone to see or hear that might cause trouble?

Gersh plays for a long time, smoking cigarettes with Viktor until the room is a warm haze. The tips of their cigarettes worm back, the ashes fall to the floor—like the dust from that drill hole. Nina focuses instead on the love she feels around her, not only between her and Viktor, and Viktor and Gersh, but now Gersh and Vera, too. Until very late they stay there, drinking tea from Gersh's cheap metal samovar. It is as if all four of them are waiting something out, as if none of them wants the night to end. Morning has sprouted, pale and winking, by the time they say good-bye.

LOT 41

Art Nouveau Plique-à-jour Enamel and Diamond Butter-fly Hatpin, the plique-à-jour wings edged with rose-cut diamonds set *en tremblant*, body and green enamel head set with old European, old mine, and old single-cut diamond mêlée, engraved legs, silver and platinum-topped 18kt gold mount, 3 1/2 × 2 1/2 in. (*en tremblant* mechanism rigid). $10,000–15,000

Note: For a similar example signed by Eugène Feuillâtre and auctioned in these rooms, see Fine Jewelry, Beller Galleries, Auction 1462, lot 326, Sept. 1990

CHAPTER EIGHT

In the wee hours of Monday morning, the blizzard that had been making its way across the country blew into the Commonwealth. White tufts fell in great busy swirls, a big billowing curtain of lace; by Tuesday the storm had been declared Boston's largest on record. Grigori arrived at the department later than usual, hindered, like everyone, by the snowdrifts everywhere.

He had not spoken to Evelyn since their date on Friday. Sitting at his desk, attempting to read the newspaper he had bought at the CVS (since his copy of the *Globe* must have landed in a snowbank), he found himself trying, yet again, to convince himself that everything was fine, that he was simply unaccustomed to this thing called dating, this strange thing called a date, and with Evelyn, of all people. But then he would recall the awkward moment when he at last said good night—and Evelyn bowing her head as she closed the door, as if in acknowledgment of their folly.

From the ballet they had walked to the lounge at the Four Seasons, where Grigori, more anxious than he had expected, must have drunk too much. All the while he told himself his unease wasn't anything about Evelyn; it was from running into Drew Brooks. How awkward that had been, there in the theater lobby. Still feeling agitated as he huddled with Evelyn in a niche by the window, he drank too many whiskeys, and when toward midnight he walked Evelyn from the T to her apartment, taking her arm to make sure she didn't slip on the ice, and she asked if he would like to come in for a cup of tea, it hadn't occurred to him not to.

She was wearing that skirt with the slit at the side. It wasn't the first time Grigori had seen the skirt on her, but only in the niche at the Four Seasons had he noticed the way that a sliver of Evelyn's thigh peeked out at him. When, in her apartment, next to Grigori on her leather sofa, Evelyn placed her hand on his elbow, Grigori had looked shyly down, and his gaze landed on the skirt's slit. Though he quickly looked up again, it was too late, Evelyn's eyes had followed his. She kissed him then, as Grigori's thoughts rushed forward, the awareness that he was kissing someone, someone who wasn't Christine, and that this was what people called "moving on," this feeling of surprised curiosity—and then Evelyn was asking, "Is it all right?" and Grigori had to acknowledge that, without meaning to, he had pulled away.

He ought to have understood at that point: these situations were delicate and could not be rushed. Instead, flustered, he had mumbled an apology and tried to kiss her one more time, to prove that it was all right. But when she responded, he became suddenly daunted, and Evelyn, clearly sensing his hesitation, said with great generosity, "We can take things slow." Her hair had become disheveled. Grigori was dismayed by his behavior.

And to think that none of this would have happened, he told himself now (giving up on the newspaper), if he hadn't run into Drew Brooks. Then Grigori might not have felt so anxious, and drunk all that Bushmills. Or if he and Drew had at least come up ahead of time with some basic statement to explain their acquaintance . . . Grigori wouldn't have worried, then, that he might have to make up some small lie to tell Evelyn, in order not to have to share anything about the auction house, or the pendant, with her. That was the core of the problem, Grigori realized, suddenly and quite clearly, with his feelings about Evelyn. He could not imagine telling her his secrets.

Well, these things take time, he told himself, placing the newspaper in the bin for recycling. He peeked out into the hallway. Evelyn's door was closed; she hadn't come in yet. Grigori felt a small pang of some emotion he could not quite name, and went back to his desk to retrieve his telephone messages. There was only one. Everyone used e-mail instead these days.

The message was from Drew Brooks.

"I just wanted to let you know," came the self-assured voice, "that we have the official lab results back, and the necklace is indeed genuine Baltic amber."

Relief washed over Grigori. But then of course Drew Brooks added that she had "another question" for him, "if you could call me back at your earliest convenience."

So much for relief. Frowning, Grigori took up the telephone, to dial the auction house. Another woman's voice, coming from the hallway, caused him to pause, his heart racing. But, no, it wasn't Evelyn. It was just Carla talking to Dave.

Stop being so antsy, Grigori scolded himself. It would all be fine. He and Evelyn were two mature adults, there was no reason they could not pull this off. Yet all at once it seemed too difficult—how to face her, what to say. After a moment's contemplation, Grigori put on his coat and headed out to the snow-beached avenue, to board the B train to Back Bay.

SCENT OF AUTUMN, of mud and first frosts and wood-smoky air. The Bolshoi until midnight, and late meals at the Aurora: salt fish, thick slices of salami with garlic . . . *The Fountain of Bakhchisarai*—with Nina as Zarema and Vera as Maria—is a grand spectacle as usual, with its exotic costumes and Tartar hordes. The new piece,

The Bronze Horseman, is more serious, about the necessary sacrifice of the individual for the greater good of one's country.

Gersh too has new work performed that autumn, 1949. A sonata for cello—the gorgeous, aching sound of yearning. To Nina, the music conveys something about Gersh himself, the depth of mystery and tenderness she has always sensed hidden in him, despite his brazen talk. The following week, reading *Pravda*, Viktor shakes his head.

"What is it?"

"Oh, this critic. His review of Gersh's piece."

"May I see?"

Quietly, under his breath, he says, "Opportunism. That's all it is." He hands Nina the newspaper.

The article is more of an essay than a review, an argument for the qualities that Soviet music ought to display—and the many ways that Gersh's piece has failed. *Deeply marred by the influence of bourgeois decadence, completely devoid of social context, this new work is a disturbing testament to its composer's servility to the West.*

Gersh the reviewer calls an "anti-patriot" and, farther down, that other word, the one heard more and more these days. There's even a little ditty about it going around—quietly, sardonically:

If you don't want to be known as an anti-Semite
Be sure to call a kike "cosmopolite."

Probably Nina shouldn't be surprised by this review, after so many similar articles. Plus there was that long, stern editorial in *Kultura i Zhizn* . . . But the fact of it glares at her: Gersh has been singled out. It's official, in print—no question, now, as to how others are to view him. Yet Nina says, "I don't understand." Because despite all these things the reviewer states about Gersh's piece, its many faults, all that Nina heard was beautiful music.

Viktor says, "One is entitled to one's opinion, of course."

Nina feels a sudden, fleeting fear, of what this might mean for Viktor, and for his friendship with Gersh. The two of them have known each other for nearly a decade. Nina knows well how much Viktor values Gersh: his wit and intelligence, his boldness. He is Viktor's most outspoken friend, and Nina suspects that irreverence is part of what draws Viktor to him, those qualities he wishes he too possessed. She senses, too, Viktor's genuine appreciation of Gersh's music, a respect unhampered by any competition or envy, as he might feel with fellow writers.

Perhaps there is something they ought to be doing for Gersh. Sometimes support from someone respected can make a difference: decrees are rewritten, verdicts reversed. Other times, though . . . you might as well dig your own grave. Nina folds the newspaper in half, as if to silence the journalist's complaints.

When she enters their little dressing room the following evening, she can see that Vera has been crying.

"It's Gersh," Vera says tearfully, and Nina supposes Vera too has read the *Pravda* review. She spends much of her free time with Gersh these days, and it's no secret to Nina how strong Vera's feelings are. Sitting by his side at the concert, she even looked nervous for him despite her usual cool veneer. Afterward her face glowed at such applause—the crowd clapping in unison, insistent even after Gersh had taken multiple bows, so that he had to go onstage again and accept more flowers.

"I telephoned him yesterday afternoon after rehearsal ended early to ask if I could stop by. When I got there, he acted so happy to see me—but then what does he have to say? 'You know, you should try to give me more warning before you come over. What if I had a girl here? What am I to do with her when you turn up?' "

"He's teasing, Verochka."

"I know." She shakes her head. "It's not the first time he's done it. I try to go along with him. I just said, 'You mean you *don't* have a girl here now?' He said, 'She's hiding in the cupboard, poor thing. See what you've done?' " Vera gives a tired laugh. "I'm stupid to cry about it, I know. But I keep thinking he'll stop. It's hard, trying to act like I don't care. Really it hurts me."

"Of course it does. I don't know why he has to act like that." But as she says it, Nina is recalling how Viktor first referred to him, "a ladies' man." Maybe it has to do with pride, with his old sense of himself as free and unattached. Maybe that's why he acts as though Vera has no special claim to his affection—in order to retain some former notion of himself. Really anyone who has even glimpsed him with Vera these past two months can see he is hopelessly in love.

"Why do *you* think he does it?" Nina asks.

Vera says, "Fear. I think that talking like that convinces him he won't be trapped by love."

"Right." Nina too senses fear there, despite Gersh's seeming confidence. What she doesn't say is what Vera herself must surely sense: that it isn't love, or being trapped by love, that he is afraid of.

THAT DECEMBER IS Stalin's seventieth birthday, with all kinds of celebrations. As part of the festivities Mao Tse-tung makes a visit; to mark the occasion, the Bolshoi has prepared a special revival of *The Red Poppy*, about Tao-Hoa, the Chinese teahouse dancer who gives up her life to save the Soviet captain. Vera says the Bolshoi production is much more lavish than the Kirov's.

The city has been thoroughly done up for the festivities, the buildings decorated with red flags and banners, and platforms set up in the squares for dancing. An enormous floodlit portrait of Stalin, held aloft by big blimp-shaped military balloons, floats above the Kremlin, shedding its light on the streets below. When Nina and Vera join Viktor and Gersh after their performance, music is blaring from the loudspeakers in Manezhnaya Square, and all around them people are dancing, many women together, and separate groups of men. Viktor and Gersh look dapper in their dark hats, and Nina feels suddenly joyous—the crisp air against her face, and her love for Viktor so full, it may as well be the sky. Viktor's and Gersh's cheeks and noses are rosy from the cold, or perhaps from drink, or from dancing.

"Don't I get a dance?"

Zoya, in her curly goatskin coat. Nina watches, wondering, as Gersh gives an awkward hello. Though she doesn't seem surprised to find him with Vera, Zoya does look a bit hurt, eyes slightly downcast as she bats her curled lashes. Nina momentarily feels for her, that she is not too proud to reveal her feelings. And that unlike so many people, she is not one to pretend—now that Gersh is in disfavor—to no longer know him.

When Nina asks how she is enjoying the celebration, Zoya's face lights up. "Oh, it's all so wonderful! Did you hear his speech?" She looks truly moved, beautiful, even, her eyes sparkling. Nina almost understands when Gersh says, "Here, noodle, join us!" That flash of attraction again, in Zoya's face, as Gersh takes her hand. But now he lets go and begins a silly dance, kicking out his legs as if about to do the *kazachok*. He is this way often these days, joking, frantic.

Vera's expression is aloof. "I don't understand," Nina says under her breath to Viktor. "Zoya and Gersh."

"I suppose she still has her sights set on him," Viktor says, "though surely she can see it's a lost cause." A drunk man goes careening by, knocking into them. To Zoya, Viktor says, "Please, may I have this dance?" She smiles gratefully as he whisks her away.

They look quite cute together, Nina has to admit. She wonders about Zoya, if Gersh truly has, or had, feelings for her, or if she is some kind of cover for what he really feels. For now, though, he and Vera are together, dancing close, quietly, their faces serious, as though something important has been discussed.

When the song ends, Viktor thanks Zoya for the dance, and Zoya explains that she must run off; actually, she is meeting some comrades at the other side of the square. Despite everything, Nina can't help but admire her pluck.

A new song has begun, and Viktor reaches out for Nina. The music chimes as they begin to dance, as he and Gersh spin Nina and Vera between them. Nina feels her coat whirling around her calves, her head tossed back, laughing, as she and Vera are passed back and forth, one and then the other.

DREW BROOKS WAS there at the auction house, talking to another woman by the front desk. Something unaware about her, the way she carried herself, leaning with her back against the counter, in a green dress. With a light nod she led Grigori into a little room almost like a closet, with a small round table and two plastic chairs.

"I'm sorry to have rushed away the other night," Grigori told her, taking a seat, having thanked her for her telephone message. "It's just that my friend doesn't know that I've brought anything here. Nobody knows. If it should happen again—"

"I'll just say I approached you about clarifying a Russian document someone brought to us. How's that?"

He considered. "That works."

"It actually relates to my question. You said that you teach Russian."

"I do."

"You know I've been trying to find out more about the origins of the amber suite. Trying to see how far back I can trace each of the pieces. It's possible I might be able to go all the way back to whoever they were originally intended for—if it was anyone specific. It's quite a challenge, and I haven't been able to get much of anywhere yet, but most famous makers kept ledgers where they listed everything they produced, as well as the buyers. Lenore doesn't seem to think we'll have much luck finding anything for the amber, but who knows? The Boston Public Library is good at requesting this type of information, and with so many archives online, I'm thinking we might be able to find something."

"Really?" Grigori heard the eagerness in his voice.

"The thing is, *if* I'm ever able to find anything, I'm assuming it's going to be written in Russian. In which case, perhaps you might be able to help me."

"Certainly." To think that there might really be some sort of confirmation . . .

"I wish I could read it myself." Drew gave a little smiling shake of her head. "That Russian class I took was so awful!" She laughed. "What I really wanted to learn was Finnish. Even though my mother was born in Finland, she grew up here, and . . . I just feel sad not knowing the language. But of course it's impossible to find a Finnish class, because what use is it to know Finnish? Anyway, when I couldn't find a Finnish course, I took Russian instead, since my mother's father was Russian. But I'm basically no good with languages."

"Many people aren't."

Her eyebrows lifting, Drew said, "The teacher said I was useless."

"I can't imagine a teacher saying that."

"Well, what she actually said was that 'it' was useless. There was no point in my continuing in her class, because it was useless." She gave a laugh.

"My dear, it sounds like your *teacher* was useless."

Drew smiled, and there was something lovely in the modesty of her face. Then she straightened her shoulders and, in a more businesslike voice, said, "Anyway, we'll see if I'm even lucky enough to find any official records for the amber."

"And if you do, are these things necessarily . . . unequivocal?"

Drew gave a little shrug. "They can be quite specific—how many of each style, and for whom." She paused. "It's amazing, when you realize that the original amber set probably included even more pieces than these three."

"Is that so?"

"I wouldn't be surprised. A full parure around that time would have meant a bracelet on each wrist, plus a ring and another necklace that unclipped to become a brooch. And depending on the era, some clasps and buttons, or aigrettes and hairpins. If not a tiara."

Grigori tried to picture it. "And no one thought this overkill?"

Drew laughed. She told Grigori how amber of this kind, with once-living specimens preserved inside, had been the vogue in Victorian times, and that those who had the means would have specifically commissioned such jewelry. "Your piece is clearly nineteenth century. That's when gems began to be inserted in open settings—much less heavy, you can imagine, than wearing all these things embedded in a solid foundation." It was this sort of information, Drew explained, that she would be including in the supplemental brochure that she was preparing for the pre-auction dinner. Perhaps she hoped that if she reminded him, Grigori might suddenly have something to share with her. "Anyway, I'm still looking for anything else I can find out about the amber."

Grigori pictured the vinyl bag, the handwritten letters, the black-and-white photographs. The hospital certificate with its Soviet insignia and some sort of serial number, and the time and place typed so firmly, you could feel the letters beneath your fingertips; where a name ought to be was just a thick black line and yet another address. Only a system so thoroughly bureaucratized could be so utterly dysfunctional.

He nearly smiled, to think what Drew might make of these things, though of course he couldn't show them to her. He hadn't even dared show them to Nina Revskaya. Well, yes, he had, long ago—or would have, had she given him the chance. "You've a lot on your plate here, don't you?" was all he said now.

"I like it that way. With the research, it's like an ongoing history course. I learn something new every day."

Grigori felt something close to envy, wondering if he could say the same for himself.

"Actually, some of the things that have made the strongest impression on me haven't even had anything to do with the auction itself."

"Really?"

Drew paused, seemed to be remembering. "One time we were auctioning porcelain, all kinds of beautiful things, tea sets and vases and figurines. A good portion of what we had that time had come from one person, a woman whose mother had collected little porcelain tchotchkes. Some of them were quite sweet, actually, little animals, swans, rabbits, things like that. I was with the assessor when they went through the mother's collection, and each piece had a bit of masking tape on the bottom with a name on it. There were three names, I still remember them, Anne and Lise and Clara. The ink was very trembly, you could tell that whoever wrote it—the woman who had died, the mother, I suppose—had had a tremor in her hand. I never found out who Anne and Lise and Clara were, but I imagined they were granddaughters or nieces. They weren't the name of the woman who had brought the figurines in, and all I could think about for weeks and weeks was that the girls those pieces were intended for never got them. That the woman's will wasn't followed through."

Grigori wondered aloud, "Do you think the writing might have been from before that? That maybe the woman who had died was Anne or Lise or Clara? Maybe they had eventually all been passed along to her."

"No, the tape was new, I could tell. You know how it gets dry and yellowed after a while." She seemed to be remembering. "What moved me most was just seeing the names on the masking tape, in her handwriting—the aunt's or grandmother's or whoever she was. I kept picturing this old sick woman knowing she was going to die, going through her things, deciding which of them she wanted to give to Anne or Lise or Clara. She had written each name out so purposefully."

Embarrassingly, Grigori felt tears coming to his eyes. He was recalling Christine, on a horrible autumn day two months before she died, going through everything with him, writing lists of things she wanted to give to Amelie, and college memorabilia she wanted to donate to her sorority, and then, most horrible of all, taking the time to describe for him the sort of funeral she would like to have.

"I didn't mean to tell such a depressing anecdote." Drew lowered her gaze. "Sorry about that."

"Oh, no, please, I'm the one who should apologize. I'm keeping you from your work." She was leaning lightly on her forearms, with one leg reaching forward so that her foot was just past Grigori's ankle. Feeling all at once that he had stayed too long, Grigori stood and pushed in his chair.

"Again," Drew Brooks said abruptly, following his cue and standing, "if you think of anything I might include in the supplemental—"

"I can check to see if I have anything." He heard how brusque his voice sounded.

"Thank you, I appreciate it," Drew said quickly. She shook his hand and, before letting go, added, "Sometimes it's surprising what people find."

"Now, who exactly are you?"

She asked him in Russian, aware that she was smiling—just a tiny smile at the corners of her mouth—at how shy the young man looked, standing there in the front vestibule. A boy, in a way, still in possession of a youthful lankiness. Thickly curling hair from the humid day. In a low voice he began to speak, ducking his head slightly as if in effort to not be so much taller than Nina.

"My name is Grigori Solodin." Diffident, he hung back behind the glass door that Nina held only partially open; clearly he did not expect her to recognize the name. "I believe you and I . . ." His hesitation, his deep eagerness. He believed, he managed to state, that he and Nina might be related.

Puzzled was what she felt. No clear idea, not even a guess, of what he could mean. Yet already she had begun to tremble, that sudden weakness that arrives with terror. So really she must have known, she told herself afterward. Perhaps Grigori Solodin, too, sensed this. There came a rush of words, so painfully eager. "I was born in 1952, in Municipal Hospital Number 3, Moscow." He named a date in May, waiting only a brief moment to see if it held any significance for Nina. But Nina could not react other than to be stunned by the fact of this young man before her, bending down now to take from his backpack a large envelope, unclasping it. "Here, I can show you the certificate. It lists a home address." He blurted the address even as he was pulling the document out.

That was when Nina understood, clearly, who this young man must be. Her entire body trembled now as she said simply, firmly, "You are mistaken."

His blinking eyes, his desperation as he reached again into that big envelope. "You see, I have other evidence of our connection, if you'll—"

"I'm not the person you want." With that she pulled the door shut, her heart racing, and turned to hurry up the stairs.

It was a week later that she received the letter—a "cursory explanation," the young man called it—requesting that he be allowed to show her more precisely what he meant. What was the worst that might happen, he asked innocently, if Nina simply took the time to examine what he had to show her? But of course she could not look. She had escaped all that once already, could not willingly place herself back there again. Holding a match to the pages—two of them, handwritten, one atop the other—Nina watched the retreating edges take the flame. The letter dropped into the kitchen sink, where it became a curling brown flower, shrinking and spouting fire, and then a single great burst of flame, until nothing was left but fragile gray skin crumbling in the basin.

As for Solodin's most recent letter, Nina still had not answered it. Even now there really was nothing to say, just Go away, please, leave me be. That palpable wanting, his need to know—the very opposite of Nina. Perhaps she might explain it to him that way, very generally, nothing personal: *Like many of my compatriots, after Stalin's death . . .* Or, *My whole generation, with the wool pulled over our eyes . . .* Or, *Being disabused of so many misconceptions . . . It is simply overwhelming.*

Already Nina had had the blindfold torn off, that bright painful light. Why hunt for anything more? The truth of this man, no longer young. Nina knew enough of his convoluted story; there was no reason to hear him out. Already she was plagued by memories, more of them each day, images so vivid, it was as though she were back there again, instead of here in her wheelchair by the drafty window, wearing her woolen dress and cotton tights and soft fuzzy slippers from L. L. Bean. She sighed. Even a year or so ago she wouldn't have worn such slippers in the presence of another human being. They were a mauve color, of artificial fleece. Tama had given them to her, a few Christmases ago. At the time Nina had been appalled, at what they stood for and at how Tama must see her: an old woman with no need, on most days, for any more serviceable sort of footwear.

As if on cue, a cold throb overtook her joints. She closed her eyes and waited for its grip to release. Such betrayal, after so much of her life spent strengthening herself, constant exercise to ward off injury.

A life so centered around routine that Nina still felt at ten o'clock each morning the nag of knowing she should be at her position at the barre. All those years of stretching and strengthening and limbering up. In the end none of it had helped.

The end. Though she might use such language, she really did not see this as the end. No, it did not feel like the end at all. Not with this thorn, Grigori Solodin, still in her side. Though hopefully the auction would take care of that. And then something good: Shepley was coming to visit. Not for two months yet—not until April—but April really wasn't so far away (although the icy air coming through the open slit of the window made it seem otherwise). He had called the other night, said, "What's this I hear about a major auction of a certain famous ballerina's jewels?"

"How do you know this?" She was surprised; surely there couldn't be much interest beyond New England.

In fact there had been an article in the *L.A. Times*; Shepley clipped it and mailed it to her, a single column, not very long, but it was news nonetheless. "I'm proud of you, Nina," he had told her on the telephone. "It's extremely generous of you."

"Well, you know I never wear them. They live in a vault."

"Yes, but I also know how you are when it comes to these things. You're possessive—like me." Shepley laughed, the soft, self-effacing sound Nina loved. "We're the same, you and me, because we can't help ourselves. We can't help falling in love with beautiful things."

AUGUST 1950. PRECIOUS days of tomatoes, of big green cabbages. Air close and steamy, like a breath. The four of them drive past the outskirts of the city, along yellow dirt roads, in the brand-new car Viktor has purchased. It was even posted in *Pravda*: "V. Elsin, poet and Esteemed State Artist of the RSFSR, and P. Lisitsian, soloist of the Bolshoi Theatre, each bought Pobeda automobiles." The car bumps along in a cloud of dust, past locals tending their gardens and kolkhoz peasants threshing barley. Beyond are pine-covered hills, and copses of birch and alder. Tall grasses line the road, and already the air smells oniony, of weeds and reedy flowers. And then they are in the forest, pine groves all around. At a partial clearing, bordered by a high fence and rusty gate, is the dacha.

"Straight out of a folktale," Nina says, looking up at the steep roof edged in gingerbreading, and the small windows framed with wooden shutters, curtained with bits of white cloth. It is the second summer that she and Viktor have owned this little cottage, with its old furniture and worn wooden floorboards. Most other dachas in this village are owned by the Literary Fund, doled out to writers on a merit basis—which is how Viktor first came to stay in this one, off of one of the most secluded roads. But he wanted to be able to visit whenever he chose, and to invite whomever he pleased, and so last year he managed to purchase it. Other writers have even settled here full-time.

They unload bags and provisions: canisters of paraffin, sacks of potatoes and carrots, fat heads of lettuce, thick-necked bottles of Zhigulevskoe beer, round jugs of Napareuli wine. With her valise under one arm, a watermelon under the other, Nina inhales the scent of pine and nudges open the squeaky gate; it stretches a spiderweb into a nearly invisible net. "Thank you," Viktor says, marching right through the web, past the small, half-shaded stone terrace, with his cache of canned fruit and vegetables from Eastern Europe. Gersh follows, balancing the various sacks and boxes, but Vera pauses next to Nina to look at the house, taking a deep breath of the woodsy air. "There's the river," Nina says, pointing just beyond the patch of woods.

The air swells with the hum of insects. "It reminds me of summers when I was a boarder at the ballet school," Vera says. The country sunlight reveals the reddish highlights in her hair. "They used to take us to the Black Sea. The ones who couldn't go home, I mean." *Orphans* is the unspoken word—or children from Alma-Ata and Chelyabinsk and other places too far to travel home to. "We stayed in wooden barracks, and slept on stacked bunk beds, and I never wanted the top bunk, because there were always spiders on the ceiling."

Nina says, "There are probably spiders here too."

"Oh, they don't scare me anymore."

The dacha is spare, its walls appropriately flimsy, its toilet outdoors. Whitewashed walls. An iron washtub. A stack of firewood next to a brick stove with a tall chimney pipe. Hazel-switch fishing rods in the corner. Cane-seat chairs, kerosene lamps, a cupronickel samovar. Metal-framed beds with hard, straw-stuffed mattresses. Soot from so many burned candlewicks. The *banya* is out the back, so that they can go from there right into the river.

Nina loves the gentle slap of bare feet on the wooden floor—not a sprung-wood one, but it will do for indoor practice. Sunshine seeping through the scrappy white curtains as early as three in the morning, and sifting through the trees all afternoon. The bright yapping of sparrows and magpies. Shared meals under the pines, water fetched from the spring, the ground moist, the air delicious, the river green and cool.

The evening glare spreads orange coins across the water. There are swims in the river, and volleyball matches. Though plenty of group activities are offered over at the Writers Recreation Center, Nina and the others remain here, quietly together. Viktor has vowed to write a poem a day, and Gersh works from sketches of a new piece, whistling melodiously. Vera hums along, often simply sitting beside him, or reading, her long bare legs tucked up under her skirt, lighting the lantern at nightfall. Nina wonders if Vera is as glad to be free of Nina's mother as Nina is to be away from Viktor's, whom poor Darya continues to care for, while Nina's mother makes her own rounds and visits with friends at Bear Lake.

And so this is a month of perfection, of leisurely freedom, of lazy afternoons spent on the terrace in long, wandering debates that spin off into the air without conclusion. Wildflowers sweeten the air, and butterflies tumble by—nothing like the exquisite pin Viktor gave Nina for their anniversary, but no less magnificent, with their nearly translucent, brightly spotted wings. Gersh and Viktor spend hours on the terrace in the wicker chairs, looking quite satisfied in their striped pajamas as they argue lightly back and forth. Gersh teases Viktor for being an "Esteemed State Artist." It's one of those honorary titles that didn't previously exist, and that span the whole range of cultural pursuits, not just the finer arts. "Cheap incentives," Gersh calls them, and names a singer they know who is always traveling all over the Republic to this and that region, collecting as many titles as he can. But the fact is, "Esteemed State Artist" is the reason Viktor is allowed to travel abroad and can afford a dacha like this one. If he or Nina ever becomes a "People's Artist"—the highest title possible—there will be even more perks.

"You know very well that I have nothing against popular entertainment," Viktor says, clearly hoping to incite. He enjoys these debates with Gersh, the kind most people won't engage in. "What's the point of creating anything, no matter how beautiful, if it doesn't manage to speak to the people? If it never *reaches* the people?"

"You sound like Zoya!" Gersh says, as Viktor surely expects him to. He can mention her today, because Vera has gone off on one of her long walks, gathering mushrooms. By the gate, her hand resting on the iron fence, Nina moves through her daily barre exercises. She hasn't skipped a day of training. Even a week of missed practice could mean bruised toes and aching limbs when her muscles are forced to work again.

"This utilitarian view of art makes my insides squirm," Gersh says. "You know that, of course."

"Why do you put up with her, anyway?" Nina calls.

"Who?"

"Zoya!"

"She makes me look good, don't you think?" Gersh says in his teasing voice. In a lisping imitation, he adds, "Upright citizen. Party spirit and all that. Perfectly commendable, actually."

Nina doesn't laugh; even in his mocking, Gersh seems uncomfortable. Perhaps Zoya really does feel to him like some kind of badge of approval. There has been more anti-Semitic commentary: editorials in the press, even another swipe at Gersh himself by one particularly belligerent critic whom Viktor has nicknamed "the Rottweiler." More than once Nina has glimpsed the slogan "Down with the Cosmopolites!" Maybe Gersh really does see Zoya as a protector of sorts.

"I'm not joking," Viktor says. "I mean what I said. About reaching the people. There's a reason front-row seats cost only three rubles at your theater, Nina. Life is hard, people are tired. You bring them beauty. You make them proud. You remind us of all we're capable of—that we ourselves are a work in progress, creating a great new society. Why do you think our Iosef Vissarionovich himself prefers the biggest, most colorful productions? He knows it's the monumental stuff—the most colorful scenery, the brightest costumes—that has the strongest impact."

"Exactly," Gersh says, "this is exactly the problem! There's no room for complexity, for sensitivity, for anything the slightest bit challenging. Instead we're supposed to pander to the audience. When, really, how are they ever going to learn to appreciate anything truly profound? Everything always has to be exaggerated. And you know why: because people need to be *cued*. They need to be *told* what they're supposed to think—"

"They're tired," Viktor says. "They work hard, they—"

Gersh cuts him off. "They need to have it made absolutely clear to them how they're supposed to react."

"I'm not sure it's that," Viktor says calmly, though Nina can tell he is wondering. "I think it has to do with . . . making things straightforward—simple, available to everyone."

"I'd hardly call the glamour of Bolshoi productions 'simple,' " Gersh puts in. "All that pomp and glitter. As if it has anything to do with everyday life. You're awfully quiet over there, Nina, by the way."

"I'm considering what you're saying," she calls back. She has begun her foot exercises, grabbing with her toes the heavy braided rag rug she has placed on the ground in front of her, pulling it toward her and then, with the toes of her other foot, grabbing it again to try to drag it back out to where it was. "I mean, isn't that the way theater ought to be—magnificent?" It's true that Bolshoi productions are outsize, majestic, nothing restrained about them. Swirls of color, brash acrobatics. For a few hours, the audience exchanges real life for the plush velvet seats of a glittering auditorium, its five tiers of red and gold balconies, and glowing candelabras, and gilt ceiling and ornately draped Tsar's Box, and giant chandelier suspended regally, dripping with crystal. For those few hours there is beautiful music, and dancing that will restore anyone's faith in the world.

Gersh says, "Perhaps, but—"

"You underestimate our populace," Viktor tells him. "I don't think they need to be told how to feel. Great art communicates instinctively. One can't help but understand it."

This Nina too believes. It is when she is dancing—not marching in a line or singing Party ballads on the tour bus—that she feels, truly *feels*, the common humanity of the world. Only onstage, performing for the public, is she aware of herself as a comrade in a great nation. And yet . . . she recalls her night as Odile, the audience's

wide eyes as she performed her technical tricks, like some circus dog.
Their automatic applause, not at her musicality or artfulness, but at
that long string of show-off fouettées. That's not what it means to be
an artist. Nina knows this deep down. She has witnessed the exhila-
ration that Ulanova, her favorite ballerina, creates when she dances,
how her nuanced movements seem to lift, palpably, the audience to
a higher plane. What Nina would do to achieve that same level of
artistry, performance that is itself life-affirming . . .

"That's your problem," Gersh is telling Viktor. "You're a
romantic."

"A Romantic? Not at all!"

"Not your poetry. I'm talking about your outlook, your faith in
the greater good. In your leader. You idealize everyone."

That's the thing about being out in the woods like this, Nina
thinks to herself. One can talk this way, unrestrained. No one
around to hear you.

"I don't idealize," Viktor says. "It's simply a matter of perspec-
tive. We are inventing a new nation, a new great people. It's a difficult process. You choose to see the negative side of this. When really
there's much that is positive." Nina loves this about him—his opti-
mism, his gentle wisdom and genuine hope.

"Yes, of course," Gersh says. "Because you're still able to do what
you love and have it matter. Not to sound grandiose, but really, let's
be honest, there's nothing left for me in this country. I have no future
here. Everything I compose now is for the desk drawer."

He's probably right, Nina thinks to herself. No orchestra would
dare play his work now. No one will record him. Yet she hears herself
say, "That can change. You know that—it can change overnight."
Because that, too, is true.

That night the four of them make mushroom soup and potato
hash, and drink so much wine that Viktor, when their glasses are at
last empty and the sound of crickets fills the air, grabs his abdomen,

groans with pleasure, and says, "I'm sorry, Nina, we may have to forgo lovemaking tonight."

"Look!" Vera says, nodding lazily toward the open window. "Fireflies." She is wearing a white linen dress with folk embroidery, and leaning back into Gersh's arm. In the pale white linen, with her glimmering hair and the flickering light of the kerosene lantern, she looks almost mothlike. Gersh pulls her closer, nuzzles her neck. In moments like this, his crossed eye makes him look somehow dashing.

"Ach!" Vera pretends to pull away. "You smell like a bachelor."

Gersh pulls her close again. "I say we all go for a swim."

Viktor says, "With all this food in me? I'll sink."

But Nina drags him up out of his chair. "Come on, I'll save you."

The river is just below their slope of forest, a sudden clearing lit brightly by the moon. Tied to a log at the edge is the canoe they sometimes take out. Nina regards the soft black mirror of the water, its smooth, dark skin. Black shadows all around. She and Vera undress with care, but Gersh and Viktor simply strip down and run like children straight into the water. Nina walks forward to where the shoreline ends, the earth soft with silt, and continues in up to her waist, then leans forward to submerge her arms, as if slipping them into long evening gloves. The water is surprisingly warm. When she dives in, she feels herself enveloped. Reemerging, she leans back, lifts her feet, and floats on her back. Above her the sky is dark black, an endless stretch dotted with tiny stars.

The sound of night, the thick, rich quiet—and the hooting, every few minutes, of an owl. Nina still hasn't grown used to this quietness, the hidden, elusive sounds of nature, instead of Moscow's loudspeakers broadcasting patriotic songs out over the streets day and night.

Gersh has returned for Vera, who is still close to shore. "Come here," he says, wading toward her.

Viktor paddles on his back until he is next to Nina. His fingers touch hers, wriggling in the water. She wiggles hers against his. Gersh has begun to hum, a song Nina recognizes. Now Viktor puts his hands underneath Nina's shoulders and pulls her along, swinging her slowly through the water. "I love the sound of the crickets everywhere," she says. "Like they've overtaken the world."

Viktor is quiet for a moment, then says, "You know what it is? It's the sound of vastness."

Leaning back in his arms, pleasantly exhausted, the sky embedded with stars, Nina feels—actually feels—the vastness of the world, that it stretches on and on, and that she and Viktor and Gersh and Vera are the merest part of it. She senses, for the first time, how far away one can be from one's own life, how contentedly distant. The gaping enormity of the universe, its endless possibility . . . She feels it, an aura, an inkling: the illusion of absolute freedom.

BOOK II

LOT 50

Tiara. Rhinestone and Austrian crystal, h. 1 3/4 in., dia. 5.5 in., plated in sterling silver, comb tines on each end. $800–1,000

CHAPTER NINE

In his mailbox in the Department of Foreign Languages, Grigori found a single piece of paper, folded.

His heart gave a little kick. Could it be a response at last? No, no, of course not, ridiculous to even hope. Even if Nina Revskaya did decide to write to him, surely it would not be like this, in the open, without an envelope. That squashed spider . . . Perhaps the note was from Evelyn, an invitation, some friendly suggestion. She had been away at a conference much of last week but had sent a few chatty e-mail messages. Grigori recalled that she was due back last night.

Unfolding the piece of paper, he saw that it was from Zoltan. Another photocopied page from the diary. February 1962. Zoltan would have been just twenty-nine years old; perhaps by then, after six years there, he considered London a permanent home. Grigori wondered if, in rereading these pages, Zoltan longed to be that sought-after young man again, instead of the eccentric old one he had become. Zoltan's thickly slanting letters, handwriting from over forty years ago, rushed forward:

Thursday. Gray and rainy but I like it, I do, it seems to express, I think, all the beauty and sadness of being merely human, so many of us plodding along in our overcoats, aware and unaware of who we are and our place in the rainy world. Went to a luncheon put on by a member of the House of Lords who thinks himself a poet. Who am I to contradict him, though I do wish he would use less alliteration. Samuel was there with his latest model girlfriend. I thought I knew her, then realized it was her face I had seen, without ever speaking to her, on so many advertisements and magazine covers. All around, in fact, were recognizable persons: MPs, and the blond folksinger whose name I can never remember . . . Something came over me, a longing for the wet air outside, I can't explain it, only that I felt I had to separate myself or I would become less real, less genuine. So I took my leave, early and perhaps rudely, but with that priceless feeling of sudden, exquisite freedom. It was as I was leaving that I saw the Butterfly herself, Nina Revskaya, with her sharply pretty face and dark hair. A sadness about her that I find quite beautiful, something just under the surface. Though she can't yet be forty, age shows in her hands—big, painful-looking knuckles—and in her eyes, which are a magnificent green, bright and sharp yet somehow equally pained. She surprised me by following me to the coatroom. I didn't notice until I turned around, ready to put on my coat, and there she was in a green wool dress with a fur collar. I wanted to tell you something, she said. When we spoke at the Christmas party, when you asked me about my husband and his poetry. I want you to know why I think that.

She sat down on the divan all in one movement, a Z folding itself primly, hands together on her lap, no space between her knees or ankles. "There was a day one time," she said, "when I showed frustration at the situation in my country. My husband did not share my anger. I yelled at him, 'How can you be this way? How can you act as if nothing is wrong?' He walked away, because of course it was dangerous to do what I was doing. Later that day, my husband came and sat down next to me and said to me, so quiet, he said, 'Don't you see, I have to believe in him.' He meant Stalin. He said, 'I have to believe. Otherwise, how can I get up out of bed in the morning?'"

Her face barely moved as she said this, but her intonation changed, so that I wondered if as she said it she was hearing his voice. She stood and I would like to say she looked unburdened, but she did not. She wished me good day and walked out of the room.

Having reached the end of the passage, Grigori closed his eyes. He felt deeply and abruptly sad, and somewhat guilty, as if having spied on someone. It was not mere sadness for Nina Revskaya and Viktor Elsin, nor for Zoltan and his faded diary. His sadness, he realized, was for the poems he had loved, for the innocently wistful herders of goats and sheep, the dreamy landscapes and vivid forests, the weary yet satisfied peasants whose bright hopes never seemed desperate, just pure. Surely there was some truth in them. Because if Elsin hadn't believed . . . what would it have felt like, to write poems he knew were also a form of propaganda? Was it with cynicism, too, that he had written them? It wasn't a vision Grigori liked to have of Elsin, and it always evaporated before fully taking hold. Then again, what else was a poet to do? Either you made the most of the rules and regulations, or you . . . what? Did an Esenin: slashed your wrists and wrote a poem with your blood, and then hanged yourself for good measure.

Or you escaped, like Zoltan. Lived to tell the truth. It was one of the reasons Zoltan's work mattered so greatly, each poem a message that had jumped a wall, burrowed a tunnel out of prison, survived to tell the rest of the world its news. So many others—other people, other poets—never made it. Even Zoltan's newer work, Grigori reflected, would be marked by that experience. If only someone would publish it . . .

Grigori sat down, put the page on his desk. If Viktor Elsin had really felt that, really believed, or *had* to believe, as he told his wife, then what could he have done, really, to have ended up where he did? Not that the charges would even have had to be true. It was enough to simply associate with the wrong crowd; one need not be guilty of any specific political offense. Of course, it was more attractive to think that Viktor Elsin had in fact acted subversively than to admit that he had simply toed the line. Grigori had long found a certain thrill in the thought that Elsin had, despite his seemingly naïve good faith, ultimately rebelled. *Black velvet night, pinned wide and high by pinprick stars . . .* It was the opening phrase of "Night Swimming," an uncharacteristic poem, and the one Grigori had put such stock in so many years ago. The rhythmic imbalance of his translation still bothered him—but the images and their precise wording were what had mattered most.

NIGHT SWIMMING

Black velvet night, pinned wide and high
By pinprick stars. Faces under moonlight.
Faint echoes float atop the river.
Our reckless splashes toss them here and there.

How very young we were, one floating year
Ago. Wet tresses draped our ears.
And in the air, the hum of crickets chanting
Apologies we could not, did not, hear.

Gone, gone, the forest's past perfection:
Patchwork shade, pine needle carpet,
Ocher-resin drops of sun. The air
Hums . . . Unseen, the nightingale, too late,
Thrums its stubborn song—caught somewhere
Between the deep black water and sky.

It was one of Elsin's final poems, and one of the least typical. So much melancholy. But could one call it seditious? If looking for seditious material, perhaps, that tone of regret, of loss, the water and sky so black. Yet it had made it past the censors—though that meant little in the scheme of things. Such decisions (what passed, what didn't) could at times seem nearly random; an editor might have been owed a favor, or a work was allowed into print but the number of copies, or their distribution, suppressed. And even if this poem had been explicit—or the opposite, if Elsin had never written a problematic word—what could any of it prove? Neither possibility would necessarily indicate that Elsin had done something, had acted on any thoughts, any doubts. *Unseen, the nightingale, too late . . .*

And even if he had . . . well, then *what* exactly had he done?

This pattern of thought was an old one, a loop Grigori's mind had followed many, many times. It never landed anywhere new. Yet now he felt oddly hopeful, as if the pattern might be about to break. This feeling had to do, he realized, with Drew Brooks, the way she had sounded when she told him, "I'm thinking we might be able to find something." Grigori still heard her voice in his mind, the hopefulness and possibility of her words. Had she perhaps managed to get hold of any of those jeweler's archives? Grigori felt a sudden urge to pick up the phone and dial her number. But not a full week had passed since he last spoke to her, that day at Beller. And he would have heard from her, wouldn't he, if she had found out something? *No news is good news*, he told himself—though what did that saying mean, really?

THE FIRST SCANDALOUS thing at the ballet the following season, autumn 1950, is the night one of the prima ballerinas falls. Of course dancers fall—an overzealous leap, an off-kilter pirouette, one must take risks. But this one has passed her prime; she is overweight and warms up with hot showers rather than exercise. The next thing everyone hears, she is out on medical leave.

The next day's rehearsal call has Nina listed separately from the others. In an upstairs practice room she is sternly coached by the ballet mistress, and on the following week's schedule her name is written at the very top, next to "Giselle." Giselle, the pinnacle of classical dance, from the story about the Wilis, ghosts of girls jilted on their wedding day; in the woods at night they emerge from their graves in their bridal attire and dance until dawn—but any man caught in their path must dance himself to death. For years Nina has longed to perform Giselle's *déboules en diagonale*, to spin hopelessly into insanity and then death. Now an extra line of little hooks is added at the back of both Giselle costumes, taken in to Nina's frame. She receives new pointe shoes and, for her act 2 pair, hammers the toes until they are soft and pulpy, so that they will make no sound on the stage. She wants to create the illusion of ghostly lightness—the nearly silent steps of feet that seem not to touch the floor.

Waiting for her entrance, she feels her legs begin to tremble. With her first steps, it is as if she has been set on fire, nearly numb and at the same time so hot, her face must be bright red. This opening section requires as much miming as dancing, lots of shy little runs away from Albrecht, delicate skips and hops. Girlish in her pretty peasant dress, Nina calls upon her own recent past, how it felt to be young and naïve and newly in love, the surprise and doubt and elation. *He loves me, he loves me not*—she plucks the daisy, tosses it away, Albrecht sitting next to her on the bench. Not until she has accepted his love and circled the stage with him in joyful leaps does the last of Nina's tension dissipate. Her body carries her along expertly, spinning serenely, the graceful arch of her back as she makes slow twirls on one foot and then the other. How well her feet know this floor, the steep rake of the stage, every tiny nick in the wood, each trapdoor and footlight and patch of colored tape. When it comes time for the

little hop on one toe nearly all the way across the stage, Nina's confidence is such that she tosses Albrecht a little kiss halfway through.
She feels her comrades watching from the wings, rooting for her,
critiquing her—knows Vera (who as Queen of the Wilis won't be on
until act 2) is looking on from a spot in the back, while Polina, by the
rosin box, does a last warm-up for her scene full of teasing jumps; a
perfect coquette, she is dancing the "Peasant Pas de Deux."

Now Nina has arrived at one of the most difficult parts: the "mad"
scene at the end of act 1, when Giselle learns that the handsome peasant boy supposedly in love with her is really a prince—and already
engaged to the duke's daughter. Shocked, horrified, she looks down
at the gold necklace Bathilde has given her; she tears it off, throws it
to the ground, and runs to her mother's embrace. To show Giselle's
sudden unraveling, Nina has prepared by imagining how she would
feel to be tricked like that, recalling how Viktor too first presented
himself to her—a man of simple upbringing, the woods his home—
before revealing the truth. As if in a trance, her gaze distant, her hair
fallen loose and dark against her pale face, Nina dances as though
lost, moving in halting, distracted steps, imagining how it would feel
to really be Giselle, breaking down, her mind and her body.

Tremendous applause at the close of the first act, even louder
after the difficult adagio in the second. Mother is there in the audience, happily flapping her program at Nina, but Viktor witnesses
none of this. He is home with Madame, checking her pulse, laying
cool washcloths on her forehead; she has worked up a fever and is
delirious, prostrate on her bed. Though Nina supposes she ought
to be worried for her, she knows, too, that by the time the night is
over, Madame will have miraculously recovered. It is not the first
time the old woman has fallen ill the moment Nina is to debut a
new role.

Nina tells herself it does not matter that Viktor is not here to
see it. There will be other nights like this, tonight is only the

beginning. . . . And then the performance has ended, the audience is applauding, a long, loud ovation, their claps becoming synchronized, persistent, so that Nina must take repeated bows. Only offstage does she briefly burst into tears—of relief and exhaustion.

Within just a few performances it seems she was meant for this: the audience cheers her entrances, and tosses flowers at her feet, and calls her back out so many times, she is still bowing after the orchestra has left, their seats and music stands abandoned the moment their duties have been satisfied. The concert hall is packed, patrons leaning out over the boxes as if to try to get closer to her—yet becoming perfectly still, engrossed, as soon as she begins to dance. Viktor is there, too, now that Madame has finally given up her illness and given in to her daughter-in-law's success. *Pravda* salutes Nina's "great artistry and exquisite lightness" and calls her "the Bolshoi's newest star." Within weeks she has been officially promoted.

Principal dancer: a ballerina at last. Fetching her pay from the cashier's window at the end of the month, she is handed double her old salary. And when she passes a Bolshoi advertisement on the street, it is her name in big bold print on the poster. Yet at first it all feels so tenuous; why, it might have been Vera's name, or Polina's, up on that bill, had the director decided to choose one of them instead. Probably they too have had that thought. Or perhaps they too can see, no matter their feelings, that it is Nina whose name deserves to be up there.

Blur of days and nights, of weeks and now months, as she learns new roles, one after the other, Kitri instead of the Queen of the Dryads, Princess Aurora instead of the Lilac Fairy. Her curtain call has become that of a star, the entrance just a bit slower, more stately, taking her time. She is allowed requests—extra safety pins and greasepaint, and more clips for her hair—and before performance nights spends all day in bed with her feet up on a pillow. Already she has learned to ignore the envy and faint malice that waft her way from some of the other dancers.

Her partner is Petr Raade, beloved by the public, with a haughty bearing and the most daring of jumps. Other times she is partnered by Yuri Lipovetsky, another great showman. Four years ago, on a night when Stalin himself was in attendance, Yuri was called into the Great Leader's box for a private meeting. This story Nina has heard numerous times, Yuri describing, in great detail, how Stalin sat there behind a table, very serious, with a bowl of hard-boiled eggs in front of him. "He told me," Yuri informs anyone who will listen, "that he found my style 'reflective, especially in the shoulders.' "

For four years, Yuri has been trying to tease some meaning out of this comment. When he asks Nina for her interpretation, she dares suggest that perhaps it doesn't mean much at all. After all, Stalin doesn't possess a dancer's vocabulary; perhaps he was simply trying to think of something to say.

"He's our great leader, Nina, he must have meant something."

"But he isn't a dancer. Maybe he didn't know quite what he meant. Or how to say what he meant."

Yuri squints at her. She has been too bold, to suggest that the Great Leader didn't know what he was talking about.

"What I meant was—"

"I know. But still, it must mean something."

Tête-à-têtes like this, with one of the most famous stars of the Bolshoi . . . Nina dances premieres now, and receives fan mail, and watches performances from a red armchair in the spacious, satin-lined director's box. Yet her routine remains the same, back and forth to rehearsals and performances and the obligatory political hour. Sewing satin ribbons onto her slippers, soaking the heels in warm water, bending the shanks back and forth. Mending the holes in her stockings, carefully pulling the threads back up with a tiny hook. Mondays—her day off—she spends what time she can with Mother, and in the evening scurries from one solo recital to the next, and at last rests her feet very late, dropping into bed limp as the day's

lingerie. Time with Viktor has been reduced to mere scraps of morning, of late night, and the occasional precious afternoon in between.
She loses track of which man Polina is in love with, of what is happening between Vera and Gersh. Though they still have their nights
at the Aurora—vodka, spicy radish salad, cold celery and beets with
sour cream—Nina is rarely able to join them, since, despite dancing in
fewer Bolshoi shows, she now performs on her nights off, too. It is how
the top dancers earn more on the side: private concerts and parties,
and solos at the cinema before the films start. And so on her days "off"
Nina dances even more than other days. And of course there are more
diplomatic events of the sort where she first met Viktor.

She is even given a new dressing room, larger and at stage level,
shared with the one other young premiere *danseuse*. Back into her
little sack go the contents of her dressing table, her eau de cologne
and good luck charms. Vera and Polina are not present when she
cleans out her drawer and removes her sweater and leg warmers,
tights and leotard, from the peg on the wall.

She takes a last look at the little room where so many of her
dreams—of the ballet, and of romantic love—first became real. And
yet it is just a bleak little space, with its bare lightbulb and austere
walls. The yellowed newspaper articles by Polina's aesthetician are
no longer tacked up, shrine-like, in her corner; Polina has instead
begun following Vera's much simpler beauty regimen (lanolin soap
and lukewarm water) as if it might turn Polina into a beauty, too.

Something else important happens that year—and continues,
Nina notices. Something that has nothing to with the ballet. The city,
life in their city, is improving. The shops on Gorky Street have more
goods than last year, and food is no longer scarce, plenty of crabmeat
and caviar. The fabrics, even the cuts, of dresses have improved—are
of better quality and more varied. Mother even accepts a new skirt
Nina buys for her, of a lovely flower pattern. When in November the
new shoes arrive from Czechoslovakia, there is an array of colors

and styles, in canvas as well as the usual squeaky imitation leather.

No more live wires dangling here and there. Buildings are repainted, loose stones reset, holes in the sidewalk filled. New apartment houses are rising everywhere, immense "high houses" with big square towers that grow in tiers, taller than anything Nina has ever seen. Across the city, construction cranes stretch into the sky like the skeletons of some prehistoric animal.

Just as Viktor always says—he was right after all. After so many years, things really are, finally, better.

Worker girls are repaving the streets. Passing Manezhnaya Square, Nina watches them unloading bricks from trucks, shoveling gravel, pouring hot asphalt, steam reaching at their ankles in the brisk air. They are her age, these girls—early twenties, perhaps younger—in flimsy skirts, headkerchiefs tucked into the collars of their quilted jackets. Some drive steamrollers slowly along, like royalty atop ceremonial elephants. But of course they are nothing like royalty; they are country girls brought in from the steppes, living in barracks on the outskirts of the city, carried back home each evening piled onto freight trucks like so much cargo. . . . As Nina hurries by, she is acutely, uncomfortably, aware of them lugging and lifting, smoothing the hot asphalt, transforming the square with their own physical force.

She reminds herself that she has her own burdens; all week she has felt the weight of a predicament of her own. She turns away to avoid the sight of the girls mopping their faces with their neckerchiefs. Off to the side a girl is leaning on a shovel, her head down. Though Nina tries not to look, she can't help but see. The girl's shoulders heave as she cries silently.

When Nina arrives home that evening, Viktor, reclined on the settee where he always writes, is holding a glass of liquor, looking tired and somehow sad.

"What is it?" Nina asks. "What's wrong?"

"Oh, it was to be expected. It can't be helped." He takes a swig from his glass. "The necessary speeches." The Writers Union meeting, he must mean. His voice drops very low. "Hard to sit through, though. A very long speech."

"About . . . ?"

A lazy nod, eyes half closed, as if she ought to know.

Of course: the cosmopolites. "*Bezrodnye kosmopolity*" is the phrase one hears, more and more these days. That and "alien bourgeois elements." But it is that first one, "rootless cosmopolitan," that Nina finds most telling. The usual officially cryptic language, such a brilliantly awkward substitute for "wandering Jew." Nina lowers her head as Viktor continues, in a whisper, "All the while Leo Stern was right next to me, just sitting quietly. Having to act as if it wasn't about him at all."

"It's not your fault."

"I know that."

"What I mean is, there's nothing you can do."

"Of course not." His voice returns to normal decibels. "It has to be said. Antipatriotism . . ." A loud sigh. Viktor gulps from his glass. "We have Tolstoy, we have Mayakovsky, Gorky. Our work doesn't need the West. What we need, as Comrade Stalin himself has said, are Soviet classics. 'Revolutionary clarity' . . ." As he takes another gulp of liquor, Nina sees that his hand is shaking.

"It's all right," she tells him. "You can't be expected to . . . defend people." But as she says it, she hears another thought: that someone *might* do that—someone with a death wish. That must be why she is saying this; she is telling Viktor, Don't even think of speaking out. Don't put yourself in danger. Stay safe. For me.

"I happened to see Gersh yesterday," he tells her. "By chance, on Prechistenka Street. We were walking toward each other. I saw him just when he noticed me—and he ducked his head and looked away. He was going to walk right past me. I'd been over at his place two days ago! I went up to him and said What are you doing? He said, 'I'm trying to make it easy for my friends to ignore me.' "

Nina closes her eyes. "Oh, Gersh . . . He knows we wouldn't do that."

"There was another article in the paper," Viktor says. "Yesterday. Not about him, specifically, but his name was mentioned."

Nina realizes that she is avoiding looking him in the eye. There is nothing more to say—not here, at least, not indoors, so many people around. She joins Viktor on the settee, pulling him close and laying her head on his shoulder. She waits in silence, until she is sure he has nothing else he wants to say. Now is as good a time as any to tell him.

She had planned on doing so somewhere outdoors, the only place one can have a truly private conversation. A walk outside, just the two of them. But to suggest that now, the mere words "Let's go for a walk, what do you say?" might provoke all sorts of anxieties, wondering what she could want to discuss—and she doesn't want her news to be treated as much at all.

She takes a preparatory breath and glances toward Madame's door. The light is off; she must be sleeping. Just outside their door, someone is talking on the hall telephone, saying, "Yes, but—" and sighing, over and over.

Very quietly, Nina tells Viktor what she still hasn't quite accepted herself. "I'm expecting."

Viktor's face changes—brightens so visibly, it takes Nina by surprise. "Sweetheart. How . . . utterly magnificent."

Nina looks down. "But I can't have a baby," she whispers. "Not now. It's impossible. It's not the right time. I've been principal barely three months."

Viktor doesn't understand just how difficult it is to return to dancing after a pregnancy—the toll that childbirth takes on the body, how it alters it, permanently, despite so much physical fine-tuning and careful refinement. Not to mention the lost time, so many months away from her career and training, and in these prime years. Even so, Nina never would have thought she would make this decision. Just a year or two ago the idea of having a baby with Viktor made her feel warm inside, something romantic about the very idea—not just of a child but of a family, their own family, creating one together. Now, though, it is clear to her that that dream will have to wait, and that this must be what it means to be an adult: the difficulty of choice, of decisions that really do matter.

Viktor readjusts his expression. "Right, of course." He breathes loudly through his nostrils. "Yes, well."

"I wanted you to know." Her voice is nearly silent, she whispers so softly. "I've arranged an appointment. Monday." The procedure is illegal, could mean two years in jail—but everyone does it. Well, everyone who can pay for it. Nina knows from other ballerinas whom to go to, how to proceed. Viktor gives a small nod, and it occurs to Nina that she must have chosen to tell him now, here, in this building teeming with people, on purpose: to avoid a long discussion, to have it over and done with.

Viktor reaches out and pulls her toward him, slowly, across the settee. "Come here." For the first time Nina sees in his face the very quality he always—only he, no one else—has seemed to lack. Resignation. The resigned look of tired eyes, of heavy shoulders.

Nina lies alongside him as he places his arms around her, a strong grip that is somehow more than physical. Closing her eyes, she feels herself enveloped. Only when she has fully settled into Viktor's warmth does it occur to her that his embrace, the affection in these arms, is not just for her, but for the tiny almost-being inside her.

PERHAPS SHE SHOULD call Tama. She was the one Russian friend Nina could really talk to, easily, effortlessly, without ever having to search for the right word, without that unwanted rhetorical distance. And even though Tama was younger than Nina, perhaps she too might have experienced, at times, this odd onslaught—memories passing before her like images on a screen. But their friendship was not about sharing secrets. None of Nina's friendships were. Growing up, secrets had been dangerous, and as for the few secrets Nina had once been privy to—well, even now she preferred not to think of them. Even after she left home, those same impulses (silence and self-protection) remained with her. She had never fully relaxed into the chattiness of girlish friendship, the giddy ease, the whoops of laughter and frank whispers that she heard around her, and even received, but simply could not reciprocate. No, it was impossible, even as those first real friends, in Paris and then London, had received her openly. Something in her had tightened, something had locked. It had taken only a few years until her body, too, was assailed by that same rigidity.

And so it went for love, too, though when Nina first began her new life she had carried within her, if only tenuously, some hope for romance. Nothing too passionate. Nothing overwhelming. But surely there was another sort of love, something less full and perhaps less beautiful, but perfectly adequate nonetheless. A light spring jacket instead of a fur coat. A nice soup and salad rather than the eight-course buffet. That would do, something simple. Something she could look forward to.

And there had been, in fact, numerous offers. In Paris, where she was at first a news item, she was nearly overwhelmed with suitors—but they were like gnats in her hair, even the most alluring. They blurred into each other, she could not focus on just one. Yet she enjoyed the attention, and told herself there would be someone. After all, she was still young, her mind open to so many new things. But her heart . . . No, even when she tried to will it open, first with big, jolly-faced Armand and then, after a dismayingly painless breakup, with sly, quiet Patrice, Nina's heart would not budge.

After that she had not even tried, really, to get to know anyone quite so well. It was too difficult to do what they wanted, to "open up," to say "what's on your mind." Not to mention that, deep down, she simply did not trust them. Not one. It was simply a feeling she had. In London she was frequently matched up with this Sir or that Lord, seated next to handsome bachelors and distinguished widowers. Her life had become even more public, her agenda always full. She dressed impeccably, wore jewels from her ever-expanding reserve, had her picture in the magazines. She felt not superior but separate, never truly among the London throng. If she were to be honest with herself, she would have to admit that she had never fully settled in, just bumped along from this to that, taught her students with devotion, attended opening nights and premieres, held teas for an expanding circle of perfectly nice but not close friends. A few of her old students she still heard from even now, though they too were now retired.

Most of the people from that swath of time had been forgotten. Nina might be able to find them in her mind if she tried, but she had no reason to. Except of course that the girl from Beller wondered if Nina had any "ancillary materials" relating to the jewels. Perhaps she did, somewhere, cards and notes and photographs—the French and British jewelers fawning over her, inviting her to model this and that, and the photographs in the socialite pages, and the days and nights so busy, there was simply no time for memories.

Instead these other figures kept returning, these oldest friends of all, unreachable and yet for long minutes each day, now, here, right in front of her.

"So, what happened with him?"

Nina jerked her head back.

Cynthia was sitting across from her on the divan, watching her intently, waiting, Nina supposed, for the soup to cook. "With Lord what's-his-name? Did you two go out again?"

Was this old age, then, at last? Not merely advancing years but true old-lady-ness, dementia, the past gradually overtaking present? She did not want to become one of those invalid old people who lost track of the days and could no longer tell morning from night and ate meals from their bed, crumbs in the sheets. "I . . . well—" She looked toward the window, out at the trees crusted with snow. Snowdust blew through the air like glitter.

Never had she even considered that senility might touch her. It was nothing she had witnessed in her own family—but then, so few had lived into old age.

Cynthia was saying something about boyfriends and blind dates, how she was lucky to have found Billy and be done with all that. Saying so, she paused to admire the small square diamond on her ring finger. Billy had proposed to her on Valentine's Day.

"My first husband wooed me with hibiscus flowers. Kept bringing them to me like it was all he had to do each day." She laughed. "Next thing you know I was married and living with my in-laws."

Nina looked at Cynthia, still in her nurse's scrubs and white shoes, as if meeting her for the first time. "You were married."

"From twenty-one to thirty-four. Three kids to show for it."

Nina wondered why this surprised her, that Cynthia should have a family of her own. Had she not mentioned this before, or had Nina forgotten?

"Charles and Raymond went to school in Florida and stayed on, but Penny's still here. It was just them and me that came to Boston." She paused a moment. Perhaps it was loneliness, the sudden awareness of having left everyone else behind, that silenced her. "Next month makes twelve years."

Nina heard herself asking, before she could stop herself, "And that is why you left? To leave your husband?"

"No, we'd already divorced. I just needed to get *off* the *island*, you know?"

Get off the island. Nina repeated this in her mind, and found herself nodding stiffly. The knot in her neck was not so bad today.

"Who doesn't want a better life?" Cynthia said. "Isn't that why you came here?"

So many questions—what was she doing, chatting back and forth like this? Slowly Nina said, "I really do not like to speak about it." Even as she said it, though, she could not help but be horrified, at the thought that perhaps she already had.

"How's the supplemental coming along?" Lenore seemed to possess a second sense for those times when Drew found herself in a brief moment of quandary.

"Slowly but surely," Drew chose to say, since it was basically true. Things had been going well. Catalog Production had staged the jewels for the photographers—attractive displays they spent hours arranging—and so far everything was on schedule. Soon another press release would go out from Public Relations, describing some of the more exceptional items. "I've just heard back from the entomologist who looked at the amber, and it turns out the pendant might be worth even more than we thought." She threw the "we" in just to be generous.

"Great!" Lenore said, not seeming to see the problem. Though Grigori Solodin hadn't given any conditions concerning his donation, Drew suspected he didn't know the pendant's full value. She waited until Lenore had left—after a few more breezy words about the brochure—to call him.

He seemed surprised to hear from her. Somewhat anxiously, she repeated what, according to the entomologist, a specialist had finally confirmed. "It's of a genus that's itself quite rare." She glanced at the words she'd taken down. "Genus *Archaea*, from the Archaeidae family. Apparently it was once common, but now it's usually only found in Dominican amber, not Baltic. Plus this one's perfectly centered, and with exceptional clarity."

Yet even when she gave him a revised estimate Grigori Solodin simply said, "Well, good, let's hope there's a bidding war. Science supporting the arts."

Drew laughed, though she found his easy generosity surprising. And then his tone changed. He wondered, he asked almost tentatively, if she happened to have found any of those logbooks. From the jeweler who had produced the amber suite.

Drew wished she had something more to report. "I've done a search on Anton Samoilov, the maker, but I haven't found any leads in terms of specific records from that house." Feeling she had somehow let him down, she added, "That said, I'm only able to read the English-language publications and Web pages. I imagine there might be other information available in Russian."

"I can do a search in Russian, if you'd like."

Perhaps he thought she wasn't working quickly enough. "I don't mean to make you do my work for me—"

"It's really no problem, Miss Brooks."

"You can call me Drew."

"Of course, excuse me. Drew—is it archives I'd be looking for?"

"Well, yes, although I don't expect the actual archive to be online—if there even is one for this particular maker. But *if* there is one, there might be a lead as to where to find it. The house of Samoilov is no longer in existence, so there's no one for us to contact directly."

"Oh. That's too bad."

"Not necessarily. A company that's still in business probably wouldn't make its archives public."

"Really?" Grigori Solodin sounded relieved. "So, then, we're basically looking for contact information. Who might have any records of sales from the house of Samoilov."

"Exactly. The jeweler, or rather the jeweler's family, might have records in their possession, or they may have donated them somewhere. A university, a museum, a historical society."

"In Russia?"

"Anywhere, really, depending on where the descendants ended up.

In the meantime, I'm trying to see what we might be able to find in this country. I already called Special Collections at the Public Library. They put me in touch with the Center for Russian and Eurasian Studies, out in Chicago, but that turned out to be a dead end. I've put in calls to various museums of jewelry and of Russian jewels—but that stuff is pretty much all about imperial jewels and the Hermitage, Fabergé, all that. Nothing owned by people outside of the royal family."

"If I did happen to find anything online," Grigori Solodin said, "a ledger or some sort of archive, what would the exact words be for the jewelry I'm looking for?"

"Oh, all kinds of phrases, 'amber drop earrings,' 'Baltic amber pendant,' 'cabochon with inclusion' . . ." Her pen was already moving as she spoke: *surmounted . . . gold fittings . . . bezel-set . . . oval frame . . . 14-karat yellow gold . . . 56 zolotnik.* "I'll have to write them out for you. I can e-mail you a list. Again, I don't mean to make you do my work. If and when you do find anything, I can of course hire a translator."

Grigori Solodin said, "You know, Drew, I *am* a translator."

"You are?" Her mind rushed, wondering if this was something she ought to have known.

"Well, not the kind you have in mind, I suppose. I'm a literary translator. Of Russian poetry."

"Oh! I love poetry."

"Do you?" Sounding truly curious, he asked, "Which poets do you like?"

"Well, I'm no English major, but I like to read poems. I took a class in college and still have all the books. I like Sylvia Plath and Howard Nemerov. And Edna St. Vincent Millay. And George Herbert and ee cummings. Oh, and I love Shakespeare. I suppose Pablo Neruda is the one poet whose work I have in translation." Jorge, a man she dated briefly the year she first moved to Boston, had given her that one.

"An excellent array."

"Nothing terribly original, I'm afraid."

"What does that matter? All that matters is that it moves you."

"I'll have to remind myself that whenever I start thinking my taste ought to be more sophisticated."

"Who started you worrying about *that*? The very fact that you read, Drew—I mean that of your own volition you open a book. Of poetry, no less!"

She laughed. "My ex-husband used to write poetry. Back when we were in college. But he had great disdain for pretty much anything they would teach in a classroom." Recalling the faith she had had in him, she felt briefly sad at how quickly, how easily, he had left his literary dreams behind when he settled in at his first job, for the communications department of a hospital. "He had all kinds of theories about verse versus prose. I remember how horrified he was when I confessed that— Uh-oh."

"What?"

"If I tell you this, then I'm confessing to you, too."

"Please, confess." He sounded like he was smiling. In her mind Drew saw the three lines in the side of his cheek.

"All right. Actually, I wonder, as a translator, what you'll think. It's that even though I love all kinds of poetry, even now, what I find I like the most . . . Oh, this is embarrassing."

"You're keeping me on pins and needles here."

"Well, what I tend to prefer are poems that . . . rhyme."

Grigori Solodin gave a brief delighted yelp.

"Not a Hallmark card type of rhyming, nothing like that. Not hard exact rhymes at the end of every line. But a more obvious matching of sound, you know?"

"Yes, I do. I know exactly."

"It's just something I figured out about myself, that I'm not always very good with free verse. I don't always know quite what to do with it. Whereas with some sort of even vague rhyme, or metrical scheme, or any kind of formal parameters, I suppose, there's at least something holding it together for me." Realizing that she had been talking about herself, perhaps for too long, Drew quickly added, "Which poets have you translated?"

She heard him take a breath. "Just one, professionally. The poet Viktor Elsin. Nina Revskaya's husband."

So that was the connection. Though she had mentioned Elsin in the biographical notes in the catalog, Drew knew little about him. But now a single puzzle piece fell into place, the reason that Grigori Solodin owned a pendant linked to Revskaya's collection. It must be because of her husband, whose work he had translated; perhaps Grigori Solodin was a collector of the poet's memorabilia. But if that were the case, why hide that fact from Drew? Why hadn't he simply explained to her his reason for owning the necklace? Drew's imagination whirred as she said, with slight embarrassment, "I knew her husband was a poet, but I didn't realize his poems were anything anyone read—I mean—that's not what I meant to say. In English, that is—I didn't realize his work was . . . available."

"No one does." That dry joking tone he sometimes used.

"I'd love to see it."

"His poetry?" Grigori Solodin's surprise was audible.

"Your translations. I'd very much like to see them."

"Oh, certainly. I can put some in the mail to you, I'd just need to photocopy them—"

"I can come pick them up. And I can bring the other things with me. The phrases for the Samoilov search."

"That would be very good."

"I can come by tomorrow, after work."

Tomorrow he was busy, and the following day she was meeting her friend Kate at a wine tasting. They settled on Thursday. "Would five thirty be all right?"

"I'll be here." Grigori gave her the department's address and told her where to find him.

"Excellent. And I'll bring you a list of phrases to look for in Russian."

Even after she had hung up the phone, she could hear Grigori Solodin's voice, that very slight accent, saying in a light, easy way, "See you."

NOT LONG AFTER her recovery, Nina and Viktor join Gersh and Vera at one of the few nightclubs in town. The hour is late enough—and the crowd sufficiently devoid of anyone official-looking—that the band has begun playing American jazz. Gersh, more inebriated than usual, recites a long Georgian toast that has them all laughing.

Then it seems the band has made an error, the rhythm is off. After a few awkward measures the music finds a traditional rhythm, no longer resembles anything close to jazz.

Nina and the others glance toward the entrance. A group of Party men, hefty in their big coats. With them are their women, each with a big silver fox neckpiece. And then Nina spots among them—sporting her own silver fox over her left shoulder, and the bright tangerine lipstick that is so popular—Polina.

Seeing Nina and Vera, Polina waves extravagantly. She grabs her man by the arm and guides him over to the table, smiling, her faint freckles glowing. "Look who's here!"

Polina introduces the man, Serge is his name. Surprisingly handsome, tall and square-jawed, smooth gold-brown hair contrasting with dark eyes; he has the stern, slightly aloof expression of a trolley conductor inspecting tickets. A bit younger than the lackeys Polina usually goes with. The prideful look about him seems to come from strength rather than alcohol and too many potatoes. Nina is surprised to note, from the reserved familiarity with which

Vera and Gersh greet him, that this is not the first time the two couples have met.

Serge too is somewhat reserved, perhaps not wanting to appear, to his fellow Party men, too friendly with Gersh. Vera has pulled up a chair from the empty table next to her, while Polina takes a seat next to Viktor. He gives her a solicitous smile, already leaning toward her—but Nina knows that is just the way he is, and bristles only slightly as Polina beams coyly back at him.

Serge has taken the seat beside Vera, asking, "And how is your Achilles?" in a concerned, somehow intimate tone. "Better, I hope?" Vera injured herself last week, not long after the article mentioning Gersh was published. Viktor teasingly calls it a "sympathizer's injury." But Nina doesn't find it funny; there are few things more frustrating to a ballerina than not being able to dance.

"If all goes well," Vera says calmly, that slight distance in her tone, "I should be back by the end of next week." She brushes her hair back with a little fluttery movement, her fingers long and thin.

"Good, good." Though Serge barely smiles, there is something fawning in his manner; it is the effect Vera has on all men, really—something wounded about her, with her great dark eyes and thin, pale frame. Even Viktor at times seems undone by her. In that same concerned voice, as if Gersh were not even present, Serge tells Vera, "I know Polina misses you on the nights you're not in the dressing room with her."

"I told him about our tongue-twister contest," Polina puts in brightly, laughing, her tangerine lips wide; she must not see anything lecherous in Serge's allusion to the dressing room. Vera too laughs, and as Polina begins to explain to the rest of them, Nina realizes, with something like shock, that Polina and Vera have somehow, without Nina even noticing, become friends.

The feeling that takes hold of her is much like the jolt she felt just a few weeks ago, when, on her night off, she went to visit Mother, only to find that she was not home. Worried, Nina waited, went out for a bit, then returned, quite late. Still in her coat, Mother had just gotten back, her cheeks rosy and cold from the night air, smiling proudly as she explained—as if it were the most natural thing in the world—that she had been at the Bolshoi; Vera had a new solo, which she had of course wanted to see.

Serge has caught the waiter's eye, raises his hand to command two more glasses and vodka for the table. Nina finds herself thinking that finally Polina has found someone who isn't quite such a lummox. She has moved up, if one can call it that, from jowly hangers-on to a more senior bureaucrat. At least, that's how it looks. Though younger than the others, this man appears to have some real power. But does Polina really want to be like those fat Nomenklatura wives? All the time Nina hears about the fall from grace of this or that government official.

With surprising speed, the waiter delivers Serge's order. They raise their glasses as Serge proposes a toast: "To tomorrow, bright budding flower."

It's a line from one of Viktor's poems—and something of a catchphrase these days. Another reminder of how popular his latest volume has become, though it still surprises Nina to hear Viktor's words on someone else's lips. His career, like Nina's, has fully taken flight, not to mention that his income has doubled. Just last month he was appointed editor of a new arts magazine, as well as writing his usual column for *Literaturnaya gazeta*. And this coming year, as a reward of sorts, he is being dispatched along with two journalists to Paris, on a "goodwill" mission.

The vodka slides down Nina's throat. Polina says, "Oh, they're waiting for us, we had better go join them." She and Serge take their leave, and the way Serge's eyes linger on Vera, Nina understands why he agreed to stop at their table.

When they have gone, Gersh grumbles, "That man looks like a trout."

"Don't be jealous, now," Vera says, though with his slightly crossed eye and lowered reputation Gersh can hardly be blamed for feeling that way. Quietly, Vera adds, "He's the sort you want on your side, you know. We ought to thank Polina."

Nina cannot help but glance toward their table, with the other men like Serge (who really doesn't look anything like a trout) and the women in their bright orange lipstick. Viktor, with a brief, dismissive sigh, as if having reached the end of some sad story, simply says, "Poor Polina."

LOT 58

Unmounted Fancy Pear-Shaped Pink Diamond. The modified brilliant weighing 2.54 cts., natural color, clarity VVS1. $100,000–150,000

CHAPTER TEN

Mounting the steep steps of the Department of Foreign Languages, Drew could hear voices, faint, growing louder. The secretary's desk was empty, but there were more voices now, coming from down the hall, English being spoken with a Spanish accent. . . . Here was his office, "Grigori Solodin" engraved in a plastic nameplate on the door. Below the nameplate, scrawled on a big yellow Post-it, was a message:

Drew,
Called to dept. meeting, very sorry. I tried your office but you'd left. Book is below. You can leave rest for me in my box. Please excuse this hasty note,

GS

Her heart, absurdly, fell. She couldn't have said why; the book was right here, propped up on the carpet against his office door. She picked it up and placed it in her leather satchel, removing the list she had typed out for Grigori Solodin. Sliding the page into his mailbox, she told herself that it was better he was not here. This way she could go straight home and have an early night, for once.

She needed a quiet evening, a good night's sleep. Tomorrow she would be up late again, flying out of Logan straight from work; Kate had found a last-minute deal and convinced her to come along, the Caicos Islands, four days, five nights, airfare and hotel included. All week Drew had been throwing things into the travel bag that sat unzipped in the corner of her bedroom, growing a messy heap.

From the other end of the hallway, she could hear voices. Now it was a French accent, and someone else cutting in, the words muted behind the door. Perhaps that was where Grigori Solodin was right now, at that meeting.

At home she found she had no appetite for dinner. She twisted open a jar of olives and poured herself a glass of wine, then curled up in the corner of the big lumpy sofa. Opening the book of Viktor Elsin's poems, she read Grigori Solodin's brief foreword, in which he explained the many difficult editorial decisions he had had to make—that as much as sound itself was important to these poems, in general he had chosen to forgo Elsin's more rigid rhyme and metrical schemes in favor of closer approximation of his imagery and phrasing. As Drew turned the page, though, she was seized by an old, familiar fear, one that had begun all the way back in elementary school and that, perhaps thanks to Eric, she had never quite overcome: that the poems might be beyond her, that she might not quite understand. Even in college she had worried she might misread a poem and say something embarrassing in class.

To her surprise she found these poems—the early ones, at least—simple and delightful. Some were like songs, little ditties, sweet and joyous. Others were longer, their tone sometimes mysterious, sometimes romantic—yet their meaning, it seemed to Drew, was fairly straightforward. One later poem she liked so much she copied it into her notebook:

SUNDAY

This autumn is our first together,
Like good bread shared, the warm crusts passed
Across a table, or our shadows cast
As one, pulsing, by the lantern's flicker.

Sunshine slides down from the hills,
Over your hair. The light around you dances
In air, illuminating the yellow branches—
But we two revel in our stillness.

Let us lie down by the river,
The wind dress us in scattered leaves
And sing of its travels, its former lives,
And make the skin of the water quiver.

Drew liked its physicality, its sensuality, the natural world and
the two lovers within it, the purity of the images despite, or perhaps
because of, their innuendo: this couple conjoined, a pair, a true pair-
ing. It was the way Drew still, perhaps stubbornly, allowed herself to
view love—though really she knew better. Her mistaken marriage
was itself a product of romanticized notions, the excitement of those
first two years, of being "in love": the late nights and long mornings
together, love notes tucked into books and slipped under doors, that
one tortured telephone call and fevered reconciliation, and, finally,
after their engagement, the appealing idea that now Drew too had a
love story to tell and, like so many people around her, could be loved
in this universal, public way, with a shiny diamond on her finger.

The very recollection made Drew blush with shame, recalling
what it had felt like to be "engaged," the way the diamond caused

people to reassess her—their palpable appreciation that Drew was loved by someone, was someone worth loving. It was the sort of approval she had never felt from her parents at any of her other decisions (to major in art history instead of something practical, or to take a job at an art gallery no one had ever heard of). How thoroughly *good* she had felt at the engagement party, in her neat blue skirt and matching top with the sailor's collar, like a young betrothed out of an old movie, happy and hopeful and smartly dressed, her hair in a neat bob. At last she had done something right.

Drew tried to stop the inevitable momentum of these thoughts, that same old loop, back to what it could have meant to have remained in that other life. She might have had a baby by now—had always thought she would, had planned on it, two children, she had hoped, so that they would always have each other and not be odd and introspective the way she herself had turned out. Now, though, who knew. At her age, it wouldn't be much longer, just a few years' time, probably, before the possibility would have fully receded.

But that was the price she would pay, Drew supposed, for attaching such dreams—of children, of a family—to the fantasy of romantic love, to that distracting vision of what true love might be: couplehood based on a connection Drew had yet to feel with anyone, really. Sometimes, when she thought about it too much, she became nearly panicked, at the fact that as much as she would have liked a family of her own, she had already, in a way, made a decision. By not actively seeking remarriage, by not prioritizing that search, by resigning herself to the impossibility of such luck, she was in fact giving up that other dream.

Poor Jen hadn't had a chance when she signed Drew up for that dating Web site. As if Drew could have abided more than those few dates, the protracted meals at sushi bars and Irish pubs and "Asian fusion" restaurants, with men who laughed, surprised and slightly uncomfortable, when Drew spoke with excitement about her favorite paintings in the MFA or a movie at the Harvard Film Archive, men who chewed gum and jiggled their legs and spent spare moments playing with their cell phones. . . .

Stop it, Drew told herself, as she always did when her thoughts looped this way. She focused again on the book on her lap, even read a few of the poems aloud. They were arranged chronologically, and as the book progressed Drew found they changed slightly, remained sweet but with a nostalgic tone, sometimes wistful, sometimes closer to melancholy. She knew that these were approximations, that they would sound different in their original Russian; it was Grigori Solodin who had turned them into something Drew could understand. She found herself moved by the thought—that he had brought these poems to her, by finding the right words.

She imagined translation to be a solitary task, as solitary as the reading she herself did at home each night, and the research she did in the library and online at Beller. Or did Grigori Solodin show other people his work in progress, discuss the poems, and his translations, with them? Well, even if he did, a project like this—meticulous and sincere—came from the core, no matter how many people you discussed it with. Drew knew this from her own work. In the end there was just you and your heart.

In that way, it occurred to her, she and Grigori Solodin had their work in common: behind-the-scenes, unglamorous but necessary, and best undetected. All that effort, to deliver something beautiful to the public. Of course Grigori Solodin's work took real talent, while Drew's mainly took patience. But both were painstaking, and both required great care and the sort of focused attention that, if you allowed yourself to give in to it, and gave in to the great reward of it, became itself a form of devotion.

The thought made Drew feel less alone, or perhaps more happily alone, sitting there cross-legged on the sofa. It was the comfort of knowing that she was not quite so strange, that there were other people who found delight in private challenges and quiet lives. People who lived in their thoughts as much as in the real, physical world. It was a reminder that true dedication to one's work, to one's art, was in fact—no matter how quiet or minor it might seem—a show of faith, a commitment to life. As for what Jen and Stephen and Kate said, that Drew spent too much time in books and in her mind, well, it was probably true. But it was also true that the internal world was an expansive one, always growing, full of possibilities that the real one did not necessarily offer.

WINTER 1951. MOONLIGHT stretches the warped shadows of buildings, enormous and looming, over the square. Nina feels their presence like a weight above her as she crosses, shivering, toward the Bolshoi. Already the building is swarming with security guards. The ones at the entrance hold bayoneted rifles across their chests and, though Nina has become a recognizable face, make her show a special pass with her photograph on it, which they scrutinize coldly before allowing her in. For the rest of the night she will be made to show this pass, again and again, to enter her dressing room, the makeup room, the bathroom . . . even before stepping onstage (when she will have to tuck the stiff little card somewhere under her costume and pray it doesn't slip out).

Inside, theater people scurry around terrified, as always on such nights. Before, Nina might have felt this way too, nervous and anxious to please. After all, Stalin appears in public just twice a year, at Red Square for the May Day parade and at the air show every July; these theater visits are therefore all the more portentous. Nina wouldn't have thought anything could distract her from the knowledge of Iosef Vassarionovich himself being among her audience. But now, even as she applies her makeup and secures her bun with a squadron of hairpins, Nina can't stop thinking about Vera, about what Gersh has gone and done. . . . She tries to prevent her thoughts from continuing. Concentrate. Think only of the dance.

Tonight's ballet is *Don Quixote*, and she is wearing Kitri's flirtatious Spanish costume, the skirt layered with red frills that flip back and forth as Nina hurries to the practice room. She runs through her warm-up routine, hand resting lightly on the barre, swinging her legs forward and back to loosen her hips. Take deep breaths. . . . This is the first time the Great Leader will be watching Nina dance, and in the lead role—a technically demanding one, at that.

The door opens and Polina enters in her street dancer outfit, official pass in hand, leg warmers scrunched up around her knees (where she often complains of tendonitis). "Ugh, they're everywhere." Through the little square window in the door, Nina can see the top of a security guard's frowning forehead. By now these men are thoroughly dispersed throughout the concert hall, dressed as ushers, or in civilian clothes, even seated in the orchestra pit with the musicians.

"I didn't realize you were dancing tonight."

"I'm Vera's replacement. Her Achilles is bad again. I'm so nervous!" The room fills with the heavy scent of Polina's perfume as she stretches her legs, points her toes, one foot and then the other, and then up onto the balls of her feet for some *relevés*. Her voice tense, she adds what she has come here to say: "I suppose you heard what her so-called love has gone and done."

"He must have had no other choice," Nina says, rolling her head left and right to warm up the neck. "That's all I can think." What he has done, as Nina has just learned from Viktor, is to go off and marry Zoya.

"Clearly he doesn't love her," Nina adds. "Zoya, I mean. He just needs her as . . . you know. A front."

"What do you mean?"

"She's a Party member, well respected. She told him that maybe she could help him. With the way the tide has turned."

"She said that?"

"According to Gersh. He told Viktor that Zoya came to him with the idea—that it was her suggestion they marry."

"*Her* suggestion?" Polina's eyes open wide. "That woman stops at nothing!" As if she herself knows Zoya, and it is only natural. . . . A *tsk* sound, and a shake of her head. "She really will do anything to win Gersh back."

And yet why would she want to, Nina wonders, if things are really so bad for him? Perhaps Zoya's position in the Party protects her—as Vera wouldn't be protected, if Gersh married her instead. Thinking this, Nina says, "After all, he's protecting Vera, in a way."

That too Viktor told her—that Gersh couldn't bear to put Vera through this latest wave of darkness. Not after what she has already been through.

And anyway, Viktor added, all this would be short-lived, surely, you know politics, this sort of thing never lasts all that long. . . . Even a year or two ago, Nina might not have been able to see the situation quite so clearly.

"Well, I hate him." But Polina says it without venom. In fact she looks exhausted, deep wells of gray under her eyes despite the thick layer of stage makeup.

"Are you all right?" Nina asks. Perhaps it is just nerves.

Polina looks away. "I've been having trouble sleeping."

"Maybe Uncle Feliks can give you something." It's the pet name they have for the main Bolshoi doctor, whom every one of them has had to see at some point or other.

"Oh, I imagine it will go away on its own." Then, as if to change the subject, "I can't believe Gersh."

"For all we know it doesn't even mean much of anything," Nina says. "Maybe it's just a matter of signed papers. Maybe nothing much will change."

"I suppose." Polina is scratching her neck, and only now does Nina note the faint red splotches there. Her chest, too, Nina sees, is covered with pale red welts.

"I think you have some kind of rash." She really must be nervous; Nina has seen this sometimes, during previous visits by the Great Leader—people so excited they break into hives.

"I don't know what it is. I've had them for days. They go away, and then they come back. I thought my makeup would cover them up."

"You really should see Uncle Feliks."

"I did. He thought it was an allergy. That I ate a bad egg."

"Well, try not to scratch."

"I'm trying, believe me, I have such sensitive skin, you know."

The door swings open, the assistant stage manager calling, "Five minutes."

"No down, no feathers," they tell each other, as Nina turns to leave. Her entrance is in the first scene following the prologue. "And don't scratch!" she adds, before heading downstairs.

WAITING BACKSTAGE, IN the downstage wing, Nina looks out anxiously, across the tops of the heads of the musicians, over to the front of the opposite side of the stage. There, above the orchestra, draped with long red curtains forming a shield from the rest of the audience, is an armored side loge: Box A, where a cluster of bodyguards surrounds the Generalissimo himself. Nina sees them there and, searching, just barely glimpses him, seated behind a table. Broad shoulders, heavy cheeks, thick sweep of grayed hair. He really is here, really will be watching her perform Kitri's twirls and arch-backed leaps.

The fact is, he has his favorites. Marina Semyonova, for one. And fearless, flirty Olga Lepeshinskaya, a delegate to the Supreme Soviet of the RSFSR, no less, who despite her compact build and less classical line Stalin has nicknamed "Dragonfly." Well, it doesn't matter, Nina tells herself, as she dips her pointe shoes in the rosin box and makes sure the little drawstrings on top aren't sticking up. Already, now that the prologue has ended, she feels that combination of sweat and chill that sometimes overtakes her before a first entrance. Focus, she tells herself, take a deep breath and stay focused.

But thoughts slip in, about Gersh, and Vera. . . . A flash of recollection, Gersh on Nina's own wedding day, grinning beside her and Viktor at the registry office, in his baggy suit with its faint smell of damp laundry . . .

Focus, concentrate. You are Kitri, Lorenzo's strong-willed daughter; no one tells you what to do. You are fierce and flirtatious and in love. Let everything else fall away.

She knows it will, that as soon as she steps onstage little else will matter—that in the midst of dancing, any misery, no matter how grave, becomes instantly somehow less, lessened. Even during the war, when each day brought news of devastation, and hunger sat like a sharp stone inside her, Nina's anemic body always awoke to dance, always found some reserve of strength that she hadn't known she possessed. Sometimes she even feels rapture, becoming one with the music, no longer a person but simply movement, euphoric, a complete obliteration of the crises of the world. The physical sensation of dancing—despite the constantly sore feet and bruised legs and sweaty tights stained yellow from rosin—has always managed to erase other hardships.

Now the dressers are making one last check of her costume and hair, and the prop man hands her her frilly black fan. For act 1 the stage has been converted into a bustling town square, and the moment Nina runs confidently out from the wings and with a flourish of her hand whips out her fan, the audience begins applauding.

Nina is smiling broadly, proudly; this opening sequence is what establishes Kitri's personality, her bright self-assurance. She is a flirt and a free spirit, but she knows what she wants.

Following Minkus's spirited waltz, Nina revels in the leaps and kicks and high jumps her body loves. She feels strong and light, sure of her fast chaîné turns. She greets her Spanish girlfriends in mime and flirts with some of the young men, all the while aware that Stalin is watching—yet even as she makes her sequence of leaps around the square, slapping the ground firmly with her fan, Nina feels fully in control. When she dances her first variation, clicking her castanets defiantly, her *sissonnes* are fully split, so that as she arches her back in midair, her head points back parallel to her leg and her arm behind her almost touches her outstretched back foot. Petr, her Basilio for the night, hasn't let his nerves get the best of him; he supports Nina's pirouettes smoothly and for the one-handed lifts overhead is as brazen as he is secure, pressing Nina high up into the air as if such a thing is easy and utterly natural.

Between acts, she and Petr head to the backstage corridor, to wait in the side hall at the principals' table. From there they have a clear view of the door to Box A, right there at the side, and Nina can't help glancing at it every few minutes. She wonders what might happen if that door were to open, how it would feel to be spoken to by—or even to speak to—*him*. She has fantasized about it often enough, always with a little skip of the heart. She has imagined how gracious she would be, what a good impression she might make, if only she could keep from fainting. Now, though, another thought comes to her: that if only he knew what was happening to Gersh, surely Stalin could do something to help him.

Or perhaps he does know. How could he not? The most powerful man in the nation . . .

And yet, if that door were to open, would she really be able to speak out, to ask him for help? The thought overwhelms her. She tries not to think too much, tries to focus on the ballet. If only she herself possessed, offstage, Kitri's strength of nerve. . . . Petr too is quiet. He too must be wondering about Box A, perhaps thinking about Yuri's story, about being called in to speak to Stalin, imagining what that might be like.

Then their break has ended, they are back on the stage Nina knows so well, her fears falling away, and there is only the feeling of her body, dancing.

When the ballet has finished and she takes her curtain call, bowing first to the side loges as always, Nina pauses at that most important one, acknowledging that *he* is there. Then she continues as usual, to the center and then the back of the house before smiling up at the balconies. After she has acknowledged the conductor and the orchestra members, a surge of applause for their work, Nina departs from routine, turning once more to Stalin's box, performing a deep *révérence*. Only after the curtains have rushed together before her, muffling the applause on the other side, does Nina realize that she has been pleading, with her body, for him to help her.

At home, late that night, wholly exhausted, curled up in the not yet warm bed, she asks Viktor why Zoya would marry Gersh, no matter her feelings for him, no matter her competition with Vera. "She's such a social climber—at least she strikes me that way. What does she have to gain?"

From the hallway come the sounds of the man next door yelling at his wife in Armenian. "You know Zoya," Viktor says, "how she gets worked up about things. She's an organizer. A planner. It's her job, she always loves a project. Maybe that's how she sees Gersh."

The wife screams something back, even louder than her husband.

"A project." Nina recalls first meeting Zoya at Gersh's, the big to-do she made over the tea and the chipped cups, as though nothing pleased her as much as a bit of a fuss. "But it's such a bad time for him. I'm surprised she would take on a project like *that*."

"Gersh says it's because she'll do anything to not have to keep living with her parents and sisters," Viktor says. "But you know what a cynic he is."

Nina's thoughts land back at what Polina said: that Zoya would do anything to win Gersh back. Nina considers her own feelings for Viktor, the ferocity of her love, and has to conclude that really Polina is the one who, instinctually, without a second thought, without even knowing Zoya, put her finger on what is surely closest to the truth.

Viktor's hands cup Nina's face. "We're so lucky. We were able to follow our hearts. Not everyone gets that chance."

It's true, the incredible luck of it, Viktor next to her in this bed, his warm palms against her face, thumbs stroking her cheeks. Just the smell of his skin can bring her exhausted body back to life, no matter how tired she is.

"But what about Vera?" she asks. "What's going to happen to her?"

"If Gersh has his way, nothing different from what she's always had with him. Only now it will have to be on the sly. I told him I'd be their go-between."

Nina sighs, as Viktor's hands move down her skin, thumbs stroking her shoulders. "As though it's some child's game." The yelling next door has set the cat off, crying in the corridor. And though Nina's limbs tremble with fatigue, and sleep calls heavily to her, she cannot stop from reaching for Viktor, wanting no space at all between them, just the movement of his muscles against hers.

BY THE TIME the "emergency" meeting came to a close, Grigori felt he might strangle someone. If he were not the department chair, if he were not quiet, slightly aloof Grigori Solodin, if he were anyone else, he might have sat this one out, or at least left early. But no, he had sat through the entire "emergency," aware that at some point

Drew Brooks would be in the same building, expecting him, looking and not finding him there.

The meeting was, in fact, a bit of an emergency, their first-choice
hire for the new Slavic Studies slot having suddenly bowed out. They
needed to find a replacement as soon as possible, had two other can-
didates to choose from—but of course Walter and Hermione completely disagreed on which one was better suited, and spent an hour
and five minutes going back and forth about their respective picks.
They loved meetings like this, the longer the better; why decide
anything over the phone, or via e-mail, if you could hold a lengthy,
contentious meeting instead? Grigori knew he was being hard on
them, yet it was true, that was how they were, this was their life,
what made them feel good, subcommittees and search commit-
tees and "emergency" meetings. Had they no one to go home to—
Grigori grumbled to himself as he let himself into his own cold, dark
house—had they nothing better to do? No sense of time passing, of
how short life was, how quickly time sped by, especially when you
calculated it (as Grigori often had, before Christine died) in broken
toasters, or new coats of house paint, or Christmas cards indistin-
guishable from one year to the next.

He turned the thermostat up, put his coat in the closet, poured
himself a Scotch. Drew, showing up to find his door locked, the book
propped against it, or perhaps it had slid to the floor, like an old sinking tombstone . . . Well, Grigori told himself, probably she was glad
not to have to talk to some old Russian professor; probably she was
on her way out somewhere, meeting up with the boyfriend he had
met at the ballet.

From his briefcase he took the page she had typed up for him—
neatly, patiently, all the possible phrases he might look for in Russian
describing the amber pieces and the jeweler who had made them.
He turned on his computer, shifted the keys to Cyrillic. At first,
typing in the name of the jeweler and a few key terms regarding the

pendant, waiting for the search engine to whiz through its calcula-
tions, Grigori felt hopeful. A wealth of facts at his fingertips. But it
quickly became apparent, as he tried yet another possible combination of words, in every possible Russian variation, that much of what
appeared before him was repeated information, the same Web links
over and over, so that there was really not so much at all.

Frustrated, Grigori typed yet another phrase in Russian and
braced himself for the slew of unrelated information that would now
litter his computer screen. Mostly other auctions or antique dealers,
and lots of Russian Web sites. As for the house of Anton Samoilov,
Grigori found nothing like the mark books Drew had described.
When he typed in anything about archives or family logbooks, he
instead found all kinds of unrelated people by that name listed, while
a separate, irritating box kept popping up on top of everything else,
flashing on and off, with the words, *Are you a SAMOILOV? Find
other SAMOILOVs on FamilyTree.com. Free 24-hour trial.*

Clicking on the corner of the box to make it disappear, Grigori
could not help recalling the first time he had truly considered the
idea of a family history, when he was a young boy newly arrived in
Norway. His teacher had given an assignment: Go home and write
out your family tree. Grigori had at first taken on the project with
excitement, drawing a not very lifelike tree and listing all he could
from what Katya and Feodor told him of their parents and their parents' parents, the sisters and brothers and aunts and uncles. But their
information—the precise details he craved—was not nearly as complete as he had hoped. He began to wonder again, as he did every
so often, about those other parents, his birth parents. Though his
adoption had not been kept secret from him, each time Grigori asked
for more information about who those other people had been, his
parents simply said they did not know.

And so, as he questioned his mother that evening about her
and Feodor's ancestry, and added the information to his artlessly

sketched family tree, Grigori had felt that it was just a story, one that in reality had little to do with him. "What's wrong? Why do you look that way?" Katya asked, and when Grigori told her his feelings— that he could not help but wonder, could not help but feel shut out from his own original lineage—closed her eyes and gave a decisive nod. Then she stood and went into the bedroom, and brought back the stiff vinyl pocketbook. "You're a big boy now. And really this belongs to you." It contained, she added, the only information they had been given: a hospital certificate, some letters folded together into a small square wad, two photographs tucked in between them, and a few other odds and ends. No identity card. No name. Still, here was proof of an actual woman, his mother, who had indeed existed, had given him life. She was a dancer, Katya said, a dancer with the ballet—that was all the information the nurse had been able to tell them. That and the fact that the dancer (here Katya's face was long, her voice grave) had not survived.

THE NEXT DAY, Nina returns home from visiting Mother to find Vera sitting at the wooden table. Across from her, seated proudly in a bird-soiled dress, clucking disapproval, is Madame.

"Men today," she says. "They have no manners. No one holds the door for a lady. No one helps you with your coat." Shaking her head so that the big natty bun moves back and forth, the tortoise-shell comb flashing its tiny embedded diamonds. She doesn't seem to notice Nina. "A country of boors. No wonder my heart has stopped beating."

Vera looks thinner and paler than usual. When Nina tells her hello, she looks up, but Madame hasn't heard. "As for that woman, she can't hold a candle to you, I'm sure. Here, dearest, have some more tea."

Even Viktor's mother, then, can't help but be attracted to Vera.

A loud, desperate squawking issues from Madame's room. And then, as if the bird understands what she is saying: "*S'il vous-plaît!*" Lola, angry at being left there in her cage.

Only then does it occur to Nina that Viktor might not want Vera to witness this—Madame in her ancient dress, flaunting her patrician past. Vera, though, sitting so still, doesn't seem to even notice. Her eyelashes flutter when she wipes a few tears from her cheeks.

"I know how you feel," Madame says, her voice suddenly soft. "I know how it is to lose the one you love. I lost my husband. I had everything taken from me."

Vera looks so frail, those narrow shoulders, the sad slant of her neck. . . . Nina goes to her and embraces her, tells her, "It's going to be all right." But now Madame, too, appears to be crying. "He gave me these," she says with a sniffle, gesturing to her neck at the short strand of plump pearls she always wears. "They came all the way from Japan. Sea pearls, from oysters." She lifts them from her neck, and Nina can see that the string is rotting. Already a few of the pearls have shifted.

"They should be restrung," Nina says. "I can find someone—"

"I will not remove them. Pearls must be worn, or they lose their color." Proud jut of her chin. "I never take these off."

Nina says, "It's just that it looks like you might lose some pearls— see?" She reaches out to where the string is visibly deteriorated, but Madame flings up her arms.

"You are NOT to touch my hair."

In the bedroom, Lola squawks. "*S'il vous-plaît!*"

Nina pulls her hand back, looking to Vera for support, but she has shed more tears and is wiping at them desperately. The quick, small movements of long, smooth white hands. Petersburg affects, Grandmother would have said: little flurried gestures, a prideful tilt of the head. Madame, looking past Nina, tilts her head at Vera, narrows her eyes as if suddenly recognizing something. She lifts her lorgnette and squints into it. "You look like Sonia." New tears emerge from her eyes. "Her very coloring. Here, have some more tea."

During the following weeks, Vera often accompanies Nina back home from rehearsal or after performances, to wait for a message from Viktor. Though her Achilles is improved, Vera has been dancing less than usual, until her injury has fully healed. The rest of her time (apart from sleeping, at Mother's apartment) is spent here at Nina's, since Viktor's messages from Gersh are often impromptu; Vera never knows when Gersh might find himself suddenly free of Zoya, and summon her. At the table with Madame, she plays cards and sips tea, while Madame reminisces, or counts the silverware, or bosses slow, weary Darya, or declares herself without a pulse. Vera seems not to find this anything more than slightly odd, but Nina can't help being aware that now there is one more person who knows about Viktor's lineage.

"Zoya's supposed to be leaving for Katovo this evening, for a show tomorrow," Vera explains one afternoon when Nina has arrived home to find her there at the table with Madame and squawking Lola. Darya is in the kitchen down the hall, angling for a stove on which to prepare their supper. "Viktor will tell me when it's safe to go over there."

Nina wonders if Vera might perhaps, somehow, come to enjoy her new status as the "other woman."

Lola is poking at something propped on the table. Stepping closer, Nina sees that it is a framed photograph: two young women, with a young man in between them. "I've never seen that."

Madame looks annoyed to have to share it with Nina, too. "Here I am," she says, "with my sister and brother." As she says it, her face changes, softens. The young man, looking older than his sisters, is tall and slender and wears some kind of uniform. The girl to his left is equally slender, with dark, almond-shaped eyes that look away slightly, while the girl to his right gazes straight ahead at the

camera, with what looks to be the beginning of a smile. Looking
more closely, Nina realizes that this girl is Madame. But how does
that happen, she wants to ask, as childish as it sounds; how does a
girl like that, with bright smiling eyes, turn into this other person?

Madame is pointing at the other girl. "Sonia," she says, and her
voice sounds different, almost an echo.

"She's very beautiful," Nina says. As if to show agreement, Lola
pecks at the glass, and then at the shiny frame.

"Yes, she was, as well as talented. We're a good family. Strong
bloodlines—lucky for *you*. Your children will have that, at least."

At first she thought it was her imagination, but now Nina acknowledges the truth: Madame's insults have become worse. Ever
since meeting Vera.

Pretending not to notice, Nina says, "Your brother was quite
handsome."

Madame nods, and her eyelids droop as if to prevent unwanted
visions. "Now you've met my family." Her voice is soft. "Killed. Replaced by boors. The Armenians next door . . ."

Vera reaches over to pat Madame's hand, as Madame so often
does for her. Feeling suddenly in the way, Nina goes to lie down on
the bed.

"Viktor's been at the office since early this morning," Vera says,
as if aware of Nina's feelings, trying to include her. "The office" is
that of the magazine where Viktor is the poetry editor.

"They work him so hard," Madame says, and sighs loudly. "At
least they're sending him to France next month. All my dresses were
made there." She nods toward Nina. "It's a shame he won't be taking
you along."

Nina pretends to ignore this, though really these trips, to places
she has never been, pain her. It isn't just the separation; she hates not
being able to picture, in her mind's eye, just where Viktor is. At least
when he travels to places like Peredelkino, or the cities where Nina

herself has toured, she can, in the moments when she most misses him, imagine him there.

That night, when Viktor arrives home and Vera, with visible relief, has gone around the corner to Gersh's, a funny thought comes to Nina. She says it aloud, an hour or so later, when Madame has gone back to her room and shut the plywood door. "If I didn't know better, I'd think she'd been sent to spy on us."

Viktor laughs, setting his clothes neatly aside, readying himself for bed. "Quite a mole she'd make!" Then comes a long sigh. "I don't know what I'd do with myself if I were her." He slides under the covers, gives a dramatic shiver. "If you'd done that to me, Nina. Gone off with some other man instead of me."

Nina raises her eyebrows. "You know perfectly well the worry was the other way around." Though she trusts Viktor's love for her, at times it takes all of her strength not to wonder—about whom he meets, whom he sees, during the long days that he is not with her, and what he does on the nights that she is dancing. After all, Nina knows how attractive he is to other women, and the extent to which he is fueled by that attraction. As she joins him in bed, pulling herself quickly under the covers, she puts her feet on his shins, trying to keep warm.

"I'm sleeping with an icicle," he says, with mock surprise, and Nina wants to say something funny back, but she is too tired, and then she can't help it, she is already tumbling into sleep.

LOT 62

18kt Gold Women's Miniature Dress Wristwatch. The goldstone dial with baton numerical indicators, enclosing 17-jewel manual-wind movement no. 263996, oval 18kt white gold case no. 9138 FA, lugs set with two tearshaped rubies, push crown at back, hour markers three rubies and logo, completed by a 18kt gold mesh band, lg. 7 in., 34.7 dwt (without movement), Audemars Piguet. $4,000–6,000

CHAPTER ELEVEN

For a few years, first in Norway and then in France, Grigori's imagination found much inspiration in that shiny vinyl pocketbook. Youthful fantasies about who his birth parents might have been turned his father into a sort of Robin Hood and the ballerina a secret partner in his do-good crimes—but then Grigori entered the lycée and his fantasies were of the redheaded girl in the schoolyard, his energies focused on his studies, careful *explications de texte* written laboriously on regulation graph paper, his penmanship compact with concentration. His main goal was simply to blend in, to find his own clutch of friends to smoke with after class, to swap LPs and sneak into the cinema with. He answered to "Grigoire" and, mimicking his classmates, wore a knit pullover tied casually over his shoulders. And then, just when it seemed he had mastered that persona, his parents announced the move to the United States.

There he became skilled at yet another language, dove back into his studies, focused on where he might be offered a scholarship to college. When it came to musing about his birth parents, such flights of imagination stopped altogether. There were more important activities: Grigori learned to drive a car, made weekend trips to New York City, and, most incredibly, found himself with a girlfriend, a perky brunette also on the chess team. He graduated from high school, went to college. Then, during his second year at the university, he was suddenly called back to Tenafly. His father had had a stroke, to which he would ultimately, two years later, succumb. At home with his mother, having made daily visits to Feodor immobile in a hospital bed, Grigori retreated to the bedroom where he had spent only two years, his heart now charged with a pain he had not known before. It was too awful, seeing them like this, his father incapacitated, and his mother suddenly so much older. Without consciously considering what he was doing, Grigori went to the closet where he had, after first arriving here from Paris, stashed the old vinyl purse.

He took it out, opened it, removed the contents, and laid them out on his bed, like a museum display, or a surgeon's tools. He looked at them, wondering about the hands that had once touched them. But his old curiosity was no longer there. He did not reread the letters (which he basically knew by heart), though he looked again, somewhat passively, at the people in the two photographs. Then he sat down on the bed—and felt something jut into his hamstring. He stood up to see that he had taken a seat on top of a corner of the pocketbook. He wondered what could have poked him. His hands on the outside of the bag, he felt along the vinyl until he came to a small bulge, then put his hand inside to see what was there. The interior of the bag was lined in a satin-like material—but now Grigori noted a rip at the top of that side, just under the seam of the vinyl. The tear was small; he had to turn the bag upside down and worry the object out like a mole through a tunnel. And there it was, a gold chain and, hanging from it, framed in matching gold braid, a big wedge of amber.

A sign. A secret message. As though the necklace had been hiding there. It had waited for just the right time—when the only father Grigori had ever known had unknowingly abandoned him, when there was only this other story to continue. The amber possessed its own secret. Inside was a spider paralyzed in mid-action, with something else, a large pale bulge—like a parachute, or a balloon—attached below it. Grigori stared at it for a long while, wondering.

He decided, without any real deliberation, not to tell his mother. She was still lost in her own profound grief; it could only hurt her to see Grigori focused on these other parents. And anyway, what was she to make of the necklace? Only that it must have cost quite a bit of money. Perhaps the ballerina who died was *someone*—someone famous, wealthy. Or perhaps the necklace was the only expensive thing she had owned. Quickly, with disappointment, Grigori realized that, as much as it felt like a sign, the necklace really could not tell him much at all.

Back at the university that same year, another sign, even more meaningful in its randomness, confronted him.

In the campus library, reading a book called *Socialist Realism and the Russian Writer*, Grigori came across a photograph. "Plenum of the Writers Union, 1949" was the heading. Rows of men facing the camera, looking very serious in their dark suits. In the front row, so that his features were very clear, was the man from the photographs—Grigori's photographs, his mother's photographs, from the vinyl pocketbook.

Grigori's heart gave a kick, then began pounding wildly. He brought the page close to his eyes, more certain with every passing second that it was the same man. But who was this man? Grigori began flipping through the book, nearly recklessly, pausing at every photograph in case the man should appear again. Just when he was certain that he would have no such luck, he found him. This time the man stood with two others. According to the photograph, they were editors and writers at the *Literaturnaya gazeta*, their names listed below. Grigori quickly wrote out the one of the man at the right, the tall one with the almond-shaped eyes. Viktor Elsin. The name was vaguely familiar; Grigori seemed to have heard it before. Only later did he realize where he had seen it, in two of the poetry anthologies he had perused for a paper the previous semester. For now, he did what research he could, spent hours in the dark basement of the library snapping cartridge after cartridge into a microfiche machine, sliding the flat tips of roll after roll of shiny brown film through the wheel, so that the illuminated screen filled with decades-old newspaper and magazine articles. There he learned what little he could of Viktor Elsin's fate, as well as surprising information he could not have even hoped for, would not have dared dream up on his own: that Elsin had been married to the ballerina Nina Revskaya, who— he discovered after more frenzied searching of microfilm—currently resided in Boston, Massachusetts.

"SHE'S REARRANGED THE furniture," Vera reports, a few weeks after Gersh's marriage to Zoya. Vera, Nina, and Polina are with a small Bolshoi group in Berlin, Nina's first time in this ruined city, streets not yet rebuilt, darkened buildings and bombed-out plazas still piled with rubble. At their hotel (an underheated structure on an oddly empty boulevard) the three of them are finishing an afternoon meal. Not in the dining room—no money for that. Even with her promotion Nina has only a meager travel salary. Like the others she has stuffed her suitcase with food from home, biscuits and canned beans and sauerkraut, a few hard dry sausages. Anything to save a few kopecks. In Vera and Polina's room, she has warmed the beans on a portable burner, so that the place smells like a campsite. And though her own room, shared with the other young *premiere* danseuse, is larger and on a quieter floor, for a moment, eating the beans and biscuits here with Vera and Polina, it feels like the old days (only less than a year ago, really) when they were all three of them eager first soloists, sharing the stark little dressing room.

"Zoya's clothes all lined up on a rack," Vera continues, calmly, almost passively. "The apartment is basically *hers* now. Oh, and did you know she collects recordings of Stalin's speeches? Apparently she's been playing them over and over on Gersh's phonograph."

Nina laughs. "I suppose that's his punishment."

"I don't know how you can forgive him," Polina says. Something really is wrong with her skin; though the welts are gone, there are small dark patches on her cheekbones. Not bruises, exactly, more like hives, but a gray-black color instead of red.

"It's because I feel sorry for him," Vera says. "It's clear Zoya has had her eye on his apartment from the start. She's just using him, so that she doesn't have to live with her family anymore."

So that's what Vera has decided to tell herself, or what Gersh has convinced her—and perhaps himself—to believe. Well, probably it is one facet of the truth. As Nina contemplates this, Polina looks at the clock and says, "We should get going." This afternoon is their one chance to sightsee; in other words, to shop. Though they are confined to the Soviet sector, there is a good chance that with the American, French, and British sectors so close they might find goods unavailable back home. "I'll go check in with Arvo"—the Komsomol representative traveling with the troupe. They are supposed to keep him informed of their every coming and going.

"Oh, let him figure it out," Nina says. After all, chances are that one of the small contingent of East German chaperones, whom they met at the welcoming dinner yesterday and who seem always to be hovering about, will be waiting for them in the lobby.

But no one is there when they hand their keys to the sharp-faced sentrywoman stationed at the elevator, nor when they leave the building and step out into the cloudy gray day. Vera simply shrugs her shoulders, and Polina seems to relax, as they make their way along the run-down streets. Nina notices the way people look at them as they walk by, wonders if it is their clothes that make them stand out, though their clothes aren't all that different, really. But no, it isn't their clothes, nor is it their being Russians; it is that they are so clearly *dancers*, with their poised, open-stance ballerina walk, and their hair pulled into high chignons. Polina especially has the exaggerated, ducklike stride of a dancer, when really there is no reason to walk that way—except that that walk, too, is part of Polina's very identity. It occurs to Nina that each of them has a signature gait: Polina's is self-conscious and somewhat forced, her turnout coming from the ankle rather than the hips, while Vera is blessed with natural turnout, her steps easy and light on high-arched feet. Nina knows she too has her physical quirks—the long neck and proudly held head and relaxed yet perfectly erect posture, shoulder blades pulled back instinctively so that her spine forms a strong vertical line. Quite a contrast to the marketgoers shuffling around them, hunched forward as if to burrow their way through their errands, or to duck from the cold.

With little difficulty, the three of them find the stage apparel shop they have been told of. What they most want are nylon tights, which won't sag at the knees like the silk ones from home. But this shop is sold out. After they have stocked up on grease sticks and face powder, the shop's owner writes down another address where they can find what they want, he explains with a shrewd look, eyes narrowed, pointing out the U-Bahn stop and describing, through gestures and broken Russian and little knowing nods, how to get there.

They board the subway feeling adventurous, the car so crowded they have to stand. Two stops later, though, nearly everyone in the car shuffles off. Nina looks out at the sign on the wall of the tunnel, big black letters with the name of the subway stop. Below, something longer is written, the words too long and foreign for Nina to make sense of. "Why do you think so many people are getting off?" Polina asks nervously—and the door slides shut.

Only as the car lurches forward again does Nina allow what the reason might be. Her heart speeds at the thought; she doesn't dare speak. The next stop is the one the shop owner told them, and they are there soon enough. With Vera and Polina, Nina steps out to the platform.

They emerge from the subway to a bustling street, oddly bright though the sky is as gray and cold as before. Shop windows glow with neon signs, and above them, big and clean, are billboards such as Nina has never seen, colorful and spotlit even though it is daytime. People everywhere; even their coats and hats look brighter, somehow. "That's why everyone had to get off." Nina says it even though it is clear from Polina's and Vera's faces that they too understand.

"We're not supposed to be here," Polina says.

"We didn't know," Vera whispers, eyes wide as she takes in the scene before them, the people walking at an easy clip, unworried, and the buildings that, while still somewhat derelict, are cleaner and free of rubble, with lights illuminating their windows.

"Well, we're here now, we might as well find what we came for." Nina tries to sound confident, though in her mind she hears the repeated warnings of Arvo and their East German hosts, that they are not to leave the democratic sector, that evil Western capitalists might kidnap them at any turn. In a voice of forced calm, Nina reads out the shop address while Vera searches the map. "It's this way," Vera says, finding the street sign. Nina and Polina follow her. At the corner, though, they come to a stop.

In front of them is a vegetable kiosk. And there, heaped at the end, like something out of a fairy tale, is a stack of bright yellow bananas.

Polina and Vera too stare, as Nina allows herself to fully take in the scene around her, people walking calmly without the least sign of wonderment at the bright shop windows, the billboards, the bananas. Their easy chatter and relaxed faces, the quick, optimistic clicks of shoes on the sidewalk . . .

"We're just following directions," Polina says defensively, turning away from the bananas. Nina fights the urge she has—to spend her money not on tights but on this gorgeous, exotic fruit. But Vera is pointing at a narrow side street. "That's it. We might as well go in." After all, they simply want to buy dance supplies.

The address the shop owner has written down is a tiny place, something of a junk shop, no sign out front. Inside are all kinds of wigs and tights and costume materials and fabrics they never see back home. Not just costume jewelry but also real jewels and perfumes and coffee beans and English cigarettes. The owner is an older woman with her hair in a very long gray braid. No one else is with her. Nina and the others lose themselves for a long while, calculating dreamily, deciding what to splurge on. Nina purchases fabric for her mother, cigarettes for Viktor, and tights for herself, while Vera and Polina continue sorting through the fabric. When the woman hands over Nina's change, she presses something into her hand.

"In case you need it." The woman's voice is so soft, her German-accented Russian so quiet, Nina might have dreamed it. But the woman's hand is adamant, insistent in its pressure, forcing something into Nina's palm. A little slip of paper. Nina is so taken aback she doesn't dare look at it. She just nods thank you and slips the tiny note, with the money, into her pocket.

"Look," Polina calls from the other end of the room. She is holding up a pocket watch. "For Serge!"

Nina's heart thumps anxiously, the slip of paper in her pocket like a lit match. She tries to distract herself by going over to see the watch. "You two are serious, then?" she asks as calmly as she can.

"He's such a wonderful man, Nina, I feel so lucky." Polina turns to call to the old woman, to ask how much for the pocket watch.

All the while that Polina is bargaining down the watch for Serge, Nina wonders about the slip of paper in her pocket. What is it, and why has the woman given it to Nina, of all people? As curious as she is, she doesn't dare peek at the paper yet.

When they have bought all they can afford, they head straight back to the subway, aware—without daring to speak of it—of their transgression. Nina finds herself trying not to look at the bright shop windows, at the different fabrics of coats and hats; she is ashamed of her own wonderment, and of the way these sights disconcert her, something wrong about it, that the "evil capitalists" she has been told about should look so content, their streets clean, with vendors hawking bananas—and no queue at all, no desperate rush. When she and the others have boarded the train back to their stop near the Lustgarten, Nina feels relief.

Only after they have emerged from underground, as they make their way along the street to their hotel, does Nina venture to say, under her breath, what she has been noticing—if denying to herself—since leaving the junk shop. "That woman there seems to be following us."

Without looking up, Vera says, "The one in the gray hat?"

"You noticed her too, then." Nina feels herself begin to tremble. Could it have something to do with the note in her pocket? And what about Vera and Polina—when they paid for their goods, did the woman press something into their palms, too? Or was Nina the chosen one, simply because she was the first to make a purchase? Nina wants badly to ask them but doesn't dare. "It was an honest mistake," she says, to calm herself. "If she really is following us, then she must have seen that. She saw that we were just trying to shop."

Quietly Vera asks, "You don't think she thinks we were trying to . . . leave?"

"Well, of course not." Polina says it with affront. "Why would we ever want to do that?" But she still looks frightened. After all, now she *knows*. She has seen what's there, on the other side. She too saw the ripe bananas, and people walking past as if it were nothing extraordinary at all.

Nina thinks of Sofia, the other Bolshoi soloist, who was at the last minute pulled from the trip as a travel risk. Rumor said it was because she had relatives in West Berlin; only now does Nina understand.

Her voice emphatic, Polina says, "Everyone knows it would be an insane thing to do." She seems to have turned paler; the odd black spots on her cheekbones stand out even more.

Nina says, "I'm worried about your skin."

Polina shifts her eyes. "Uncle Feliks says just to be patient and it will go away." Then, as if uncomfortable talking about herself, she says again, "Really, you'd have to be crazy to want to *leave*."

In a low, flat voice, Vera says, "They find you and break your legs."

Polina looks frightened.

"No matter where you go." Vera's voice is soft, measured. "They have agents all over the world. It doesn't matter how far away you get. And then, what would you do, in some country where you don't know anyone, and you can't even dance anymore."

Nina has heard as much, although it always sounds extreme. Why punish a mere dancer, as if she were some sort of secret agent? Nina has to force herself not to look back and see if the woman in the gray hat is still behind them.

In a small, terrified voice, Polina says, "I'm worried it's me."

"What do you mean?"

"My fault that woman is following us." Polina's steps have slowed, and her voice is very quiet. "Why me? I'm just a ballerina. I only have a few close friends, no one really tells me anything personal at all."

"Keep walking," Vera says, while Nina makes what sense she can of Polina's comment. Under her breath Vera asks, "Did someone ask you to do something?"

It happens often enough, even in the ballet: people being asked to write things, reports. Nina has heard of this, been warned of a few people in particular, mostly those younger or less accomplished— character dancers, or perpetual coryphées who can't quite break into the top tier. If informing will help their careers, then they will keep their eyes and ears open—though what could they overhear, really? Nina hasn't ever considered that it might directly affect her. And after all, she hasn't done anything wrong.

Vera is biting her lip, looking almost angry.

"You know me," Polina says. "I like everyone, I can't help it, it's just the way I am. Do you see why it's hard for me?"

Nina dares to look Polina in the eye, understanding, now, the hives, the anxiety, the nervous looks. "Have you . . . done anything?" Even as she asks the question, she is wondering what Polina possibly could find to say. How could she know anyone who would do anything truly wrong?

"I only write very general things," Polina whispers. "But they keep telling me it's not enough, I'm not doing a good job." Tears have started.

"But if you're telling the truth," Nina says, "then what more can they ask of you?" Vera looks steel-eyed, no such question on her face. Maybe, Nina considers, it is only Polina's perception that she is supposed to be doing more than she already is. Perhaps Polina has misunderstood. She's always so eager to please.

And then the thought occurs to Nina: Have I said anything, done anything? Laughing about Stalin's speeches . . . Even that comment about Arvo . . . Nina tries to recall exactly what she said, how it might have sounded to Polina. How it might sound on the page. And that slip of paper from the old shopwoman . . .

"I didn't have anything to do with Sofia!" Polina blurts out, her eyes suddenly wider. "Honestly, I didn't. There's no one I could ever bear to hurt. There's no one I don't like."

Nina's hands are trembling, while Vera hushes Polina, tells her to keep her voice down. "Can't Serge help you out? Get you off the hook, so that you don't have to write anything anymore. It's his job, after all."

"His job?" Nina asks.

Polina's voice drops. "He's with the State Security."

The secret police. Before Nina can ask if he is an agent or an administrator, Vera adds, "He must have some sort of pull. Surely he knows someone who can do something."

"But won't it sound like I'm complaining? I'd hate for him to think I'm unwilling to help. I don't want to disappoint him."

Nina says, "You're a ballerina, not an informer."

"I suppose I could ask him," Polina whispers, and a small whimper escapes. "It's just—I love him, I really do. I don't want anything to go wrong between us." Even in a whisper, there's a wailing sound to her voice. "I feel so sick. I'm sick with it."

They have reached the hotel. Vera holds the door open for Polina while Nina, feeling around in her pocketbook, finds her handkerchief, onto which she sprinkles some eau de cologne. The woman in the gray hat and scarf lingers outside.

Vera has led Polina to a chair in the hotel lobby. "Close your eyes and take a deep breath," Nina says, laying the kerchief over Polina's forehead. "It's going to be all right."

It isn't until many hours later, when they have danced and showered and eaten and are back in their rooms, that Nina finds a moment alone to look at the note in her pocket. On it is printed, in small but clear letters: *Passports, i.d. Ernst 11 6275.*

THE REST OF that year, the year Grigori turned twenty, was filled with Elsin's poetry. Grigori returned to the vinyl bag and its contents, the photographs and letters; the pendant remained his secret. He read all he could about Elsin and Revskaya, and like a sleuth pieced the puzzle together. And then came the disappointments: Big Ears' dismissive response to his essay, not to mention—after his careful and timid approach—Nina Revskaya's angry green eyes.

But his efforts were not wasted. If nothing else, he now had his topic of study; the socialist realist poetry of Viktor Elsin was soon to become his subject of expertise, and won him a student travel grant—his first trip back to Russia. In Moscow, using the address and bit of information he had gleaned from the hospital certificate, he sought whatever records he might find. The frustration of trying to access those records, a search that, on that first trip, proved futile, was like nothing he had ever experienced. Even when he returned two years later—as a chaperone on a student exchange program—to repeat the attempt, the ordeal was dismaying. First he waited all morning for the burly woman at the housing records office to finish whatever she was doing and pay attention to him; when at last Grigori was allowed to explain his reason for being there, the woman announced that it was her lunch hour. When she returned much later to find Grigori still waiting, she allowed that any files she might be able to locate for him were only accessible, for some reason, between nine and ten thirty in the morning. And so Grigori showed up the next day at the appointed time, only to be told that the woman was not in that day and that, since she was the only person in charge of housing records, no one else could help him. When he returned on the third day, the office was inexplicably closed.

"You look grumpy," Evelyn said now, as they made their way in Grigori's Volvo to the home of Roger and Hoanh Thomson, both colleagues of theirs at the university. "Don't worry, we don't have to stay long."

"Sorry, no, it's—I was just remembering something."

Evelyn gave him a sympathetic look. Probably she thought he was thinking something sad about Christine. She had been very patient with him ever since Valentine's Day, had even made a point of saying she was glad that they were "taking things slow." Grigori sat up straighter and tried to look cheery. It was a cold Saturday evening, the first of March, and they were headed to the Thomsons' yearly faculty party in honor of International Women's Day. (Really it was meant to be celebrated on the eighth, but spring break was next week and most people would be away.) This was an event to which "Grigori and guest" were annually invited simply because he and Hoanh—who tutored French and Vietnamese and dressed in aggressively tarty outfits—had offices on the same floor. Though she was not particularly pretty (bad skin, and something cold in her small brown eyes) Roger clearly thought her a sexpot, and everyone at the university (well, perhaps not Evelyn, who knew about fashion) acted like she was, since she wore lots of makeup and form-fitting clothes more revealing than anything they themselves ever dared. Even to this party most of them would surely turn up in rubber boots and baggy turtlenecks and goofy all-weather parkas intended for trekking the Himalayas; you would think they were in the middle of a blizzard. Not Evelyn, of course. She had styled herself in a sleeveless silk blouse, a slim black skirt, and those high-heeled leather boots she looked particularly good in.

"That sounds good," Grigori had told her when she asked if he wanted to carpool. That was how she put it, "carpool to Roger and Hoanh's," as if even phrasing it some other way—"Would you like to go to the party together?"—might not be "slow" enough for him. Of course, no matter how she phrased it, their colleagues would whisper when they showed up together. Fine, let them talk. It didn't matter.

"Oh, brother, I forgot about the no-shoes policy." Evelyn looked put out as they came upon the sad-looking lineup of dirty boots and sneakers and salt-stained galoshes arrayed on a layer of newspaper in the foyer. The Thompsons' home—a roomy apartment on Medfield Street—was toasty, the fireplace emitting its woodsy scent. "My whole outfit is about the boots." Evelyn gave a good-natured laugh, unzipping the slender boots, and slid them off, as Grigori silently stepped out of his loafers. Though he too found the no-shoes policy inhospitable, something stopped him from showing sympathy for

Evelyn, even when he saw how small she now became, a good three inches shorter in her sheer-stockinged feet. "Well, here goes," she said, opening the door. Feeling guilty and ungenerous, Grigori held it for her to go ahead of him.

"Welcome, Greg, and Evelyn, I salute you." Roger greeted them and handed a tiny bouquet of pinkish rosebuds to Evelyn. This too was part of the tradition, little posies for all the women, and on Roger and Hoanh's stereo music by female artists only. By the door was a framed declaration of International Women's Day and a dona-tion box for the Girls' Fund of America.

"Mmm, this way I can keep smelling them," Evelyn said, care-fully pinning the posy to her silk blouse, as Roger hung their coats on the wall rack. "Thanks, Roger."

The other guests stood around in fuzzy socks and pilly sweat-ers, drinking Roger's homemade coffee liqueur. Deplorable, thought Grigori—though his trousers too were somewhat rumpled. New England winter . . . Yet even Christine, in the long last winter of her illness, had not fallen into the torpidity of perpetual poly fleece.

Roger said, "You're looking lovely, Evelyn, I must say." It was true; the shimmer of her silk blouse made her eyes look even brighter, and she held herself straight and proud, in that petite, fit way of hers, unlike so many of the others here, lumpy in their heavy sweaters. "So, you know the ropes. Drinks, et cetera, over here, edibles over there. " Roger indicated the table over by the window, said, "Oh, my bride is beckoning," and went over to where Hoanh was standing in a tight, stretchy dress that somehow managed to accentuate her pubis.

Grigori was glad not to have to talk to them. The truth was, he couldn't stand Roger, a sociologist who studied fripperies such as "the social impulse" and even got away with teaching a course on "friendship." There was a falseness about him, a posturing, and that embarrassingly transparent pride at having managed to marry a skinny Asian fox of his very own. Something so practiced about him, always a new sleek tie, or suits he wore with Converse high-tops. In better weather he rode an old Schwinn three-speed to work; he had spent months researching retro bicycles before having it shipped from Chicago. Even this apartment seemed a pose rather than genuine, the African masks and Vietnamese water puppets carefully commingled with a circus poster, a London transit map, and photobooth Polaroids in which Roger and Hoanh made faces of forced jollity. Atop the living room bookshelf, record albums were propped for display—Joan Baez, Laura Nyro, Patti Smith, Joan Jett—though really all of the music was coming from one of those iPods advertised everywhere these days, plugged into a speaker system in the corner.

"Do they even own a turntable?" Grigori asked petulantly.

"They're for decoration," Evelyn said, and pinched his arm. "Stop being a humbug."

"But it's my defining characteristic." He filled a shot glass of the homemade liqueur and handed it to her.

"Ooo, yum, it's good, Grigori, you should try it. Hello, Zoltan."

"*Kezét csókolom.*" Zoltan had taken Evelyn's hand and kissed it.

Grigori reached out and shook his hand. "I have to admit, Zoltan, I'm surprised to see you here." Zoltan always made a point of saying he had no time for "the petty one-upmanship of academic banter."

But now he said, "I decided I must, since it will be my last one."

"What do you mean?" After what he had been through with Christine, Grigori could not help worrying; perhaps Zoltan too had received bad news from a physician.

"Ssh." He pulled them away from the drinks table and whispered, "This is my last year on the faculty. As chair of the department, you are now officially the first to be informed. But please don't tell the others yet. I'd hate for anyone to think they have to do anything, you know, a big party or ceremony or what have you. I'd like to avoid any commemorations."

A doubt entered Grigori's mind, that his colleagues, or the university administration, could be quite so generous. He would have to come up with some appropriate way to show their gratitude. Zoltan added, "Believe me, it's better this way. Just slip off quietly into the night."

"But where will you go?" Evelyn asked, and Grigori understood what she meant—that the academy, with its steadfast faith in intellectualism and its own arcane scholarship, was the only place for a man like Zoltan, whose artistic devotion was rarely so passionately embraced in the quotidian world. After all, universities themselves were museums of a sort, places where people like Zoltan, and others who did not quite fit in, could comfortably ensconce themselves for decades—entire lives, even—worrying away at whatever esoteric subject they chose, until their hair had receded and the last of their youth disappeared.

"I plan to return home," Zoltan said.

"Home?" Evelyn asked, but Grigori knew what that must mean.

"Hungary," Zoltan said. "A cottage on Lake Balaton awaits me."

Grigori asked, "How long have you been planning this?" and, hearing a hurt tone in his voice, added, "It will be bleak without you here." He meant it. Who else was there to argue about Mahler with, to compare translations of Baudelaire, to commiserate over the sorry state of the fiction in the *New Yorker*? Zoltan could become red-faced over a doltish *Times* book review, it didn't matter whose book or what subject. He would telephone Grigori when a particular recording of Schumann was being broadcast, and showed deep affront if a student claimed never to have heard of Diaghilev or Brodsky or Vanessa Bell. "I'll miss you," said Grigori.

"Me too," Evelyn said obligingly.

"You will, and then after a while you won't." Zoltan poured himself a Scotch with shaky hands. "As for me, it's time to go home."

"I didn't even realize you had planned to go back."

"I hadn't. But when I started looking back at my journals, it's funny, it jogged something in my mind. I began to remember things. I'd put so much out of my mind. This Christmas, I was on the T, seeing people's decorated trees through the windows, and I thought for the first time in decades—decades!—of a bonbon we used to have, wrapped in crinkly paper. We decorated the Christmas trees with it. And for a full day I couldn't remember the name. That was when I knew it was time to go home."

Grigori nodded. He knew that feeling, that urge—and yet what was home, now, for Grigori? He had been asking himself this since Christine's death. Lately he had even considered moving—not leaving Boston but finding a smaller place, perhaps a condo somewhere.

"What's the word?" Evelyn was asking. "For the Christmas candy."

"*Szaloncukor!*" Grigori glimpsed the glee of a child in Zoltan's eyes. "I think it will be an amazing thing to go back to a place I once had to run from. That now I can say what I want, without any worry for my safety. Or perhaps it won't feel that way; perhaps it will be a reminder. Living here, one forgets what it was like. Not just for me. For any intellectual. Always some mortal threat or other. Always watching your back. Simply for being who you were—appreciating what you appreciated, understanding certain things."

It *was* amazing, what Zoltan, in his perhaps small, perhaps quiet way, had accomplished, even if he was but a footnote to the list of triumphs of art in the face of authoritarianism. And buoying to consider that as Zoltan's literary executor Grigori might too be part of that chain of hands, if only he could secure a translator and publisher for Zoltan's later work. It would be a long project, that was certain—but then, what was life, really, without such challenges?

"Though this country has been my home for a good while," Zoltan said, "it's a different kind of home. I'm not sure I ever quite belonged. I was reading my journal this morning—I don't know, Evelyn, if Grigori has mentioned that I'm writing a memoir. I was looking back at entries from when I first arrived in America, and it was so curious to see what I'd noticed back then that I no longer notice at all. I'd been in London quite a while by then, and didn't realize how differently the United States would strike me. But from the minute I stepped off the plane, the difference was visible."

"How so?" Evelyn asked.

"Oh, everyone rushing about, gesturing to each other, the physicality of it. Here everyone is always in a hurry."

"No one in England was ever in a hurry?"

"They don't show their emotions the way people here do. Americans don't hold back. They swear and curse and slap each other on the back. I hadn't seen anything quite like it before."

Grigori was nodding, recalling that sensation of newness. "For me it was the houses. I'll never forget first time I saw a suburban American house. I couldn't believe how big it was. And that there were extra rooms that people didn't even use. 'Guest' rooms." He shook his head and laughed.

Zoltan nodded. "This country has been good to me. But it doesn't hold the indentation of my body on the mattress, if you see what I mean."

"Yes, well, nor does it mine, I'm sure," Grigori said.

Evelyn said, "You egotists," and laughed.

"Egotist!" said Zoltan. "I've been in the splendid company of one all week, actually. I'm reading Berlioz's memoirs. Talk about an ego."

He began to describe the book, but Evelyn said, "I hate to be rude, but my feet are freezing. You two continue. I need to get over to where the carpet is."

Grigori could see, now, that she was shivering. "You poor thing," Zoltan told her. "Do go warm up."

Watching Evelyn make her way toward the fireplace, Grigori felt again his own self-reproach; he ought to accompany her. She looked diminished without her sleek boots. He blamed himself as much as he did Roger and Hoahn. How must it feel, to have a person agree as easily and willingly as Grigori had to "take things slow"? Well, he was simply trying to be careful and not rush things.

Natalie Gluck, one of the sociology professors, had come up to the drinks table, and now Zoltan was telling them about Berlioz's early fitful love affairs, until Grigori was no longer following. He was thinking, he realized, of Drew Brooks. She had called him yesterday. Grigori was sorry to have gotten the message too late, after business hours. A warm chattiness to her voice on the recording: she had meant to call earlier, she said, but this week had been so busy; she had gone on vacation and was still catching up. . . . Grigori liked her self-assured manner, her energy and poise. He liked the very fact that Drew used the telephone instead of e-mail, that she was not afraid, like so many younger people, to encounter a human voice at the other end of an appeal. "I've been reading your translations," she had said in her message, sounding truly interested. "I'd love to discuss them with you."

Relief washed through him. After two weeks of hearing nothing from her, he had begun to wonder if by lending her the book he had saddled her with another task; perhaps she felt she could not speak to Grigori until she had read it. Or she had tried to read the poems but was uninterested. Or even disliked them.

But she had devoted a good deal of the past month to Nina Revskaya's life and treasures. It made sense that she might be drawn to Elsin's poems. Grigori wondered, now, nodding along to his colleagues' conversation, how she might react if he simply told her the truth: about the necklace, about the poems and letters and photographs in that vinyl purse. Just give them all over to her, for the catalog or pamphlet or whatever that thing was that she was working so hard on producing. She had read the poems, after all. Perhaps she would be intrigued to see how the poems and letters matched up.

No, no . . . But, then, why not? He could go there, show them to her. Though why should she care? No one did. . . . And yet—the thought came to him now—perhaps she might.

Grigori's colleague Bill Muir had approached him, was talking to him, the usual chitchat, shaking his head at the president's latest ultimatum. "They've supposedly started dismantling their missiles," Grigori said hopefully, if mainly out of some grudging need to contradict Bill. "Maybe Hussein will follow through after all."

"Right. And the Sox will win the World Series." Bill Muir shook his head again, and made some typical, tiresome comment about the president, how there was just one more year of this madness and then they could be rid of him. Grigori was able to commiserate politely, heard himself speaking, heard Bill answering—and yet he was aware of not being here, really, not with his soul. He had no interest, he had lost heart, could not commune with these people, his own colleagues. When had it happened? When Christine died, or just now? He had been here too long, perhaps, in this department, teaching the same subjects, attending the same conferences, presenting paper after paper on Viktor Elsin and his cohort. Only now it seemed meaningless, all of it meaningless, these colleagues around him whom he at times thought of as friends—but now he simply did not care.

Bill must have noticed; he excused himself and wandered away, while Natalie and Zoltan discussed bullfighting, and Billie Holiday, and then Mallarmé and Verlaine. Grigori listened without joining in. I ought to engage more, he told himself. I ought to go chat with Evelyn.

She stood not far from him, conversing with the new sociology professor, Adam somebody, athletic-looking and fair like Evelyn. There was a hole in her stocking where her toe had poked through. Even from here Grigori could see the toenail, painted a dark shiny purple color, like a bruise. And though Evelyn appeared to be enjoying the conversation, she held her arms across her midriff, hands over elbows, as if to comfort herself. Grigori felt a surge of tenderness for her. There were different ways to love a person, he told himself; there were different kinds of love. With a fresh drink in hand, he turned to make his way toward her.

MARCH 8, A holiday, though still a workday. Usually men give flowers, but Viktor has given Nina a tiny gold watch, the most delicately functional object she has ever seen. Swiss, bought on his visit to France. The band is a gold chain slinky as a water snake, the face of the timepiece a tiny shining thing Nina has to squint at to read. Its near inutility is the very embodiment of luxury.

Having removed the watch for rehearsal, she is now placing it back on her wrist, trying to catch the clasp at the end.

"There you are." Breathless, Vera, already in her street clothes, has found Nina in her dressing room. "It's Gersh. He had a call this morning—from Stalin's secretary." She pauses, as if unable to believe it. "Telling him to come to the Kremlin."

Nina feels her eyes open wide. "What about?"

Vera just shakes her head. "It can't be good news." And with desperation, "Can it?"

"What time was the meeting? Has it happened yet?"

"This afternoon sometime. But I can't go over there to wait for him, because Zoya might be home."

"I'll tell Viktor. If nothing else, he and I can be there when Gersh gets back. And I'll tell you anything I find out, as soon as I can. I promise."

And so Nina and Viktor are in Gersh's apartment with Zoya that evening when Gersh returns from the Kremlin, his face tired but only somewhat drawn. Zoya, who has been pacing anxiously for hours, rushes to him. "What happened, what did they say? Did you meet him? Did you speak to him?" Her tone changes on the word "him," reverent, eager.

"Just his secretary. But it wasn't a conversation, really. He simply read a decree to me."

"What decree?"

"Nothing new, really, same as always." Gersh looks suddenly exhausted. "But then he handed me this." He holds out a typed page.

Zoya quickly takes it from him, and Nina and Viktor read over her shoulder. It is a memorandum, from the deputy chairman of the Committee on the Arts. "Under the aegis of the Council of Ministers of the USSR," Gersh has been expelled from the Composers' Union.

Zoya's curls quiver as she shakes her head. "It's because of what you said about bel canto. That must be it." To Nina and Viktor she explains, "He can't help it—you know how he loves Rossini and all that." Her voice is sad yet matter-of-fact. In a harsher, brisk tone directed at Gersh, she says, "I told you to get rid of those Donizetti records."

"Yes, ma'am."

But Zoya doesn't look angry so much as galvanized. "It's a misunderstanding. Don't worry, it will just take some turning around."

Amazing, that nothing seems to frighten her, that she never becomes disheartened. She rarely appears the least bit confused by the things happening around her. Nina, on the other hand, has felt puzzled by so many things recently. Not only this latest harsh treatment of Gersh. As much as Nina used to think she knew whom she could trust, lately it seems impossible to ever really truly know what other people are up to. What Polina told them, in Berlin last month, about being asked to inform . . . And the note from that woman in the junk shop. Was Nina supposed to pass the information along to Polina and Vera? Or was Nina singled out for some reason—because of how she looked, like a person who might need or want that information? Did her eyes say that? Did she look needy, or wise? For the hundredth time she wonders if Vera and Polina each received a little slip of paper, too. In the end Nina just rolled hers into a tiny pill and shoved it into the corner of one of the compartments of her makeup case, too scared to show anyone, especially after learning about Polina.

Not to mention that the woman following them turned out to be one of their assigned escorts, an East German named Bergit, who reported them to the Komsomol representative for having gone outside the designated bounds. All three of them were scolded harshly, in front of the rest of the troupe, for leaving their pre-scribed territory, and then the company manager gave another lecture, reminding them that there was nothing they could have needed to buy that was not available in the democratic sector, and that they might have been kidnapped by evil capitalists. And so Nina, Polina, and Vera were made to stand in front of the group and explain that they had been wickedly misdirected and were re-lieved to have been able to return safely within Soviet bounds, and that never again would they so much as risk finding themselves in the nondemocratic world.

The lie of it, the pettiness—after all that they saw just two subway stops away. Surely some of the others knew the truth. And yet, like Polina said, you would have to be crazy to leave, why even risk it? *They find you and break your legs.*

Now Zoya is telling Gersh he might write a letter of apology; that might do the trick. "I'll of course help you and all that. I'm not a bad writer myself." Glancing back at the memorandum, she says, "I wonder if Stalin himself saw this."

She sounds almost awestruck. After all, she is a vocal devotee of the great leader. On the wall where previously there was only a very small oval mirror, she has hung a framed section of a *Pravda* article from last year:

> If, encountering difficulties, you should doubt your own
> strength, think about him, about Stalin, and you'll find
> the necessary confidence. If you feel tired at a time when
> you should not, think about him, about Stalin, and your
> fatigue will leave you. . . . If you have planned something
> big, think about him, about Stalin, and the work will be a
> success. . . . If you are seeking a solution, think about him,
> about Stalin, and you will find it.

"I'm sorry," Nina says, awkwardly, "but I have an engagement, I have to go now. Viktor, I'll find you back at home."

She leaves the room with an exhale of relief. But her heart drops again when she thinks of the news she has to pass along to Vera.

FIRST THING MONDAY morning, Grigori went to find Drew.

She looked up smiling, came out from behind her desk to shake Grigori's hand in that confident, professional way of hers. "Nice to see you."

"Likewise. I see you took some sun over your vacation."

"Oh, good, I thought whatever tan I'd managed had already faded." That easy smile. "The catalogs have just gone out. You should be getting yours in the mail, today or tomorrow."

So it was happening, events were now in motion, the auction would truly take place. Perhaps when he received the catalog Grigori would fully believe it.

Drew was shuffling through her big leather bag. "Thank you for lending me your book."

"Thank you for reading it. It's rare that my translations have much of an audience."

"I'm impressed. The poems feel perfectly natural in English. If I didn't know they were originally in another language . . ."

Feeling somehow humbled, Grigori heard himself say, "I suppose they've been a good bit of my life's work. So far."

Drew nodded as if she already knew this. "I love them. Not just the poems on their own. Also knowing about Viktor Elsin. I've been thinking about some of them, just imagining. I was wondering about the later ones. His style changed so drastically."

Grigori nodded. "I've written papers about that. It's the sort of thing we academics seize on, for lack of more meaningful occupations."

Again, her laughing smile. "And . . . what conclusions have you come to?"

"Oh, you don't want to get me started."

"Yes, I do." She was looking him straight in the eye.

"Well, I think his stylistic changes had to do with changes in his personal and professional life. That new subject matter dictated a change in approach. Not that the poems say any of this explicitly. But you know he was arrested shortly after those last poems were written. There's been speculation that he might somehow have been involved in some sort of subversive activities."

Musingly, Drew said, "I suppose Nina Revskaya would know."

"Yes, well . . . perhaps. She hasn't ever said so."

Drew flipped to the back of the book. "This last poem especially. It's so haunting."

"Riverside," the least typical of all, no metrical scheme, no attempt at all to rhyme. It was Viktor Elsin's final poem.

RIVERSIDE

I.

These woods contain glorious secrets.
Pitiless wind, its message garbled
by wood smoke at summer's end. A rattling
hazelnut tree: Encore, encore! Time
lifts into air. Shoreline runnels. Revenant.
Black empty sky, no snarl of stars,
no indefatigable moon. The pines weep.
Restless branches give faint signals . . .

II.

Distant stars: tiny drops of dew
on a giant spider's web.

III.

Under spruce-cover, a colony
of mushrooms hides from that bright
jewel the sun, smiting the wind.
Ancient tears, like hearts, harden.
One can never be prepared.
Over roads dust hovers.
Astonished faces of flowers.

"He must have written it quickly," Drew said. "Or maybe it just
feels rushed."

Grigori nodded. Particularly that third stanza, the way it so rap-
idly diminished, as if running out of words, out of time. Saying so,

he pointed at it and felt the pleasant sensation of his arm brushing Drew's.

"And that second section," she said. "It's almost a haiku." She looked up at him. "A big overpowering net."

"Or maybe the spider allusion," Grigori said, "represents some all-powerful, menacing evil."

Drew said, "The dew, right after the weeping pines, makes me see teardrops. And then those tears again in the final section." She paused, thinking. "Do you think the censors maybe found it subversive, somehow?"

"I haven't been able to find any documentation of that precise charge. But if one looks for subversion one can find it here. This line here, for instance. Be prepared, that was the Young Pioneers slogan. The Communist youth group all children were supposed to join."

"Like the Boy Scouts. It's the same slogan."

"Exactly. So to say, 'One can never be prepared'—"

"Might be in reference to—"

"Or not. But he tucked it in there." Grigori felt himself nodding again, so glad to have an ally. Was that it, was that the feeling he sought but found so elusive? Even with Zoltan, who understood his work as well as his background, Grigori did not necessarily feel a *closeness*; never had he told Zoltan anything terribly personal, nor had he wanted to. And with Evelyn he felt friendship but not the closeness of a companion. What a failure he had been at the party on Saturday, unable to rally; dropping Evelyn at her building afterwards, he had given just a quick, guarded kiss.

"The penultimate poem, too," Drew said now. " 'Night Swimming.' " She turned the page back. "It seems to be mourning some loss of . . . innocence, maybe, or faith in . . . goodness."

"Yes. In the world as a good and honest place." Now was the moment. Grigori willed himself to be brave, to dare to show her what he had once shown awful, condescending Big Ears. He cleared his throat. "I have some letters."

Drew looked up, eyes wide, pools of brown flecked with green.

Grigori's heart punched at his ribs. "If at some point you find time to read them," he added, turning to remove the folded letters and the typed translations from his briefcase, his heart still punching, "now that you've read these poems, you might find some similarities of phrasing."

He gave her the original letters first. She touched them as if they might crumble in her fingers. "Who wrote them?"

"They're signed, 'Yours always,' and this one, 'Yours and yours only.' But I have reason to believe that the author is Viktor Elsin."

"Really?" Her eyes opened even wider. She flipped back to the top of the first letter. "And do you know whom they're addressed to?"

Big Ears shaking his head, that horrible condescending face. That Grigori had dared to do this much, already, dared to suggest . . . Not to mention how Drew might react to his possessing Nina Revskaya's mail. "It simply says 'my dear.' "

"Have you shown them to Nina Revskaya?"

A deep breath. "I tried to. She didn't want to see them." Grigori found himself using those same phrases as always, *It could be painful for her to look back . . . no interest in the past . . .*

But it felt wrong, this time, wrong not to be telling Drew the truth. "A long time ago," Grigori allowed himself to admit, "I tried to show them to her. She wanted nothing to do with them. Or me. It took me another year to get up the nerve to write her. I wrote her a letter, trying to explain." It was too much, he could not say much more. "She didn't answer."

Drew looked perplexed. "But why wouldn't she?" And then, "Oh, I see."

"See what?"

"They're love letters, is that it? To someone else—"

"Oh, no, no, that's not it, I don't think so. Well, yes, one is a love letter, in fact, but, well, that's why the necklace, the amber . . ." But it was easier to simply show her, let her see for herself. "I brought you these translations of them."

Drew was looking back at the originals, flipping them over, squinting at the handwriting. Grigori could see her frustration at not understanding, at not having learned from that Russian class. "If they're her husband's letters . . ." She looked up, took the translations from him. "You're saying that some of what's in the letters matches up with these poems?"

"One of the letters, a section of it. I think." His courage faltered. "Don't worry, I don't mean to force my own obsession on you. I just thought it might be of interest to you, if and when you have time. Not now, of course. I—I see how you busy you are."

She put the translations down beside her on her desk. "I'll have time tonight. You've made me very curious. Maybe between the two of us—" She stopped, seemed to be thinking. "Maybe together we can figure it out."

Grigori wanted to tell her that she was very kind to take an interest, and that she had brightened his day. Instead he did something, it seemed just to happen, to occur, his hand lifting slightly, reaching for her hand. He touched her long fingers, enfolded them in his palm. She was looking at him calmly, and now with his other hand he reached up, toward her hair, touched the skin of her temple. Lightly he traced the side of her face.

A long flat beep—the telephone. Drew pulled away.

Grigori said, "I'm sorry, I didn't mean to—"

"I don't need to answer it." But she hurried to her desk and grabbed the receiver, said "Drew Brooks," in a rushed way. "Oh, hi, yes, sure, just one moment, I'm just finishing up here." She looked shaken.

I've done something awful, Grigori thought to himself. I must explain, I must apologize. But he did not understand, himself. As soon as Drew replaced the receiver, he said, "Please excuse me—"

"That was Lenore, I'm supposed to be at a meeting. I completely forgot. I'm sorry to . . . run off." She swallowed visibly, her eyes shifting away as she added, "I'll have to—get back to you."

"Oh, yes, well, but—really, there's—no need." Grigori turned to retrieve his coat, which he pulled on desperately. "Please accept my apologies." He hurried out the door.

LOT 71

Baltic Amber Bracelet, c. 1880. Five $^1/_2$ in. cabochons, each with inclusion: fungus gnat (Diptera: Mycetophilidae); dark-winged fungus gnat (Diptera: Sciaridae); moth, with bleaching; sand fly (Diptera: Psychodidae); unidentified insect. Colors range from butterscotch to honey. Each cabochon bezel-set in 14kt yellow gold braided frame with the 56 zolotnik gold standard hallmark and maker's mark AS in Cyrillic (Anton Samoilov, Moscow) partially obscured, 63 × 55 mm with clasp and safety chain. $2,000–3,000

LOT 72

Baltic Amber Ear Pendants, c. 1880. Two $\frac{1}{2}$ in. cabochons, each with inclusion: fungus gnats (Diptera: Mycetophilidae), good clarity. Each cabochon bezel-set in oval 14kt yellow gold braided frame with the 56 zolotnik gold standard hallmark and maker's mark AS in Cyrillic (Anton Samoilov, Moscow). $1,000–1,500

LOT 72A

Baltic Amber Pendant,* c. 1880. 2 in. cabochon with
inclusion: arachnid (*Archaea absurda*) with egg pouch.
Exceptional clarity. Bezel-set in oval 14kt yellow gold
braided frame with the 56 zolotnik gold standard hallmark and maker's mark AS in Cyrillic (Anton Samoilov,
Moscow). Braided chain, lg. 30 in., closes with secure
working spring ring clasp. $20,000–30,000

*While this item does not come directly from the collection of Nina Revskaya,
we believe the full suite to belong to an original set by Anton Samoilov.

CHAPTER TWELVE

The mail that afternoon contained a letter from Shepley. He always chose big blank greeting cards with reproductions of oil paintings on the cover. This one was something nineteenth-century French, a dark-haired, long-dressed woman with a parasol. Inside, Shepley's print was small and neat:

My dear Nina,
This woman looks like you, don't you think? Robert thinks
so too. Listen dear, I have to push back my Boston trip,
should be able to come in May. April has somehow become
ridiculous, and then that final week I need to be here: it
turns out I'm to receive an AWARD. Nothing glamorous,
a "local hero" thing—but it would be rude to skip it. Wish
I could see you before then. I hope you'll put this card on
the table beneath the Bonnard print. The colors will match
perfectly, if I'm remembering right.

With love,
Shepley

Nina tried to stop frowning, even as she rolled her wheelchair over to the wall where the Bonnard was. It was nothing she ever took time to look at, but she placed the card atop the table as Shepley had instructed. An *award*, a local hero thing . . . So that's how it is. This is how it will be. Well, I'm no fun to visit, really. Who can blame him? An *award*.

"You sure you're all right?"

Cynthia, sitting in the salon, had looked up from her magazine to wrinkle her forehead at Nina.

"I am all right." Merely speaking caused a claw to scrape through her.

Cynthia frowned, unconvinced, then returned to her magazine. She liked cheap ones overrun with celebrities. In her slight, haughty accent she said, "This stuff puts my diamond ring to shame. You never told me you had so much loot."

That was how Nina came to understand that it was the auction catalog Cynthia was looking at. It had been printed up and was now officially on sale to the public; Beller had sent one along in the mail for Nina. Only now did she note that it had made its way onto Cynthia's lap.

"Loot. Well, I no longer wear any of it." That icy claw scraped again. The doctor always told Nina he had seen worse, that one woman had spent twenty years so stiff, she could not bend even to sit in a wheelchair, and had to lie about all day strapped to a board. "It seems my fashion now is slippers."

Cynthia laughed, perhaps at how spindly Nina's legs looked. "Well, I can picture some of these on you pretty well. These ones match your eyes."

Nina did not look over. "You may take that home with you."

"Really?"

"You may take it."

"You think that's going to get me to leave? No go, sugar. I'm still waiting for your dinner to cook."

At least the auction would be over soon. Just three weeks. Maybe then the memories would leave her. Nina sighed, more loudly than she had intended. Could one die of pain? Nina had never spent much time wondering how she might die, though she found herself chronicling, these past years, the ways that her various friends and acquaintances had begun meeting—more frequently now—their demise. Sophie, a dancer in Paris, had died of leukemia. Beatrice had Alzheimer's, though she wasn't even old. Edmund had been perfectly sprightly until ninety-two and then broken his hip; after that it had happened quite fast. And poor Veronica had gone crazy (there was no other way of putting it) and lived off of public assistance in Leeds.

Nina told herself that at least her mind was all right. Well, she thought so, now that she had put aside the tablets, told Cynthia it was her own choice and that she could handle the pain. She had been a dancer, after all.

But it was funny what had happened without the pills, how in a way everything else, too, had become sharper, her mind searching for distraction, anything to detract from the pain. Yesterday she had found herself talking for a long time, with great effort, telling Cynthia about the war years, about performing for the wounded in one of the military hospitals, the horrible smell of the burn unit, a smell that still sometimes haunted her.

Nina wheeled herself over to the window, looked out at the spindly trees. Not long until they would begin to grow buds, though one would never guess it now, their crooked branches like a network of veins in the sky. The days had begun to grow longer, Nina had noticed. Normally she liked the gradual lengthening of the days—but now it just made her more aware of waiting. If only Shepley were here, if only he were coming to relieve her. An *award* . . .

"You want me to start another CD?"

Bach had been playing. How long ago had the music stopped?

"Yes, please, Cynthia, thank you."

It was but a minute before Glière came through the speakers, the opening bars of the *The Bronze Horseman*. Another wave of ice rose through Nina's limbs. But she closed her eyes, and sat, and listened, and for long moments in her mind, danced.

APRIL 1951. AIR still gray and cold, only the flowering gold of mimosas brought in from the Caucasus and sold by street vendors to brighten things up. Snow and rain become sleet. Roads are filthy, nearly impassable, full of potholes and enormous puddles. Pedestrians splattered with mud.

When Viktor arrives home earlier than usual, just as Nina is about to leave for work, she takes one look at his face and asks, "Are you sick?"

Slowly he says, "They fired Gersh from the conservatory."

Nina closes her eyes. The beginning of the end. Since every citizen must work, unemployment is a criminal offense. "I don't understand," she says, searching Viktor's face for an explanation. "Who's in charge of these decisions?"

Viktor is still standing there in his coat. "I'm going over there. He's going to need us. Perhaps you can tell Vera."

"I don't know if she's dancing with me tonight. I'll try to find her."

"I'll see if she's at your mother's. Come to Gersh's when you finish up."

Making her way across the wet asphalt of the square to the Bolshoi, Nina feels none of the usual excitement of such nights, though tonight she is to dance, again, for Stalin. This time it is a visitor from Laos he is entertaining; like all foreigners, the envoy wants to see *Swan Lake*. Melodramatic, show-offy *Swan Lake*. What did such things matter, frivolous fantasies, when all around horrible, inexplicable events were taking place? So long ago, the days when Nina found nothing more lovely than the swan-girls stretching forward to bow over their legs as they surround Odette . . . Now it just feels like a sham.

The theater is in a tizzy as always, the same stern-faced guards, the same nervous bustle, but this time Nina hardly feels enthusiastic. She hurries through the long corridors in search of Vera, past carpenters hammering last-minute repairs, cobblers stitching slippers in the shoe workshop, wig makers curling and combing out wigs. A cluster of mechanics, weighted down by their tool belts, is sharing a smoke in a side hallway. Nina doesn't find Vera anywhere.

For much of the first two acts of the performance, Nina manages to forget, for entire scenes, about today's new misfortune. But during intermission, as she sits with Petr at their table in the back hallway, the real world comes flooding back: Viktor's face when he stepped into the apartment this evening, the slump of his shoulders. Awful thoughts rain down, as Nina keeps her eyes on the door to Box A. She is willing the door to open.

If Comrade Stalin himself walked out and found her here, she could speak to him, tell him what has happened. *You know, of course, the composer Aron Simonovich Gershtein* . . . And yet, wouldn't he already know? How could he not? But then how could he let such a thing happen?

Suddenly Petr's eyes open wider. Nina follows his gaze, to the door of Box A. The door has opened. Nina's heart seizes, and Petr sits up straighter—and she knows this is not merely wishful thinking or a mirage. Flanked by two bodyguards, out steps Stalin.

Something formidable about him, thick chest and neck, pride in his stance. The slow stateliness of his walk, his left hand tucked in somehow. Overwhelmed, Nina feels herself about to look away— but he is looking right at her, has seen her seeing him, is approaching their table slowly. Dark, piercing eyes, and that glistening shock of gray-black hair, combed up and back. A firmness about him. He really is a man of steel, just as his name says.

Now he has stopped in front of their table, looking down at them. The guards hang slightly back.

"Butterfly," he says slowly, "a most impressive performance. You make us proud of our great nation."

His accent is more noticeable up close, almost intimate in its familiarity. His very tone exudes wisdom, and Nina, standing up to curtsy, bows her head and hears herself mumble something—but it is not what she wants to say, what she wishes she could say. If only she can find the strength to ask him.

Her ears are throbbing. Already he has turned to Petr, is saying, with that same simple boldness, "And you, Petr Filipovich."

Petr stands quickly, bows his head and shoulders in submission, his entire body trembling. With Petr standing like that, Nina sees, with surprise, that Stalin is not as tall as she thought. Up close, his skin is pockmarked.

"Comrade Stalin is most pleased," he continues. "A very interesting portrayal. Yes. If only there could be more . . . convergence." He smiles, and Nina sees his yellow, broken teeth.

Petr stutters something, but Nina's ears are ringing. She cannot quite hear his response, as Stalin wishes them well—and then he is walking away, guards on either side, and it is almost as if he were never even here, except that Nina's face is still hot.

Her one chance to say something, her one chance to ask. And she has failed. Failed herself, failed Gersh.

Petr has gone pale. Wrinkling his brow, he looks at Nina. " 'More convergence . . .' " He repeats the phrase, questioningly, once more, and then again. After a few minutes, during which neither of them makes a sound, Petr says, "You know, I think he's exactly right."

WHEN SHE ARRIVES at Gersh's apartment, after midnight, both Gersh and Zoya are in surprisingly good spirits. "It so happens I just bought him the complete works of Lenin," Zoya says. "Now he'll have time to read it!" But surely she must be frightened. After all, she is his wife; none of this can reflect well on her.

Viktor is drinking vodka, and Nina joins them at the table, Gersh asking about the performance. "Oh, it went fine, I suppose." She does not mention Stalin's presence, or their conversation, if one can call it that. She is too ashamed, certain she could have done something. The others speak lightly, of this and that, yet it feels like a vigil, like they are waiting for something. Nina wishes she could lie down and sleep.

A knock on the door. Gersh and Viktor do not look surprised, though at this hour it can mean only one thing. Zoya, her eyes fearful, goes to the door. "Yes?"

It is the building manager, and with him two men in dark suits. One of them wears a holstered gun around his waist.

"I've been asked," the building manager says in a somewhat timid voice, "to bring here representatives of Unit 4 of the Moscow Criminal Investigation Department." The men pluck identification cards from their jacket pockets and flash them at Zoya. Then the taller, armed one takes out another card, which he explains is a search warrant.

Zoya begins to cry. "Go about your business," she manages to say, then returns to the table and drops into her chair.

Quietly Gersh says, "I suppose I should pack some things."

"Oh, I'm sure there's no need for that!" Zoya says, as the two men tell the superintendent that he is free to leave. They begin their search.

Nina whispers to Viktor, "Should we go?"

Under his breath, "Not until Gersh tells us to."

He must have expected this. He must have known. That is why Viktor wanted to stay here so late. Because these things do not occur during the day. Like the old joke: "Thieves, prostitutes, and the NKVD work mostly at night."

The men are going through the drawers and cabinets, shuffling through papers, receipts, notebooks, letters. Taking their time, a nasty meticulousness about it all. They have left the door open, and in the dark hallway the few neighbors still awake pass by with wary curiosity, peering in passively, a distant look—as if they have not shared kitchen, bath, and toilet basin with this man.

"I can't imagine what they're looking for," Zoya says, her voice bewildered, frightened, yet somehow disingenuous. "I don't know what they think they'll find. I just can't even imagine . . ." Nina takes her hand. It is cold and damp. As Zoya repeats, "I just can't imagine why they would come here," Gersh leans over, very casually, and whispers something to Viktor. He slips something into his hand. Nina sees Viktor give a nearly imperceptible nod.

Soon an hour has passed. One of the men is sorting through sheet music from the drawer of the piano bench. The other is flipping through a series of bound scores. The janitor, a yellowish, sicklooking man, has come by and leans against the doorframe, watching with curious indifference as the men pluck books and notebooks off of shelves, and manuscripts from the piano. "There go my notes on Beethoven," Gersh says lightly when the shorter man shoves a wad of papers into his briefcase. A horrible pain has started at the base of Nina's head. Outside the window the sky is still dark.

The janitor wanders away but comes slinking back every quarter hour or so, while Zoya bustles about, as if there is something she ought to be doing, her forehead scored with frown lines. She seems to want to be helpful but clearly does not know how, keeps stepping aside as the two men rummage through the cabinets and bookshelves. This is by far the quietest Nina has ever seen her, and Nina finds herself thinking, guiltily, absurdly, So *this* is what it takes to shut her up.

The throbbing pain has reached the crown of Nina's head, a horrible splitting sensation. The men are still going through the bookshelf and bureau, one item at a time, more manuscripts, now, these ones rolled into tubes like diplomas. The janitor, back again, is trying to catch their eye. When he does, he says, in a voice that tries too hard, "We owe our safety to you. I can't tell you how grateful I am to know that—"

"Get out of here!" Nina yells. The janitor just raises his eyebrows. Then he turns away slowly, seeming pleased to have gotten a few words in.

At last the men have finished. There is no sign of fatigue on their faces, though the room is ransacked. They fill their briefcases with Gersh's notebooks and papers, and take a bottle of liquor, too. The shorter man asks for Gersh's passport, which he then slips into his own breast pocket. In a light, not unfriendly voice, the one with the gun turns to Gersh and says, "If you'll just come along with me to headquarters for a minute."

Gersh gives the smallest nod, unblinking, as Zoya jumps up. "If he really must go, then may I come along?"

"Oh, there's no need for that." The man with the gun says it in an easy, almost friendly, way, as if she has offered him a favor.

"Well, then, here, let me get something together for him, oh dear . . ." Zoya has gone over to the larder, takes out some sugar and ties it into a linen serviette. "Here, take this sausage." She thrusts a hard salami into Gersh's palm as if it were a block of gold. Her face has gone white. She must really not have thought this possible.

"Good-bye," Gersh says flatly, nearly sardonically, as they lead him out the door.

"I'll see you very soon, then!" Zoya is dabbing petitely at her eyes. Viktor nods at Gersh. Nina has no words, just watches him step out into the hallway.

Only when the men have left does Zoya fully begin to fret. "They found his diary, did you see? Oh, I just hope he hasn't written anything unwise! Oh dear, oh dear. You know Gersh. He doesn't mince words!"

"He kept a diary?" Nina asks, wondering if it has anything about Vera in it.

"Oh, not like you and I would keep. More of an artist's notebook, actually, thoughts on art and music and all that—oh, I just hope he hasn't written down anything imprudent. You know how silly he can be!"

Nina stares at her. Because what could Gersh have written that would be bad enough for him to be taken away? For all she knows, Zoya herself—crazy patriotic Zoya with her recordings of Stalin's speeches—could be the one who told those men about the journal. And yet she really does seem upset. Well, of course she is: How incredibly hard it must be to love two opposing things, to want so badly to believe in them both, simultaneously. Nina's headache grows suddenly stronger, with the thought that there could be something about Gersh that they don't know.

"Well, I know it will all be all right," Zoya says pertly. She seems really to believe it, though a few tears wet her cheek as she bats her curled eyelashes. "They mean well, I'm sure they do. They were perfectly polite—although they did leave a mess and all that! Oh, I just hope he's comfortable enough for now."

"Do you want to lie down, Zoya?" Viktor asks, his voice so slow and sad, Nina can't tell if he is sympathetic to Zoya or simply tired. "I can watch over things here, if you like. Or leave if you'd prefer some privacy."

"I don't know how I could sleep," she says, and bends down to start picking up some of the papers and books strewn on the floor. "Oh dear, do you think they'll come back?"

"Most probably." Viktor sighs. "They'll want to make sure they didn't miss anything."

"But what more could there be? I suppose we should check. Look through everything. Oh, dear, who knows . . ."

"I can help you," Viktor tells her.

"Thank you, Viktor, yes. Oh, I just hope he's all right on his own there!"

"I should go," Nina says, looking at Viktor so that he will understand what she means: *I must tell Vera.*

Out the door into the surprise of an early spring morning, air suddenly sweet after yesterday's rain. Pale sun brimming faintly like a dully glowing bulb. The thin scratchy sound of thatch brooms against the sidewalk—it must be close to seven, the old women have started their sweeping. Nina's headache grips her scalp and forehead like a too-tight cap. *If you'll just come along with me to headquarters for a minute.* The throbbing makes her squint as the sun stretches its pale light across the sky. The snow has fully melted, tiny streams in the cracks of the sidewalks, black rushing gullies at the side of the road. In front of the Metropole, a taxicab's bright green lights beckon. But Nina needs to feel the air on her face, her feet on the ground. She walks past storefronts with cardboard displays in their windows, past the corner kiosks setting up their candy and drinks and sandwiches, past the long block of *doma kommuny*. Bad news, bad news . . . All at once everything is rotten, even this world she had thought was *better*. The new sidewalks are sagging, the new paint already flaking, like nail lacquer from the Cosmetic Trust. When she turns onto the boulevard near her old home, the big, stocky worker girl hosing the sidewalk lets the water pour right over Nina's feet.

Just like that horrible janitor. Everyone is so awful.

Her wet shoes make slopping sounds as she arrives at her old alley. Dirty water spills out from the rusted drainpipes, and the smell is wet and dank. She has to step on planks that have been laid crosswise, to avoid the muck everywhere. Above, industrious early risers are already up and about, airing out their rooms, washing windows. She passes a woman scrubbing out the muddy entryway, filling the alley with the smell of carbolic. The cleaning, the rushing drainpipes, the pale white morning glories crawling up the balconies in spindly strings . . . It was spring too when Vera's parents were taken away. The memory returns, suddenly and with great clarity. Yes, of course. These mass arrests, always in spring or autumn, are seasonal, as vegetables and holidays are in other countries.

Now she is inside, making her way up the dark stairwell to her old apartment. She wonders if Vera was able to sleep at all last night, and if Mother is already up. Taking a deep breath, Nina prepares to tell them the news.

ALL DAY DREW had simply to think of him and she could feel it again. She wanted to tell someone, call Kate, or Jen, tell them how his touch felt, how, almost lovingly, he had touched the side of her face—

Of course it was ridiculous. They had a business relationship, and he was an older man, probably twenty years older! There was a heaviness in his touch, not just of weight but of magnitude. It was not simply the way he had touched her; it was something about his eyes, laughing but in a slightly sad way. His eyes, she decided, said something about having lived, something about humor and sadness being inexorably intertwined, no matter the depth of sadness, the depth of experience.

"Eyes full of life." It was a phrase Grandma Riitta had always used when recalling Drew's grandfather, Trofim. This phrase Drew now appropriated for Grigori Solodin. But he had looked so shaken when she pulled away. Well, how could he not be?

If only there were someone she could talk with. But Jen would just ask all kinds of dangerous questions, like How can you even be absolutely, one hundred percent sure he's not married? . . . And Kate would be horrified at how much older he was. Not to mention that he was a client, Drew had a professional relationship with him, would continue to have one until three weeks from today. She must reel herself in, take a deep breath. And yet let him understand: that it was all right, what he had done. She trusted him, as much as she was afraid.

For a while she simply thought to herself, wondering, not doing a scrap of work. To think that she had felt something, finally, and with the most improbable man. Just like Grandma Riitta and Trofim. . . . She nearly laughed to herself, and looked down at her garnet ring. Grandma Ritta would have understood. Thinking this—of Grandma Ritta's love story—Drew had an idea.

It took her a few moments more to decide. Then she picked up the telephone and dialed Grigori Solodin's number.

As soon as she spoke, he said, "I'm so sorry, I hope that—"

"There's no need to be sorry." She hoped her voice made that clear. "I just want to be . . . professional."

"Of course, yes, please don't—"

"I'm calling about something else. Unrelated, actually." Personal business, she heard herself saying, aware that even in this telephone call, on the Beller line, she was crossing a boundary. "There's a diary I've always wanted to read. Just a small one, not many pages at all, but it's in Russian. It belonged to my grandfather. My mother's father. My mother has it now, since my grandmother passed away. But she doesn't speak Russian, either. I've always wondered what it says." That her mother never seemed to have had much curiosity about the diary was one of the many things that continued to baffle Drew, though she had long sensed a faint fear surrounding it, at what it might contain: the man himself, her mother's father in his own words, undiluted by Riitta's loving recollections.

"I'd be more than happy to take a look at it." Quickly he added, "If that's what you're asking."

"I'd be very grateful."

Grigori sounded relieved, even surprised, as he said, "Of course if the handwriting is difficult, I might not be much help. But I'd be glad to give it a go."

Drew said she would have her mother send it to her. "I've always imagined I'd eventually show it to my children." Saying this, she realized she must not quite have given up hope that she might indeed start a family. "Or at least pass it down to them. The way my grandmother told me stories about him."

"Were you very close with her? Your grandmother."

"Yes. She's my kindred spirit, in a way. I still think of her every day." After a moment she heard herself say, "I wish I could talk to her about . . . things."

Grigori's voice was very quiet. "Drew. I—" He took a deep breath, seemed to be thinking, and Drew felt a sudden terror, of what he might say. "What I showed you today. The letters. They were family documents, too. Like your grandfather's diary. I ought to tell you that."

"From your family?" Drew's thoughts sped, wondering what the connection might be.

After a moment Grigori said, "You see, my interest in Viktor Elsin, my research on his work, comes through a family connection. I first became interested in him for that reason. I have other documents. Some photographs. I would love to show them . . ."

Though his voice faded, Drew understood that he was asking her something, that what he had told her was difficult, and that it was her turn to help him. She heard herself saying, "I'd like to see them. That is, if you want to . . ."

He quietly told her yes.

DAYS LATER, ON a chilly spring afternoon, Nina joins Zoya in the long line at the information office on Petrovka Street. They are trying to find out if Gersh is still being held there; he never did make it back from headquarters. So far, Zoya has been able to find out only that he has been arrested for "anti-Soviet activities." At least, that is what Viktor has passed along to Nina. She hopes to find out something more today. Though the information office won't open until ten thirty, Zoya has been here since five in the morning, so as to be closer to the head of the line. Sure enough, by the time Nina joins her there at one o'clock, there are hundreds of people along the sidewalk. Nina counts, since there is plenty of time.

Thick knots of gray fill the sky. Without sunlight, the day feels even colder. Nina has brought Zoya some berry soda and biscuits, which Zoya ingests eagerly. "It's really so nice of you to wait with me," she keeps saying. "Although I'm not much company, of course. Before you got here, I kept falling asleep standing up! I hate to get up so early, you know, but yesterday I didn't get here until seven and had to wait eight hours, and then just as my turn was about to come up, the woman in the window announced it was closing time!" All Nina can think is that what she suspected must be true, after all: Zoya must really love Gersh. "All I wanted to know was had they sent him away somewhere."

The smell of the air is oddly familiar. Nina tries to think what it reminds her of. Every once in a while the people behind them push up against them, eager for the line to move ahead. The first time it happens, Nina's immediate thought is that she has been recognized, that some fan in the line is about to cause a scene—but she has tied a big kerchief over her head and in fact is barely recognizable.

"Anyway, I've been able to use my time all right," Zoya says. "I've been writing a letter, to see if that won't take care of things." She takes a sheet of paper and a pen out of her purse. "Maybe you can help me."

"I'm afraid I'm not much of a—"

"Dear Comrade Stalin—or is that too impersonal, do you think?" Zoya makes a mark on the page with the pen, begins again in a plain, proud voice: "Dear Iosif Vissarionovich—sounds better, don't you think? More direct. Dear Iosif Vissarionovich—oh, and copy to the arts commissioner, too, don't you think?" She makes another note to herself. "Dear Iosif Vissarionovich, I am writing you regarding an urgent matter pertaining to my husband, the respected musician and composer Aron Simonovich Gershtein. First let me tell you that I am an active and responsible citizen who has been a member of the VKP since 1947. I was born and raised in Moscow and did my studies in the Party History department at the Institute of Red Professors. Following graduation, I went into government work, first with the Scholars' Aid Commission, then with the Higher Education Committee of the Moscow City Education Department. I now work for the department's lecture bureau. . . ."

Nina listens as Zoya reads on, lists in detail Gersh's educational and professional background, each fact noted as an example of his patriotic spirit. Every once in a while she stops to fiddle with phrasing. Her voice is earnest and hopeful, so that Nina recalls the letters she and her schoolmates used to write to Chairman Kalinin when they were children. *Hello Uncle Misha!* and lots of encouraging information about what they were up to in school, before making some simple request. *Give my regards to Uncle Stalin and the others . . .* Such earnest faith. Now, though, it seems childish.

"Despite his many years of dedicated service to this country, through his work as a professor and as a composer, my husband has been arrested under Article 58. And yet I assure you, as you would surely see yourself, that nothing my husband has ever done or said, nothing he has taken part in or even read, has even the merest link to any sort of counter-revolutionary agitation."

Nina has to wonder. "Do you think there's something we don't know?" She says it softly, since she knows what it means to even think it. "Something he was up to?"

"I'm his wife, I would know."

Nina bristles. Do you know that he was still seeing Vera? she wants to ask. To calm herself she breathes in deeply, and notes again the familiar-smelling air.

Zoya says, "The only thing I might not know is if his family might have somehow . . . I don't know them, you see. He says his parents and other relatives are gone now. But maybe they were, you know . . . part of the class system. Who knows, really? Even if they were, we're supposed to be free of our fathers' sins. This is a new world, after all—oh, that's a good line!" She takes a minute to scribble something onto the paper.

The training studios at the Bolshoi—on exam days, or during auditions. That's what the smell reminds Nina of. The smell of cold human sweat.

"I assure you," Zoya reads on, "my husband, like myself, has always lived his life as part of the fight for a great new society. Since we were born we have been taught to be always truthful, always honest and forthright—"

"Excuse me, Citizen, but do you know which line this is?" A woman with only a few teeth is tugging on Nina's sleeve.

Again Nina's first thought is that she has been recognized. Even with the kerchief obscuring her face, she and Zoya stand out among the many people in this line, their coats not quite as thin, their shoes not quite as worn.

"Is this the information line, or the parcel delivery line?" The words sound awkward due to the woman's missing teeth.

"This is for information," Zoya says briskly, pointing. "You need to go over there."

"Thank you, Citizen." The old woman shuffles away—and Nina sees where the backs of her felt boots are worn out.

"Where was I—oh, here. Truthful, always honest and forthright, always prepared to fight the enemies of socialism. My husband has lived these credos fully and faithfully. . . ." Soon Zoya is listing every major performance of Gersh's work, every award he has ever won. Probably Nina and Viktor ought to be writing on his behalf, too, though there is always that other worry, that they might themselves be punished "for loss of political vigilance." And meanwhile, people like that old woman with the worn boots . . . Who is there to write a letter for her?

Zoya's letter is long. Not till the end of the third page does she say, "I thank you, Comrade Stalin, for your attention to this most urgent matter, and I look forward to continued service as a most devoted and enthusiastic member of our great Party. Always prepared in the struggle for the workers' cause, et cetera. . . ." Zoya nods to show that she has finished.

"It's a good letter," Nina says, wishing she could feel as hopeful as Zoya.

"Well, we'll see." Zoya gives a small, tired sigh. "Thank you for waiting here with me. It's really very kind of you."

Nina feels a pang of guilt. Because it isn't kindness, really. She simply wants to be able to tell Vera whatever she can find out. Where Gersh is, or where he is going to be. It astounds her to think that everyone in this line is wondering the same thing, is here because someone they know has been arrested, and that like Zoya they don't even know where he has been taken. Watching as each person has his or her turn at the information window, Nina can see, easily, which ones have been told their loved one isn't there anymore. They are the ones who hang their heads, or cry loudly, then go to wait in line at a second window to find out which camp their loved ones have been sent to.

At last it is Zoya's turn. Yes, he is still here, the woman in the window tells her in an almost cheery voice; she could be a ticket taker at the cinema. "He hasn't been transferred yet, but he has been sentenced."

Ten years "with correspondence privileges." When Nina relays this news to Vera, later that afternoon, Vera says, "Well, I suppose that's a relief." Her face is swollen from crying, faint bluish circles around her puffy eyes. " 'Without,' and you might as well kill yourself."

"Why do you say that?"

"Because then they can just kill you. They can do whatever they want, without anyone really knowing what's gone on, since you can't write letters or anything. But if you have correspondence privileges, then other people might have at least some sense of what's happening to you."

It still surprises Nina, how Vera hands out this information, as if she has some special source, as if her parents' experience automatically allowed her this knowledge. Well, probably if Nina's parents had been sent away, she too would have paid attention to this kind of information. Vera has no problem comprehending things that Nina is only now acknowledging.

"How long, did you say, until they send him away?"

"I'm not sure, but he'll still be there tomorrow, at least."

"Then I can bring him a package." Vera goes to the little table beside her bed and opens a large Palekh box, takes out some money, and finds a clean handkerchief to wrap it in. "I should try to find him some socks and underwear, too. And some onions—for scurvy." As businesslike as Zoya.

It takes two days for Vera to leave her package for Gersh. "You should see the employees at the drop-off," she tells Nina, when she has finally succeeded. "They open up your parcel and take everything out and hold each thing up to the lights like scientific specimens. They tested the onions as if they were buying them at the market." She laughs, a sad, weak sound. "I'd tucked a letter inside one of the socks, and the woman found it. She started yelling at me, 'What in the world do you think you're doing?' So loudly the people behind me were staring. I said I just wanted to make sure the letter didn't fall out. She said, 'Now we'll have to read it, make sure there's nothing in it. . . .' Oh, Nina, I worry what they're doing to him in there."

"What did the letter say?"

"Oh, just that I loved him and that we were working on securing his release, that surely someone can pull some strings." She looks away, and Nina wonders if Vera really believes that.

HE TOLD HER to come to his office after work tomorrow. That way, he considered, they could speak without Drew having to worry about her supervisor, and yet they would not be alone, would have to behave professionally, no risk of Grigori embarrassing himself again. The Asian Languages division was holding a meeting at five, and the place would be teeming with professors.

All the same, Grigori kept worrying that he had somehow dreamed Drew's phone call. A personal request, nothing to do with the auction. He supposed it was an olive branch, simply to show that she did not intend to have him arrested. Unless this was all some terrible trap, to catch him out, make him look like a fool for having felt, in that awful moment, that there was some connection between himself—dour Grigori—and this bright-faced young woman.

She showed up in a coat of pale yellow that seemed to herald spring. Before he could thank her for coming over, she said, breathlessly, "I think I see what you mean. About the letter and the poem. The descriptions of the amber and of the forest."

"You see it, too, then?"

"They match up. Well, in a way. The image is so similar."

"I think you'll, well, here"—he took up the photographs—"hopefully it will all make sense." He might have shown her the hospital certificate, too, but it was in the safe. And yet, to tell her that part, about his parents, about his mother bringing him the vinyl purse . . . Surely it was too much. Grigori felt, already, his courage waning.

"May I see the photos?"

A mute panic spread through him: that showing them to her—exposing Nina Revskaya, in a way—was an act of meanness, done behind Nina Revskaya's back. No, he quickly decided; as long as Nina Revskaya continued to insist that none of it was hers, then all that these documents could ever be, really, were relics.

Drew held the photographs with slim, neat fingers. Both pictures were slightly worn, lines near the corners where they must have been folded by accident. But the images themselves were very clear. The first showed two couples seated on a settee, looking relaxed and happy. "This is her, isn't it?" Drew said. "She's so elegant. In a way, her face hasn't changed much. It's just . . . harder. Older." After a moment, Drew asked, "Is this her husband?"

"Yes, that's Viktor Elsin." Looking virile and jolly, he sat at one end of the settee with a cigarette held nonchalantly in his fingers. Next to him Nina Revskaya looked almost prim, her shoulders and neck straight, her smile small and slightly impish.

On her other side was the man Grigori had eventually identified as Aron Gershtein. His slightly crossed right eye had helped with that. "This was his friend, an accomplished composer." Looking up everything he could about Viktor Elsin back in college that first year, Grigori had learned that some thought Elsin's arrest might have been related to that of Gershtein. Grigori had therefore read up on Gershtein too, and subsequently recognized him as the other man in this photograph. "He survived years of persecution."

"What was he persecuted for?"

"Oh, it was simple anti-Semitism. After the formation of Israel in '48, Stalin decided he had a new enemy. He was old and becoming more paranoid, and of course Israel was allied with the United States. So he revved up the anti-Jewish campaign. As a result, people like this man here suffered."

In the photograph he was laughing. Leaning into him was a beautiful woman with big dark eyes. It had taken Grigori longer to figure out who she was. Only after much research had he learned that Gershtein had married an active Party member, an employee of the Moscow Education Department.

Even as he explained this to Drew, she kept her eyes on the photograph. "It's amazing," she said. "It's as if they still exist. There's so much life in this picture. You can see it in their faces. They're in love." Her expression was sad and serious.

"Both of those men ended up incarcerated, probably not long after this photo was taken. A year or two at most." Saying so, Grigori felt like a killjoy.

"And Nina Revskaya defected." Drew nodded gravely. "And this woman"—she pointed to the woman next to Gershtein—"do you know what happened to her?"

"No, but she probably would have become, by association, an enemy of the state."

Drew made a little sighing sound. She seemed to be having trouble looking away. "She's so beautiful."

Before he could stop himself, Grigori offered that he found the woman looked a bit like Drew.

"That's quite a compliment!"

Something inside his chest did a small flip, at the delight in her eyes. For a moment she seemed about to speak—but then she looked to the other photograph. This one had been taken out of doors, in front of what looked to be a dacha. Seated there were Nina Revskaya, Viktor Elsin, and another woman. Nina and Viktor looked much more serious in this one, almost stiff, their eyes tired and gray underneath. But the woman next to them, skinny and long-necked, had a big bright smile. There had been someone next to her, too, but the way the photograph had been cropped, only the side of his arm and his hand were visible.

"Someone wanted this guy out of the picture," Drew said. "Who is this woman, do you know?"

"I do not." He had tried to find out, had looked through numerous photographs associated with Elsin and Revskaya, but none showed any woman resembling that one.

Drew was again examining the photograph. "Do they know what eventually happened to him?"

"According to my research, Elsin was sent to the Vorkuta gulag and died there a few years later. It was surely a miserable existence."

Drew looked at the photograph for a moment longer before asking the question Grigori had been expecting. "And you have these photographs because of your . . . family connection?"

Grigori said what he had prepared. "It's a long story, but, through a series of events, I was given, many years ago, a woman's pocketbook that contained these photographs as well as the letters I showed you." He waited a moment before adding, "It also contained the amber pendant."

"Oh!" And then, "But whose pocketbook—"

"Exactly. I was told it belonged to a dancer. A woman who gave birth to—" But he could not do it, he could not say it. Why not? Just say it, Grigori, tell her what you think. A fool, to think he could just open up like this . . . "A relative of mine, who was then adopted." He closed his eyes, furious at himself, at his cowardice. "This relative was told that the dancer, his birth mother, had died."

Drew's eyes had opened wide, her mouth opening slightly. "You think . . . the birth mother—the dancer . . ." He could almost see her mind working. "That's why you tried to show them to her. To Nina Revskaya."

"Tried, yes."

Drew was still thinking. "And if I showed them to her . . ."

"Perhaps you might have more luck. But, Drew, that's not the reason I'm showing them to you. Not to make you do that. Not to make you do anything for me. I hope you understand that. I decided to share them with you because I felt I could tell you. I—I want you to know that I have them, and why I have them." He was already feeling embarrassed. "I supposed, since you've been so involved with the auction, you might be interested."

A look in her eyes like a question mark. She was still figuring, calculating. Why not just tell her, Grigori, that you're that child, that boy?

"This auction," he said, "what started it, I fear, was . . ." He decided to begin with November, the second anniversary of Christine's death. But what came out was his grief, how he had loved Christine more than he had understood, that sometimes one forgot what it meant, really, to love, the way the tide of a marriage advances and retreats, and how it was to watch her fade into some other person at the end, still Christine but also someone he did not, could not, quite know. Drew sat still and expressionless as Grigori continued, explained that he had already lost his parents, felt that loss every day, really, and now that Christine was gone realized just how much these things mattered, not just family but love, connections—and that time was short, he had in his possession these belongings, and Nina Revskaya was still alive. "And so I wrote to her. I included in my letter a photograph of the pendant. Because surely it's one of a kind, surely she would recognize it, no one else could have the same one. If indeed it is part of her set."

"And instead," Drew said, nodding slowly, "she decided to get rid of hers. I see now." And then, "I'm sorry."

She seemed to mean it. Grigori was touched. But there was a knock on his door: Evelyn leaned in. "Hey there. Some of us are going out for drinks—"

Drew looked up, her face registering who this woman was, as

Evelyn said, "Oh, sorry, you're with a student. Give me a knock when you finish up."

Drew's face fell. Evelyn had already turned away, not recognizing Drew, leaving the door half open behind her. His heart thudding, Grigori could hear Carla in the hallway saying, "Oh, Evelyn, if you could sign these thesis forms . . ."

Grigori tried not to frown. But suddenly everything felt wrong. Drew had stood and buttoned her coat. "May I take these, then?" she asked of the photographs, her voice flat and businesslike.

"Yes." Grigori was having trouble looking her in the eye.

"I mean, may I show them to Nina Revskaya?"

Grigori heard himself say, "You may."

"And the letters?"

He nodded as she put the photographs into her bag.

"Don't worry," she added, her voice still flat, "I wouldn't force anything on her. I would just see if she might be willing to look at them. Maybe talk about them."

"Just don't expect much," Grigori told her, his heart still heavy somehow. "She clearly has her reasons for not wanting to see them. I don't suppose it makes any difference who brings the subject up." Drew was standing close to him. Nervously, he added, "Who knows, perhaps all of it's meaningless."

"I doubt that." She was looking straight at him, the way she had when he had held her hand, touched her cheek.

He thanked her and, determined not to behave imprudently, held his hand out firmly to shake hers.

Drew shook it briskly, hesitating for the slightest moment before saying good-bye. Already she was heading for the door. Grigori could hear Carla, just outside, asking Evelyn where she had her hair done.

Then Drew turned, her eyes dark. In mere steps her body was against Grigori's. Grigori pulled her close and, as she leaned into him, refrained from whispering something long and embarrassing.

In the hallway, Evelyn's voice said something that caused Carla to laugh.

Then Drew stepped back, gave a small nod, and went quickly out the door.

DAYS OF WAITING, time so thick, you could touch it. Now that Gersh has been transferred to the prison camp, Viktor and Nina make sure to stop by the other wing of their building as often as before; perhaps Zoya, still living in Gersh's apartment, has more news.

He has been placed in a psychiatric rehabilitation camp, not far from Moscow—which Zoya attributes to her epistolary efforts on his behalf. "I think quite highly of the place, actually," she tells them after her first visit there. "Very progressive and all that. Impressive, how it's run."

"But why is he in a psychiatric camp?" Nina asks. "I still don't understand."

"Oh, the director explained it. It turns out they found some things in his diaries, you know, about the French Impressionists and Picasso and all that. But it's all right, it's just a mistake, poor Gersh, he's been confused, that's all. It will just take some instruction, re-learning, you know. It's really not a bad place at all."

Viktor's face is expressionless, while Nina tries to make sense of what Zoya has said. Why should it be a crime, to have such thoughts? How could that be serious enough to send Gersh to a psychiatric prison?

"Oh, and I have other news." Zoya gives a coy smile, waiting for them to ask. "His sentence has been reduced. To just five years."

"Already," Viktor says. "That's wonderful."

Wonderful. Nina can't bring herself to agree. *Only* five years— of watery kasha each morning, bread and water at noon, a scant ladle of soup at night. That's what they fed Nina's uncle, according to Mother. But of course this is one of the tricks, Nina sees now;

a sentence is reduced, so that the prisoner and his family become grateful rather than incensed, thankful rather than outraged. The same thing happened with her uncle. But even a reduced sentence was not short enough. He died before they could send him home.

"It's a very good place, actually, the rehabilitation camp. The director has a degree in psychiatry and all that. There's a whole system worked out, to help the patients. Poor Gersh! I should have noticed the signs. His views were quite mad, actually, I just didn't know. But it's all right, they're going to help him."

Surely she doesn't believe this, Nina thinks to herself. Surely she is just pretending. Yes, that must be it; it is an act, a performance, this too is a dance. A dance they all have to do, carefully saying the right things.

Or does Zoya really not understand what Nina sees, more clearly every day now, a thought so awful and yet she is every minute that much more sure of it: that this is all some big horrible, nasty joke.

AT HOME AFTER rehearsal one afternoon a few weeks later, Nina finds Madame at the table as usual. But instead of counting the silverware, she has in front of her an open cardboard box. Inside, Nina sees, there is jewelry: amber, framed in gold. Big thick beads, like candies on golden foil.

There are three pieces: necklace, drop earrings, and a bracelet. Nina wants to touch them, feel their weight in her hands.

Seeing that the array has caught her eye, Madame gives a pleased smile. "They needed polishing."

"Are they yours?" Madame has always complained about her jewelry being stolen after the Revolution, says that all she owns are her earrings and pearls and the tortoiseshell hair comb lined with diamonds. "Where did they come from?"

"Viktor brought them."

"Viktor?" Nina leans closer, because she sees, now, that the beads are more than just amber and gold. Inside the earrings are tiny flecks that, as she brings them to her eyes, look like midges.

"You may use my lorgnette." Madame hands the little spectacles to Nina.

Magnified, the insects' wings are clearly visible. Holding the lenses over the bracelet, Nina finds more midges, and a tiny fly, and then a tiny moth, its body visibly furred, its wings nearly translucent.

"Viktor brought them?" Nina wonders when, since he has been away much of the week, resting and writing at Peredelkino. Hopefully the change of scene will cheer him. He has been so glum since Gersh's arrest, drinking more than usual. Nina hasn't said anything to him about the drinking. But she worries.

"He wanted to keep them in my room, to hide them—Oh—" Madame makes an exaggeratedly startled face, as if she has just remembered something. "I believe it was supposed to be a secret."

She is visibly glad to have ruined the surprise. It seems she cannot help herself, every now and then, from poking at Nina in some way, seeing what she might get away with. Just last week, apropos of nothing, she turned her head away and said, as if to herself, yet purposely loud enough for Nina to hear, "I preferred Lilya."

Though Nina feels a familiar surge of anger, she reminds herself, as always, that there is nothing she can do about it. What does it matter, really, that Madame has shown her the amber? The surprise doesn't matter so much; what touches Nina is the simple thought that Viktor has seen these jewels and thought of her. Their anniversary is in just a few days, as Madame knows. The amber must have been incredibly expensive. Perhaps Viktor feels he has to outdo himself each time.

"Oh, well," Madame says theatrically. "Now you've seen them, what can I do? We'll just have to not tell Viktor."

Nina bites her lip and doesn't reply. Holding the lorgnette over the necklace, she inspects the bead. It is larger than the others. Inside, caught in action as if just moments ago, is a clearly visible spider, and below, like a tiny balloon, its egg sac. The way it is puffed out, just beneath the spider's body, it looks like a single big white egg. A tiny creature in the midst of creating new life—stopped forever by the very resin that preserves it. Nina looks at it for a long while, aware that she is witnessing the final moments, the dying act, of another being. Then she hands the lorgnette back to Madame and thanks her politely, making sure not to seem at all bothered by her having spoiled the surprise.

THEIR THIRD ANNIVERSARY is a staid affair. "To love" is their toast, raised tots of good vodka brought back from abroad—Viktor bought it, Russian vodka, but for export only, better than any for sale here. Viktor swallows his glassful in one gulp, says, "Love is all we have. I understand that now."

The first thought Nina has, though, is that for her there is also the dance. Dance and love. They may be all she has, but they are also all she needs.

Viktor nuzzles her neck. "Let's start a family, Nina, hmm? What do you say?"

A family. Children, a child. "I've tried. I'm just . . . having trouble." Now is simply not the right time. It would put a stop to her career right when she is at her peak.

Looking very serious, Viktor says, "I suppose it's common for dancers sometimes. To have trouble."

"Yes, but don't worry. We have time." She feels a wave of guilt, that she is unwilling, now when he so needs her, to give him this one thing he wants. With every passing month she sees more clearly how certain feelings and actions become decisions, rather than the other way around. Because really she would love to start a family, if only it did not mean that other sacrifice. How nice it would be, in a fantasy world, to have both.

Now Viktor is reaching under the table, and produces a small cardboard box. "Your present."

It isn't the box Madame had out the other day. This one is square and much smaller. Nina unwraps it to find yet another box, of beautiful shiny green malachite.

"Viktor, it's lovely."

"Open it."

Ah, so this is a double gift. Nina lifts the lid, which is some other stone—dark shiny black, inlaid with malachite—and looks down. There, inside, is a pair of little round sparkling green earrings.

She has no trouble looking surprised.

"When I saw them, I saw your eyes."

Emeralds. "They're gorgeous." She can imagine how much these must have cost. She is moved by Viktor's thoughtfulness, and by the great beauty of these dazzling green stones.

Even so, she can't help but think of the amber set, and wonder what Viktor might be saving it for.

LOT 89

Malachite and Onyx Box, c. 1930. The onyx lid with malachite intarsia, ribbed body set with beveled onyx panel, 3 3/4 × 3 × 1 1/8 in., signed Russian guarantee stamps and maker's mark (minor crack to bottom panel). $900–1,200

CHAPTER THIRTEEN

Cynthia went right back to the catalog the next evening, saying she needed to wait for the pork to thaw. Nina sat patiently through all sorts of questions, how heavy was this tiara, is this photograph the actual color of that stone, who gave you this opal ring. . . . For brief moments it felt almost good to recall times other than those early memories, to describe her travels, her move from Paris to London, the photo shoot where she wore the ruby necklace, the pearl bracelet the Earl of Sheffield gave her when she went with him to Wimbledon.

When the buzzer sounded, Cynthia gave a start. "You expecting someone?"

"The girl from the auction house. She has a man's name."

Cynthia went to the intercom to allow her in. She had already retreated to the kitchen to chop vegetables when Drew Brooks stepped inside, her cheeks rosy. "Hello there."

"So cheerful," Nina said, aware that she sounded disapproving. "Please, take off your coat."

"Thank you for taking the time to meet with me again. Oh, and I see you received the catalog, good. I brought another one with me, just in case."

"No need."

"I'll take it!" Cynthia called from the kitchen.

Drew looked surprised to hear someone else in the apartment.

"That is my nurse," Nina meant to say, but it came out, "That is my Cynthia." If only the pain would leave her be, not interfere with her mind. Before Nina could correct herself, Cynthia had hurried out to say hello.

"Very nice to meet you," Drew was saying in that professional way of hers, and Cynthia said, "I won't shake your hand, I've been handling garlic."

"We are here for business," Nina said, as coldly as possible, but it did not seem to faze either of these two. Drew appeared glad to be rid of the extra catalog, and Cynthia returned to the kitchen and set back to her chopping—though Nina could hear the knife slow down every so often, whenever Cynthia decided to listen in.

Drew had taken out the documents she had mentioned earlier, ones she hoped she might use in the supplemental brochure. Photographs and some letters. "An interested member of the public lent them to us," she said, somewhat evasively, and then looked carefully for Nina's reaction.

Interested member of the public. What did that mean? Solodin again, or was there someone else, now, too? Nina leaned forward until the knot of her neck seized. Two photographs, black and white, not at all faded, though they had been slightly crushed at the corners. Drew had laid them out on the coffee table, with nervous glances at Nina. "I of course wouldn't use either of them without your permission. I thought you might recognize them, or recall when they were taken."

Just seeing the four of them there on the sofa, so happy, laughing . . . Whose room was that? Not hers, and not Gersh's. They must have been at a friend's place some evening, some kind of party. After days of vivid memories, Nina was relieved not to recall this one. "It cannot have been later than spring 1951. This man here, the best friend of my husband, was arrested that spring. I never saw him again."

"I'm very sorry," Drew said, sounding sincere. Her expression was surprisingly sad. She was not a bad person, really. Just young. Nina felt suddenly mean, for having been cold to her earlier.

She thought of Gersh, the scenes that had overtaken her so miserably these past days. If only she could expel them—would that, could that, expel the pain? A deep sigh only made her shoulders ache. "I did not understand. The anti-Jewish campaign I knew, but first I believed that Gersh—this man here—must have done something. I was ignorant, you see, I was a dancer, I did not care about any other thing. I closed my eyes. I did not want to wonder why people were taken through doors and never seen again." It felt good to say it, even to someone like this girl, who surely could not understand.

Vera's gaze in the photograph looked dark and haunted. "This girl here, she too had a hard life. Her parents were arrested, and she moved to Leningrad. In the Great Patriotic War her city was ruined, so many people she knew died. And then the man she loved most in the world, this man, was taken away."

Nina shut her eyes briefly. "She was my most close friend." Dancing around the dusty courtyard, going up onto their toes . . . "But we each hurt the other."

A perverse hope came over her: that Drew would ask, How? What did you do? and that Nina might unburden herself. Maybe that would stop the recollections, more of them each day, encroaching. But all Drew said was, "She's so beautiful."

Of course. Typical. Nina pulled the picture away, covered it with the other photograph. Squinting, she took in that other world, which easily made itself understood. "This one. This is August 1951. I recall making this. At the dacha. My friend took it. It was not her camera. It belonged to . . . him." She pointed just beyond the photograph, to the space on the coffee table where the remainder of the picture would have been. She remembered very clearly who had been there. But who had cut him out of it? Whose photograph was this?

"Who is she?" Drew asked, tentatively, pointing at Polina.

"I suppose she too was my friend." Nina felt her eyes well, though really she and Polina had never been close. She turned her head, as much as she could, away.

"I also have these letters," Drew said, nervously. "I thought you might . . . recognize them."

The tears blurred Nina's vision, as Drew unfolded the sheets of paper and placed them before her. And though the handwriting might have been vaguely familiar, it was nothing Nina recognized. She was horrified to feel one of the tears roll down her cheek. Stiffly, she raised her hand to brush it away.

"I do not know these letters. Please take them away. You may use the photos. I give you permission." But the pain was too much. She simply could not look any longer.

THIS YEAR THERE are just three of them in the Pobeda. It has rained for days, and the wet clay road is slippery, the wavy fields of rye glistening. The spruces seem taller, thicker, greener. But the dacha looks the same as always, white lilies lining the stone terrace and, just beyond, magpies with long flashy tail feathers pecking at the ground. Something must have gone to seed.

Now the rain has started again. Vera cooks a barley soup while Viktor goes out to fill a bucket with wet raspberries, to eat before they grow moldy. Nina burns wood in the stove, so that the air around them becomes deliciously smoky, and feeds crackling pine-cones to the samovar.

That night she lies in bed awake, pale light seeping in between the slats of the shutters. An awful summer this is. Gersh gone, and Viktor so glum and drinking too much, and Vera sad and thinner than ever. And then there is Nina's guilt, at having made a promise to Viktor that she does not want to keep. Everything rotten, everything wrong. She is finally falling asleep when a nightingale starts up, somewhere close to the window. *Ta-ta-ta-ta-ta-ta-ta-ta-trillll* . . . Loud, its pitch clear and strong, precise as a metronome. The song reminds Nina of Gersh, his clear, perfect whistling.

A ghost. That's what it feels like, though Nina doesn't believe in ghosts. *Ta-ta-ta-ta-ta-ta-ta-ta-trillll* . . . So adamant. Nina finds herself silently speaking to Gersh. What are you trying to tell me? Please tell me. Please explain what happened. What exactly did you *do*?

Rising early the next morning, she decides to try to make a punch with the leftover raspberries, before they turn. The rain has stopped and the sun is strong, the air uncomfortably humid. After bathing in the river, Nina quickly feels hot again. Sunshine and shadows sift through the trees.

Viktor rises much later, comes into the kitchen rubbing his eyes. Glad not to be alone, Nina wishes him good morning.

"Is it? I barely slept what with the racket of that bird. Oh, hello, Verusha." Vera has trailed in sleepily behind him, though it is past ten o'clock. Flecks of hazel in her dark brown eyes. Viktor takes the water pitcher and heads outside to the well.

"Did you hear it, too?" Vera asks.

Nina almost laughs. "How could I not?"

"I couldn't help thinking . . ."

"I know. Me too."

"It's as if he's right here. Which makes me worry. Because if it's his *soul*—"

"He's not dead. They're not killing him there."

Vera looks skeptical. "How do you know?"

Nina has to stop herself from repeating what Zoya has told them, always so brightly, after her visits: *An excellent program, actually, very progressive and all that.* Gersh is permitted a weekly letter home and has even been allowed a call on the telephone, his reward for being a "star worker."

"Yoo-hoo . . . !"

Out on the terrace, Polina, wearing dark sunglasses, stands with Serge, waving at the window. "I told her we'd be here," Vera says under her breath. "I didn't think they'd visit."

Viktor, back from his wash down by the pump, is already greeting them, and Nina and Vera step out to join them. Already Nina feels tense. Ever since she has known whom Serge works for, not to mention that whole business last year about writing reports, she has felt on her guard around Polina.

"We're on our way back home," Polina says, "but thought we'd stop by. What a lovely spot." She and Serge have been at a nearby government sanatorium, she explains, as Viktor urges them to make themselves comfortable. Though he doesn't appear bothered by their visit, Nina supposes Viktor is a better actor than even she truly knows. Serge kisses Nina's hand exuberantly, then takes Vera's gently, as if in wonderment at being allowed to touch it. His lips graze her skin so lightly, it seems he hardly dares allow himself the pleasure. Yet his voice is almost cool as he says, "So good to see you." He has brought yellow lilies "for the house," but presents them to Vera. Polina gives a proud look, as if to say, See what a gentleman he is? Hard to find, a true gentleman, these days. Well, it's true. . . . She looks quite glamorous in her sunglasses. Yet even in this summer heat she wears a thick layer of makeup—quite a contrast to Vera's naturally clear skin. Perhaps she still has to cover the last of those odd gray patches. There must still be something upsetting her. . . .

"You wouldn't believe all the different kinds of lilies there," she is saying, of the sanatorium. "And hazelnut trees all around. Oh, it was so lovely!"

When Nina goes inside to fetch the punch, Vera follows her in. "We need one more chair."

"What do those two want with us?"

"I suppose they just wanted to say hello. I'm sorry. Maybe I shouldn't have told them." Through the window, Nina sees how re-laxed they look sitting there with Viktor, fronds of light filtering over them. Vera joins them, bringing the extra wicker chair with her.

"You've had a good holiday, then?" Viktor is asking when Nina returns with the punch and a tray of glasses. Serge leans back and with a slow, calm hand lights a briar pipe just like Stalin's.

"Oh, it's so comfortable there," Polina says ecstatically, "you wouldn't believe it. On one hundred *desyatinas*, full of aspen groves."

Serge says, "She's been practicing her dancing daily, I can report."

"I have to, especially with the yummy meals there every day. You could stand to do some gymnastics, yourself, you know." She play-fully taps Serge's midriff. "You're getting a belly."

"I play croquet. That'll have to do."

With a happy sigh Polina says, "I'm no good at it, I'm afraid." As Nina pours the raspberry punch, Polina takes off her sunglasses, to polish with the edge of her skirt. "Serge bought them for me."

"I've been admiring them." Nina wonders where they could be from, if Serge has been abroad, or if he bought them at one of those special shops, the kind reserved only for high-up government folks. That must be where he found the camera hanging from his neck—a big shiny one poking out of an open leather pouch.

Now that everyone has some punch, Serge says, "A toast." Some-thing aggressive about the way he raises his glass, that quick, gruff confidence . . . "Glory to great Stalin."

They repeat his words, and drink the punch, and then Viktor comments on the impressive camera.

"A Leica," Serge says. "I'd love to take a picture of all of you."

"We're all so well-dressed," Nina jokes, gesturing at her thin cotton housedress and Viktor's striped pajama bottoms. Vera too is in a housedress.

"Here, you four get together, pull your chair up, please, Viktor. You, too, Polina, just a bit closer."

Viktor has his arm around Nina, and Vera and Polina on his other side. The camera clicks, and Polina suggests that Serge might like to be in the picture. "Here, you sit here," Vera tells him, "I'll take it."

Serge takes a seat next to Polina, encircling her with his arm, and gazes ahead at Vera. A click, and the pose is over. He lets his arm fall away.

"Oh, there's the river," Polina says. "I can see it from here."

"Care for a last dip before you're off?" Nina hears how it sounds, as if she wants them gone. Well, it's true. She cannot relax with Serge here, Serge and his camera.

"I'd love a swim—it's so hot! Serge, will you come?"

He seems to be waiting to see what the others say. "You go ahead."

"I'll join you," Viktor says gallantly, and Nina feels a surge of love for him. But she does not join them, not wanting to leave Vera alone with Serge. Already, now that Polina is out of earshot, he is telling Vera, "Your hair looks luscious today, I must say."

Vera laughs. "It's because it got wet yesterday in the rain, and then Viktor braided it."

"Viktor! I thought that was a woman's job."

"Yes, well, if you'd seen the braid," Nina tells him, "you'd have your hunch confirmed." She has to laugh. Though the braid was messy, Viktor wove it tenderly, something almost fatherly in his attentions. Nina finds it sweet, the way he seems to be making a real effort to be there for Vera. He made a point of telling Nina, after Gersh's arrest, that it was up to them, now, to show Vera that she is loved, even without Gersh here.

"I slept with it braided," Vera says, "and when I took it out, this is what happened." Waves like the rye fields yesterday.

Nina begins to clear the glasses and empty punch jug off of the table, going in to the kitchen as many times as she can justify, in order to avoid Serge. At last she hears Viktor's and Polina's voices coming up the hill, Polina jabbering happily about all the special things available for guests at the sanatorium where she and Serge stayed. Quickly Serge takes Vera by the arm and says that though Polina needs to be in Moscow, perhaps he might return and visit again. He lets go of her arm before she can reply, and jumps up to greet Polina. "It's time we were off." Not until they have pulled away in Serge's dusty car does Nina breathe a sigh of relief.

That night the nightingale returns, quite late. *Ta-ta-ta-ta-ta-ta-ta-ta-trillll* . . . Steady and clear as taps on a piano keyboard. Haunting as it sounds, Nina is grateful for the song, for its insistence, its persistence, as it sings throughout the night.

THE NEXT DAY, Nina and Vera sit together in the *banya*. It is a small wooden room just behind the dacha, not far from the river, so that they can easily go back and forth. Dark walls and in the corner a big stove with river stones piled up around the pipe. Steam rises in billows each time Nina ladles water onto the hot stones. Lying down on the wooden step, she feels the hot air envelope her, the heat extreme, nearly painful, filled with the scent of birch leaves. On the step across from her, Vera lies on her back, propped up by her elbows.

"Why do you put up with him?" Nina feels the heat touch her mouth when she speaks.

"Who?"

"Serge. He's positively lecherous with you."

Vera is briefly silent. "Maybe he can help us. Gersh, I mean. Serge knows people. Maybe he has some sort of pull."

Nina considers this. "But why would he want to do anything to help *Gersh*?"

"Because I'll ask him to. He likes me."

His shyly lewd tone, his eager eyes . . .

"There might even be a way to have the charges erased." Then

Vera's voice becomes nearly tearful. "I can't stop worrying about him. Gersh, I mean. What do you think they're doing to him there?"

Poisoning his mind, probably—but Nina bites her tongue. "He's strong, Verochka."

Vera gives an odd, achy-sounding laugh. "So many men have offered themselves to me. Cried over me. Made all kinds of promises. Yet I love this strange one with a funny name and a crossed eye, and who wouldn't even marry me."

Nina tries to make light of it. "Think of it this way: it spared you a mother-in-law."

A long, sad sigh from Vera. "I know you don't get on with yours. But she's been kind to me."

"Well, you've seen how she manipulates Viktor," Nina says. "And how she talks to me. I'm déclassé, you know. She has to keep reminding me I married 'good stock.' It's the only way she can convince herself her grandchildren won't be tainted."

Vera seems to be considering this. "Will you give them to her?"

"Grandchildren?" Nina sighs loudly. "Ugh, Vera. I'm pregnant again."

Vera says nothing.

"I guess today is the first day I'm admitting it."

"Again," Vera says, slowly, and then, "Don't you douche?"

"Every time, with vinegar, it doesn't work! And that sponge thing from Budapest is useless." Nina lies still for a minute, suddenly hotter from her outburst. Well, it is the price paid, she supposed, for the tyrannical power of the attraction she still feels for Viktor—the electricity that still arcs between them. "It doesn't matter. I'll make an appointment as soon as we get home."

Vera says, "Do you want children, ever?"

Children. As always, the word itself warms her, brings with it the aura of childhood: such pureness, the one innocent time in life. To grasp again that purity, to love, again, in that uncomplicated way, laughing in the courtyard, Vera's hand in hers at the Bolshoi audition . . .

"Children, yes. But pregnancy, childbirth?" Nina wishes it were less complicated. "You know what Alla told me, about when she was in labor? There she was, screaming in pain, and what did the doctor say? 'Relax.'"

Vera laughs.

"Alla told her it was impossible to relax when she was having a hole drilled through her spine. So you know what she told her to do? 'Recite Pushkin to yourself.'"

Vera says, "I remember one of the dancers in Leningrad telling me her labor went on for so long, the doctor threw himself on top of her, to try to push the baby out."

"Ugh!"

"She didn't even want a baby. But she didn't realize she was pregnant until six months."

"Luckily I at least don't have that problem," Nina tells her. "One girl I knew, before you came here, didn't know at all until one day she had a miscarriage. Turned out she was already at five months."

Vera asks, "But you can tell?"

"I get this heavy feeling in my abdomen. And then my breasts hurt. After the first time, now I know what to look out for." She shakes her head. "But I can't bear to tell Viktor again. He was so happy the first time. He thought I wanted to keep it. The next time I didn't even tell him. And I told him we could try this summer. I feel horrible."

The steam is settling again, so she stands up to ladle on some more water, and is briefly dizzy. "Of course not having children is one more thing his mother holds against me. You know what she told me? That all my jumping around onstage was what was keeping me from getting pregnant."

After a moment, Vera says, "She puts vodka in the tea."

"Viktor's mother?" Nina sits back down on the bench. "Really?" Lying down again, she says, "I can't believe it," although of course it makes perfect sense. Always feeling "flu-ish" . . .

"I can't believe you didn't notice."

An edge to her voice. For a moment Nina thinks she must have misheard. She looks over to Vera—still reclining passively, as if she has said nothing of note.

"I've been busy working hard for almost two years straight," Nina says, trying to remain calm. "I don't have time to notice every detail of other people's lives." But already her adrenaline has surged. "I dance nonstop. I don't take 'leave' here and there. I don't have Uncle Feliks write me a note every time a tendon hurts." It's the truth. Nina dances on sprained ankles and jammed kneecaps. The last show of the season she performed with a broken toe—froze it with chlorethyl and wrapped it tight, and then danced a four-act ballet flawlessly.

Vera's posture has changed, stiffening as she props herself up. But Nina cannot stop herself. "I have work to do. I don't have time to always . . . push myself into other people's business. Prostitute myself with whichever man offers himself to me."

"I'm not prostituting myself!"

"What do you call it, then?" Nina sits up, too quickly; her head rushes.

"Caring! Trying to help someone! Thinking about someone other than myself!"

"I think about people other than myself!" The two of them shouting, like anyone, no better than the awful apartment neighbors at home . . .

"Do you?" Vera's voice changes. "Do you really?" Her tone flat, she says, "But you're a ballerina, a star. How can you possibly have time to worry about other people? You're so busy all the time. So busy you haven't even noticed that your mother is . . . dying."

Wincing in the burning air. "What are you talking about?"

A slow, concerned exhale. "She's ill, Nina. The doctor came just before I left." Vera waits a moment, seems to be thinking. "It's probably just a matter of months."

"Months?" Nina feels faint, damp with sweat. "Were you ever going to tell me?" And then, as if it is Vera's fault that her mother is ill, "Why didn't you say something?"

"I assumed you would have noticed how sick she was. I thought you would have noticed the great change in her. But you've been running around so much, and resting up so much, and thinking about yourself so much, you've barely had time to check in on her. Even when you do, you don't really *see* her."

Nina has begun trembling. Because it's all true. She barely sees her anymore, Mother in her skirt full of flowers. . . . "Yes, I'm a bad daughter. You're the good one." She stands up and swoons from the heat. "I have to go."

Vera says, "That's not what I'm saying. I'm just—"

The air stings as Nina pushes toward the door.

Outside she quickly wraps herself in a rough, stiff towel. The river below looks green, the droopy willow dipping its reflection as a troop of ducks drifts passively along. Nina feels how bright red her skin must be—with shame, she thinks, hurrying back to the house. "Viktor!"

"What's wrong?"

"I need to go home. Right away. I'm sorry. I'll take the train back, if you'll take me to the station." A fresh sheath of sweat has surfaced, and she wipes it away with the towel, too roughly, scraping the skin on her arms.

"Nina, stop that, you'll rub your skin off. What's going on?"

"I need to help Mother. She's ill. You can stay on, I'll know more soon. But I have to go."

. . . .

THOUGH SHE TRIED to read through the page proofs with care, Drew had to stop repeatedly, to refocus, each time she became distracted by the odd turn of her heart. Sometimes she even found herself shaking her head, as if that might clear it of those other thoughts. Leaning into him, the weight of him. At certain moments it seemed impossible that she had really done that, leaned into his body, stepped up to him like that. And then she would recall how good it had felt to do what she so rarely allowed herself—to act on her feelings.

Really, she reminded herself, there was no time for personal disruptions. Between coordinating with Miriam in Exhibitions and dealing with Public Relations and giving various small jobs to her new assistant, there wasn't time for much else at all. If she could just sign off on the galley proof of the supplemental brochure, that would be one less thing to worry about. The printer would send back five hundred copies on good thick glossy paper for next week's pre-auction dinner, where it would be perused in distracted boredom as attendees waited out various speeches and the clinking of glasses and whatever other activities had been planned. Then the folded programs, printed out on good, thick paper, would be tossed away with the rest of the garbage.

Funny, how none of it seemed to matter so much, now. Not the auction, or the jewelry, or proving anything to herself. What mattered was that she might be able to find something out for Grigori.

Just this morning Drew had contacted yet another "expert" whose name she had been given, and who might know something about where to find the jeweler's archives. No matter that it was something of a pipe dream, or that there was little chance she would discover anything in time for the auction. Normally Drew would have looked forward, at this point, to putting the entire project behind her. Now, though, she wanted to keep trying, to find something that might help Grigori figure out if what he thought about Nina Revskaya was correct.

A family relation of his . . . a family connection. Drew found her thoughts following that same well-traveled route, from Nina's bracelet and earrings to Grigori's pendant—all of which now lay sealed in unceremonial clear plastic baggies, awaiting next week's preview. The pendant, Grigori Solodin's pendant, and the spider with a pouch like a parachute underneath it . . . The letters Nina Revskaya said were not hers . . .

Drew's heart sank all over again, recalling how she had caused Nina Revskaya to cry. Just by showing her those two photographs . . . In fact Drew herself had felt shaken, at the reality of those pictures, at their silent reminder: that the people we are closest to can disappear like that, even the people most rooted in our lives, the ones we think of as constant. Jen and Kate and Stephen; her mother, her father. They too, like Drew herself, would at some point exist merely in images— photographs, recollections.

At the thought, Drew pulled her shoulders back, shook her head again. Photographs—the supplemental, the final proofs. There were still blank spaces where the pictures would go. Drew turned to her computer to make a final check. First came a photograph of the young Nina Revskaya leaping, her legs a horizontal line in midair. Then a newspaper clipping announcing her defection, and then a glamour shot from a Van Cleef & Arpels photo shoot. Next Drew had added the image of Nina Revskaya and her husband, cropped from one of Grigori's photographs.

For the final page of the brochure, on the back, Drew had selected a candid image: Nina Revskaya and three other Bolshoi dancers, leaning against the barre in a practice room. Drew had found it on the Web, where there were archives of such photographs, dancers in rows at rehearsal, or off to the side, watching a teacher's demonstration. It was these unposed photographs, especially ones of the corps, that

Drew found most intriguing, the way they captured who these dancers were—just girls, most of them, with still-young bodies and youth
in their eyes, the nameless girls no one remembered anymore. They
really were nameless, some of them: every once in a while a photograph
would list an "unidentified dancer," so that Drew found herself pausing,
wondering about these girls who, despite having been part of one of the
world's best ballet companies, had been excluded from historical record.

As she double-checked the image that she had selected for the
back page, Drew noticed something. The woman to Nina Revskaya's
right. Something ethereal about her, and familiar. That dark look in
her eyes. Drew thought for a moment, then turned back to the folder
containing the items Grigori had lent her. She felt sad all over again as
she found the photograph with the couple she had cropped out for the
brochure. Yes, she was right: this was the same woman—the one Nina
Revskaya had called her best friend. So she too was a dancer. According to the online archive, the woman's name was Vera Borodina.

Clicking back through the computer windows, Drew returned to
her cache of archival photographs. Indeed she was able to find two
others of Vera Borodina, one of them particularly beautiful, a still
from *Swan Lake*. So she too had been famous—or at least on her
way to being famous. Behind her, in the dark background forest,
were five other swan-girls, the nameless ones—wishing, Drew supposed, that they might one day play the lead swan.

Then Drew realized something: she recognized someone else
now. One of the "unidentified dancers," a skinny girl with a long
neck. Drew looked carefully at the on-screen image and then back at
the other black-and-white photograph from Grigori, the one in front
of the dacha. Yes, this was her, the girl whom Nina Revskaya had
called a "friend." They too must have become friends through the
Bolshoi—although this skinny girl must not have gone on to have the
same success as these other two.

The thought occurred to Drew that she could ask Nina Revskaya her friend's name. Then maybe Drew could figure out a way to e-mail the people who had archived these photographs, and let them know who this girl was. That way she would no longer be an "unidentified dancer." The thought was almost enough for Drew to telephone Nina Revskaya. But she didn't dare, not after the other day, how quickly Drew had upset her. Besides, there was too much else to do. And anyway, in the end, whether or not anyone would know this girl's name probably didn't really matter.

NINA SETTLES BACK in her old apartment, where she cares for Mother as best she can, even while she too is recovering—from the surgery that has taken care of her own condition. It was best to have the procedure done before Viktor's return, to rest up in her (now Vera's) old iron cot.

She has hired Darya to come by each day after she leaves Madame's, to help with the cooking and cleaning. Mother looks much thinner, older, in her skirt of faded flowers. Her body worn out, her smile black where her teeth used to be. Those once-proud shoulders now hunched, from so many treks from shop to shop, from waiting in lines and in offices and her seat at the Bolshoi . . . A mother's life, one long errand. One enormous chore. Like those worker girls Nina sees along the roads, and loaded up onto trucks at the end of the day, atop sacks of cement, to be driven home like so many planks or logs or metal beams . . .

Nina remains there until the end of August, when Viktor returns and helps her move Mother to their apartment, into their bed. He and Nina will sleep on a mattress on the floor. Mother has already become much more feeble and soon lies in bed all day. At times she barely seems to take in her surroundings or note what is happening around her. "Is it catching?" Madame asks when she emerges— for meals only, now—from her room, sniffing the air for microbes.

Never has she deigned to say good day to Mother. Darya too seems intent on ignoring her. Though Nina has continued to pay her extra, Darya refuses to do any more than her usual cooking and cleaning here in Madame's household. It takes over a week for Nina to figure out why: Madame has instructed Darya not to.

Her rage boils up all over again—but she is tired of fighting, tired of her own constant, simmering anger. It is all so petty, yet so all-consuming. She still hasn't spoken to Vera, has no energy or urge to reconcile. And yet when Viktor describes their days at the dacha, he seems completely unaware that the two of them have quarreled. Vera must not have said anything about what happened.

"Fortunate in a way that you didn't stay. You would have had to put up with that Serge character."

"He came back?"

"Twice. I don't like him." Jealousy in his voice. Only now does it occur to Nina that she perhaps did something unwise, leaving Vera and Viktor there together. After all, as devoted as Viktor might be, it seems no one is inured to Vera's allure.

"Where has she gone to?" Madame asks one day in September, when she has emerged from her room to eat some of the watery soup that Darya has cooked. "That beautiful Vera. It's ages since I've seen her."

Nina's own mother, too, misses Vera, and has more than once asked when she will visit. "She's busy these days," Nina says as an excuse, aware that, other than looking after Mother's apartment, and Viktor's solicitous checking in on her, really Nina has no idea, anymore, of what Vera is up to.

THEN ONE NIGHT Viktor does not come home.

Nina lies awake very late. Has it happened to him too . . . because of Gersh . . . Has something horrible happened?

When she dares to wake her mother-in-law, to ask if she knows where he has gone, Madame scolds Nina, loudly and angrily, for disturbing her sleep. She doesn't seem worried that her son has not returned.

It is nearly four in the morning when Nina hears his key in the door, his footsteps entering the darkened room. She has to stop herself from shouting. "Where were you? What happened? Are you all right?"

"I'm fine. Look at you, you've gone pale. What's wrong?"

"What's wrong? You don't come home until four, don't tell me where you've gone. I thought you'd been—I didn't know what to think."

"I told my mother, didn't she tell you?" And then, "I took Vera to visit Gersh."

Of course Madame didn't tell her. Nina bursts into tears, too exhausted, too shaken, to be fully angry. Viktor puts his arms around her, whispers, holds her, it's all right.

When she has managed to stop crying, she rubs her face against his chest, wiping her tears on his shirt. She hates the sound of her own sniffling. But now that she has calmed down, she is able to think more clearly. "You took Vera?" Softly, so as not to wake Mother. "I thought they only accepted family visitors."

"Yes, well, they're open to persuasion."

Nina raises her eyebrows, as Viktor adds, "It seems there are ways to finagle a visit."

He steps back, sits tiredly in one of the wooden chairs. Did he bribe someone, or forge something? Again Nina tenses, at the thought that he has put himself in danger. If only she could stop being furious at him. "Is Gersh all right? How is he?"

"According to Vera, not terrible."

"You didn't see him?"

Viktor shakes his head. "Vera was the only one allowed in. As 'family.' "

"Family." Nina considers what this could mean, and drops wearily into the chair next to Viktor. Perhaps Vera's putting up with that horrible Serge has paid off. "I still don't see how she managed it. What about Zoya?"

"It seems now that they've gotten a new director, Zoya has stopped showing up."

Nina raises her eyebrows. So, it's true, then, what she and Viktor suspected: that it was the previous director, and not Gersh, whom Zoya was so keen on seeing. "Just when I'd convinced myself she really loved him."

"Maybe she did." Viktor shrugs his shoulders in a way that annoys her. How can Zoya be so fickle? How can a person's love just skip from one person to another? When Viktor puts his arm around her, Nina lays her head against his, searching for comfort. If only she could stop feeling angry with him. If only she could relax, and believe that everything is all right, that Viktor hasn't compromised himself by helping in Vera's ploy.

Only after they are in bed, her head on his shoulder, does Nina ask, not sure if she really wants to know, "What was it like there?"

"I told you, I don't know, I didn't see."

Viktor sounds annoyed, so that Nina too feels a surge of irritation. "Why did you go all the way there if you didn't even see him?"

"To take Vera. I told you." He pulls away, rolls onto his side.

Nina tells herself that this is better than arguing, better than erupting into a true fight. And yet she feels dissatisfied. Perhaps Vera is just an excuse. A ruse, a way for Viktor to go . . . where? To do what? Nina thinks back to when she first met him, shapely blond Lilya at his side, and to the pleasure he takes, even now, in women's company. Of course a man with his success has admirers. Thoughts swirl in Nina's mind so that she cannot sleep. Everyone is suspicious to her now. As if the earth were no longer solid but some shifting thing, no foundation at all, nothing to stand on. Every day there are fewer people she can trust.

IT WAS A day or two after Drew Brooks's visit that Cynthia, having put the soup on, came out from the kitchen and, instead of going back to her magazines or the auction catalog, took a seat across from Nina's wheelchair. "I've been thinking about what you said to that young woman the other day. About your friend. You sounded like you wanted to talk about it."

Honestly, this woman could not just simply cook a soup. . . .

"Her life was hard. She suffered."

Two days straight, now, of bad memories. All today Nina had tried to distract herself—put the Bach CD on again and flipped slowly through a book on Gauguin, a big coffee table album she had not bothered to look at for years, all kinds of wonderful pictures for her to focus on. The pain slid in all the same. "Sometimes I tell myself that her suffering was her punishment."

Cynthia's eyes opened wider. "She'd better have done something pretty horrible, then."

Nina considered this, thought of her own body and how it had betrayed her. "I do think we receive what we deserve. Look at me: in this wheelchair."

Again Cynthia made a surprised face. "I don't care *what* you did, no one deserves to be stuck in that thing."

This straightforward statement—instead of the typical voyeuristic pity—and the light singsong tinge of Cynthia's island accent had a strange effect. Nina began to cry.

"Oh, sugar. Here." Cynthia reached over and dabbed up some of the tears with a tissue.

To Nina's surprise, the tears continued. Slowly she told Cynthia, "I did to her something heartless."

"You only tell me if you want to. If it will make you feel better."

If she could shake her head, or just let it drop dejectedly onto her chest, Nina would have. But the knot at the back of her neck was so tight now. No longer her grandmother's lovingly tied scarf. These days it was a noose, a stranglehold. "Nothing will ever make it better. It is too late."

Cynthia dabbed up more tears. "It's never too late. My father always said, whenever you think there's nothing you can do, you need to think again."

"Please, Cynthia, do not try to kill me with your good nature."

Cynthia laughed, and as if by magic, the knot at the back of Nina's neck loosened, just the slightest bit. But she decided not to mention that to Cynthia, lest she continue to put forth her father's platitudes.

EVEN WHEN REHEARSALS have begun again in late September, Nina and Vera do not speak; whenever they see each other at the Bolshoi, Vera turns away, looking bashful, almost guilty. Well, she ought to be. It still doesn't make any sense to Nina, why Vera would have tried to keep Mother's illness a secret from her. Yet it confirms that mystery that Nina first sensed about Vera, back when she first appeared in the little dressing room two years ago. Something enigmatic about her. What does she do with her free time, now that she has no secret visits to Gersh's room, no card games with Madame? All alone in Nina's old apartment, the entire room to herself . . . Apparently she visits Mother only when Nina isn't home.

Nina finds herself avoiding Polina, too, speaking to her only when they happen to cross paths at the Bolshoi. The rash has returned, hives on her neck, and blackish marks on her cheekbones, so that Nina assumes Polina is still being asked to report on people. But what information could she have? Nina cannot help feeling sorry for her, how thin and anxious she looks.

It is early October when Mother drifts away for good, Nina hovering above her, listening for a heartbeat or a breath. For a brief moment she again hears something, her mother is still here with her, but then Nina understands: it is her own heart she is hearing, the relentless thud of final understanding, that it really is over. Only later does it strike Nina that, unlike so many others, Mother has managed to die on her own, a natural death—from illness, not starvation or war or imprisonment or some other inhumanity.

At the funeral service, under a cloudless sky, in the small nearby cemetery, Nina and Vera barely speak. Now, though—having lost the person they have both lived with and loved as a mother—their silence seems preposterous. Nina is relieved when Vera lingers behind afterward, as they walk slowly away from the lowered coffin laden with snapdragons.

Nina allows Viktor and the others to go ahead, and waits for Vera to near. "I'm sorry," Vera says. "I loved her. I want you to know that."

"I know." In her mind she hears her mother's voice, the soft way she always answered Nina's knocks at her door: "Yes, yes, yes," and the shuffle of her slippers as Nina let herself into the apartment.

"I've been thinking how if it weren't for her, I wouldn't have this life. Not just in Moscow. I mean my career."

The Bolshoi audition. Nina nods. "I was thinking about that, too, the other day. How we followed her like two little ducks to the ballet school. And going through the rotating doors at the Metropol."

Vera closes her eyes briefly. "You and I went around that same door, but I've always felt when we stepped outside again, we stepped into two completely different places." Her parents, she must mean, what happened to them, and her move to Leningrad, and the Kirov school.

Nina says, "I think the men must have been flirting with Mother, don't you, letting us go around in the doors like that? She was so slender and pretty." She wants to be able to smile again, to laugh. To hear her mother's soft voice, *Da, da, da* . . .

Vera's eyes are still sad and dark. "I know I should have told you right away that she was sick. But you have to understand . . ." Her voice trails off, and she looks away.

"Understand what?"

"It wasn't . . . *that*." Vera lowers her head, looks at the floor.

"What do you mean, *that*?"

"I mean that the doctor—didn't really say that. That she was dying. I thought she looked ill, but the doctor . . . He never told me that."

"You mean you . . . made it up?"

"I must have sensed it, she looked so poorly."

"So instead of simply telling me that my mother looked ill, you . . . you said *that*." Clenching her jaw, Nina exhales loudly through her nose. "You said it, and it became true."

"I didn't *will* it."

"What kind of person makes a . . . a . . . *trick* out of someone's life or death?"

"It just came out! I suppose I knew it, somehow. And I was angry, you were having all your success, while I was the one—"

"Right, right, I know, you were the one caring for her, seeing her daily, while I was off being the bad daughter. Just like with Viktor's mother. I know it, believe me. Everyone loves you more."

"That's not what I'm saying. You don't understand. I really did love her."

"And she loved you. More than you even know." Nina feels she might explode. And then she hears herself blurt out, "She's the one who sent you those telegrams."

For a moment Vera looks confused. And then, "That's not true."

If only Nina could erase her own words. She feels like a skunk, or some other creature unaware of its full repulsion.

From Vera, a sound, small like a whimper, escapes.

Nina rushes away, past Viktor and the others, out to the street, where the old women are sweeping with their twig brooms. She is shaking, nearly dizzy, alarmed by her own cruelty. It is the first time she has ever felt within her something so awful—this enormous capacity for betrayal.

LOT 93

Platinum and 18kt Gold Diamond and Topaz Barrette.
With pairs of bead-set round diamonds alternating with
sets of three topaz beads with milgrained edging and engraved sides, joining a bar clip, lg. 8 in. $4,900–5,400

CHAPTER FOURTEEN

The days just before an auction were always stressful, the phone ringing constantly with last-minute inquiries (was this ring fourteen- or sixteen-karat gold?) and Drew's voice mail clogged with unofficial bids. Not to mention the flurry of previews, waves of people eagerly seeking out their vast and precise desires. All afternoon the gallery had swarmed with the usual mix: women trying on necklaces and rings and admiring themselves in propped-up mirrors, while auction employees told them what good taste they had, and parents and husbands and fiancés looked on, and grave-faced dealers squinted over the magnifying loupe for closer inspection, checking for imperfections. Among the mix this time were dancers, too, wispy long-necked women, some quite young, pointing at this and that as they peered into the glass-covered display cases.

The events director kept giving brisk orders to the interns; the pre-auction dinner was tonight, and there was much setting up to be done. From her desk Drew could hear the interns scurrying back and forth, while out on the sidewalk St. Patrick's Day revelers, some in Celtics jerseys, some with tall squishy brimmed hats emblazoned with shamrocks, and some wearing shiny green metallic beads, made their way from some pub on to the next, though it was barely afternoon. With the city of Boston on official holiday, it seemed everyone was out in the street.

Before now Drew had simply viewed Evacuation Day as an excuse for people to take the day off and join their friends at the bar. But now it struck her as significant that on this same day in 1776 George Washington's army had forced British troops out of Boston—peacefully, without a single casualty. Today's newspaper spelled out more ominous headlines: "U.S. Prepares for War" and "Diplomatic Efforts in Iraq Fail." One article said the president planned to send troops over in a matter of days. The drunken laughter on the street outside seemed wrong somehow. And yet, as another wave of revelers made their way past her window, Drew supposed that they too might not be quite ready to believe the headlines, might still be holding out the merest hope.

At her computer's little binging sound, Drew looked down from the window. An e-mail from Stephen, asking if she wanted to meet for a beer. Below it were two unopened messages from her mother, one with the subject line "oops!" Drew clicked on it warily, since most of her mother's missives were either forwarded warnings about some sort of computer virus or random cheerful updates about people Drew either barely knew or did not care to hear about. This one read, "Sorry about that, I meant to forward to Dad, not you . . ." Below was a link to an article in the *Seattle Times*. "Eric is quoted!" her mother had written to her father.

It was an article about cooking classes for couples. Eric and Karen had been taking the pastry course; they were considering cake decorating for next time. Of course Drew read the article. Curiosity compelled her to, the same thought as usual briefly sweeping through her: That could have been me. That life could have been mine. *East Coast transplants Eric Heely and Drew Brooks, a married couple in their early thirties, originally intended to take a culinary course on deep-frying . . .* The steady ease of couplehood, just your average married couple, doing the kinds of things that couples do.

Then the thought was past her, drifting away. Drew found the delete button, to erase the message—but saw that another e-mail had come in.

> Ms. Brooks:
> Paul Lequin forwarded me your message regarding the
> logbooks of Anton Samoilov. All of my family's books are
> in the archives of the Minnesota Russian Society. I have
> told the Society about your research and have forwarded
> them the amber descriptions you gave to Paul. The archivist
> there is Anna Yakov. Please feel free to contact her at
> Yakov.Anna@MRS.org. Best of luck to you,
> Theresa Samoilov-Dunning

Drew gave a little yelp and quickly typed a message to Anna Yakov. And though her next impulse was to want, very much, to call Grigori and tell him this news, she knew she ought to wait. She had not seen him since that day in his office, had not even spoken with him; she had decided to contact him only if she found something definite to show him. A possible answer, something to offer. First, she would have to see if in fact this message led somewhere, if she really might at last be able to find something out.

AUTUMN CHILL AND whiffs of winter, dead leaves skirting the ground. Bitter drafts surge through the Bolshoi's corridors and stairwells. At class each morning, Nina takes her spot at the barre, not looking toward the other end, where Vera too stands in her usual place. They rarely pass each other in the hallway, since their dressing rooms are on different floors; Nina finds it easy to go a full month without speaking to Vera.

Polina, who used to stand next to Vera at the barre, has changed places, over to the other side of the practice room, in front of the mirror no one likes because it makes everyone look slightly heavier. Not that that should bother Polina; she is skinnier than ever, her muscles visibly tense, buttocks and thighs tightly clenched before lowering herself into that first plié. Even the way her fingers grasp the barre, when really they ought to be simply resting lightly atop it, reveals her tension. Going back and forth from the rosin box, she sometimes looks almost sickly—but whenever Nina tries to catch her eye, she looks away. One morning, hammering a large hunk of rosin into smaller bits, Polina looks furious, seems to be taking her fury out on the yellow chunks as she grinds them into a powder.

Something is happening; something bad is happening. Yet as much as Nina knows it must be true, she does not know, exactly, what "it" is. She tries to float above it, stay true to her most basic tenet: think only of the dance.

Late one afternoon she returns from rehearsal to find Viktor at home, seated at the wooden table. Already Nina can see that something is wrong, the way his jaw flexes. He is clenching his teeth, so that Nina has to ask why he is looking at her that way.

"It's time we discussed what you neglected to tell me."

"What do you mean?"

Pain in his eyes. "Apparently your rushing home to take care of your mother this summer wasn't purely out of concern for her health."

"It most certainly was!"

"Really? And you didn't have your own medical concerns to attend to?"

"But—" How could he know that? "Viktor." Nina feels suddenly exhausted. "I'm sorry. But you have to understand, that wasn't the reason I came back. I really did need to help Mother. But I realized I was pregnant and needed to take care of it—"

"Interesting choice of words."

Nina lets herself drop into one of the wooden chairs, too tired to think of any clever retort. "Let's not fight about this. You know my mother was sick. I didn't lie to you."

"You didn't tell the truth. I had to wait to hear it from my own mother."

"Your *mother* told you?" Rage shoots through her, at the same time that Nina wonders how Madame could know such a thing.

Then she remembers. Vera.

"Why did you do it, Nina?"

What she says, in a whisper, is nothing she has ever consciously thought before. "How could I bring a child into a world like this?"

Victor leans back into his chair, as if to observe her more clearly. "What's that supposed to mean?"

This world where the people one loves are taken away in the middle of the night. Where they are hounded nonstop and cannot marry as they wish, and have their very reputations, their professions, stolen from them. "Gersh," she says simply.

Viktor gives a pained sigh. "It's just temporary. A necessary . . . wrinkle. You know what they say: 'You can't make an omelette without breaking some eggs.' Things will change when everything gets sorted out."

"How can you even say that? Is Gersh just an egg? Is Vera? How can you even repeat something so—"

"Of course they're not. All I'm saying is—"

"Oh, stop it!" Nina is surprised at her own voice. "I don't understand how you can keep this up." As if there isn't something horrible going on all around them. Only in thinking it does Nina realize that this really is the way she feels, and that it is the truth. She must have sensed it for a long while, now—that there are horrible unspoken things taking place all the time.

A sound, the plywood door swinging open. Madame stares at them. "What are these raised voices? Are you a bunch of brutes?"

"It's all right, Mama," Viktor says tiredly. Nina feels she might scream. If Madame hadn't told Viktor, they would not even be having this discussion. All because Madame told him. Madame, who would do anything to get rid of Nina . . . *You're not Lilya.* Ordering poor tired Dasha not to cook for Mother . . . Showing Nina the amber jewelry, to ruin Viktor's surprise . . .

Only in recalling the amber does Nina wonder if that was what those jewels were for: Was Viktor waiting for a baby, was that when he was planning on giving them to her?

"As bad as the Armenians." Madame shakes her head and returns to her room.

Nina's cigarette case—where she keeps a folded handkerchief instead of cigarettes—is on the table; without thinking, she grabs it and throws it at the door. It hits the wall instead, and lands on the floor with a pathetic tinny plunk.

"Oh, stop it," Viktor says in a tired voice. He walks over to the bed, sits down heavily.

Nina is putting on the coat she has only just taken off.

"Where are you going?"

"To work."

"You just got home. You're not even performing tonight."

"I need to practice." Really she just needs to get outside, away from Viktor, away from Madame. Viktor makes no move to stop her. When she leaves, he is still sitting there, leaning forward, his head resting in his hands.

She decides to rehearse. She will use this surge of anger, of adrenaline, in the only good way she knows—turn it into spins and leaps and quick, strong jumps. It is all she can do, all she knows how to do. Her hands still shake as she enters the Bolshoi.

Though this evening's performance is not for another two hours, the hallways are busy with costume deliveries and dancers scurrying up and down the stairs. Nina means to go straight to her room for her exercise clothes, then to an empty studio where she can work. But she finds herself continuing past her door, up the stairs, along the next hallway, to her old dressing room.

Vera must have visited Madame while I was away. She must have told her, on purpose, to turn her against me. Nina raps loudly on the dressing room door.

No answer. Vera might not even be dancing tonight. Nina wants to shout at her, to leave an angry message, to break something . . . Anything to rid herself of this awful feeling. She flings the door open with such force that it slams against the wall.

In front of her, at eye level, unmoving in the air, are two limp, silk-stockinged legs.

Looking up, Nina's eyes find a form long and thin, like a trussed goose on a peg in a kitchen. Polina, in her tights and leotard, her head at an unnatural angle. Lying on its side below her on the floor is the old wooden stool.

Only when she has regained her voice, recalled how to use her legs, does Nina scream. Running into the hall, she finds the first person she can. And still it takes a good hour for her to truly understand—to comprehend as reality—that Polina is dead, that she has done this thing to herself, with a long wool scarf looped around her neck.

All week whispers hiss through the corridors of the Bolshoi. *Dumped by her man, don't you know, dropped her like a hot potato. . . .* But how could she kill herself, Polina of all people, in that most unpatriotic, un-Soviet of acts? *You know Polina, there was nothing more for her, no will to live. . . .* But why here, the Bolshoi, of all places? *She thought it was Vera, don't you know, thought Vera was the reason. . . .*

Vera, meanwhile, has not been here even once. *Barely gave him the time of day, but you know how men are, they like the chase, and after all, persistence pays off. . . .* She is absent the following week as well. *Her Achilles, you know, but really some people think, well, I won't say anything, that's how rumors get started.*

And of course there is that most obvious of facts—that it wasn't Nina, but Vera, who was supposed to be the one to discover Polina.

IN THE DINING room, sitting at the table set with woven place mats and linen napkins and the good heavy dishes he rarely used for himself, Grigori smiled, pleased, as Zoltan declared the meal excellent. "You never told me you were a chef, Grigori. I hate to admit that I hadn't thought it possible."

"Christine taught me a few tricks." Grigori had seared two big salmon filets he then sprinkled with dill and garnished with a slice of lemon. Steamed rice and stir-fried broccoli were the accompaniments. "But I don't often cook for just myself." He did not add his next thought, which was that only in these past days had he found himself, suddenly, very hungry.

As he took another bite of the salmon, he fought the unfamiliar urge that kept creeping up. To mention Drew, to simply say her name. But of course he stopped himself; at the very word, it might all dissolve. Not to mention that he and Zoltan never spoke of such things.

"I realized something today," Zoltan said, munching. "It's a funny thing, how working on this memoir, and reading through my old diaries, has crystallized some of the ideas I've had over the years. Or perhaps that's not quite it. Perhaps it's that I'm seeing my own thoughts from a distance, across a bridge of time. Their repetitions and choruses. Page after page of this odd young man's thoughts. And that odd young man was *me.* I see the things I wrote about, and whom I wrote about, and you know what has become absolutely clear to me, Grigori? Though I suppose I've thought it, or known it, innately, all along. That there are only two things that really matter in life. Literature and love."

Grigori grinned. "I might have to agree with you." After all, he felt like a new person ever since Drew had reached out to him. And friendships like his with Zoltan at times seemed all he could really count on. The same way that he could always count on Chekhov, Eliot, Musil. There was one horrible day, toward the very end of Christine's illness, when, suddenly and utterly aware that she was on a terrible lonely journey where he could no longer reach her, Grigori had sat down to reread *The Death of Ivan Ilyich*, and afterward had felt—not comforted, not at all, it was such a sad story, but that he understood something, understood in another way what Christine was going through. And so he hadn't felt quite so alone.

"I remember before I left Hungary," Zoltan said, "understanding so completely that literature could save me as much as it could get me killed. Of course it's not like that here. But isn't it funny, that in some ways the price one pays for freedom of speech is . . . a kind of indifference."

Grigori nearly told him his latest news: that it looked as though he might already have found the perfect translator for Zoltan's poems, a Hungarian American who had expressed interest in Zoltan's work years ago, at a conference Grigori had attended. He was proud of remembering her, a professor in Syracuse. But he kept quiet, since he had yet to secure a publisher, and that could take some time.

"Of course," Zoltan was saying, "you can't be wary in poetry. In any art. Just like with love. It's all or nothing." He chewed on his broccoli. "That's why love too is dangerous. We stand up for love. We take risks. Well, you of all people know about that—your own Soviet Russia, an entire nation rearranged to discourage love for anything other than one's country."

Because love caused people to think for themselves, to look out for themselves and their loved ones. Nodding, Grigori said, "Love makes people strong, we do all kinds of crazy things for love." In his mind he saw Drew stepping up to him in his office, reaching her arms around him as he pulled her to his chest . . . and the Department of Foreign Languages right on the other side of the door.

"Exactly," Zoltan said, triumphantly. "That's what makes it more important than anything else." He chewed a bit and added, "Except literature, of course."

Thinking aloud, Grigori said, "Sometimes I think that's what keeps me in academe. It's one of the few places in this country where you don't have to always fight to convince other people that literature and art matter." With a sigh he added, "Zoltan, what am I going to do without you here next year?"

"Exactly what you always do," Zoltan said. "Sneak cigarettes in your office and hold too few department meetings."

Grigori laughed. But he was serious when he said, "The truth is, I feel less and less connected, somehow, to the university these days. Less engaged." He wondered if it had to do with Drew, with the way he felt in her presence, and how meaningless so much else of his life now seemed. Drew's arms around him . . . Still, he ought to be wary. It might be too much, he might scare her away. Or weigh her down. Why burden her with my secrets? Really I don't see how she could love me, she hardly knows me. I barely know her. She's still young. And me, fifty years old!

All day his thoughts had followed this path; he thought with faint guilt of Evelyn, and of the expectations of Christine's friends, and of everyone in the department, that it would simply be too strange, how could it ever work, so improbable, and people would talk. But then he would ask himself, what did he care about people *talking*, people with nothing better to do than *talk* about other people. . . .

And yet when he thought of what it would take to get to know someone again the way he knew Christine—such a steep road to climb, to get that close to someone again. It really was all or nothing, Zoltan was right. But to get from here to *all*, to knowing and loving someone completely . . . It seemed impossible, how did people do that, share everything of themselves, all over again?

And yet, now Grigori wanted to, wanted at least to try.

THE SEASON IS busy as usual, Nina dancing at her peak. Dance itself is her kindest partner, now that her friendships have fallen away and her marriage tensed. She has avoided Vera all winter, eyes quickly averted the few times she has passed her in the hall or backstage. And then for a long while Vera was out on medical leave, her Achilles again, this time for surgery, with a requisite six weeks of recovery. But her Achilles must not have healed well; Vera still isn't back.

Meanwhile Nina has been on a number of brief tours, to Riga and Kiev and Minsk. Now it is May, the air sweet, leaves a bright yellowy green. Viktor has gone out to the dacha. He says it is because he needs to get out of the city, but Nina knows it is their life together, their cramped quarters, that he needs escape from. He has even timed his return so that he won't be back until after Nina has left—tomorrow, on another mini-Bolshoi tour, just the "stars." It is what they call a "quickie" tour, three theaters in three days.

And so, when the wife from the apartment next door raps on the door and says there is someone on the telephone for Viktor—someone from the hospital—Nina at first thinks that something has happened to him. It takes her a moment to understand the question, to tell the voice on the clunky black telephone, "I'm sorry, he isn't here. He won't be back until next week."

"I'm calling because his name is listed as the emergency contact on Vera Borodina's file. She isn't doing well. If he could come in—"

"I'm afraid I don't understand."

"Vera Borodina is here, and we are . . . fearful for her recovery. If Mr. Elsin is able to come in—"

"I'll come." Nina's heart is racing. "Just please tell me where to go."

At the hospital she is sent up to a room full of many occupied beds. Vera's is in the front corner of the room, tucked behind a tall screen. Vera is pale, her eyes closed. In a daze, Nina wonders how long she has been seriously ill. "What's wrong with her?" Nina asks the orderly who has brought her here.

The orderly shushes her, and pulls her more fully behind the screen, to hide her. They are not to have visitors here; Nina has paid to be allowed up. Before she can repeat her question, the orderly has hurried off.

With her skin so pale, Vera looks nearly angelic, her hair shiny and only slightly matted. Nina takes her hand and is relieved to feel a pulse.

"Verochka, I'm here."

A twitch of her face.

"You can hear me? Vera, what happened?"

No reaction. Still holding her hand, Nina tells herself that the strength in her own body will carry over into Vera's. If she doesn't let go, she can make her healthy again.

But now the doctor, a short, stern-looking woman, has come to check on her.

"But what's wrong with her?" Nina asks.

"Hemorrhaging. It seems to have stopped for now. But we can't be sure. Some people are predisposed to it." She makes a quick pen mark on the piece of paper on her clipboard.

"Predisposed?" Nina looks at Vera, whose hair curls slightly from sweat. "I don't understand."

But the doctor has already gone on to another bed, the one right across from Vera's—no screen to separate it—flipping to another page on her clipboard. Nina would like to sit somewhere, but when she steps out to look for a chair, there are none, just bed after bed, and a stocky, wide-hipped nurse bustling forth. She has with her an infant—a crying infant, as if there is not enough noise and discomfort in this room already.

"He's a hungry one," the nurse says, handing the little thing to the woman in the bed across from Vera's. Nina watches her help bring the child to the mother's breast. "No, no," the nurse is saying. "You're doing it wrong, he can't latch on at that angle." The new mother readjusts the infant. "I can't do it."

The nurse gives a huff. "Oh, so you're going to let him starve?"

Nina looks up at the nurse, and at the overwhelmed mother, and only then does it all make sense. She peeks around the cloth barrier, looks quickly at the bed next to Vera's, and the next, and the next. "Oh, look, he's staying on now," the new mother is saying, relief and joy in her voice. "Look, there's the milk!"

The big-hipped nurse says, "There, you see? He knows just what to do."

"Excuse me," Nina asks anxiously, as the young mother suckles her infant. The nurse turns toward her briskly. "My friend here. Did she have a baby?"

"Of course she had a baby. This is the maternity ward, isn't it?"

"But . . . I don't understand. Where's the child?"

"In the nursery." And then, almost mischievously, "You can see him if you like."

Him. A boy. In a stunned voice, Nina says, "Yes, please."

When the nurse returns, she holds a tiny baby wrapped snugly in white cloth. Nina peers warily at the infant, expecting a walnut-faced creature like the one across from her. But as the nurse, with something like reluctance, hands over the small bundle, Nina sees that this baby is beautiful. Instead of closed puffed slits of skin where eyes should be, this baby's eyes are open, searching, a bewildered blue. This tiny being is clearly a person, fully human, his nose and chin surprisingly defined. "Why, he's perfect."

"Yes, he's a handsome one. I did his hair." Though the child has only the finest—nearly invisible—whisper of hair, the nurse has given him a crisp, minuscule part.

Yes, he is a real being, a living person. Nina searches his face to find Vera somewhere in it. Vera and . . . who? Whose child is this?

Nina asks the nurse.

"Just a big line where the father's name is supposed to be." Clearly the nurse does not approve.

Vera in the *banya*, saying, "So many men have wanted to marry me. . . ." And how she was willing to put up with that awful Serge. As if he would ever help Gersh. Serge, who dropped Polina *like a hot potato* . . . But no, surely Vera wouldn't do . . . that. The apartment all to herself as soon as Mother moved out . . . The truth is, it's been so long since Vera and Nina have spoken, the father could be anyone, really. Nina shakes her head.

"That's right," says the nurse. "So much for this little guy, no father's name on his certificate." A new law has reclassified illegitimacy, making such children second-class citizens.

Nina watches the child, bewildered. Turning to the nurse, she asks, "What's your name?"

"Maria. Three more, and I'll have seen my one-thousandth baby here."

"Mmm." Nina nods, but she cannot keep her eyes away from the child, how sweet and helpless he is. The swaddling cloth comes up over his chin. She tugs the cloth down a bit, revealing the top of the baby's tiny muslin shirt. Yes, his mouth is Vera's, exactly—but minuscule and moist and perfect, the same way his nose is perfect, the same way his eyes are perfect. Nina touches the baby's cheek. "Why, he even has a tiny dimple!"

The nurse, Maria, says, "Just like a movie star."

He squirms then, and lets out a cry. "I'll need to take him back, now."

Still squirming, the child cries out again, catlike, painful. Maria takes him from Nina and bustles out of the room.

Her eyes closed, her breath light, Vera looks even more pale now, as if the nurse has scared the color right out of her cheeks. "Verochka," Nina says, stroking her forehead, "why didn't you tell me?" Vera's eyelids flutter as if to open, then close again. Nina takes her hands in hers. "You didn't have to do this, you know. Did you want to?"

Maybe she didn't notice until it was too late. Or maybe she wanted this child. But how could she, if it is of that horrible Serge . . . No, surely she would only keep the child if the father was someone she loved. Nina brings her mouth closer to Vera's ear. "I would have helped you, if I'd known."

Now Vera's lips move. Words too faint to make out. Nina asks her to repeat it, and waits, but Vera says nothing more.

Now the nurse has returned. Frowning, she puts her hand on Vera's forehead. "She's burning up." Briskly she turns to Nina and says, "I'm sorry, you'll have to come back later." She lifts the side of the blanket to glimpse Vera's body, then turns toward the doorway and calls out another name.

"But . . . Is she going to be all right?" Nina is pushed aside, as a doctor and another nurse rush in.

No one answers her as they hurry to Vera's rolling bed and whisk her with them out the door.

BOOK III

LOT 100

18kt White Gold and Sapphire Buckle Bracelet. The wide strap prong-set with cabochon sapphires weighing 250 cts., lg. 7 ⅛ in., Bailey, Banks & Biddle. $5,000–7,000

At first Maria thought she was the only one who had noticed the patient's cream-colored pocketbook. Leather, a buttery color and soft, you could tell just by the way it folded in gentle pleats up at the clasp—two small flat gold knobs that hooked together like tiny hands. Maria had been eying it ever since the woman first started hemorrhaging, when it was already clear her chances of survival were slim. But then there was an awful moment when Maria noticed Lydia, the orderly, eying that same purse. It was just waiting there for someone to take it.

The moment runs through Maria's head again as she makes her swift way from the maternity ward out of the building, onto the broad, dusty boulevard. With Lydia, you knew it was simply money she was after. Maria, though, wanted the purse. Beautiful, the leather so fine, who knew where one could find such a thing, let alone afford it. If only she had thought to move it, hide it . . . Instead, she had noticed Lydia, who turned to see Maria watching her and glanced nervously back at the purse. That was when Maria decided to approach her, and the two of them made their bargain.

In the privacy of one of the medical closets, they quickly emptied the bag, at first just a few papers and keepsakes the poor woman had been carrying around with her. Much of the stuff wouldn't fetch any money at all. Photographs, a stained handkerchief, a pink lipstick down almost to the tube. But at the bottom were a fancy hairbrush, a gold makeup compact with mirror, and a matching perfume flask. The wallet was a new one, of matching creamy leather. Gifts, these things must have been, from someone with money and means. Or maybe the woman herself had bought them. Apparently she was a ballerina, one Lydia said she recognized, although Maria had never heard of her. Not a bad amount of money in the wallet, either. Lydia kept rifling through the little slits, in case there might be something more, while Maria did the same with the inside of the purse.

That was how she found the necklace.

A big smooth stone. Sliding it out from the slim inner pocket, Maria stopped herself. She could not quite see what the stone was but did not want to risk having Lydia see. The glimmer around it looked like real gold; it could really be worth something. She might make more selling this than any one of those other things. And so she decided: this she would not split with Lydia.

She was about to slip the thing quickly back into the side pocket, but Lydia said, "Let me see?" and grabbed the purse from her. Quickly Maria shoved the necklace into her own purse, a shiny, poorly constructed thing of black vinyl.

When Lydia had gone through all the contents of the leather one, she began to gather everything up, promising to split whatever she made, fifty-fifty. A glimmer of doubt, that Lydia would keep her word. Instead, Maria suggested that Lydia take the wallet, the money, and all other valuables (the comb and compact and perfume case), and that she—Maria—would keep what she had originally wanted more than anything: the purse.

"Here, just swap hers with mine, for the record. Put anything you don't want in here, and I'll put my things in that one"—she gestured toward the beautiful cream-colored bag. Then she switched the contents of her own vinyl bag with the leather one, careful not to let Lydia see the necklace. The problem was, Maria hadn't quite seen it either, as she dumped her things into the leather pocketbook. She turned the vinyl bag upside down, right above the leather purse, and gave it a good shake. Then Lydia transferred the woman's non-valuables to the cheap vinyl purse, and the two of them were finished with their transaction.

Maria runs through those moments again now as she continues on her way, walking briskly in the warm spring air, her head covered in a paisley kerchief, a pocketbook over each shoulder, arms crossed below her midriff, coat concealing the most precious bundle of all. Already she has stopped once, in an alley, to go through the leather bag, and then the vinyl one—but she still cannot find that necklace. Well, it doesn't matter. She has a much more important task at hand, and hugs her precious bundle tightly to her chest. Near the Krasnye Vorota metro stop she turns onto Kotelnicheskaya and her pace quickens, brisk squeak of her shoes with each step. The sound reminds her of baby birds, hungry and chirping incessantly, abandoned in their nests. She lets out a great sigh, as she has many a time, in the face of such tragedy. No matter how many times it happens, she has never grown used to it—the perfunctory dreariness, the flat factuality, the extreme nonnegotiability of death.

Soon she has come to one of the nicer high-rise apartment houses, where a woman named Katya lives with her husband, Feodor. According to the friend who first introduced them, telling her their plight, Katya is a chemist, and her husband is a geologist. It is for them that Maria has paid Boris in the hospital records office to make sure to take care of any documentation.

Katya's face, when she ushers Maria into the apartment, is a mix of smile and worry lines. She is well into her forties but wears her hair in a thick braid tucked up into a wide barrette at the base of her head. She kisses Maria, peers into the bundle, and begins to cry. Maria cannot tell if these are tears of joy or sympathy. The child is still sleeping.

"You're sure there are no relatives?" Katya asks.

"There was just the one friend," Maria tells her. "After identifying the body, she ran off."

Katya says, "I imagine she must have been in shock."

Maria shakes her head. "A snobby one, she was. Turns out she's famous, another ballerina, according to one of the nurses. *I* didn't recognize her. I told her she could keep her friend's things. . . ." She hears the evasion in her voice, adds, "She didn't want anything."

The maternity dress and stretched-out stockings Maria has left in a bin in the hospital. And as for this poor child, well, everyone knows an orphanage is a rough place, especially for a bastard child like this one. There is no doubt in Maria's mind that she is giving him a better future, a mother and father, legitimacy and love.

Katya's face has relaxed, finally able to accept her luck. "May I hold him?" she asks.

"He's yours." Maria passes her the delicate bundle, his tiny chest rising ever so slightly with each tiny breath. "Oh," Katya says, and begins to cry again.

Maria places the vinyl purse on the wooden table beside them. "Her belongings are here. The only things she had with her."

Katya doesn't ask any more questions. Not in the face of such a gift, this answered prayer. She looks down and kisses the baby on his forehead, while Maria waits, not wanting to ruin the moment by asking for her tip. Then Maria hears Feodor's footsteps behind them, and Katya turns to show him that a miracle has finally occurred.

ANNA YAKOV WAS out of the office until the following week. Though Drew's heart sank to find the automated reply in her in-box, she had managed to locate a telephone number—only to discover that it too went straight to Anna Yakov's mailbox. So it was not until Monday that Drew received the fax. *I believe this is it*, Anna Yakov had written in hasty script. *Sorry for the delay.* The following page, scored with lined columns and profuse with penmanship, appeared to be a photocopy of a page from the logbook. Though written in thick ink, the handwriting was slightly faded from the transmission. The fax itself was clear enough to read—if only Drew had been able to read Russian. For a moment she just stared at it, hard, searchingly, as though simple patience and effort might somehow make the words intelligible to her.

"Hey, Lieutenant, good news."

Drew looked up to see Lenore standing at her door.

"I've already had three messages complimenting us on the supplemental," Lenore told her. Drew was gripping the fax so tight, she realized she was wrinkling the flimsy page. "All old ladies, of course." Lenore laughed, while Drew placed the fax on her desk as if it were nothing at all.

Ordinarily she would not have waited an extra second to report her news. Now, though, she felt strangely as if the page, whatever information it contained, had nothing to do with anyone here, as if it were not about the auction at all. No, it was nothing Drew cared to share with Lenore. What she said instead, in a casual, musing way, was, "You know, I think it's probably time you stopped calling me that."

Lenore raised her eyebrows. "Calling you . . . Lieutenant—is that what you mean?"

Drew nodded, smiling lightly at how good it felt to speak her thoughts, her feelings. She had never seen Lenore look flustered before.

"Well, of course. Certainly. I never realized . . . I'm sorry, Drew. If you had told me it was a problem . . ."

Smooth and easy, Drew said, "Now it won't be."

Lenore stood up straighter. "Good point." She gave a professional smile, said she'd see her at the ten-thirty meeting, and left.

Feeling a great lightness in her chest, Drew turned back to the fax that sat waiting on her desk. Eager and wary, she picked up the telephone to call Grigori Solodin.

ON HER HOSPITAL form, for next of kin, Vera had written "Viktor Elsin."

This fact won't give Nina's mind a rest, even after Nina has signed the necessary forms and left the hospital. Well, now that Mother is dead . . . Not my name, but my husband's . . . *Just a big line where the father's name is supposed to be.* I know we had a falling-out, but still . . . Next of kin.

She goes directly to her old apartment—Mother's apartment, Vera's apartment—to see if there might be some indication there, some clue as to exactly what happened.

The room looks different, sparse without Mother's things. Same old bed, and the wooden chest where Nina's own clothes, folded carefully, used to be. In it now are blankets, mittens, winter scarves, the woolly smell of winter. Here is Vera's big travel trunk. Nina opens it warily but shuts it at the first glimpse, unable to face the sight of Vera's clothes.

The first place she decides to search is underneath the cot. Indeed there is a box there, with a little latch that hooks over the edge. Nina slides it out, brushes off a layer of dust, and unhooks the clasp. The box is full of folded papers, which Nina quickly shuffles through, searching for letters. Or love notes.

But these are professional communications, ballet contracts, receipts for earnings. Below are other formal documents, and a series of mailings that appear to concern Vera's parents. Nina returns all of them to the box and places it back underneath the bed.

She stands up, wipes the dust from her knees. On Vera's bedside table is a bottle of perfume and a large Palekh box. The table has a small drawer, and though it might simply be decorative, when Nina pulls on the little knob, the drawer surprises her by sliding open. Shallow, containing some nail clippers and a flat little metal container. Nina removes the metal lid to find inside tiny pieces of torn yellowed paper. Trying to make out the typed words, she realizes that she knows what these bits of paper are—what they once were. There is an awful ripping feeling in her chest. She puts the lid back on the tin and shuts the drawer, feeling guilty all over again.

But she goes ahead and opens the Palekh box. Inside is a shallow tray, nothing in it. Not quite expecting anything, Nina lifts the tray. Underneath, to her surprise, she finds a gathering of amber beads.

She lifts them out, a bracelet and a pair of earrings. *The* bracelet, *the* earrings—the ones framed in gold, the ones Madame displayed on the table that day. Only the necklace is not here; Nina's heart winces as she realizes that Vera must have been wearing it.

Vera, wearing it. Vera's bracelet and earrings.

Nina's heart plunges. No—no. No, of course not. How could it be? It can't be.

Well, of course it can. Of course. What was she thinking, leaving the two of them there together at the dacha?

She drops the bracelet. No, maybe it's not true, maybe she is wrong. Because how could they? How dare they? Her entire body is trembling.

It wasn't enough to turn Madame against me, wasn't enough to turn Viktor against me. . . .

No wonder she didn't speak to me, didn't dare look me in the eye.

And Viktor, is that where he's been: not the writers' retreat but the hospital, with his Vera. . . . But no, that can't be, they would not have called for him at home, Nina would have seen him at the hospital. . . . No, they must have been keeping it a secret, not letting on to anyone: *Just a big line where the father's name is supposed to be.* A secret—their secret. All the time that Nina has been working so hard, and been so trusting. She feels, now, her heart cracking. Yes, that is what is happening, that is just how it feels, her heart cracked in two, like a nut.

The next thought that comes to her, swiftly and absurdly, is *My life is over.* Because how can she go back? How can she continue to live?

She will strangle him, throttle him, stab him a thousand times. She understands, now, how a person could do such a thing. Her fury has turned her skin hot, her face burning.

The two people left in her world, the two people she loved most . . . Together, behind her back. Yes, this is how it feels to be betrayed: her chest ripped apart, her heart torn out. The pain is physical—immense, gaping. Now she hears a wailing sound. It is her own voice; she has begun sobbing.

For a long time she sobs, until her voice has become hoarse and her eyes hurt from crying. Yet even when she takes a deep breath and sits very still, quiet and exhausted, her thoughts continue to race.

She will have to leave Viktor. Move out—but where is there for her to go, other than this apartment right here? This room full of Vera's belongings. This place where Vera and Viktor must have been meeting, the two of them together, here where Nina and Mother once lived together so innocently.

I have to leave this place, leave this life.

You can't leave, no one can, you know that.

I hate them, hate them with every ounce of my being, I'm full of hate.

I have to leave, thank God we leave tomorrow.

I can't look at them ever again.

I'll leave and never come back.

They find you and break your legs.

I'm leaving this place, for good.

Impossible. How does one do that? How does one escape?

They break your legs. And then what will you do, no money, and you can't even dance . . .

Nina looks down at the bracelet and earrings and decides. She takes them, drops them into her purse.

Rushing out of the building, she feels as if she is in a movie or a dream, not her real life. She walks the streets in a daze, past the bored-looking troops stationed at the intersection, passively blowing their whistles long and loud, past the vendors of ice cream and vodka and round watermelons, past the old woman with the scale where people pay to weigh themselves—and it seems an abomination that the world can continue on like this, so easily, when these awful other things have occurred.

As if to prove her point, walking toward her is Serge. Of all the people in the world . . . Nina hasn't seen him since Polina's funeral, where he stood far back, perfectly still, head slightly bowed yet somehow still proud, a long face but not a tear in his eye. He wears his usual stern expression now, though he looks somehow less prideful, less sure of himself.

His greeting is unsmiling. "Nina Timofeyevna, good afternoon."

The possessive way he kissed Vera's hand . . .

"I don't suppose you know she's dead."

"Who's dead?"

When she tells him, his jaw slackens and his face goes pale. For a moment she thinks he might faint. "No, it can't be. How could it be?"

Nina hears herself telling him "birth" and "hemorrhage," and Serge says, "I . . . I didn't even know she was expecting." He is doing something Nina has never seen anyone do, tugging the skin at the tops of his cheeks, just beneath his eyes, as if to see more clearly. Little upside-down triangles of skin, and his mouth hanging open. He lets go, shakes his head, as if that might help him understand. "It's been so long since I saw her. We'd grown close, she and I. But she told me she couldn't see me anymore." Pained sadness in his face.

"Well," Nina says, her voice tight, "it seems she took up with someone else."

Serge squints at her. "Oh." A small, sharp nod of understanding. "I should have known, when I saw them together over the summer. You weren't there. You—"

"My mother was ill. I had to go to her." As if it were her fault, as if Vera could ever have loved Serge. Only now, witnessing Serge's quick nod of comprehension, and his eyes narrowed, calculating, does it occur to Nina that Vera must have said that on purpose— about Mother being ill—in order to get Nina out of the picture. So that she could be alone with Viktor.

"I saw it with my own eyes," he says, his jaw flexing angrily, "but I just thought—I suppose I just didn't want to believe it. The bastard. I'm sorry, Nina. And now she's dead."

"She's dead," Nina repeats, to convince herself, but all she sounds is furious.

"Bastard," Serge says. "His fault." A tight, angry look, shaking his head at himself. "I should have known. He was so affectionate with her there at the dacha, it was obvious, and still I didn't— Because the way he acted, he just didn't seem to be . . . hiding anything."

And that's not all he's hiding. Spiteful thought. For a split second, Nina thinks she might say it aloud. Because all she feels is spite. Madame, behind the flimsy plywood door . . . Even though she stops herself, Nina supposes it is already too late, that she has said it, already, in so many words. That she is saying it right now, with her fury.

Serge's eyebrows rise just the slightest bit, as if reading her thoughts, and Nina feels immediately ill. Already it seems wrong, an accident. As soon as Serge has hurried away, she turns into an alley and retches, still shaking as she wipes her mouth on her sleeve.

. . . .

WHEN SHE SAID, "It's good to see you," he had to smile. Grigori wanted to touch her, to at least shake her hand, but she seemed somehow nervous—or perhaps simply excited, at what she had to show him. She made sure there was a good foot of space between her body and his as she took the faxed page from her desk and held it out to him. "Does this look like the right thing to you?"

"Let's see. The columns say 'date,' 'items,' 'price,' and 'buyer.' "

"Sounds right."

He began with the top entry. "Date, June 7, 1882." Looking up, he explained, "That would be the prerevolutionary Russian Orthodox calendar. Twelve days behind ours . . ." He cleared his throat, suddenly nervous, and continued. "Bracelet, five beads, each with insect specimen and 56 zolotnik triple-twist gold frame."

"That's it," Drew cut in. "That's got to be it."

As he read the price aloud, he realized his heart was pounding. "Next it says, 'Amber drop earrings, two beads, each with insect specimen, and 56 zolotnik triple-twist gold frame.' "

"That's right too." A flush had come into Drew's cheeks.

" 'Amber inlaid brooch, 56 zolotnik triple twist gold frame . . .' Hmmm. '56 zolotnik triple-twist hairpin with small amber cabochon.' "

Drew leaned closer to him. "Is there a necklace there, too?"

Grigori ran his finger down the column, searching. "Ah, here. 'Amber pendant, large bead with spider specimen, in 56 zolotnik triple-twist frame.' " He took a deep breath, his eyes continuing down to the bottom of the final column. Aloud, and with surprise, he read, "Buyer: Avrim Shlomovich Gershtein of Marosejka Street, Moscow." He took a step back, as if there were more there, to be read more carefully. "Huh."

Drew was looking at him. "Avrim Shlomov . . . ?"

"Gershtein. It's the last name of Viktor Elsin's close friend. The composer in the photograph I showed you." His mind was racing now. "These people could be his ancestors." Again he heard himself say, "Huh."

Drew quickly went back to her desk and was rummaging through some folders, while Grigori asked himself what this page might mean. Viktor Elsin's friend . . .

"Here," Drew said, "is this him?" She held out the photograph Grigori had lent her; in the supplemental brochure that had been mailed to him, Gershtein and his wife had been cropped out of the picture, so that the brochure showed just Nina Revskaya and Viktor Elsin. Pointing at the original in her hand, Drew said, "This is him, right?"

"Yes."

"So, the amber must have been something *he* owned, that had been passed down to him from his parents or relatives. These pieces were his. Or became his at some point."

Grigori nodded, but it was an automatic movement rather than one of comprehension. "Yes, he must have given them—or sold them—to Viktor Elsin. Probably when he was arrested." He thought for a moment. "Gershtein must have given them to Elsin for safekeeping before he went off to prison, and then Elsin gave them to Nina Revskaya, and she took two of the pieces with her when she left Russia."

Drew gave a small nod. "But why would she take only two of them?" She paused. "Maybe Elsin gave two of the pieces to his wife and the pendant to someone else."

"But who else?"

"The person whose bag you have. The person who had those letters."

Grigori realized that she thought he knew more than he claimed to. Well, of course. He had not told her that he did not know who, precisely, his "relative" was. "But you see," he tried to explain, "I have reason to believe that the pocketbook belonged to Nina Revskaya. I'm quite sure it did."

Wrinkling her brow, Drew asked, "But couldn't it have belonged to someone else? And the letters, too."

Just like Big Ears, incredible . . . Grigori felt a surge of impatience, while Drew, oddly calm, said, "I think we need to take one step at a time. Starting with what we know for certain. And that's the fact that these jewels originally belonged to the Gershtein family." She looked back at the photograph Grigori had given her. "What would you do if you were this man and owned this set of women's jewelry that had been passed down to you?"

Grigori said, "Give them to my wife." He pointed to the beautiful woman next to Gershtein.

Drew said, "Nina Revskaya told me she was an old friend, that they were very close. They were both dancers. Maybe—"

"No, actually," Grigori corrected her, "Gershtein's wife wasn't a dancer. She worked for one of the government offices." It was one of the few facts about her that he had been able to learn in his research.

Raising her eyebrows, Drew thought for a moment, and then said, "Well, in that case, this wasn't his wife. She was . . ." Drew leaned back toward her desk to look at something she had written down on the blotter. "Vera Borodina."

Questioningly, Grigori repeated the name.

Drew clicked on her computer, and a photograph emerged, as she moved her seat so that Grigori could see the image on the screen, a beautiful woman slouching against a barre in a ballet studio. The woman was indeed the same one in the other photograph. "Her name was Vera Borodina," Drew said, "according to this archive."

"But that's not the right name." Grigori felt momentarily dizzy. "No, you're right, this isn't his wife. This must be . . . someone else."

"Vera Borodina." Drew said it adamantly. She did not appear to see anything confusing about any of this. "Do you think the bag you have might have belonged to her?"

"No, no," Grigori said gruffly. "No, because then that would mean . . ." But his mind was not quite working. "I'm sorry. I'm finding this confusing for some reason."

Drew said, "Maybe Gershtein gave the pendant to Vera Borodina, and the bag you have was her bag, and those letters were written to her. Not to Nina Revskaya."

Grigori thought back to what Katya had said when she first handed the bag over to him—that his mother had been a ballerina. "But—the poems." He closed his eyes. "I'm going to have to think about this for a minute."

"Maybe we should look back at the letters again. To see if they could have been written by Gershtein." Drew did not look at all upset at the proposition. "And I should call Nina Revskaya, in case by some chance she knows any Gershteins in her husband's family." She paused. "But it seems improbable, doesn't it? Do you think maybe her friend gave them to her? For safekeeping?"

Grigori realized that he was grinding his teeth. "I'm sorry, I need to get some air."

"Are you all right, Grigori?"

"No. I'm not." He turned to leave, but not quickly enough to miss the look on Drew's face, of shock and hurt.

SHE ARRIVES HOME, her legs still quaking, to find Madame asleep in her chair, forehead on the table, the loud drunken rheumy snoring Nina has grown used to. Lola sits quietly on Madame's big thick messy bun, pecking at the tortoiseshell comb.

Sitting there so smug. *Viktor brought them. It was supposed to be a surprise.* The meanness in her smile.

Nina wants only to grab her travel case and leave. It is my fate, she tells herself. There is no other way now.

She will take refuge in the Bolshoi, and from there go straight to the car that will take them to the airport. And then . . . But her hands are shaking, her whole body shaking. *They find you and break your legs.*

Surely she can do this, other people have done it. You can do anything you want with sufficient money, sufficient bribes. And your wits about you. She hurries over to the box where she keeps her valuables. Places the emeralds in her earlobes, catches the gold watch around her wrist. Glances over to make sure Madame hasn't woken. Her fault, that Viktor went back to his old ways. Her fault; she is the one who told him, who turned him against her.

Leave this place. Leave these people.

Into the small pot of cold cream in her makeup case she submerges her wedding brooch and diamond studs. The amber and her little malachite box she tucks into the toes of two thick wool socks, which she adds to her packed valise. Lola watches her quietly, and gives another peck at Madame's tortoiseshell comb. The one with the tiny diamond flecks . . . Why, yes, thank you for reminding me. Nina marches over and lifts the comb from Madame's bun. After all, these might come in handy. Lola gives a squawk. That preposterous survivor. "*S'il vous-plaît!*"

Despite a loud, drunken snore, Madame does not even lift her head. And only then does the thought occur to Nina.

You are NOT to touch my hair!

With sudden clarity, Nina touches that messy bun. Gently she begins to loosen it, carefully pulling apart the sections of grizzled hair. It does not take much searching. Nestled within a knotted clump she finds first one and then another of what she ought to have always known were there.

Soon she has found five stones, one of them quite big. Madame is snoring even more loudly now. Nina takes three of what might be diamonds, one of them shaped like a tear, another a yellow shade, and tucks them into her brassiere. Security, for later. The other two she leaves on the table for Madame to find. Then she pulls on her coat, grabs her valise and theater case, and hurries to the Bolshoi, where her ride to the airport awaits.

"WHY DO YOU ask?" Nina said into the telephone. The receiver felt especially heavy today, the weight directly absorbed by her knuckles.

"Because an amber pendant, bracelet, and earrings of the exact description of the ones in this collection, along with a brooch and hairpin, were originally purchased by Avrim Shlomovich Gershtein in Moscow in 1882." Drew Brooks sounded different today, her voice almost shaky. "If that is a name in your husband's ancestry," she continued, somehow timidly, "it will allow us to be certain that indeed those pieces listed in the archives are those in your possession, and that the pendant is therefore of this same suite."

Nina felt a horrible humming between her ears.

"Gershtein," Drew was saying, slowly, as if Nina were impaired. She began to spell out the name.

Had Gersh given them to Viktor, or had Viktor bought them from Gersh? Nina could still picture Madame's gleeful whispery little smile, *Viktor wanted to hide them in my room*, her feigned surprise at having given up a secret. What if Viktor had been hiding them for Gersh? Not for himself, not for Nina. What if they were from Gersh, for Vera?

"Ms. Revskaya?"

Nina had to close her eyes. Of course Viktor had not been "hiding" the amber from Nina but from others in the apartment, the way one places anything of value aside in a safe spot. Of course. But then why had he not told Nina about it? Probably he had meant to. Probably he would have, if Nina had been home when he first brought the amber back from Gersh's. But greater issues had consumed them both: Gersh's arrest, his sentencing, his transferral to the psychiatric prison . . .

The pain inside Nina's chest was awful. If the baby was Gersh's—only that would explain why Vera did what she did. Which would mean that she really had in fact visited Gersh at the prison camp. She must really have been alone with him, that was why Viktor wasn't there, wasn't with them, he was telling the truth.

Oh, Viktor.

Or was *that* how Vera had managed to visit Gersh: favors for Serge? Awful Serge, there on the sidewalk. Such hazardous providence.

But no, because if the baby was Serge's, then surely Vera would not have kept it. Unless, perhaps, she was not certain whose child she was carrying.

And yet, if the child was Gersh's . . .

"Ms. Revskaya!"

Gersh's baby, and Vera's—and Nina had done nothing for him, just turned her back, hurried out of the hospital, left him there. When I knew his parents better than anyone . . . Viktor and I were his only connection to them.

"I'm going to hang up now and call an ambulance."

"No. No need for ambulance. Please." But she could feel her heart galloping, a horrible panicked feeling. Fate, it could not be helped. But oh, Vera. Dear Gersh. And Viktor . . .

"Are you really all right?"

"Please. Just wait. Let me . . . think." But no, it wasn't *fate*. How could she not have seen that? Serge right in front of her . . . Not fate but circumstance. Distrust everywhere, whispers and secrets. The world around her: little betrayals every day. Probably she had never fully trusted Viktor, not as she thought she had. Probably that sliver of doubt was always with her, lodged inside her, as it was inside everyone, about everybody else.

Not fate but simply inevitable.

Drew said in a pleading voice, "Really, I would feel better if you'd let me call a doctor."

"My nurse will be here very soon. She comes at five." Nina could hear how weak she sounded.

"Well . . . all right." Drew sounded fearful. "But please call me if you need any help before your nurse arrives."

With what energy she had left, Nina said, "Yes. Good-bye."

ALL AFTERNOON GRIGORI tried to understand. If what Drew suggested was correct, then the man whom he had thought his father might be another man altogether. The composer Gershtein. And the woman he thought was his mother . . . But then why did Nina Revskaya have two of the amber pieces? And why had she acted so oddly toward him? Not to mention what she had said in the News 4 interview, about the amber being from Elsin's family. Why would she have said that, if it was not so?

Perhaps Viktor Elsin had not told her the truth—that the beads had been given to him by (or taken from?) Gershtein. Or, no, maybe it was Gershtein himself who gave them to Nina Revskaya, maybe he was in love with her. But no, not with that other, beautiful woman leaning into him in the photograph, and his face lit with love . . .

Already the rush of thoughts and suppositions had caused his head to pound. Grigori took some Tylenol and went to his desk, to read, yet again, the original letters—the ones he had for so long believed to be written by Viktor Elsin. For one thing, there was the "please forgive me," at the beginning, which Grigori had always supposed to be from some marital spat. And that "big net so wide and inescapable"—which he had often pictured like the spider's web in that other, final, poem. Well, perhaps that might be a bit of a stretch. . . . But what about this, the same image as in "Night Swimming":

. . . refuge under a tree. And then the ground was damp and you worried you wouldn't get the sap out of your skirt. I can still smell the pine needles, winter hidden in them, cool and delicious, the checkered shade of those branches.

Grigori did not need to see the "Night Swimming" poem in front of him to hear the echo of that letter: *Patchwork shade, pine needle carpet, ocher-resin drops of sun. The air hums* . . .

Surely it was the same hot bug-filled summer day. The shade gone from "checkered" to "patchwork," and the same pine needles. The "ocher-resin drops of sun" surely recalled the tree sap:

I sometimes think, *that* is what I live for, days like that, perfect. But of course there was the tree sap staining your skirt. That tawny resin, slow-motion tears, as if the tree itself knew the future.

Of course lots of people described drops of liquid as tears. A poet, Elsin had in "Night Swimming" turned the sap into "drops of sun." Just as in his very last poem, where he referred to "that bright jewel the sun" and "ancient tears, like hearts, harden"—all of which, Grigori was certain, revealed Elsin's view of both the sun and the sap as amber. . . . *The amber, framed in gold.* What the letter called "little drops of sunshine." There was poetry in that letter. Perhaps nothing outstanding, but it made sense that a poet—the poet Viktor Elsin—had written it.

Then again, the letter was so sad, its reference to "the future" so dismal. . . . Elsin would have had to have written it after something bad happened. The arrest of his friend Gershtein . . . Wasn't that what that last poem referred to, the "Pitiless wind" and "rattling hazelnut tree: Encore, encore!" A musical reference, surely, as in "Night Swimming": "the air hums . . . Unseen, the nightingale, too late, thrums its stubborn song. . . ."

Grigori realized he was holding his head, fingertips pressed into his scalp. As if the pressure, the grip of his fingerpads, might release some new insight. He considered the way the letter had been signed, "Yours and yours alone"—how could Gersh have signed a letter that way if in fact he had both a wife and a girlfriend? Then again, people did not always write the literal truth. Especially in a letter of apology.

The checkered shade of those branches and the pine sap staining her skirt. *Whose* skirt? Could there have been more than one woman there? Or two couples—the ones from the other photo, the dacha photo, including whoever had taken it. *The impossible perfection of that summer . . .*

Stop, Grigori. Remember what Drew said: start with what you know.

He knew the letter had been written by someone, to a woman he loved. If it were Gershtein, that would explain the mournful tone, of having lost someone—the woman he did not marry, the beautiful one in the photograph. That could make sense.

Could the letters have been sent from prison, was that why they were so remorseful?

Our dear V. says you might take a friendly jaunt together.
Lucky we are, to have such friends! But please, dear—only
if the weather is clear. And don't forget to bring ID. A song
keeps running through my head, the one about the husband
missing his wife like a wave misses the shore—over and over
again. That's how I miss you.

A friendly jaunt. Grigori had never troubled himself much with who "dear V" might be—so many names started with that letter, it was pointless to try to guess. What struck him now, though, was a new possibility: that the V stood for Viktor Elsin. And then there was the one sentence Grigori had long wondered about: Don't forget to bring ID. An odd, probably pointless warning, in a time when no one ever left the house without their papers. ID would have been a given, as automatic as a wallet in your pocket. No need to state it outright. Unless it was code for something more particular. In which case "only if the weather is clear," too, began to sound like code. Grigori closed his eyes, overwhelmed, his head still pounding.

Both possibilities made sense to him, now that Drew had brought Gershtein into the picture. He certainly did sound like a man caught in some way, a man banished or punished. But the poems—they were Elsin's. About that, at least, there was no doubt.

A thought came to Grigori, an odd one, but he stopped to consider it. Might Viktor Elsin have read the letters and borrowed the phrasing?

No. Impossible. He was a poet, he didn't need to pilfer from others' correspondence.

But they were the same images. Or, if not quite the same, similar . . .

Similar enough to create a hypothesis, to write a paper that was given an A. But did that mean Elsin had stolen from Gersh? The poems were certainly different from his others. But not so different as to indicate that they had be *copied* . . . And why would he ever do that?

Maybe he hadn't meant to do it. But he had read the letters— delivered them, perhaps? As an emissary to the prison?—and the images remained in his mind. After all, this was his closest friend. . . .

Or maybe he hadn't read the letters at all but had been present, with Nina Revskaya, who was such close friends with that other ballerina. And so Gershtein too had been there, two couples, at the dacha, at the river, taking refuge from the sun under a pine tree.

Grigori realized that he was chewing on his lip. Taking a long, slow breath, he tried to calm himself. But he could not stop, and found himself looking again at the photographs he had taken back from Drew, his own photographs, which he knew so well, and that he had been so relieved to show her. He tried to reimagine it all, rewrite the story in his mind—though really he didn't look like Gershtein any more than he looked like Elsin, or Revskaya or the other woman, for that matter. Well, his chin looked a bit like Elsin's. But then his eyes—they definitely had something of Gershtein in them, he had to admit. And his mouth, wasn't there something in Vera Borodina's mouth that was exactly like his? And his cheekbones—so much like Nina Revskaya's.

He nearly laughed at the idea, four parents now, instead of just two. Six, if you counted Katya and Feodor. His dear parents, the most real ones of all, whom he sometimes, just every now and then, wished he might see again. Well, then what did the past matter? His life was here now. Drew was here, had been right next to him. And he had stomped off.

Grigori looked at his watch. Though it was after five, he quickly reached for the telephone, to try calling Drew at work. When her machine answered, he left an apologetic message—but it wasn't enough, he knew that. He felt suddenly desperate. Turning to his computer, he found the telephone index for the Boston area. Though there were three Drew Brooks in the city of Boston, only one was not listed as part of a couple. Grigori immediately dialed that number.

Drew's voice came up on the answering machine. At first Grigori's heart sank, not to have reached her. But at least, he told himself, he now knew that this was the correct number, the right Drew. His Drew. Checking the address once more, Grigori put on his coat and went to find her.

CYNTHIA DROPPED HER purse and her nurse's bag and hurried over to Nina. "Sugar, you look awful."

"Then my look is how I feel."

"Why didn't you call me? Did you call the doctor?" Cynthia had already reached out to take Nina's wrist in her hand, and began to check her pulse.

If Vera really did visit Gersh in the psychiatric camp, and Viktor really did take her there, then Viktor had not, after all, been having an affair with Vera or anyone else. No, Gersh had asked him to hold the jewels so that Zoya would not take them, so that he could pass them along to Vera. And Madame—why, she thought she was simply spoiling Nina's surprise. Just her usual mother-in-law antics. Probably she had not known at all how much confusion she would cause.

"Your pulse is low. But not in the danger zone." Now Cynthia was looking through her nurse's bag, and plucked out a thermometer, removed the tip from its sterilizing wrapper. "When did you start feeling sick?"

When she did not bother to answer, Cynthia stuck the thermometer in Nina's mouth.

"We might have to go in," Cynthia said. "To the hospital. I'm not taking any chances with you." She continued to say such things, about doctors and tests and the pallor of Nina's skin, but Nina stopped listening. She was thinking about Viktor, how she had hated him, so much, in those hours following Vera's death. How she had loved Vera too, and how she should have known, must have known, in fact, deep down, all along. Was that why I ran away from that young man, Grigori Solodin, so eager there at my doorstep, those years ago? I must have known that, too—known that he could do this to me, reveal to me this truth.

As long as she had not known for certain, it had not felt quite so awful when she found herself, reluctantly, unwillingly, thinking of what Viktor must have gone through because of her. If I hadn't left that night, things would not have looked at all suspicious. There would have been nothing to prove, nothing to make him look guilty. I gave them a reason, nothing Serge needed to make up. When really there was no reason for me to leave, no reason at all. Because I knew perfectly well how much Vera loved Gersh, I knew what she was willing to do for him. But then there was Serge, horrible Serge, right there on the sidewalk . . . Vera saying, *He said he can pull some strings.* The chance, the randomness of it—that he should be there at that very moment.

If only I had never seen him, our lives might have been different. The look in his eyes: anger and grief and retribution. And Polina, like a ghost floating in the doorway . . .

Nina was aware of something desperate happening within her, a frantic searching for a way out—some way to convince herself that none of this was quite so awful. Thoughts flew, glimpses of what might have been, and of what had happened instead. Well, there was Inge, she told herself, feeling only the slightest relief. If Nina had never left, she would not have been able, after all was said and done, to secure Inge the position in Bonn. That at least was something.

Cynthia had reached over, was wiping Nina's tears, trying not to knock the thermometer from her lips. Nina did not mind; the pain of movement had become too much for her, each time she used even the smallest muscle.

When she had removed the thermometer and was certain Nina was not about to keel over, Cynthia pulled up a chair beside her and took a seat. Then she simply reached over and took one of Nina's cold hands in her hers. The look on her face was very still, and Nina thought to herself, with surprise, This is what compassion is.

"You are very kind to me, Cynthia. I do not deserve it."

"Are you going to go on about that again? About deserving and not deserving?"

"I made a horrible mistake."

"And I said to you the other day what I know about mistakes. That it's never too late to try to fix them."

"Of course it is too late. These people are dead." All of them, from mistakes, not just Viktor, and Vera, but even Vera's parents, *The neighbor told me* . . . Even Nina's own uncle. A trail of bodies. Of course it was too late. These people were gone, every one of them, for no good reason, and all that was left of them were memories—in the mind of a woman so frail she could not survive a day without the help of Cynthia. "I cannot wipe my own tears, how am I to fix my mistakes?"

Cynthia just squeezed her hand.

Vera's hand in hers, at the Bolshoi School audition . . .

Nina closed her eyes. "Who else, after I die, will even remember these people? They were real people." It sounded silly to say it that way, not what she meant at all. What she meant was that it seemed a crime that their thoughts, their lives—the very fact of their lives, the truth of their lives—were lost along with them. No one to preserve the truth of who they were. Who they had been. Thinking this, Nina felt a sudden jolt.

"Cynthia," she said, eyes opening wide, her body filling with energy. "Please bring me to my writing desk." Some thoughts arrive so clearly, it is as if the answer has always been right there inside you.

"Is this good?" Cynthia asked as she rolled Nina's wheelchair into the study. "You sure you're feeling better?"

"Yes, thank you. Thank you very much. I am going to need your help with some things." She thought for a moment, and uncapped her pen. She had a letter to write, along with an official note, and telephone calls to make, and for a brief moment she wondered where to begin. There was so much to say. More than she would be able to say, surely, in just one communication. But one had to start somewhere. Nina leaned forward and brought her pen nib to the paper.

Dear Grigori, she began. *I want to tell you about your beautiful mother.*

. . . .

THEIR FIRST STOP is Berlin, where Nina and Yuri are to dance high-lights of *Sleeping Beauty*. They will not even have time to watch the performances following theirs; they are to leave immediately follow-ing their slot, straight from the theater, in order to be in Warsaw by tomorrow morning.

Nina wishes she had had time to plan. Time to think things out. The malachite box she has transferred to the very bottom of her the-ater case, where the little pill of rolled paper from the old woman in West Berlin with its bit of information (old now, maybe even too old) still hides, along with her good-luck charms and needle and thread and hairpins and tape and tubes of greasepaint—and the pot of cold cream, to which she has added Madame's gemstones. The tortoise-shell hair comb is there, too, along with some old, plain, diamond-less ones. The amber Nina has stitched into the seams of her thick cardigan sweater. Should anyone need some urging, she is prepared.

"You're daydreaming again." Yuri gives her a friendly tap on the top of her head. They are in the warm-up room, Yuri in his princely outfit, Nina sparkling in her tutu and tiara, her neck and back pow-dered, leg warmers pulled up over her thighs to keep her muscles from tightening up.

"Sorry. Don't worry, I'm ready."

She repeats these words to herself even after they have finished their pas de deux and variations, even after the audience, on its feet, has thrown bouquets and bravos at the footlights, even after she has hurried backstage to the "star" dressing room she has been assigned for the evening. Right next to the big communal one where the corps dancers dress; Nina can hear them through the door that separates their room from this one.

A quick rap on the door to the hallway. The company manager, calling out, "No dawdling! We leave in twenty minutes!"

Nina closes her eyes, tries to think. If she leaves this city, with its less stringent patrols, its proximity to freedom, already her chances will have diminished. She has the little scrap of paper, and knows where she might find that woman, the shopkeeper. No, she must not go on with the others. She must figure out some way.

If she leaves this room, she will be seen. Nor is there anywhere in here to hide, except of course the adjoining shower stall—the first place anyone would look. And if Nina goes through the other door, to the corps dressing room, well, for one thing it is teeming with dancers, and will be occupied by someone or other for much of the time.

"Twenty minutes!"

The door between that room and Nina's is of cheap wood that does not fit correctly into the door frame; light shines through the gap in between, the bustling sounds from next door seeping through the crack. Nina can hear one girl's voice as if next to her, saying something excitedly in German, and then another girl laughing. They must have the very last dressing tables, at the end of the row.

She brings her eye to the gap. The view is clear, if somewhat dimly lit: a cramped, busy room with a large circular costume rack in the center, and all along the walls dressing tables framed by bare lightbulbs. A mess of clothing and costumes all around. Twenty or thirty girls pulling on stiff flat white tutus, placing little feathered wreaths on their heads, the feathers reaching down toward their cheeks. *Swan Lake.* That's right: one of the Bolshoi's ballet masters is the resident *régisseur* here this year, and set the show for the Berlin company earlier this season. Tonight they will be performing act 2.

To think that only five years ago Nina was one of those girls. Sometimes it feels like just yesterday, eagerly searching out her name on the call sheet, the glee at each small advancement, from swan-girl to cygnet, from understudy to alternate cast. And yet nothing is the same now as it was then—though five years is not long at all, really.

Not long at all.

Like yesterday.

And so the thought comes to her. She puts her eye to the door, where the crack is, where she can glimpse the two nearby girls talking and laughing. Young, most of them, probably new recruits, recent graduates. Not much else to guess about them from their faces.

Nina's mind works fast, wondering, planning. When the other girl steps away, Nina tries to read the face of the girl who remains near the door, as if in one glimpse she might know whether or not to take this chance. Something about the girl's eyes, her expression, suggests to Nina that her idea might work. No time to consider if she is right or not; the other girl could return at any moment. Nina puts her mouth to the crack. "Psst!"

The girl doesn't seem to have heard her.

Nina stops, thinks again. Impetuous . . . "Psst!"

The girl has heard. She stops mid-action, looks toward the door. Nina opens it just the tiniest sliver. "Come!" she whispers, hoping the girl understands. "Quick!" And then, for just a split second, she brings her head to the space in the door, opens it a tiny bit wider, so that the girl might see her, see who she is. "*Bitte!* Come quick!" Then she steps back and closes the door again, lest someone in the other room notice.

For a moment nothing happens. Then, from the other side of the door, comes a whisper, very quiet, in German-sounding Russian. "What you want?"

"*Bitte*, help me. *Bitte*, come here."

And then she has an idea, and turns to her makeup case, to find one of the loose stones, the biggest diamond of all, pressed into the little jar of cold cream. Nina wipes it off and then opens the door again, just the tiniest bit, so that the girl might see the diamond there in the palm of her hand. In Russian she says, "I'll give you this."

Though the girl does her best to appear to be nonchalantly fiddling with her tights, her eyes, shifting toward the open sliver of door, widen when they see the diamond. Clearly she has never seen such a thing close up.

"*Bitte*," Nina whispers. "Please help me."

Silence again, for what seems a full minute. And then, quick as a fly, the girl slips into Nina's dressing room, the door swiftly shutting behind her.

DREW'S BUILDING WAS at the summit of Beacon Hill, where, Grigori knew, even expensive apartments had small rooms with low ceilings and ancient plumbing and no laundry facilities. After all, this was the oldest and most historic part of the city, in some ways the very center of Boston—just one T stop over the river to Cambridge, or an easy stroll across the Common to Downtown Crossing, or a quick walk to Back Bay. Standing on the red-brick sidewalk, searching for Drew's name above the antiquated-looking doorbell, Grigori was aware of himself as part of a continuum that had begun long before this land had been filled, before the first cobblestones were laid, before the first warped windowpanes looked out onto these same narrow streets. How many other confused, lovelorn, perhaps foolish men had stood on this same hilly street, perhaps at this very same corner, or in front of this same old building, even, bracing themselves for disappointment?

"Hello?"

Her voice—Drew's voice.

"It's me. Grigori. I came to apologize."

An excruciating silence. But then her voice said, "Come upstairs."

When he reached the top of the stairs, there she was in the doorway, in the dress he had seen on her once before, a green knit thing, though her boots and stockings were off, just her bare feet on the scuffed floor. Grigori stood back, afraid to approach her. "I'm very sorry to have stormed off like that. It's not like me."

She motioned him in, saying nothing.

"I had to go look back at those letters," he explained. "What you were saying about who wrote them, and to whom . . . It makes sense. Though I still have questions about the poems, I suppose."

She nodded, said flatly, "Here, come sit down."

He took a seat next to her on the big, somewhat lumpy couch. "But you see, when I told you a relative had given me that handbag with the letters and photographs and the necklace, what I didn't say was that the person who gave it to me was my mother. My adoptive mother. She told me the bag had belonged to my birth mother."

"Oh." Drew's face changed. "I see now."

"That's why I feel so foolish. All this time I've thought I was . . . someone else."

Drew gave a slow nod.

"I'd created a mythology around my past. I was always looking back, trying to build on something that it turns out wasn't even true. And . . . my parents died when I was young, you see, and as much as I missed them, I was lucky when I met my wife, she became my family—and then I lost her. And now today it's like losing someone again, in a way. Losing that other family I thought I had." He thought for a moment, gave a small laugh. "It's foolish, I know. But I had this other concept of who I was. All because of who I thought my birth parents were."

"It isn't foolish. It's perfectly natural. But how does it change things, really?"

"I suppose all it changes is my faith in my own deductive powers." Grigori gave a small laugh. "I misread so much. Everything, maybe."

Drew's eyes looked up at his. "I'm looking for a likeness. Seeing if I can find the Gershtein and that beautiful ballerina in you." A small flat smile. "But what I see is you."

Such incredible kindness. Grigori felt something almost painful in his chest. "You know what I wish, now?" he asked. "I wish I'd kept that pendant."

Her face fell.

"What's wrong?"

"You don't really mean that, do you?"

"Well, no, not really. Since then I might never have met you. I just meant that"—he thought for a moment—"Well, what if I did want to . . . withdraw it from the auction? Is that possible?"

"Well, yes. With a penalty fee. Thirty-five percent of the mid-range estimate. So for the pendant, let's see—"

"No, no, don't worry." He felt silly for having become sentimental all over again, when the whole point was to rid himself of the thing. Yet he couldn't help asking, "People *do* do that, then? Withdraw things."

Drew nodded. "And sometimes items are withdrawn because they're lost, or not lost, necessarily, but if inventory control can't find it, we're not going to try to sell it. But, well . . ." She looked down, her forehead wrinkling, and for a moment Grigori worried she was considering purposely losing the pendant. She would do that for me, he found himself thinking, fantastically, knowing it wasn't exactly so.

"Please, Drew, don't worry. I said I'd donate it, and I want to. I do. I only wondered because, it simply occurred to me that . . . it would look very nice on you."

She smiled broadly, the lines fanning from outside her eyes.

"Now you know," he added, "the full scale of confusion when it comes to my family background. Tell me about *your* family. Do you have siblings? Are you close to your parents?"

She told him about growing up an only child, and about her father, a businessman, born and raised in British Columbia, and her mother, born in Finland but raised in New York. In some ways the most powerful bond she had felt, growing up, had been with her maternal grandmother. "I don't quite know why, but I always felt close to her. And my relatives always say we have the same personality. Although she had a completely different life from me." Drew told him about her Grandma Riitta's rural childhood and move to the city, and how following the death of her one great love—Drew's mother's father—she had married a second time. A doctor specializing in pulmonary conditions, he was invited to practice at a hospital in New York. "That's how they ended up in the States."

Drew gave a small start. "Which reminds me. The diary I told you about, my mother's father's. It arrived today." She jumped up to fetch it—but sat down again, seemed to be thinking. "You know, in a way it's kind of wonderful, what you've found out today, about who your real parents are. Or who we think they might have been."

"Is it?"

"Yes. Because even though it didn't work out for them, in the end, it can still work out for you. You have the chance to live out what they didn't. To create your own life. Your own family."

There was a tearing sensation across Grigori's chest, his heart breaking at the same time that it was refilling with something. He reached for Drew and ran his fingers through her hair. His body remembered, now, what this had felt like, what he had forgotten, the ache of wanting, of needing this other person, running his fingers down her back, touching the small bumps of her spine, becoming lost in time, hours like minutes. At some point, Drew stood and led him into her bedroom, and what amazed him was the ease of it, even as it seemed that what they had begun was something utterly exceptional that no one had ever quite attempted before.

NOW THAT SHE is in the corps dressing room, she can hear the company manager calling her name, on the other side of the door, slamming in and out of the "star" room. It isn't long before he, the

Komsomol representative, and the theater manager are making their way through the halls, tromping up and down the stairs. They have twice looked into the corps room, to the protest of the dresser and a few half-naked girls. They didn't explain what they wanted, whom they were looking for—an effort, perhaps, to preserve the illusion of nothing having gone terribly wrong. Both times Nina, already in her swan costume, the feathers of her headwreath reaching down over her ears and cheeks, was bent over her toe shoes, re-stitching the tips of her shoe ribbons into the sides, her shoulders hunched in a way that feels utterly unfamiliar. The big round clothes rack in the middle of the room, full of frilly tutus hanging upside down, helps obscure the view. To Nina's right, underneath the corps girl's coat, are her shoes and sweater and makeup case.

Already she is feeling doubtful. And guilty, at having bribed that poor German girl into her scheme. What is the worth of a diamond, no matter how big, if the girl is caught, if anyone finds out that she has helped Nina? Nina's heart sinks with worry for the girl as much as for herself.

She mustn't lose her nerve. Affecting great attention, she leans over her legs, massages her calves, while all around her dancers preen. For the first time in her life she appreciates the great narcissism of ballerinas, each girl in this room interested solely in herself, her costume, her hair, her makeup, barely noticing the others. Whenever it seems someone might be looking her way, Nina fiddles with her feathered headband, with the bun of her hair, always something up around her face, even as she and the rest of the swan maidens are herded out toward the backstage door.

Then there is some kind of commotion at the other end of the corridor. Nina recognizes the Bolshoi manager's voice. "What's that? Are you certain?"

"She left," a man's voice, thickly accented, replies. "Franz just told me. A woman with the exact same coat you described."

A third man's voice protests something in German. "He didn't know," the second translates, as his fellow German continues. "He says . . . he could have sworn it was a dancer he sees all the time. She looked like she was going home for the night."

The Bolshoi manager's voice says, "Quick, let's go."

Nina feels something inside her release, though surely the building is still teeming with patrols. Not to mention that she is now trapped in the pack of girls backstage, a crowd of swans awaiting their entrance—and that as much as she might try to hide among them before slipping away, she must still be recognizable, should anyone take the time to look at her. But no one here has ever seen Nina close up, and surely everyone's focus will be on the two principal dancers (first Siegfried, then Odette in her grand entrance) rather than on the many swans surrounding them; the love duet is a main highlight, and true stars never lose an audience's attention. Even if some balletomanes in the audience might notice Nina, the theater guards most probably don't know what she looks like. And with the manager and his assistant gone, there will be fewer people here who have ever seen her in person. If only she can find some way to slip out.

The Berlin girl, her savior, has told Nina her number in the lineup—by stroke of luck toward the rear of the corps, no "Dance of the Little Swans" for her. The girl must indeed be a novice. Nina takes her place as if stepping back in time, back to her early days, giddy and nervous, the mass rustling of crinoline and tulle. But tonight the fearful trembling that the swans must enact is, for Nina, *real*—not simply nerves but true fright. She is, she realizes, petrified.

For the first time in years she will have to dance in unison, the carefully coordinated positioning of arms and legs, even the tilt of her head, her every movement matching those of her fellow swans— no standing out, no personality or flair, the very opposite of a prima ballerina. In a way, tonight's role is the greatest challenge of her career: how to unlearn all of her training, to conceal the very qualities that have made her a star, to be good enough but not too good. She prays that her body will know what to do, will submerge itself, suppress its expertise—and that no one looks too closely at the new swan there in the back. For the moment, it seems possible. Even right here, crushed close to one another in the back wing, the other swan-girls are too preoccupied with shoe ribbons and hairpins to notice an unfamiliar face among them. The stagehands, too, are so busy with their work, negotiating props and lights and curtains, that not one of them pays attention to the dancers.

Nina keeps her head down, pretends to be adjusting her feathers. If any of the other girls should notice her, she tells herself, she will give a confident wink, as if it has all been planned, nothing but a little prank. But there is no need: here is their cue, and with the rest of the swans, Nina drifts onto the stage.

THE FAMILIAR BLOCK of sunlight stretched across the faded purple blanket. Hurrying past, grabbing her purse, Drew said, "It's going to be crazy all day, you know." Though the auction was not until four o'clock, she had much to take care of before then.

Grigori nodded, taking his coat from the lumpy sofa. "A friend and I were planning to stop by the auction. But don't worry, I know you'll be working."

Drew had to smile, seeing him there. "Come find me afterward. I'll just need another hour or so to finish things up."

As natural as it felt to say this, she felt a ruffle of something else, something between fear and excitement, and a kind of disbelief, that this was her, Drew, that she had taken this step toward a new person. Even to be with him now, here in her home, brought her a feeling not just of warmth but of exposure—her self, exposed and vulnerable. Scraped clean, that was how she felt: her old skin peeled off, and new, tender skin exposed. As much potential for pain as for tenderness and love.

Grigori helped her into her coat, pausing to look at her with a small smile. They were about to step out the door when he stopped. "You wanted to show me something. Your grandfather's journal."

"Oh, that's right!" The package had arrived just yesterday, a small padded envelope posted by her mother. It seemed ages ago that she had mentioned it. Today itself seemed miles and miles away from yesterday.

The journal was a small, square booklet slim enough to fit in a coat pocket. Showing it to Grigori, Drew felt moved just fanning through the many blank pages at the end. "He died not long after he started it. I remember my grandmother showing it to me."

Grigori held it gingerly, looking at the first written page, and nodded as if to say that he could do this. "May I take it with me?"

She told him yes, and they left the building, stepped out onto Myrtle Street to find the air almost warm, full of a sweet spring humidity. Parents were walking their children to the playground, their coats open to the breeze. You would never have thought that it had snowed just two days before, one of those last-minute March dumpings, thick wet heavy flakes that create a big mess before quickly melting away.

Feeling his warm hand in hers, Drew turned with Grigori down Joy Street toward the Common, so that he could take the Green Line home. And though Drew would have liked to ride the train with him for the brief two stops to Beller, simply to remain in his company a bit longer, she decided to walk. With the bright sunlight and the air nearly warm, she wanted to savor—without a crowd of strangers and rush-hour noise around her—this new, oddly calm elation, the bewildering sense that she had somehow, at last, landed where she was meant to be.

. . . .

THE BODY REMEMBERS.

Like a cat remembers the way home, instinctively, Nina thinks afterward, back in the dressing room, hastily slipping her tutu down from her hips. Each movement came to her like breathing, like drinking water, perfectly naturally. Never has she felt so grateful to her body, to the familiar heat of the stage lights, to the haunting music that her muscles know by heart.

Now, though, her hands fumble as she rushes to pull on her skirt and shoes and cardigan sweater. The other swan-girls have only brief minutes longer onstage; Nina simply could not risk staying on any longer, with the curtain call so soon to come. She can hear her own breathing, quick and anxious, as she slips her arms into her new coat—the corps girl's coat, not at all as nice as hers, but of course that is the point. She needs to vanish yet again. At least there is no sign of the company manager or anyone from Komsomol; they must not have returned since leaving to search for her.

Seeing an exit arrow at the end of the hallway, Nina takes up her makeup case and ventures into the corridor. She hurries to the first intersecting hallway, a smaller, narrower, darker one, and steps into it, waiting. Soon she hears voices, a small group coming along the other corridor. When they have passed, she peeks out, watching as they leave the building. Indeed there is a guard there, although he does not stop anyone in the group, seems to know them, or at least knows that they are not Nina.

Now the corridor has filled with the bright girlish voices of the corps. Finished for the night, they bustle back to the dressing room. Just a few more minutes pass before they emerge yet again and begin to leave the building, clusters of them giggling and chatting as they head down the hallway and out the door. Perhaps none of them noticed Nina after all. No, there's sure to have been someone. . . . Her thoughts skip back and forth, her pulse racing, as she waits. When a larger group of dancers comes along, she decides, as they pass her, to try.

Quickly she steps out and bustles along behind them, just another faceless dancer eager to leave for the night. Now they have reached the door, where the armed guard awaits. Act natural, don't hurry, you're a ballerina leaving work, with your little case of necessities. . . . When the girls directly in front of her laugh at something, she smiles broadly, as if she too finds it funny. And like a dream she drifts right past the tired guard, who does not stop to question a single one of them.

LOT 108

Sapphire and Diamond Dinner Ring. Square-cut sapphire encircled by 10 small diamonds (total weight $1/3$ ct., color grade I, clarity VSI) and 20 sapphire baguettes (total weight $2/3$ ct.), solid yellow 18kt gold band, size $6\,1/4$. $960–1,090

CHAPTER SIXTEEN

I t wasn't until she arrived at work that she realized she had forgotten her garnet ring.

For a moment Drew felt suddenly, utterly naked. It was the first time that she hadn't noticed at the last minute and gone back for it. To forget it completely, today of all days . . . Drew knew better than to be superstitious, yet even as she shrugged off this small lapse—and sat down to turn on her computer, bracing herself for the latest onslaught of e-mail—she felt somehow unarmed, not to have the ring with her.

At the top of her in-box was another forwarded message from her mother. This time it was a fund-raising message from her mother's friend Laurie, whose son would be running the Boston Marathon to raise money for AIDS orphans in Uganda; there was a link to a site where you could donate to his fund. Though the message itself was innocent enough, Drew found herself recalling the most recent tidbit that had slipped from her mother's lips: that Eric and Karen, who was apparently a long-distance runner, had started training for the Dublin Marathon next fall. Annoyed all over again, Drew for a moment considered writing her mother yet another brief, brisk reminder that, if she must send such e-mails, they ought to go to Drew's private account.

Yet something prevented her—stopped the impulse itself. It had to do with Grigori. Not just her happiness at the thought of him, but also what he had told her yesterday, about his parents, his adoption, about his longing and confusion, and that long, ultimately ungratifying search. How lucky Drew was to have this mother of hers, this constant, reliable, if at times irritating presence in her life—this mother, like so many mothers, beloved and blamed. Lucky she was to have experienced, through her mother, the twisted intricacies of deep, and deeply complex, love.

After all, her mother had probably suffered these feelings too. Drew thought of Grandma Riitta, that even she—with her strong will, her inescapable straightforwardness, her permanent cache of intimate stories—must have at times exasperated her daughter. Wasn't that partly why Drew's mother had so stubbornly ignored much of her past? Had turned away from her native language, away from her own history. Had erased any last residue of foreignness, and named her daughter "Drew."

Thinking this, Drew felt something other than her usual resigned understanding. She picked up the telephone and dialed her parents' number.

When her mother answered, the first thing Drew did was to thank her for having sent the journal. "I've already given it to someone to translate."

In a brisk, light way, as if it didn't really matter one way or the other, her mother said, "Well, you'll have to tell me what you find out."

Drew said what she had been considering. "I thought we could read it together."

Her mother's surprise was audible.

"I thought I'd bring the transcript when I come visit," Drew continued.

"Oh! Are you coming here, then?"

"I could come for Dad's birthday." The idea had just now crystallized. "Since it's on a Sunday, and I have that Monday off, for Patriots' Day."

"Patriots' Day . . ."

"And for his birthday present I was thinking—"

"He'll be delighted you're coming!"

Drew waited for her mother to say that she too was delighted. And even though, as the conversation continued, she did not say those exact words, the tone of her voice seemed to reveal that she did, in fact, feel that way.

GRIGORI DRIFTED THROUGH the morning as in a dream. Funny how one thing, one wonderful thing, could alter everything, make it seem that nothing in the world, no goodness or luck, was too much to wish for. After all, if this could happen to him—if love could happen, again, for him, Grigori Solodin, widower aged fifty—then why not other good things, for other people, too?

As if to confirm this, his voice mail contained a message from an editor interested in Zoltan's poetry. He had started a new translation series under his own imprint, at a reputable press. "I've long been a fan of Zoltan Romhanyi's work and am really thrilled at the prospect of publishing his new poems," his message said. "Let's make it happen."

Full of a lightness he could not quite recall feeling before, Grigori was aware of something else in his heart, another kind of letting go. It had to do with the letters, with the poems, with the way those images matched up. If indeed the letters were not Viktor Elsin's, Grigori still might never know whether Elsin had ever seen them, or had perhaps even borrowed images from them. But what mattered more, he felt now, was the fact of the letters themselves—that they were real, someone's real life, someone's real words. *Whose* life, *whose* words, was not something he might ever solve with any concreteness, as much as he still desired some kind of certainty. But that desire had been eclipsed by a greater one, and by an understanding that Grigori must have already possessed all along. An understanding that such uncertainties were part of the mystery of this life, and would always coexist with those things that are certain: his love for Christine, and now Drew, and his friendships, his passions. Of course Grigori could return to the poems yet again, make an even more obsessive study of them, try to answer the question for himself, if no one else. But the question, though still a teasing, perplexing one, no longer nagged at him. His body itself felt lighter, unburdened.

Turning to his desk, he took up the little journal Drew had given him. He had only a few minutes before his lunch meeting, but he could at least take a cursory look, to see if the handwriting would be discernible, how difficult a task it might be.

Between the covers was that typical penmanship of Soviet schooling, small, no margins at all, using every inch and both sides of each page.

I write this Diary for Elli my daughter two days old.

    I was born in 1910 in a village just north of Ukraine not far from Sumy. Not a bad size village tho believe me any stranger who ever set foot there was news. You see we was real far from any city or even a town and not easy to find if you wasnt looking. A real pretty place tho with big old trees bowing their heads at you when you rode along the brown dirt road. Winters was sometimes rough but come March youd see little green points poking up out of the ground so hopeful and know you made it like a miracle to another Spring.

    Didnt get much schooling past grade 6 on account of Papa died and Mama needed me and my brothers to take

his place. Thats too bad cause I liked school specially reading and writing even tho there was barely any books and
just one teacher to teach us anything worth knowing. But
we was good at farming and had good luck. Time I was
15 we was able to lease more land and even hire help at har-
vest. We done pretty well meaning we had plenty to eat even
if we never did have any money left. Me being oldest I was
the manager so to speak. Buildt some barracks and hired
farmhands and run the place pretty good if I do say so. But I
never liked ordering folks around so when there was problems I wrote joking messages and little rhymes and left them
around like they was love notes.

Grigori realized that he was smiling. This man, too, was a writer.
Amazing, really, that he—Grigori—was able to hear that man's
voice now, and so clearly, so many years later. The voice of the man
without whom there would be no Drew.

Then we started hearing things just a little and then more
about people having to give up their farms and tractors and
even their homes and work together on kolkhozes. Heard
about it but didnt see it. Then one spring when I was 21
some men they come to the village and next thing you know
the richest peasants the Shevchenkos and the Ilyichovs was
gone on account of they was Kulaks. Kicked out and most
of what they owned took from them. The rest of us well we
was scared but also angry and I got some meetings going to
plan what to do if those men come again.

It took two more years but they did come back and that
time we was ordered to give up all our grain and then our
animals and machines. We put up a fight let me tell you but
in the end they just comfuscated our land and packed us

away to way up north. Mama and my brothers and their families was allowed to travel together but me I was arrested for being Head of Household not to mention a Dangerous Counterrevolutionary Activist.

Mama died on the way. It was winter and so they couldnt dig a grave but when the men in charge seen she was No More they made them leave her on the side of the track like she was a sack of rotten turnips. My brothers sent the letter saying so.

The trip up north was my first train ride. Weeks and weeks and then I was put in a Labor Camp with a bunch of other so called criminals. Shared a cell with a guy named Lev not a bad guy but its how I learned that just cause you get to know someone dont mean you get to like him. The only way we even knowed we was close to Finland was some of the men we worked with spoke that language (your language Elli).

Grigori was aware of his heartbeat having quickened, and of that other, rare and startling, sensation: the certainty that he was on the brink of something. He glanced at his watch. The meeting would have to wait.

In the camp we was put to work in the mine. An amber mine. Spent my days in a pit a hundred feet deep and so wide it might of been a village. My work was digging up the so called blue earth but really it was grayish green. Crusty clay like the roads at home right when the rainy seasons over. All inside the greenish gray like currants in Mama's dough was pieces of amber.

Spent most days shoveling. For a time I got to work in the washing plant where you get the amber out of the crust and that wernt too bad. Even tho we was mostly sick and always hungry I made up songs and told jokes to keep us on our feet.

Maybe its bragging but you know what they called me? The Happy Forced Laborer. They said I was crazy to laugh even tho they laughed too when I got things going. But really I dont like to remember life in that place so let me just tell you I spent 12 and a half years of my time on this earth there.

Elli theres something else I skipped from this story. Its that before we was taken away from the farm I had a wife Masha and a daughter Liza and they both was still there in the village when I left. Then one winter they both got diphtheria and was No More. Even if I hadnt seen them for five years I still saw them in my head. So you see you really are a gift to me who had nothing to go home to cause he lost everyone even his first daughter your sister who youll never know but through this Diary I write for you.

My brothers died too of colds gone to their chests the letter said. Anyways when my time at the camp was up I had nothing to go home for. Hopped a train with one of the Finns and rode it long as we could. Got off and found our way. He helped me get across and then well I just wandered. Thats when I seen your lovely mama walking along the muddy road.

I want to tell you about all that. But I been sick a lot on account of breathing in the dust from the amber mines. So I will take a break now and next time tell you all about making a new life here with your mama.

This worlds given me nine lives
First as a babe at my ma's sweet tit
Then as a boy in a house full of flies

Then a big brother and then a young man
By the lake where the bullfrogs saw my first kiss.
Next I farmed 25 desyatinas.
The land took orders not from me but the sky.
Been husband to a girl with braid on her head
And Pa to a daughter with cornflower eyes.
Then came the prison. A lot of winters shivering
And watching time crawl by like a slug.
This lifes the Ninth. This family my sweet nest.
Each days a place to hang my new warm coat.

A verse for Elli. Wrote by your Pa

The rest of the book was blank. At first Grigori just sat there gazing at the old dried ink. It's true, was his thought: we are all connected. And it took fifty years for me to understand this. . . . He realized that his eyes were teary, and wiped them with his handkerchief. It must be the abruptness, he told himself, that is making me cry: another life cut short. Turning back to the opening page, he looked to see when that first entry had been written. There was no date.

Grigori began to read again from the beginning. Amazing how just a few brief pages revealed so much about the person who had composed them: his outlook, his good nature, and, despite his lack of schooling, his ear for language. Those empty pages at the end were no longer simply blank but painful in their blankness. The curiosity Grigori felt was as strong as what he had felt for Elsin's poems, yet less needy—simply eager. This other man's words, pure and unaltered, the man himself pared down to what little language he had . . . His words were concerned not with art but simply truth, and therefore contained, in their own way, the beauty of art.

This man, Drew's grandfather. Her mother's father, an unschooled man, a farmer, a prisoner. A man with a sense of humor, a man who understood the worth of taking the time to write down one's thoughts, one's life. How many other men like this, unknown and uneducated, had left such documents behind? Grigori thought now of the KGB archives that had recently been opened, the many confiscated diaries and letters it must contain, records as important as any of Viktor Elsin's poems. How many other people's stories must be lodged there, unread but waiting. Waiting for someone like Grigori to take a look, and to let the world know.

Full of a new energy, Grigori set to work typing out his translation of the little journal's pages. It would be his gift (the phrase that went through his head was "my first gift") to Drew.

AT THE AUCTION house, the seats were already filling by three o'clock that afternoon. People kept peering about as if they might get a glimpse of Nina Revskaya herself, though surely they knew better. Drew recognized a few of the regulars, tradespeople and private buyers: the handsome dealer from D.C. who specialized in diamonds; the middle-aged woman who always bid on about twenty necklaces but rarely ended up buying any; the young millionaire who brought a new girlfriend to every auction, whether it was jewelry or furniture or wine; and the skinny bald guy who never bid on anything, just stood around at the buffet table eating the free hors d'oeuvres. Today the caterers had put out crudités, very thin cinnamon cookies, and big percolators of coffee. One of the water pitchers already needed refilling. Drew notified the intern.

She had not spoken to Lenore since the morning. But as the auction start time approached, it seemed the day's excitement and stresses (the assistants at first hadn't been able to find the extra chairs, and there was some small mix-up with the catering) appeared to have at last gotten to her. The lines of her forehead were suddenly prominent, deep worry marks between her eyebrows.

Now, though, as the clock prepared to strike four, Lenore straightened her shoulders and walked confidently to the shiny wooden auction block, where a laptop computer and two full glasses of water awaited her. And though she still held her mouth tight, the worry lines seemed to magically recede. Everyone else took their places: Mark, the stocky young gallery guard, at the top of the stairs, and Drew, along with a dozen other women and two men, all of them employees like herself, at one of the long banks of telephones at the front of the room. With such heavy interest, they needed everyone on. Drew had been assigned to a bidder in Florida, paddle number 201. He was an Argentinean who lived in Miami Beach—was, in fact, this very minute, lying on a towel on the beach, smoking a cigarette; even through the cell phone Drew could hear him taking a drag. "What's the weather like there?" he asked, and Drew could tell from his tone that he knew about the freak snowstorm—one last brief dumping that quickly melted away—earlier this week.

"Not bad," she said, defensively, thinking of her walk to the T with Grigori that morning, the pleasant breeze and open coats, Grigori's hair curling from the humidity. "Spring's almost here. Some afternoons it's almost warm."

As she spoke she glimpsed Grigori walking in, with an older, somewhat disheveled-looking man.

"Here it's gorgeous," the man in Florida was saying, taking another loud drag on his cigarette. "Lately it's been too windy for my taste, but today, perfect."

Drew could see Grigori looking for her. Leaning forward just slightly, so as not to call too much attention to herself, she reached a hand up above her head. It worked; he saw her, as she gave just the slightest twist of her wrist before running her hand through her hair. Grigori cocked his head at her, smiling, so that she glimpsed his dimple lines. Then she heard the small clicking sound of the microphone coming on and looked up to where Lenore was adjusting the laptop computer. Behind her, the big projection screen lit up, a bright blue light.

SITTING NEXT TO Zoltan, Grigori had to stop himself from looking back at Drew every minute or so. He had only a partial view of her, since she was seated all the way at the front wall, but he kept finding himself looking her way, perhaps to convince himself that she really did exist. With Zoltan he surveyed the rest of the room, the many people milling about, open catalogs in hand. Standing at one of the high round tables was a well-dressed young man with his arm around a woman in a tight sweater dress that stopped just below her buttocks. The way she clung to the young man's arm, Grigori wondered if the two were there to bid for an engagement ring. Behind them, at the top of the stairs, a gallery guard—a young man looking very serious and yet somehow pathetic—stood stiffly, stockily, the sleeves of his suit jacket just a tad too long.

At the podium, the auctioneer was shuffling some papers. An attractive woman wearing a tight dark lacy knit sweater, she appeared to be in her forties, slender and French-looking, her hair pulled back in an easy knot. The room quieted down when, in a cool, smooth voice, she welcomed everyone and instructed them to turn off their cell phones. "Unless of course you are using them for bidding." A faint, ambiguous accent—or rather, affect, like the announcers on the classical music station.

Grigori watched as the screen above her displayed a photograph of the first item: a pair of sparkly gold bangles. "Lot number one. Two twenty-four-karat gold bracelets inlaid with diamonds. I have a bid here now"—she was looking at her computer—"of ten thousand, looking for eleven." She spoke quickly but smoothly, her vowels wide open, nothing slack about her. "Is there any advance over the ten thousand?" A woman in the front row raised her paddle. "I have eleven to my right now, looking for twelve. Who will go to twelve?"

A young man at one of the telephones gestured, and when the auctioneer called out again, a very fat and somehow sloppy-looking man leaning on a table in a corner lifted his paddle. "Thirteen," the auctioneer announced. "Are you all in all done at thirteen?" Grigori found himself leaning forward through the pause, until the woman in the front row raised her paddle. "Fourteen—in time. . . ." The fat sloppy man kept coming back in immediately after the woman, nodding as the price quickly increased, until finally he just shook his head at the auctioneer. "Are you all in all done at eighteen?" the auctioneer briskly asked the woman in the front. "So it is. Sold to paddle 310."

"So, that's how fast it goes," Zoltan whispered, and Grigori thought to himself, Yes, that's how easily these things will be dispensed of, even that necklace that I thought meant something. That I treated as if it had some sort of power. When really it is just an object, to be picked up with a mere nod of the head. Gone at last, to anyone in this room.

"It is yours," the auctioneer was saying into the microphone, already finished with the second item.

As the next few images appeared on the big color screen, people wandered in and out, and helped themselves to coffee, and stood around reading the addendum or flipping through the catalog. The man in the seat in front of Grigori kept track of every winning bid, writing the price in pen next to each item in the catalog. Next to him was a woman who seemed intent on a number of things, but each time bid just once before chickening out. At the bank of telephones, "Samantha's bidder" kept gobbling things up, while "Brian's bidder" popped in only now and then. Drew had not done any bidding yet, but Grigori kept looking over, to see if he might catch her eye.

She looked contemplative as she watched the auctioneer. Grigori

felt again, as he had throughout the day, an almost physical awareness of having been lifted past grief, and past so much other heaviness, by surprising and generous forces: the passage of time, of
course, but also Drew and the auction, and Zoltan here, and, why,
Evelyn too. He would have to tell Evelyn, of course, where his heart
had led him. Already he sensed that she herself understood the truth
of it—that the two of them were not meant to be anything more,
together, than what they already were to each other.

It took close to an hour for the auction woman to come to the
amber set. But at lot number 71, the amber bracelet, the projections
overhead went blank. Just the empty blue void of a computer screen.
"This item," the auctioneer said, her voice calm and easy, "has been
withdrawn."

A disappointed sound came from some of the crowd. Grigori
looked over to Drew, to see if she had known about this. The expression on her face told him no. "I assure you," the auctioneer was
saying, as a man in the front row stood up noisily and made his way
out of the room, "that this was a last-minute occurrence. Otherwise
we would have done our best to inform you in advance." She took a
long gulp from her water glass, and Grigori was impressed to see that
her hands did not shake. He could imagine what it might feel like, to
be in her position. Replacing the glass on the console, she said, "I'm
sorry to report that the same goes for the next lot, number 72, the
Baltic amber ear pendants. Those too have been withdrawn."

A woman in Grigori's row sighed loudly and stood up to leave,
as Grigori wondered what these two withdrawals could mean. The
auctioneer shushed some people who were whispering, and said that
lot number 72A, the Baltic amber pendant, was still available. Pro-
jected onto the wall was that big reddish-brown bead in its wreath
of gold. The trapped spider and its puffy white pouch looked enormous, and somehow enormously lonely, up there like that. Grigori
felt his heart rush as the auctioneer opened the bidding.

Right away paddle number 99 went up—a white-haired man in a baggy sweater, standing near the first bank of telephones. When paddle number 176 immediately followed, number 99 popped right back up. This back-and-forth continued until the price had reached twenty-six thousand.

"Do I hear twenty-seven?"

From the bank of telephones, a bid came in. When the auctioneer asked for twenty-eight, more employees at the phones joined in, as if members of some club. This flurry continued until the price was at thirty-five thousand. The auctioneer called out for thirty-six.

For a moment there was nothing. But then, not far from where Grigori and Zoltan sat, in the group of seats to their left, a new paddle was raised. "Paddle 102."

When the auctioneer asked for thirty-seven thousand, paddle 176 made a more tentative reach. But 102 held firm, even when 99 came back in and forced the figure up to thirty-nine thousand. When 102 went to forty, everyone turned to see who this headstrong person was.

She was, Grigori noted, the only black person in the room, middle-aged and skinny, her mouth set firmly yet somehow serenely. Grigori was mortified by the thought that swept through him—that she did not look like the sort of person to have the money to bid like this, or even to be at this auction. A racist thought, horrible. Just because she was black, could she not bid at a jewelry auction? But no, that wasn't it at all, Grigori realized with a strange, perplexed relief. It was not her skin color but her clothes. Most of the people here wore silk scarves and fitted blazers, stylish heels and clean, un-scuffed boots, but this woman was wearing nursing shoes. Those bright white fake leather ones with the thick laces. And her coat was a shiny pink rain jacket sort of thing. Nor did she have paddle 99's scientist-type look. Even the auctioneer's smooth, calm expression became slightly skeptical, or perhaps just surprised, as the woman steadfastly raised her paddle.

. . . .

AT FIRST DREW wondered if she might be a shill. Not that such things took place at Beller—at least, not that Drew had ever known of. But the way the woman in the pink vinyl coat suddenly jumped in, and kept raising her paddle, so adamantly, while the man near the telephones briefly fought back, a look of shock on his face, made Drew wonder. From her seat at the bank of telephones, all Drew could see was the raised arm, a thin dark female hand and a bright pink sleeve. No, this was no shill; this person was in it to win.

Other than that, there was not much drama for the rest of the auction. The man sunbathing on Miami Beach did not win any of his bids, and his tone through his cell phone when he said good-bye seemed to blame Drew. By six o'clock all of the snacks had been eaten up and some of the women who had come together in groups, just to have a look, had left to go shopping at Prudential Center. Drew kept glancing over to see if Grigori was still here or if he and his friend had left. And then at last the auction was finished, and everyone stood and stretched and prepared to make their purchases.

Drew wanted to say a quick hello to Grigori, just shake his hand, feel his palm on hers. She stood and looked for him, momentarily losing him in the crowd. And then she heard her name, and Lenore saying "Yes, just one moment, she's right over here."

Drew turned to see the woman in the shiny pink coat approaching her, her hand outstretched. Only then did Drew see and recognize her face.

"Miss Brooks, nice to see you again." That slight accent, as Drew reached out to shake her hand.

That was when Cynthia explained Nina Revskaya's request, about whom the amber was to go to, and that she had with her here a guarantee from the bank, and a letter for Drew—as well as a second letter, for Drew to pass along to Grigori Solodin.

. . . .

SINCE DREW HAD said it might take an hour or two for her to finish up, Grigori decided in the meantime to accompany Zoltan back home. A leisurely but energizing walk to Kenmore Square, the air refreshingly mild, and though Grigori wished he might have said something to Drew before heading out, he had seen for himself how busy she was, knew she would understand why he had not hung about trying to get in a quick word or two.

Outside, evening was just beginning, the sky ahead of them pink with sunset. "I wonder how it feels," Zoltan asked, "to give up something that way. A collection one has spent one's life amassing. And then in a matter of hours it's broken up forever, all these disparate people hurrying away with their booty. What used to be yours."

"I imagine," Grigori said, "it might feel quite good. To be rid of something you've had enough of. It's the reason I've never really collected anything, I suppose. The burden of it."

In truth he had felt, for a brief moment, when the woman in the pink plastic raincoat won her bid, that he might cry. Not so much because he wanted the necklace back, as because of what it represented, those two unfortunate people who, whether or not they were his true parents, had paid the most exorbitant price of all—for living out something illicit, when really they were just living out their lives. *Each piece has its own little world inside. They remind me of the dacha (all those insects!) and the sun in the late evening, the way it would just drop right into the lake.*

"Yes, I see what you mean," Zoltan was saying. "Although I myself find it hard to give almost anything up."

Grigori said, "I think it would become oppressive, having a collection, having to always add to it, and take it with you no matter where you end up—no matter who you become. Even when you've grown out of who you were before."

"Hearing you say this," Zoltan said, "it occurs to me that I *am* a collector in a way. Of my own life. I've kept a journal since I was sixteen, and here I am at age seventy still adding to it, not to mention reading it, carrying all these volumes around with me, cherry-picking this and that out of it for my memoir."

Grigori thought of the little diary in his pocket, Drew's grandfather's, and the translation he had typed out this morning. "You've reminded me of something wonderful that happened today. A discovery of sorts. I think it may have even led me to a new project."

"Really?"

As they approached Zoltan's building, Grigori told Zoltan about the journal he had translated, and his thoughts about those other diaries, written by Soviet citizens, that he might be able to find in the KGB archives. "Of course it will take some doing. But it seems worthwhile, doesn't it? A whole new set of voices, no longer silenced."

Zoltan's approval of this idea made Grigori all the more eager, even as he stood there on the sidewalk wishing his friend good night. Around them evening was emerging, the streetlamps—tall and slightly glaring—punctuating the fading sky. When Zoltan had gone inside, Grigori turned and made his way back toward Beller, wondering if Drew would be free yet from her duties.

When he arrived, the front windows were dark, and through the entrance he saw that the receptionist's desk was empty. It seemed that everyone had gone. Grigori was about to press the doorbell when he saw something move in the dimly lit vestibule—Drew, standing up from a bench. She did not have her coat or bag with her, and for a moment Grigori worried that there was some sort of problem, something to prevent her from leaving. But then he saw the look on her face and, wondering, nodded hello, as she reached for the door and beckoned him in.

AUTHOR'S NOTE
AND SOURCES

This novel is a work of fiction, and while its perimeters are firmly rooted in fact, I have taken liberties with some of the information I found in my research. In particular, the unnamed labor camp referred to in the final chapter does not correspond to any actual prison camp I know of but is inspired by Victoria Finlay's suggestion, in her book *Jewels: A Secret History*, that the Kaliningrad amber mines may have been worked by gulag prisoners.

Much of the other information regarding amber has come from Benjamin Zucker's *Gems and Jewels: A Connoisseur's Guide*.

I have made every attempt to be true to the overall reality of living as an artist in Soviet Russia while creating my own version of that world. For a thorough impression of the changes in daily life in the USSR from decade to decade, I found Orlando Figes's haunting oral history *The Whisperers* extremely helpful, while memoirs by Nadezhda Mandelstam, Ilya Erenburg, and others were rich with insights into Soviet cultural life. (Ehrenburg also provided the anecdote about Zhdanov's musical advice, while Sergei Dovlatov's

Ours: A Russian Family Album included an account, echoed in Gersh's storyline, of the writer Zoshchenko trying to "make it easier" for friends to pretend not to know him.) In particular, Emma Gerstein's *Moscow Memoirs* painted a vivid picture of life as a Jew and an intellectual in literary society and included anecdotal inspiration for the character Zoya.

Zoya's letter to Stalin is modeled on letters excerpted in Lewis Siegelbaum and Andrei Sokolov's *Stalinism as a Way of Life.*

I am also thankful for the many travelogues, diaries, and unofficial cultural studies by Westerners who went behind the Iron Curtain in a particularly difficult period and took the time to record their impressions, however partial and idiosyncratic. Lydia Kirk's *Postmarked Moscow* was an especially rich source of information (including the childbirth anecdotes in the *banya* scene), as was Harrison Salisbury's *Moscow Journal: The End of Stalin*, which supplied the *Krokodil* jokes in chapter 5.

The joke "Thieves, prostitutes, and the NKVD work mostly at night" is from Robert C. Tucker's *Stalin in Power: The Revolution from Above.*

Among the many dancers' memoirs I read, Maya Plisetskaya's inspiring *I, Maya Plisetskaya* provided a particularly incisive look at an artist's struggles in the USSR and behind the scenes at the Bolshoi. For other details of the dancing life, I greatly appreciated Marie Paquet-Nesson's *Ballet to the Corps*, recollections of touring with an American ballet company in the 1950s.

I am indebted to Galina Vishnevskaya's *Galina: A Russian Story* for invaluable information about Bolshoi stage life, including descriptions of Stalin's opera visits. Solomon Volkov's *Shostakovich and Stalin* and *The Magical Chorus* presented a compelling chronology of artistic life under Soviet rule and the cloud of anti-Semitism, and provided the "cosmopolite" rhyme in chapter 8.

My details of West Berlin as glimpsed by Soviet citizens are in part based on descriptions in Nora Kovach and Istvan Rabovsky's *Leap Through the Curtain: The True Story of Two Hungarian Ballet Stars Who Escaped to Freedom.*

The extremely moving *Intimacy and Terror: Soviet Diaries of the 1930s*, edited by Veronique Garros and others, inspired the arrest scene and police station visit in book 2 and sparked the idea of including a journal entry in my novel.

ACKNOWLEDGMENTS

I had the indispensable good fortune to begin this book at the MacDowell Colony and complete it at Yaddo. Crucial support in the years in between came from the La Napoule Foundation, Ledig House, the Virginia Center for the Creative Arts, the Christopher Isherwood Foundation, the Seaside Institute, and, above all, Vassar College's W. K. Rose Fellowship in the Creative Arts.

Individuals to whom I am equally grateful include:

My constant mentors, Leslie Epstein and Margot Livesey.

The fellow readers and writers who helped me move forward from draft to draft: Eve Bridburg of Grub Street, Inc., Morgan Frank, Jill Kalotay, Leah Kalotay, Jhumpa Lahiri, Judy Layzer, Jynne Martin, Chris McCarron, Ron Nemec, Rishi Reddi, Julie Rold, Suzanne Qualls, and Ted Weesner, Jr.

For help with all things Russian: Maria Gapotchenko; Ludmilla Leibman at the Educational Bridge Project; Katherine O'Connor; and Vera Sapozhnikova, who read the manuscript with great thought and intelligence.

For details of the dancing life: Faye Arthurs and Dana Hanson; Eve Lawson; Denise Lipoli; Clyde Nantais and Jill Roberts; and Nancy Upper, who went through the manuscript with such care.

For information on auction houses, fine jewelry, and appraisals:

Elisabeth Benson-Allott and John Colosacco of Skinner, Inc.; Anne Bentley of the Massachusetts Historical Society; Linda Davis; and Julie Reber at *Antiques Road Show*.

For sharing recollections of life in East Germany and escape to West Berlin via subway: Inge Neumann.

For their help with my queries about amber and spiders: Jon Reiskind at the University of Florida–Gainesville; Naomi Pierce, Brian Farrell, and Gonzalo Giribet at Harvard's Museum of Comparative Zoology; and David Grimaldi at the American Museum of Natural History.

For answering my questions about the West Indies: Patrice Vidal.

For other research: the excellent staff of the Boston Athenaeum and the Coolidge Corner branch of the Public Library of Brookline; Brian Haskell at the Peterborough Town Library; Howard Pincus at the Railroad Museum of New England.

For helping this book finally make its way into the world: my superlative agent, Dorian Karchmar, and outstanding editor, Claire Wachtel; and Jonathan Burnham, Michael Morrison, and the excellent team at HarperCollins, especially Julia Novitch. Thank you also to Anika Streitfeld and Jennifer Joel.

For their support and inspiration, my family—with an extra nod to my great-uncle George Bolgar, the original Happy Forced Laborer.